D1337262

A STORY OF DEEP DELIGHT

A STORY OF DEEP DELIGHT

Thomas McNamee

VIKING

VIKING
Published by the Penguin Group
Viking Penguin, a division of Penguin Books USA Inc.,
375 Hudson Street, New York, New York 10014, U.S.A.
Penguin Books Ltd, 27 Wrights Lane, London W8 5TZ, England
Penguin Books Australia Ltd, Ringwood, Victoria, Australia
Penguin Books Canada Ltd, 2801 John Street,
Markham, Ontario, Canada L3R 1B4
Penguin Books (N.Z.) Ltd, 182–190 Wairau Road,
Auckland 10, New Zealand

Penguin Books Ltd, Registered Offices:
Harmondsworth, Middlesex, England

First published in 1990 by Viking Penguin,
a division of Penguin Books USA Inc.

1 3 5 7 9 10 8 6 4 2

Grateful acknowledgment is made for permission to reprint an excerpt from *Audubon: A Vision* by Robert Penn Warren. Copyright © 1969 by Robert Penn Warren. Reprinted by permission of Random House, Inc.

LIBRARY OF CONGRESS CATALOGING IN PUBLICATION DATA
McNamee, Thomas, 1947–
A story of deep delight / Thomas McNamee.
p. cm.
ISBN 0-670-81896-8
1. Chickasaw Indians—Fiction. I. Title.
PS3563.C38837S76 1990
813′.54—dc20 89-40687

Printed in the United States of America
Set in Times Roman
Designed by Cheryl L. Cipriani

For Louise

Tell me a story.

In this century, and moment, of mania,
Tell me a story.

Make it a story of great distances, and starlight.

The name of the story will be Time,
But you must not pronounce its name.

Tell me a story of deep delight.

—Robert Penn Warren
"Audubon: a vision"

PRINCIPAL CHARACTERS

1811

TCHULA HOMA, a young Chickasaw man
TATHOLAH, his father
TSATSEMATAHA, high priest of the village of Nonconnah
TAHANATA, Tchula Homa's mother
TATHONOYO, Tchula Homa's younger brother
KILLS ENEMY, chief of Nonconnah; brother of Tahanata
POTHANOA, speaker of Nonconnah
LOKANA TCHEH, mother of Kills Enemy and Tahanata
TCHILATOKOWA, Tchula Homa's older brother; war chief of Nonconnah
TINEBE MINGO, king of the Chickasaws; brother of Lokana Tcheh
HUSHTA HIETE, eldest son of Kills Enemy
MOON BEHIND CLOUD, a girl; eventually Tchula Homa's wife
WREN, mother of Moon Behind Cloud
ATCHELATA, Moon Behind Cloud's fiancé; eventually her second husband
TISHOMINGO, the Chickasaws' most venerable chief
WILLIAM COLBERT, or TCHUSHEMATAHA, councilor to the king
GEORGE COLBERT, or CHOSEMATAHA, councilor
JAMES COLBERT, councilor
LEVI COLBERT, or ITAWAMBA, councilor and diplomat

1812

NICHOLAS ROOSEVELT, a steamboat captain
LYDIA ROOSEVELT, his wife

1818

ANDREW JACKSON, general, United States Army; U.S. commissioner; eventually President of the United States
ISAAC SHELBY, governor of Kentucky; U.S. commissioner
ATCHEKOYO, son of Moon Behind Cloud and Atchelata
LAKOWEA, son of Moon Behind Cloud and Atchelata

1819

HANANATA, servant of Tchula Homa

1826

COL. JOHN D. TERRELL, special agent of the Bureau of Indian Affairs
WILLIAM CLARK, superintendent of the Bureau of Indian Affairs

1828

KIMMETEHE, a hunter
LATSE INESHKA, a hunter; cousin of Tchula Homa
NENE INESHKA, a hunter; Latse Ineshka's brother
IMMAYOTUTLA, a hunter

1832

ANGELO CORELLI, a planter
GLORY, black second wife of Tatholah

1837

MILES GLORY (though not named here), son of Tatholah and Glory

1860

GIOVANNI CORELLI, son of Angelo; a planter
CALEB, his valet
SYLVESTER [Woodson], a stable boy
BENEDICT O'CONNELL, or MR. B., overseer of Corelli plantation
AARON [Corelli], a stable boy; friend of Sylvester
UNCLE DUNCAN, stable boss
LUIGI CARBONE, cook at Corelli plantation
NATHAN BEDFORD FORREST, a slave dealer and planter; later officer, Confederate States Army
FÉLICE [Renard], Corelli's mistress
HATTIE, cook at Corelli plantation

REVEREND AUGUSTUS T. LOWDERMILK, a preacher; later a judge
JEROME, Forrest's valet
JOE JOHN, son of Hattie
BESS, mother of Aaron
AARON SENIOR, Aaron's father; called Senior
CHARITY, called CHERRY; a house servant at Greengrove plantation
JONAH JOHNSON, a slave from Arkansas
MARY MONTGOMERY FORREST, wife of N. B. Forrest
MATTIE, a kitchen maid
ISABEL, a kitchen maid

1861

ELMO, a field hand at Greengrove plantation
JACKSON, a field hand at Greengrove
DRURY, a field hand at Greengrove; Jackson's brother
ICE PICK, a field hand at Greengrove
MR. SWEENEY, overseer, Greengrove plantation
THEO, field driver, Greengrove
QUEEN, Forrest's seamstress

1863

ANDREW JACKSON WORDLAW, a Confederate deserter
SISSY, a maid at Greengrove; Drury's sweetheart

1864

SGT. OTTO RILEY, Confederate States Army; later sheriff of De Soto County, Mississippi
GEN. CADWALLADER C. WASHBURN, United States Army commander at Memphis
MISS MCCRACKEN, a teacher

1865

DR. CHRISTOPHER COLUMBUS BEAUMONT, lover and protector of Charity

1866

SIMON BOLIVAR BEAUMONT, lawyer for Sylvester; brother of C. C. Beaumont
BUTCH O'GORMAN, a white man
WILLY MCKEE, a white man

MAY CLANCY, a white woman
CLARENCE CLANCY, her son

1958

WORDLAW WICKHAM CORELLI, a boy
WILBUR COREY, an ex-convict
SECOND SAMUEL, Wilbur's dog; later Wordlaw's dog
DRURY WOODSON, Wordlaw's grandparents' houseman
ROBERTSON CORELLI, Wordlaw's father, a physician
IVY DEE WICKHAM CORELLI, Wordlaw's mother
CLAUDIA CORELLI, Wordlaw's sister; later also known as MAGGIE
SYLVESTRA WOODSON, Wordlaw's family's maid; Drury's sister
SUSANNA (SHOOT) CORELLI, Wordlaw's sister
STACKER LEE (S. L.) CORELLI, Wordlaw's grandfather
REE BILLY COREY, a waiter at the country club (later revealed: son of Wilbur)
STELLA WOODSON, wife of Drury; Wordlaw's grandparents' cook

1959

FORREST MCCRACKEN, a friend of Wordlaw
OSCAR BALLARD, Forrest's grandfather; S. L. Corelli's lawyer; also known as the Old Buzzard
CORA WHITE, Forrest's girlfriend
IVY DEE (JUNIOR) CORELLI, Wordlaw's baby sister
CORNELIA ROBERTSON CORELLI, Wordlaw's grandmother
HORACE, Ballard's houseman
OTTO RILEY, a sheriff's deputy

1960

BEAUMONT ECHOLS, Robertson Corelli's lawyer
SKEETER WOODSON, Drury's brother in Chicago
WORDLAW WICKHAM, Wordlaw's maternal grandfather
EUDORA WICKHAM, Wordlaw's maternal grandmother
COLBERT FOX, a boy
SYLVESTER WOODSON II, son of Skeeter; later known as SAXOPHONE CHICAGO
DELBERT FOX, father of Colbert; a Chickasaw Indian
LEEANN FOX, mother of Colbert

1970

MIRIAM (MIMI) FONTAINE, a singer and songwriter; later Wordlaw's wife

BUBBA BOHANNON, a friend of Wordlaw

1975

ALICE PELLETIER, Mimi's lyricist

WILY NEWMAN, a songwriter

EDMOND DELAFOSSE, Alice's boyfriend

SUSUMU (SAM) WATANABE, Claudia's boyfriend

LISA GRUENTHAL, Claudia's roommate

MARIAN JENNINGS, Claudia's roommate; art dealer and would-be writer

NEIL O'NEILL, president of Mimi's record company

HELMUT, his assistant

LIZ CHISHOLM, record company publicist

PETER AND PAUL FARR, twins, friends of Wordlaw

FLIP AND ANNIE MAYHEW, friends of Wordlaw

THE LIVING DEAD MOTORCYCLE CLUB

1977

PETER ELIAS, a piano player

AMOS JENNINGS, Marian's brother

WALTER PINCKNEY, Marian's fiancé

ALEXANDER CORELLI, son of Giovanni Corelli

HAMILTON FORREST GARIBALDI CORELLI, son of Alexander Corelli; father of S.L.

OPAL ETTA WORDLAW CORELLI, wife of Hamilton; mother of S.L.

LAFAYETTE WOODSON, son of Sylvester and Félice; father of Skeeter and Drury; grandfather of Sylvester Woodson II (Saxophone Chicago)

1980

MR. CANNIZARO, a wine merchant

TOMMY, a Mississippi highway patrolman

Part One

1811

Along the trade route that linked the towns of the Chickasaw nation with the river called Father of Waters there lay a wild and dark swamp that was sacred to the Chickasaw people. In ages past there had been at its heart a vast black lake in which the biggest alligators in the world lived, and as the generations had passed and the lake had slowly filled in, and the cypress and tupelo gum had encircled it ever more tightly, the reputation of this place as a sanctuary of primeval magic had grown.

Now the circle had shrunk almost to nothing, and a great hardwood forest, its roots a clotted web, overlay the bottomless muck in which the last of the giant alligators had long been entombed. Sometimes the swamp would groan softly in the night, and a hole would open in the forest floor through which black mud would ooze, and chill exhalations of ancient air would mingle with the foxfire.

When a Chickasaw boy of exceptional promise reached the age of manhood he would come here to meditate on the sweetness of his place in the world. Hunting was forbidden in the sacred swamp, and the animals would come close to one whose thoughts had grown sufficiently serene.

A young man was here today to find a name. He began by silently chanting the names of his family, his friends, and the other villagers, and in his mind he saw their faces. He chanted on, the names of animals, and saw them too. On the third day, in the third recitation of the bear chant, a bear came into the circle of brightly painted stones, and the young man could not tell if it was real or not.

At nightfall the wolves sang of the death and life of the deer they killed and loved. The oaks and tulip-trees shivered and bent at the top while their trunks were as immovable as the earth itself; the trees' song was of time, which is always in motion and yet never moves. The muscadine vine curled into the trees and sometimes brought them down; it, in the wind, made a music of slow victory. The great blue heron stood still in the still water, image of patience. The ivory-billed woodpecker repeated, "Persistence, persistence." The white-headed eagle spiraled down from above the clouds to light at the top of a tupelo snag with a harsh cry of courage.

Each dawn a red fox came to the circle of stones and sat down and stared at the young man. When at last he said its name aloud, "Red Fox," the fox vanished.

By the fourth night the young man no longer sensed distinction between himself and his surroundings, between himself and his ancestors, between the present and the past. He had achieved that equilibrium of spirit which was the object of the ceremony, and he remained suspended in its hushed and utter peace until the morning after the full moon, when his father came to take him home.

Bringing his eyes slowly into focus on his father's face, he felt for the first time the full depth of the change that had come about within him. His heart was calm. His hands were steady. His vision was so clear that he felt as if he had been seeing through a mist all his life and now it had lifted. No sooner than he had begun to feel all this, however, there came to him also a pang of disillusionment. Seen so vividly, his father's face was no longer, as it had always used to be, the indistinct visage of a god. It was the face of a man. A star of ice burned in the young man's heart as his father looked away.

His legs were so weak that he could barely walk. Wherever he turned his eyes, the trees leaned toward him as though they might form hands and clutch at him. Their trunks rippled like tensed muscles. The forest was loud with birds, but now their speech was unintelligible. Silver fire seethed at the edges of his vision.

Although he knew he was moving, it seemed to the young man

as if he was not, as if the forest was flowing past and perhaps even through him. The first fields of high corn, pools of sunlight glittering far away down a cave of late-summer shade, poured toward him, spilling women's song at his feet in splashes of gold.

His father froze in midstep. Ahead on the path a black water moccasin opened its white mouth. The young man ripped down and waved a willow switch, and when the snake struck he seized it by the neck. He drew his knife and with one stroke beheaded it.

"The red fox kills snakes like that, instantly and without fear," said his father, whose name was Tatholah, or Seven Pines. "I will ask the old men to name you Tchula Homa," which in the Chickasaw language means Red Fox.

As they neared the village of Nonconnah, the young man and his father met its high priest, Tsatsemataha. He too was returning from a meditation, in preparation for the Green Corn Festival, the Chickasaw people's most venerable ceremony. Tatholah told Tsatsemataha how his son had rescued him from the poisonous snake.

Tsatsemataha grunted, nodded, and moved along with them homeward in silence.

The village was full of motion and noise. Many people had come from distant towns for the festival. Women were weaving new cane seats for the old men's chairs, and singing. Children raced through the streets. Everywhere, families were gathering around fragrant pots of beans and squash for the last meal before the ceremony and its fasting began. The young man's house swam to him through the light and tumult, and swallowed him into its darkness and stillness.

His mother, Tahanata, lay curled in a blanket on the hearth at the center of the house. The air was acrid with the smoke of medicinal herbs. She had been sick for a long time.

Smiling through the stupor of her medicine, she tried to rise to welcome her son home, but she was too weak, and he knelt and held her in his arms.

Outside, framed in the dark doorway, his friends lounged under their accustomed sycamore in the windless midday shade, laughing, as they always seemed to be laughing, loud, from the belly.

The high priest stood in the square, calling into it priests, elders, chiefs, warriors, and all other men of substance. Four warriors stood at the entrances to the square to keep the uninitiated out. The young man and the other eighteen-year-old boys crowded close to the guards, trying to peek past.

It was the business of the first day of the Green Corn Festival to give thanks for the harvest, to chasten the wayward and praise the good, to effect reconciliations, and to begin the new year in purity and harmony. Late in the afternoon, after settling all the accumulated disputes of the year, the councilors called for silence, and the high priest rose to prophesy. To the young man's astonishment, Tsatsemataha told the story of his killing of the poisonous snake, explaining that this event was a portent of the Chickasaw people's coming victory over the uncleanness that had come among them. The mixed-blood men, of whom there were many now, shifted uneasily in their seats. But the priest pointedly took one very light-skinned man by the hand and said, for all to hear, "We are brothers in our way of life, and of the same fire forever. And now," he continued, "we shall have more brothers still. Young men! come here."

And so Tchula Homa was named, and became a man.

In the Chickasaw way of life one's mother's brother was as close kin as one's own father. Tahanata's brother, Kills Enemy, was the village chief. As he embraced the new-made man, Kills Enemy whispered, "We will cure your mother's illness, and our people will be great."

The men all slept in the square that night. Tchula Homa watched his father as he twitched and shivered, dreaming. In the morning Tatholah confessed to his son, and later to Tsatsemataha, that he had dreamed that the cottonmouth snake had bitten him and he had died.

Tchula Homa's father, therefore, was first among the old men to drink from the pot of button snakeroot tea, and when he doubled over, vomiting, the high priest looked on in satisfaction as the evil of the dream was purged. Because this was a day of forgiveness, Kills Enemy held his tongue and did not say, as Tchula Homa knew he believed, that Tatholah's acceptance of a Christian Bible from a white trader had brought on his wife's illness. Instead, as though to emphasize the commonality of sin, the chief swallowed a large mouthful of the violently emetic herb known as ancient tobacco and joined his sister's husband at the vomiting trench.

The next morning, the women of the village left pots of cold food at the entrances to the square. The men were very hungry, but they broke their fast slowly, careful that all shared everything.

Dressed in white moccasins, white vest, white shawl, and white turban of swan feathers, the high priest appeared from his white house on the mound at the head of the square. All fell silent as Tsatsemataha took the mother wood of oak and the father wood of pine into the house, out of sight, where with them he would engender new fire. He placed the fire under the arbor at the center of the square, and, as the flames rose crackling into the garlands of green leaves, Nonconnah's speaker, Pothanoa, walked up and down through the village calling the women out of their houses. Kills Enemy's mother, Lokana Tcheh, the oldest woman of the village, brought green corn ears and fresh fruit to the high priest.

Tsatsemataha anointed the corn and fruit with oil and threw them into the flames. "All wrongs are now righted, all wrong is made right," he chanted. "All crimes are forgiven, all sins are forgiven, all people made whole."

With his arms lifted high above his head, the high priest praised the wisdom of the Chickasaw people's old men. He urged bravery and goodness on the warriors, and cautioned the women to fulfill their obligations to purity and probity. There would be plenty of rain, he said, and good health for all, as long as the fire was honored. If rules were broken or faith not kept, the fire would exact its revenge in drought, witchcraft, illness, or enemies' triumph. "Now, women!" he said, "come, and take fire to your homes."

Six old women, including Tchula Homa's mother Tahanata and his grandmother Lokana Tcheh, came into the square, each dressed in white, each shining with oil, each wearing rattles of tortoise shell on her legs, each bearing a green bough of a different tree. The six oldest priests took boughs from the fire arbor and joined them in a dance and song. Tahanata's face, as she danced, was a leathery mask of pain.

A cauldron of the holly tea called black drink was brewed over the new fire, and the men drank many heart-quickening drafts of it in their conch-shell cups.

And now as the home fires were restored, the feast could begin. The food was the finest and most plentiful of the year: venison fried in hickory oil; bear stew with hominy; jerky with bear grease; turkey with squash; long skewers of passenger pigeon, opossum, squirrel, raccoon, rabbit; a sturgeon as big as a man, a paddlefish thick as a tree, great vats of catfish soup; steaming pots of succotash, sweet potatoes, beans; bowls of persimmons, plums, blackberries, pecans, walnuts; platters of salted sunflower seeds; baskets of pumpkin bread and chestnut bread; and, of course, hot roasted ears of the new green corn, manifestation of the earth's generosity to man. As the dishes were passed and repassed, and quiet talk flowed back and forth, Tchula Homa felt rising through his heart a sad, fierce love for these people.

The hiss of gourd rattles and the boom of earthen drums began the warrior dance. Tchula Homa's elder brother Tchilatokowa led the warriors into three concentric circles around the fire, all of the dancers dressed in white buckskin and wearing white feathers, all singing for the war-courage which had for so long been of no use to them. Afterwards the warriors fought a grand mock battle, and finally the women joined them in the three circles for the dance that brought the Green Corn Festival to its close.

The high priest pronounced the ceremonies over, and all the people began to paint themselves white. They lined up behind Tsatsemataha in strict order of rank: first the subsidiary priests, then the honored old men, the chiefs and councilors and orators in order of seniority, then the warriors in order of reputation—Tchula Homa's brother Tchilatokowa first and Tchula Homa and the other new-made men last among them—next the women, and finally the children, many carrying infant siblings in their arms. In single file they walked to the bayou called Daylight, where they all washed off the white clay and were purified.

That night, Tchula Homa saw his father melt into the forest in the company of one of the mixed-blood men.

Tahanata had allowed herself to undergo the white painting and immersion, but she had had to be carried home, and now she lay wheezing in the darkness, close to her fire. Tchula Homa stroked her forehead with a soft patch of fawnskin soaked in oil, and as the music and rough shouts of celebration mounted in the square, and the yellow bonfire light sent ghostly shadows licking down the streets and into his mother's house, he sang softly to her the old song she had used to sing when he was a baby, "Be warm, little one." In sleep, her face shrank against the skull, and its deep wrinkles seemed to disappear.

"Little brother!" called the voice of Tchilatokowa from outside. "Mother! Help me." So speaking, the foremost of Nonconnah's warriors appeared in the doorway, sank to his knees, pitched forward, and passed out. Tchula Homa's knife was in his brother's hand. Tchilatokowa's forehead was bleeding from a gash. Tahanata rose and, without speaking, stanched the wound with moss. The smell of whiskey was strong.

"Get him out of here," she said.

Tchula Homa lifted his brother beneath the arms, pulled him outside, and propped him up against a tree. "Brother," he said, slapping him softly. "Wake up. Who did this to you?"

Tchilatokowa spoke with difficulty. "Don't worry. He's in worse shape than I am." His head sank back against the tree.

Tchula Homa ran up the street and into the square. A dead man lay next to the fire, beneath the charred frame of the arbor. Kills Enemy pulled back the blanket to show the slit throat of his own eldest son, Hushta Hiete.

Tchula Homa looked into his uncle's face in the dim red light. Twice Kills Enemy's lips began to move, but each time he said nothing, peering past Tchula Homa and into the darkness. When at last he found his voice it could barely be heard.

"To kill one's own kin," said Kills Enemy, "is a crime all but unknown. Our ancestors have not given us laws specifying punishment for it. What kind of people are they who would kill their own kin? It is the kind of thing the white man does—the kind of thing we have always abominated him for. Many years ago, when I was a young warrior, the great Ugula Yacabe tried to unite our people with the Creek and Choctaw and Cherokee peoples to keep out the white man, who was inciting us to serve in his pointless wars, which gained us nothing, and bringing us whiskey, which made our warriors crazy and our old men stupid. Some of us"—Kills Enemy's eyes seemed now to focus on Tchula Homa's father, as if there was no one else there—"some of us will remember gathering near the trading post at the Fourth Bluff after our great king Taski Etoka had died; some of us will remember what Ugula Yacabe said then." Now the chief shifted his black gaze to Tchula Homa. "Young men," he said, "listen to what that wise man said. Speaker!"

Pothanoa emerged from the crowd, and quoted: " 'The morning will come,' said Ugula Yacabe, 'when our best men will have been drunk all night and will have woken to find the nation destroyed.' "

"It was self-defense!" Tatholah protested. There was a murmur of disbelief among the crowd. "People, listen: both of them were drunk, and crazy. Our chief is right about this: whiskey is to blame. My son Tchilatokowa is not a murderer."

Who, then, was to blame for the whiskey? And ought not that man to be held equally responsible for the death of Hushta Hiete?

And was not that man Tchula Homa's and the murderer's own father?

The council met late into the night, and the next morning, as the assembled villagers and all their festival visitors looked on, Tchilatokowa was tied to the trunk of the spreading sweetgum tree at the foot of the square, and Kills Enemy put a musket ball through his heart.

Tchilatokowa slumping into the ropes, the blood bursting from his chest, Hushta Hiete's staring eyes and gaping mouth and foaming severed windpipe—these images came back again and again to Tchula Homa that fall. He knew he should have been angry, but he felt only sadness.

His mother did not demand vengeance, perhaps because there were those who held her husband responsible. Tahanata herself blamed whiskey, she blamed the white man, and she blamed her people's helplessness against him.

But war, which was what her sense of justice demanded, was not a reasonable possibility. Chickasaw chiefs and councilors had visited the capitals of the white man from time to time for generations—Piomingo had gone to Philadelphia and New York more than twenty years ago—and they knew all too well how strong and how many and how bellicose the whites really were. Nevertheless, although the weakness of the Chickasaw people had been an indisputable fact for a long time, it was still not something they were able to accommodate in their thinking about themselves, and they continued to regard fierceness and bravery, however infrequently those qualities might actually be useful, as the cardinal virtues of the nation.

Why then could Tchula Homa not bring himself even to imagine retribution, vengeance no more bloody than the midnight torching of the trader's cache, flames of whiskey dancing in the forest canopy? Yet his mind would flee from even the mildest thoughts of violence.

Tchula Homa decided that he was a coward, and said so to Kills Enemy. At first his uncle said nothing, but merely poured him a cup of black drink and passed him the council pipe. Tchula Homa took a few meditative puffs, and waited. "You do not pass the pipe back," said his uncle in the near-whisper that always marked his most serious observations.

"I'm sorry, Uncle. I wasn't thinking."

"You misunderstand me." The chief murmured to his assistant, "Bring the high priest."

When Tsatsemataha came, Kills Enemy recounted Tchula Homa's confessions of self-doubt, and then described how the young man had unconsciously not passed the pipe back.

"You do not see your future," said the high priest to Tchula Homa.

"Who ever does?" said Tchula Homa, mystified.

"Sometimes," said Tsatsemataha, "we are given fleeting glimpses of our fate. These glimpses often at first may seem inconsequential, especially to the young. For generations, this pipe"—the priest took it now from the young man, and smoked—"this pipe has often known our people's future. It stayed in your hands in order to tell you that you must persevere, and that there is in you a natural authority. The hands in which that pipe lingers often become the hands of a chief. Now I have said enough." He passed the pipe to Kills Enemy, rose, and left.

"But, Uncle," Tchula Homa protested, "how can a coward be a chief?"

"Listen. Times are changing fast. Once, we and our enemies were equally well armed, and the victors were always simply the bravest; but now the white man can annihilate us on a whim. The opportunity Ugula Yacabe saw has passed us by. Now, if our people are to survive, we must parley and bargain. Courage is all but irrelevant now. Now, we must protect our world with intelligence, with negotiation, and sometimes with guile. We are destined to be an island in a great lake of white people. The time of our greatness is past, but we must remain who we are—Chickasaw people, Chickasaw nation. It will not be easy. Our people are very much tempted by white man ways."

"But there are laws against those temptations!" protested Tchula Homa.

"There can be no law that the people do not believe in," replied Kills Enemy.

Illness came to Nonconnah that autumn. Tchula Homa's mother clung weakly to life, but many others relinquished it in agonies of fever, dysentery, pneumonia. The priests searched the spirit world for culpability, but the signs were insubstantial and ambiguous. A comet with two tails was seen in the eastern sky, and although the priests could not say precisely what it portended, they all agreed that it was bad luck. Hunters lay in their houses too sick to rise, listening to the incessant rain on their roofs.

"Hand me that rattle, please, son," said Tchula Homa's father one night late, after a long day of fruitless chase. Tatholah sang the songs "Come, deer, and die" and "Wolf, tell me." As the old man shook the gourd, Tchula Homa's younger brother, Tathonoyo, brought thunder from his wooden drum, but Tchula Homa did not take up his flute.

"You do not play," observed his father.

Tchula Homa said nothing. He had begun to doubt Tatholah's ability to invoke the aid of invisible forces. He did not doubt those forces' existence, but he felt in himself no attunement to them, and he feared that he saw in his father, as in some of the other villagers, a slow decay of faith in the spirits. That, he said to himself, may well be precisely why the spirits have not come to our aid.

But why must all I think of these days be blame? Everything that crosses my mind seems to be negative—the absence of this, the insufficiency of that, the decline of the other. Why can I not love the world?

"You need a wife," said Tathonoyo.

"Bah!" snapped Tchula Homa.

Tahanata pulled Tchula Homa close and whispered to him, "Your little brother is not stupid. Listen. I know you have heavy matters on your mind. But I've just gotten a message from my cousin Wren at the capital that after she and her family were here for Green Corn, one of her daughters just couldn't stop talking about you. Her name is Moon Behind Cloud. Do you remember her?"

"No," said Tchula Homa.

"She was with that young man Atchelata," prompted his mother.

"I thought they were engaged to be married."

"No longer." His mother smiled. "You remember her."

"Vaguely," said Tchula Homa. "Very small. What happened?"

"She saw *you,*" laughed Tathonoyo.

Tchula Homa pressed his lips together and said nothing.

"How solemn you are," said his mother. "Now, listen. My cousin has managed to get some very rare medicine for me. I want you to go to the capital and get it. And while you're there, take a look at this girl. Just a look—that's all I ask."

When Tchula Homa went out the next morning to catch a horse for his journey, Kills Enemy followed him at a distance and saw how readily his own horse, East Wind, came to the young man. Tchula Homa gave the beautiful black stallion a few grapes and continued to pursue his father's swaybacked old roan mare. The chief emerged from the forest and called, "Good morning!"

"Good morning, Uncle! I didn't see you."

"I know. Take East Wind. He likes you."

"Thank you!" Tchula Homa bridled the stallion, swung to his back, and came downhill to his uncle. "I like him, too." East Wind rubbed his forehead roughly against the old chief's shoulder.

"You are going to the capital?"

"Yes, sir."

"Take this." Kills Enemy handed Tchula Homa his eagle-feathered staff. "Go to the king—he is my mother's brother, you know—and tell him I ask him to send his own doctor back here with you, for my sister."

Tchula Homa rode hard all day through forest and canebrake and swamp. Where the long miles of shadow gave way to a wide expanse of burnt corn stubble, a scout met Tchula Homa and led him through the teeming streets to the capital square. There a young warrior carrying a crimson silk umbrella took him into a high house built on a square mound of vine-clad earth—the first two-story house Tchula Homa had ever seen. The king was sitting smoking by his fire with an elaborately tattooed and very tall old man, fiercely cicatriced with battle scars, who could only have been the venerable chief Tishomingo, and four mixed-blood men. "My nephew Kills Enemy's nephew," said the king. "Your name is Tchula Homa, I believe?"

"Yes, Tinebe Mingo," replied the young man.

Tinebe introduced the first old mixed-blood man as William Colbert, or Tchushemataha. As etiquette required, Tchula Homa repeated the name in a low voice. George Colbert, Tchosemataha, was widely known as a strong traditionalist, and Tchula Homa greeted him with particular warmth. Tinebe, laughing a little, introduced James as the "whitest" Colbert—his mother had also been of mixed blood, and had taught him English, and he did not like to hear his Chickasaw name. To James Colbert, therefore, Tchula Homa merely raised his right hand and nodded. Levi Colbert, the nation's leading diplomat and political strategist, pine-straight, silver-haired, rose slowly, and took the young man's hand. "Itawamba," said Tchula Homa to him.

Tishomingo took Tchula Homa's hand; his own was dry, cool, sinewy, strong. "I bring to Tishomingo the deepest respect of the village of Nonconnah," said Tchula Homa. "And my own." Tishomingo was the greatest war chief in Chickasaw history, and an implacable enemy of accommodation with the white man. The old man's eyes looked into the young man's heart, and, faintly, he smiled. Tchula Homa lowered his eyes in gratitude.

"Leave us awhile," said Tinebe to Tishomingo and the Colberts. The young man followed the king up a narrow ladder and onto a balcony overlooking the square. "Sit down, my young friend. I'm happy to meet you. Kills Enemy speaks very highly of you."

Tchula Homa had spent his whole life in dense forest broken only by a few scattered fields, beaver meadows, and marshes; with the sole exception of the time when, as a boy, still too young to appreciate it, he had seen the Father of Waters from the crest of the Fourth Bluff, Tchula Homa had never been anywhere so big and open as the townscape and croplands of the capital; and so, looking out through the blue strata of supper-fire smoke above the countless houses and the patchwork of fields into the russet and gold of autumn woods at sunset, he felt a swelling in his chest. "This place," he said, "is beautiful."

For several minutes both were silent, passing the pipe back and forth. Then Tinebe said: "What you don't see out there is the sickness. Many of my people are ill, and my priests and doctors are at a loss to explain it." Again, a silence. "You are carrying the staff of your chief."

"Yes," said Tchula Homa.

"Kills Enemy wants my doctors for your mother."

"Yes."

"He shall have them," said the king. "But don't expect miracles. Two of my wives have died this fall." Tinebe sighed. "The Colberts want to bring us a white doctor, from far away. But I don't know."

"With all due respect," said Tchula Homa, "I think there is too much foreign influence among us already."

"At Nonconnah," replied Tinebe, "you live close to the trading post at the Fourth Bluff, and naturally there that is of concern to you. But here in the heart of our nation, the white man world seems very far away still—even while I know that that world is gnawing at our nation's extremities. Can we placate the monster by feeding it a little? Sometimes I think perhaps so. Sometimes I think not."

"I always think not," said Tchula Homa.

"Shall your mother die in the name of Chickasaw purity?"

Tchula Homa said nothing.

"I understand you want to meet Moon Behind Cloud."

"My mother wants me to."

Tinebe smiled. "And you, Tchula Homa?"

"I'll tell you after I've seen her."

Tinebe laughed aloud.

Tchula Homa was very tall even for a Chickasaw, and as he stooped to enter Wren's house he bumped his head hard on the transom, stumbled dizzily forward, put his foot in a nut basket, and, amidst scattering hundreds of acorns, pitched onto the floor at the tiny old lady's feet.

"Welcome," she said politely.

The young man gathered himself up and stood. "I bring you warm greetings from Kills Enemy, and from my mother, Tahanata, and from their mother, Lokana Tcheh," he proclaimed, too loudly. And then, too quietly, "And with their compliments I bring you this dried meat."

It was only now that Tchula Homa saw, deep in the flickering fire-shadows, the girl. She was looking at him with what seemed to be two expressions: the right side of her face grave, even stern, and the left side just short of a smile, or perhaps laughter.

"Something to eat, or to drink?" offered Wren.

"No, thank you." Having said this, Tchula Homa then observed that she was sitting there with a pitcher of hot drink in her hands, and now would not be bidden to come forward and pour him a cup of it.

"Will you warm yourself at our small fire?" asked Wren.

He sat down and considered the fire at length.

Wren had no trouble filling the silence. "This is a house of women," she said. "My husband has been dead many years, and I have only daughters. My husband was the great warrior Many Scalps, whom you've no doubt heard of. He died in battle the year Moon Behind Cloud was born. She is very much like him—fierce, but gentle. I have only daughters, three others besides Moon Behind Cloud, all married now, all to men of substance, two king's councilors and a priest, and we all have large fields. I myself grow corn, beans, squash, melons, and tobacco. I'm thinking of trying cotton next year. Have you heard of that plant? It's quite wonderful. A cousin of mine has grown it, and has made beautiful cloth. I have more land, frankly, than I know what to do with, and it is some of the best, right in the creek bottom, flooded every spring, but not too much, and high and dry all summer. I never use it all. I think one shouldn't farm too much. I think that women should stay home sometimes and work at our old-time tasks like sewing. Let me show you this. Moon Behind Cloud sewed this entirely herself, from the cotton my cousin grew. Isn't it lovely? Look at that beadwork. Of course, I suppose it's too small for a big man like you, or I'd make you a gift of it—"

Moon Behind Cloud rose now and took a seat next to her mother. She looked straight at Tchula Homa, extended her pitcher, and said, "The least you could do is drink some of this, since I went to the trouble of making it."

"Moon Behind Cloud!" exclaimed her mother. And then to their visitor: "May I present my ill-mannered daughter."

Tchula Homa raised his hand and spoke her name.

"Thirsty?" she demanded.

"Yes. A little."

"Well, this has gotten cold. I'll heat it up. I'm going to give you some soup, too."

"That's very kind."

Ever so slightly, the girl rolled her eyes.

"I have medicine for your mother," said the old woman, producing a deerskin bundle. "This is ancient medicine, very strong. She must not use too much. And she must use it only under the supervision of a doctor who knows all the ceremonies that go with it."

"Tinebe Mingo has graciously consented to send his own doctor to see my mother."

"Excellent. The Colberts, however, say that white man medicine is better than even the best of our own."

"*Mother!*" scolded Moon Behind Cloud. "There's a lot of this nonsense going around," she said then, turning toward Tchula Homa. "Maybe some great white doctor could turn me into a white girl, with golden hair tied up in pink ribbons. I could wear a long flowing dress with twenty-five petticoats underneath, and chatter like a sparrow, and ride in a carriage pulled by four white horses, and I could come back and visit among you poor savages here and feel sorry for your poverty and primitive ways."

From somber Tchula Homa this wrung a terse smile.

"My daughter's sharp tongue sometimes belies her tender heart," said the old woman.

"Pah!" said Moon Behind Cloud.

The girl was grinning wickedly at Tchula Homa. He could think of nothing to say, but only lifted his palms in confusion, and, rather wishing not to, grinned helplessly back at her.

He ate and drank in silence as the girl and her mother looked on.

"This is good," said Tchula Homa at last.

"Those are beans from my daughter's own patch," said Wren. "And she cooked them all by herself too. It's a secret recipe that has been coming down through our women for many generations."

"Mm," said Tchula Homa, quietly spitting a bean-sized pebble into his hand.

"More?" said the girl, plunging a spoon into the pot. "I might be able to find another rock or two for you at the bottom."

"No, thank you," he said, grinning again. "I really must go."

The king was waiting up for him. "Well?" he inquired.

"I got the medicine."

"And the girl?"

"She was there," said Tchula Homa.

"Of course she was *there,*" said the king. "What I mean is, how did it go?"

"Not very well, I think."

"Charming, isn't she?"

"Clever, I would say, and rather rude. And small; not strong. And there were rocks in the beans she cooked."

"But charming," said Tinebe.

"In a way," admitted Tchula Homa.

"And good-looking."

"Yes."

"You will drop by her house on your way home in the morning," said the king peremptorily.

"I really think that would be pointless. She made fun of me. I don't like her."

"Please, Tchula Homa."

"You are my king."

"Don't go because I'm your king! Go because I am an old man and know something, and you are a young man and apparently know nothing at all."

The morrow dawned in a dismal cold rain. Hunched up under his tunic, Tchula Homa led his horse through unpeopled muddy streets to Moon Behind Cloud's house. There beside the door sat a bowl of the boiled hominy meal called sofkee. It was the Chickasaw custom that if a girl were going to accept the attentions of a suitor, she would allow him to eat the sofkee, and if she wished to discourage him, she would run out and snatch it away. It had been explained to him by his village elders that this was a way for young men to avoid the humiliation of a direct rejection, but Tchula Homa had trouble seeing it that way: to him, even from this excessively whimsical girl, such a gesture would be devastating. What he had hoped, and truly expected, was that there would be no bowl of sofkee there at all. He had certainly not expressed any overt interest in Moon

Behind Cloud, and she had seemed to regard him as somewhat ridiculous. But there, nevertheless, was the bowl. He could, of course, simply have mounted East Wind and headed home, but he bent to the bowl, picked up the spoon, and held it awhile in front of his face, giving her plenty of time to appear and grab it away from him. She did not. He took a bite.

There was a rock in it.

Both Kills Enemy and Tinebe Mingo had now made it clear to Tchula Homa that they considered him a young man from whom much would be expected, and both of them took him into their confidence in discussing village and national affairs. Tchula Homa was rather mystified by all this attention, but he found that his opinions, which he gave only seldom and after judicious reflection, seemed to be much valued, and also that they were a source of some dismay.

The king prided himself on his pragmatism, and let himself be advised by the Colberts on nearly everything. But Tchula Homa came to understand that beneath that thin pride, Tinebe was unhappy, and that this was the unhappiness of the weak and uncertain. He seemed to draw strength from the young man's stubbornness. It was also possible, Tchula Homa knew, that the king was using him to define one extreme, and the Colberts to define the other, and thus between the two could make a middle way. The possibility of someday exercising influence over the entire Chickasaw nation, however, kept Tchula Homa from resenting being used. What was more, the king loved him.

Kills Enemy also loved Tchula Homa. There were no Colberts in Kills Enemy's life; his affection for his sister's son was simple. At the same time, the Nonconnah chief was not unaware of the white man, and tried to school his nephew in what little he knew of white man ways. He invited Tchula Homa often into his house to review the deliberations of the village council, whose thinking, he felt, tended to be excessively cautious. He looked to Tchula Homa for the freshness and enthusiasm of youth, yet not infrequently Kills

Enemy found himself compelled to assert that his nephew was the oldest young man he had ever known, with all the rash absolutism of immaturity but also the obdurate stuffiness of a white-haired great-grandfather. Nonetheless it was obvious that he had begun to think of Tchula Homa as his successor.

One day Kills Enemy said, "You have never seen the Father of Waters, I believe."

"No, once when I was a boy I saw it."

"Well, would you like to see it again? The trading post is much bigger now, and there's also Fort Pickering, with white soldiers and Negroes and everything. Big white man boats go by every day. It's quite a place altogether. And you will need to learn trade."

"Thank you," said Tchula Homa, "but I think I'd rather not go."

"You know, young man, in the end, we cannot hide from the outside world. It will be there whether we keep abreast of it or not. And if we do not, we may find ourselves taken by surprise. Sometimes you put me in mind of that crazy Shawnee who came to the Fourth Bluff last summer and talked to some of our chiefs at Chucalissa. You remember hearing of him, called Tecumseh?"

"Yes, I heard about him, but George Colbert wouldn't let us go to hear Tecumseh for ourselves."

"Listen to what Tecumseh said. Go get the speaker."

At the warrior house next door, an uproarious party was in progress. Tchula Homa and Pothanoa passed it in silence, turning their heads away.

"Tell us Tecumseh's speech," said Kills Enemy when Tchula Homa and the speaker entered the chief's house.

Pothanoa quoted: "Tecumseh said, 'The white race is a wicked race. Since the day when the white race first came in contact with the red men, there has been a continual series of aggressions. The white men's hunting grounds are fast disappearing, and they are driving the red men farther and farther to the west. Such has been the fate of the Shawnees, and surely will be the fate of all of you too if the power of the whites is not forever crushed. The mere presence of the white man is a source of evil to the red man. His whiskey is destroying the bravery of our warriors, and his lust corrupting the virtue of our women. The only hope for the red men is a war of extermination against the paleface. Will not the warriors of the southern tribes unite with the warriors of the Lakes?' That is what Tecumseh the Shawnee said."

"Thank you, my friend. You may go." Now, turning back to Tchula Homa, Kills Enemy said softly, "So of *course* George Colbert kept Tecumseh's words from our people: Tecumseh would have led us to suicide. Surely you can see that. The twin brother of Tecumseh, Tenskwatawa, the half-blind priest whom they call the Prophet, led the Shawnees into battle only last month, at a place in the north called Tippecanoe, against the white chief William Henry Harrison, and our red brothers were utterly destroyed. They have now lost all their lands. Tecumseh himself, meanwhile—who I believe does not even know yet what has happened to his brother and his people—has gone among the Creeks with his crazy message, and the Red Stick faction, always the stupidest of a stupid people, have allied themselves with him. Soon you will hear what becomes of these Creek fools, and then judge for yourself the wisdom of Tecumseh's counsel. Luckily, many of the more sensible Creeks have resisted Tecumseh's madness; Big Warrior has refused him. In turn Tecumseh promises that when he returns home, he will stamp his foot on the ground, and the earth beneath the Creeks will shake in anger against them. Frankly, this Tecumseh is rather ridiculous. When he returns home, he will find no ground that is his to stamp on. Here. Smoke."

Tchula Homa smoked, and said nothing. The Creeks were too warlike, the Cherokees too docile. It should not be necessary for the Chickasaws to be like either of them. All they needed to be was themselves, and apart.

"Have you nothing to say?" demanded Kills Enemy.

"I listen, and learn," said Tchula Homa.

Kills Enemy frowned.

The king too was troubled by Tchula Homa's stubbornness. The Chickasaw way of life was now inextricably linked to trade with the white man. If their leaders failed to reflect the people's own evolving values, Tinebe argued, the people would soon insist on new leadership. The Chickasaw way must change or die. Most important to him, Tinebe said, were the full-blood chiefs like Kills Enemy and Tishomingo, the guardians of ancient Chickasaw purities. Without them, he said, we cannot hope to stay apart from the corruptions of the white man world. Equally, however, we must have the full confidence of our mixed-blood leaders, who speak English and understand the whites and can keep us informed about them, because if we are ignorant of the white man he will meet us in ambush. This, Tinebe said, Kills Enemy and Tishomingo have come to understand.

The king's implication was clearly that Tchula Homa had not.

As so often, the young man made no reply.

"What, would you say," asked Tinebe, "is the greatest threat to our nation?"

"Tinebe Mingo," replied Tchula Homa, "I am only a warrior. I follow my chiefs."

"I ask you to speak, Tchula Homa. Freely."

"All right then. The Colberts."

"Why?"

"Money," replied Tchula Homa.

The first James Colbert was a Scotsman who had come to live among the Chickasaws nearly five generations before and who had eventually been accepted as fully Chickasaw. With their business acumen and worldliness, the Colbert family had managed to keep the white man at bay for a long time, and Tinebe insisted that they were now indispensable to the preservation of the Chickasaws' separateness. George Colbert had accomplished peacefully what no full-blood Chickasaw, unable to speak English or to read a white man's face, could possibly have achieved—the expulsion by United States military forces of two hundred and eighty-four white families who had taken up residence on Chickasaw lands. It was true that many of those families had quietly returned to their illegal homesteads, and were still there, but the nation's only hope for redress remained the cooperation of the white government. Tinebe knew, and freely admitted, that some of the white men considered the Colberts to be the real rulers of the Chickasaw people. But what should they care what the white man thought of their government?

Tinebe tried, gently, to explain to Tchula Homa that the changes the people were now undergoing had been made inevitable long ago. Firearms, iron axes, and horses, the king pointed out, had been part of their life since the days of their grandfathers' grandfathers, long before the actual arrival of white men in the Chickasaw nation. And did Tchula Homa wish to give up firearms? iron axes? horses? And even if he did, could he imagine the people's being so willing? And what of Tchula Homa's cherished knife? In the old days, it would have been of bone or brittle iron, and could not have been thrown without breaking.

Still Tchula Homa would not be moved, and when Tinebe pressed him again he spoke. To accept some of the benefits of white acquaintance, Tchula Homa contended, did not require the acceptance of the white man's all too obvious evils, and that distinction was precisely what the Colberts failed to consider. Wherever you look in our nation, he said, and find impurity, you need look little farther to find the name Colbert nearby. The full-blood people, even in Tchula Homa's own generation, were still fundamentally Chickasaw, and proud of it. Was not the Chickasaw horse known far and wide as the sturdiest, bravest, fastest breed in the world? Were not Chickasaw riflemen the world's best hunters? Yes, they had gained skills and tools from the white man, but they had turned them to their own, uniquely Chickasaw uses. Yet now, with whiskey and miscegenation and money, the Chickasaw people were in real danger of sacrificing their uniqueness: some of them craved property, and white acceptance, and release from the sometimes saddening realism that had made them masters of reason.

And sometimes, as he argued ardently on, Tchula Homa began to see in Tinebe's face a faint hint of shame. And the king would raise his hand to bring Tchula Homa's speech to an end, and say, "You are young."

Tchula Homa would stalk into Moon Behind Cloud's house and sit down without a word, and she would kneel behind him and rub his back and lay her head on his shoulder, with her hair trailing down his chest, and call him her bear.

Tchula Homa said nothing. He picked up his cane flute and began to play a low, mournful melody.

"You are as gloomy as a bear," she said softly.

He played on.

"Big sad bear," said Moon Behind Cloud, biting his shoulder softly, "I love you."

These nights, she would meet him in her mother's corncrib, and there, on a thick fur blanket atop the rustling ears, would instruct him in the art of love. He was an eager, passionate, clumsy, and, he felt certain, poor student.

On the now familiar ride home Tchula Homa was accompanied as usual by the king's doctor, and this time there was also a delegation of hunters from the capital who wished to negotiate a firm nationwide price for skins and furs at the Fourth Bluff, for the price paid by the government factor there had been falling steadily for the past year. But all he could think of was Moon Behind Cloud. The trees and climbing vines, black in the silver light of late-autumn overcast, made him happy. The chatter of juncos in the honeysuckle thickets made him happy. The price of hides, the fate of the nation—none of that mattered, for Tchula Homa had killed the great single *no* that had seemed for so long to be all there was inside him, and in its place there was growing a great single *yes*. Did he know her? She revealed very little of herself. That did not matter, either. He loved her.

When Tchula Homa and his party rode into Nonconnah, they saw five warriors tied with deer-sinew thongs to wooden frames in the square, with all the other warriors of the village gathered around them.

"What is this?" demanded Tchula Homa, dismounting.

"There was a white trader here this morning," said Tathonoyo.

"Why wasn't he expelled?"

"Kills Enemy was out hunting," said Tchula Homa's brother. "It was raining, and the old men were in the council house, and so when the trader got to the warrior house he just walked right in, and sold them a barrel of whiskey."

Kills Enemy strode into the square with a whip in his hand. Weeping, he began to beat the first of the five warriors.

Tchula Homa turned away.

His mother lay on her back beside the fire, wrapped in her old buffalo robe, her mouth wide open in uneasy sleep, her lips crusted with blood. His grandmother sat in the shadows, singing quietly.

Tchula Homa's father greeted the arrival of the king's doctor with cool formality. The trader this morning had spoken in glowing terms of the white doctor who was visiting Fort Pickering. He had healed not only soldiers but also many of the Indians who lived nearby. The Indian doctors, the trader had said, knew less than nothing; they did more harm than good.

Tchula Homa, however, maintained a rigid faith in Chickasaw medicine. Perhaps the doctor was not as gentle and considerate as he ought to have been, but Tchula Homa believed that the old ways' wisdom could survive the medium of an incompetent practitioner.

The doctor woke the sick woman with a sharp cry, and began to chant the songs of healing. Tahanata was shivering and coughing helplessly, but every time she tried to lie back down, the doctor would stop singing and insist roughly that she sit up.

At last Tatholah could stand it no longer. "Don't you see you're going to kill her?" he shouted. "Get out of my house! Out!"

Tchula Homa had watched this whole terrible scene without moving or speaking, not exactly paralyzed but not tempted to action either; it had simply seemed not quite real.

"Tomorrow," his father said, "I'm going to go to the Fourth Bluff to get some white man medicine for your mother."

Tchula Homa stared at him.

"Listen, son. Imagine how this feels to me. I remember your mother when she was a girl of sixteen, running like a deer. I remember when her smile went into the hearts of the best young men of our nation. But it was me she chose to marry. Marrying her made me an important man, listened to by our chiefs and priests. Now I look at her, and the woman I have loved all these years has nearly vanished into wreckage, worse than death! You think of the glory of the Chickasaw nation, but I think of my wife's suffering, this one woman's pain. If the white man medicine can make her well, what has that got to do with Chickasaw glory?"

Tchula Homa said nothing. He loved Moon Behind Cloud, and he loved his mother with all his heart, but he resolved that no individual, selfish love would ever overpower his love of his people.

"We have a lot of skins," said Kills Enemy, slapping the packs stacked tall before the overflowing trade goods house. Suddenly, just in the last couple of weeks, the few hunters who were not sick had found game plentiful. "I don't suppose you want to come with us."

"No," said Tchula Homa.

"The king's men will go with us, so the nation will be presenting a united front to the factor. There may be some hard bargaining, and it may take a while. I don't know how soon we'll be back. I'm going to ask you to act as chief in my absence."

This meant more than just temporary leadership; it implied an eventual formal designation as Kills Enemy's successor.

Tchula Homa stood before the council to be examined. The old men questioned him for hours.

"Why should we let ourselves be governed by a boy?" demanded one councilor, late in the day.

"I am a man," said Tchula Homa.

His interrogator snorted and sat down.

"I will rely heavily on the advice of all of you," continued Tchula Homa. "And I will ask myself, 'What would Kills Enemy do?' "

To this there was a murmur of approval.

"Do you want to be chief?"

"No," Tchula Homa admitted.

Somewhat to his surprise, this answer too seemed satisfactory.

Pothanoa told the ancient story of the fox pup who was eaten by the giant river snake. The pup had stayed alive inside the snake by feeding on what the snake swallowed, and so had changed into a wolf, and eaten the snake's heart.

In the silence that followed, Kills Enemy called for a vote, and with a shout Tchula Homa was elected.

His father greeted him as "Chief!"

In reply Tchula Homa frowned, drew in his breath, sighed, and said, "Father, I'm really not worthy."

"Don't be absurd! Of course you are. Who else in your generation is qualified? And nobody wants an *old* chief any more—I mean, unless it's Kills Enemy, of course. You are exactly the man."

"I wish I could feel it," said Tchula Homa. "Ever since I came home from my meditation last summer, I keep feeling somehow as if I've lost my reason. Everything seems so full of sadness, but more than sadness, almost a dread. I know there are blessings everywhere, but often they seem to me like good things just waiting to go bad. I've always thought that being a man means having a really robust, optimistic outlook on everything—you know, taking control, acting wisely, being brave. But yesterday afternoon, after the doctor had left, when I was sitting out front with Mother asleep with her head in my lap, and I was looking over at the old men in the square with the last daylight on their red blankets—they were just chatting along as always, nothing special—I suddenly felt as though my heart would break, just for the simple beauty of it all, the red blankets, the tranquility. Is that a man's feeling? And then earlier, when the doctor was here and making Mother so miserable, where was the emotion that was really called for, for her? I listened to her coughing as though she might die any minute, and I didn't feel a thing. All I could think of was the magic, the Chickasaw magic, our medicine, *my* trust in all that. That clear-headedness I felt when I finished my meditation was an illusion, wasn't it, Father?"

"No," said Tatholah. "You're your father's son. I'm the same way."

"I don't believe it."

"Well, it's true," said his father. "I've learned to conceal it, but never to control it. It's something the spirits bestow. The secret is to learn to regard it as a blessing. You see and feel more than other people, so life will be richer for you."

The next morning, as his father and his uncle mounted their horses, Tchula Homa called out, "Have a good trip. Don't let the white man rob you!"

East Wind tossed his mane and stamped. The two old men of

Nonconnah and the delegation from the capital rode slowly off, with the long string of pack horses behind them piled high with pelts.

In Tchula Homa's honor that night, the warriors of the village danced a dance not unleavened with mockery. He was deeply relieved, nonetheless, to find that no whiskey was in evidence. Tchula Homa chose not to sleep in the chief's white house at the head of the square but rather to stay with his mother.

A few days later, when Tchula Homa came home after a long session of the council, he found his mother for the first time in weeks sitting up and cooking. She was even singing softly, to the accompaniment of Tathonoyo's soft drumming.

"Terrapin soup for a chief," sang Tahanata, "cornbread for my son and my son."

"Mother, look at you," said Tchula Homa, kissing her.

"She's getting well," said Tathonoyo.

"I'm really not, you know," she said to Tchula Homa. "I just *feel* better, because I've had an idea."

"And what would that be?" inquired Tchula Homa.

"That place where you men go for your meditations," said Tahanata. "The sacred swamp. I understand it has special powers. Is there any reason why an old woman couldn't go there?"

"Mother," said Tchula Homa patiently, "it's too far. You're still too sick. Get better, and then we'll see."

"It's not forbidden, then?"

"Not that I know of."

"Well, then, let's go. I am dying, son. Let it kill me if it must."

"This is crazy," put in Tathonoyo. "At least wait till Father and Kills Enemy come back with the white man medicine."

"I'd rather go ahead and die. Now, both of you, be quiet. I need some sleep. We should try to get an early start."

Tahanata did not make it very far on foot, but she was easy to carry. As they came near the swamp, Tchula Homa and his mother met two white men with a mule train loaded with farming equipment—shovels, plows, axes, picks—and mysterious chains and instruments which the young man was later to learn were surveying tools. He knew well enough to be cautious with muleskinners, but burdened with his mother he had no choice but to confront them.

The muleskinners proved at close range to be much less fierce than their reputation. One of them, in fact, insisted, gesturing, that he had medicine that would do the old woman good. Tchula Homa sensed that to refuse it might not be wise, but his mother, still being held like a child and glaring wrathfully at the white men, let fly a volley of expletives whose sense despite the unknown language was evidently not lost on them. No inspiration of diplomacy came to him, so the young man simply turned and fled down the trail, with his mother in his arms and the white men's laughter burning into his back.

"Do you know," demanded Tahanata, "that it was white man magic that made me sick in the first place? It was one of their infernal bibles. Some missionary put it right in our house while I was out in the fields and your father was hunting."

"And everywhere you look these days there are more of them," said Tchula Homa. "At the capital, Mother, you wouldn't believe how many people are wearing white man clothes, talking about white man religion, wishing for white man luxuries. It makes me feel sick."

"It has made me literally sick. They poison those bibles with illness."

"I want to see this country rid of them, Mother."

"You are a good son."

Beyond a green-gold marsh from which clouds of geese rose braying, the cypresses towered over a maze of bayous, sloughs, and potholes. After a tortuous hour through the mud and tangled vines, they came to an upland forest where the trees were far apart and the footing was easy. In the midst of it rose a clearly man-made hill—a flat-topped pyramid. Long ago, this mound had been the foundation of the successive houses of the greatest kings who had ever lived. The bones of the Chickasaws' noblest ancestors were buried here. Along the shore of the ancient lake, there had spread a great city. Now, the lake had disappeared, and the city was gone, and only this hillock remained.

When Tchula Homa reached the top, he lowered his mother to the ground in the center of the circle of brightly painted stones. Beneath her, their ancestors slept. She smiled at her son, and said nothing.

The day had been warm, with sweet river air coming up from the southwest, and a soft blue haze above the marshes. But with evening a bitter wind slashed out of the north, and a full moon shone mercilessly clear. Tchula Homa's mother would eat nothing, and could not sleep. She coughed miserably into the night.

About midnight, the earthquake began. The ground was rent in a hundred places at once, and the huge oaks and tulip-trees came crashing down all around them, their roots hurling clots of black mud into the sky. A great bulge formed in the flat forest floor at the foot of the pyramid, and then burst like a boil. Black liquid, steaming in the night air, oozed down its sides, and then with a shudder the bulge collapsed on itself. In its place a heaving, gurgling wound in the earth emitted choking vapors in thick brown clouds. A terrible wind roared, and the earth began to roll in waves, and it was impossible to stand.

The young man and his mother clung together in the sacred circle. Tahanata was calm through it all, and Tchula Homa tried to draw strength from her.

"There have been earthquakes in our country before," she said amidst the roaring of the wind and the crashing of the falling trees and the groaning of the earth, "in our ancestors' days, when the Spanish first came and the city was destroyed by disease. And then when the French came up the Father of Waters to cut out the tongues of our buffalo, our nation had earthquakes again, though not this big, I think." For a few moments the earth was still. "You do know, don't you," said his mother, "that it was the French who exterminated the buffalo? They were the vilest of all white men. Certainly, though, the Spanish and the English were also very bad. Now these Americans, who call themselves our friends, they try to take the earth itself as though it were not a living thing, and look what happens."

She stepped outside the circle and motioned to her son not to follow. She walked down the side of the mound to the broken floor of the forest. The ground began to tremble again. "Poor earth," she said. She sank to her knees and touched it with her hands. She looked up at Tchula Homa. "Make her healthy again, son," she said softly. "You can't save me. I'm too old, and too sick. But this is your true mother, and she is young and strong, however sick she may be today, and she will still be young and strong when you're as old as I am."

They sat awake all night, the young man in the circle atop the mound and his mother at its base. The moon was huge and gold behind drifting clouds of dust. Thousands of birds swirled back and forth across it, afraid to light.

At dawn the earth quaked again, and the forest screamed with the agony of splintering trees. Hissing, steaming spouts of hot water and mud shot out of the ground. A group of young bull elk splashed through the boiling cypress flats in panic, stumbling and bellowing. In the distance, amidst the fallen timber, Tchula Homa saw a moving wave of something gray, and struggled to his feet to get a better look. He could not believe his eyes. Gray squirrels—hundreds of them, in a single mass—were pouring across the forest floor, afraid to take to the trees. With a convulsion the pyramid was cleft apart, and a black gruel flowed into the root-riddled chasm. Thunder spoke deep in the earth, and burst forth in a roar so unbearably loud that Tchula Homa and his mother clapped their hands over their ears, and still he felt as if his skull would split. An acrid gust of gas belched from a fissure, and Tchula Homa fell, choking.

When the tremor had passed, his mother was lying on her back in the mud at the base of the pyramid. He ran down to help her up, but she motioned him away. She began to sing to her ancestors. The mud sighed softly and half swallowed her.

Tchula Homa buried Tahanata where she had died, in the soft, wet, warm, still quivering earth.

1812

On that darkest and most evil of all days, the winter solstice, Kills Enemy's black stallion East Wind had come back to the village of Nonconnah, wild-eyed and unapproachable, but neither Tchula Homa's father nor his uncle had ever returned from the trading post at the Fourth Bluff. People there had told the messengers whom Tchula Homa sent that they had seen the two men on the day before the earthquake, but a number of Chickasaws camped at the base of the bluff had been swept away when the river had changed direction and run upstream.

In a sudden storm of freezing rain, a month later, a white trader was allowed to take shelter in Nonconnah. As was to be expected, he also had a little business to offer. He had brought with him the eagle-feathered staff which had been Kills Enemy's emblem of office. It had been found floating in the mouth of the Wolf River, where other possessions and some of the bodies of those who had been lost in the earthquake had been recovered. The price being asked at the Fourth Bluff, the trader said, was one beaver skin per artifact, and one prime deerskin for a corpse, but in light of the fact that several women in the village had bought cloth from him, the trader was willing to let the eagle-feathered staff go without further markup. Tchula Homa gave Tathonoyo a beaver pelt and told him to make the exchange; he himself did not wish to see the trader.

The next day, there was another earthquake, less strong than the first, though still terrifying.

The high priest said the worst was still to come. And indeed, the third earthquake, in February, was the strongest yet. With one sharp lurch of the earth Kills Enemy's house fell into rubble. The earthquake was followed by a blizzard, which kept the whole village housebound for a week. The priests consulted the spirits, and found that unknown devils were at large. Tsatsemataha prescribed a three-day ritual of purification, and said that Nonconnah must begin a new life. Ancient tobacco and button snakeroot tea were prepared, and the men of the village purged themselves repeatedly. Three women died after their ceremonial cleansing in the bitterly cold water of Daylight Bayou, and this was regarded as perhaps a sign of a successful exorcism.

The council decreed that a new chief's house be built, identical in every way to the old.

"And a chief must live in it," said Pothanoa. "Tchula Homa, our beloved Kills Enemy surely is dead."

"Perhaps not," said Tchula Homa.

"Your hand clings to his staff," said another councilor.

"Unworthily," said Tchula Homa.

"Will you serve us?" demanded Pothanoa.

"My mother," said Tchula Homa, "believed that the white man was the cause of the earthquakes. I promised her that I would work to rid the Chickasaw nation of him. This puts me at odds with the king and many other honored leaders at the capital."

"We are of one fire forever," said Pothanoa.

Tchula Homa felt tears coming.

"Brothers!" cried the speaker. "Shall Tchula Homa be chief of Nonconnah?"

"Yes!" roared the council as one.

Tinebe was pleased by Tchula Homa's election, but he thought the young chief's earthquake theory ridiculous. "The high priests of our people have explained the earthquakes," said the king. "They were caused by the comet with two tails that we all saw in the east last fall. The earth had easily rolled over the first tail, but the second was stronger, and it was this battle between the earth and the comet that caused the earthquakes."

"But *why* was the comet there in the first place?" demanded Tchula

Homa. "How many comets with two tails have there ever been in the whole history of the world? Surely such an unusual event must have a meaning. Why can't the priests explain that to us?"

"There is an explanation for everything, Tchula Homa," said the king, "but we cannot always know it. Furthermore, you, most of all, who always insist on tradition, must know that it is our tradition to accept without question the judgment of our priests."

"You remember, I assume," said Tchula Homa, "what Tecumseh said to Big Warrior the Creek, about stamping his foot."

"Yes, yes, yes," said the king wearily. "Tecumseh claims that it was his own anger that caused the earthquakes—he sets himself up as a god! He's turning out to be a rather puny god, however. Do you know that the white chief Jackson is soon going to annihilate the Creeks of the Red Stick? And you know what has already become of the great Shawnee rebellion in the north. Well? They were *destroyed.* Their lands are gone forever. *Forever.*"

Moon Behind Cloud was waiting for him in the forest, beside a deep green willow-rimmed pool where Chickasaw lovers had been meeting for generations.

When the dogwoods bloomed, it was time for Tchula Homa to take the next step into adulthood.

He took his painted ceremonial bow and found his way by moonlight and memory to the old disused corn fields south of the village, where young shrubs and other good browse were edging out from the forest. In the crown of a black oak he waited, praying. The buck, his antler-velvet haloed by the low light of the barely risen sun, answered Tchula Homa with his presence. Tchula Homa greeted him with a soft cry. Deer lifted his head and looked into the young man's face and did not start away.

This is the deer All-Deer has sent me. Forgive me, Deer. Arrow be fast and true, prayed Tchula Homa, and it was.

He field-dressed the deer, and rode with it to the capital. The king touched his fingers to the antlers, then to his own lips, and then to Tchula Homa's lips. "Now sleep," said Tinebe.

Dressed all in white, Moon Behind Cloud met Tchula Homa at the center of the capital square, beneath a canopy of flowers. On one side stood Wren and her three other daughters and their husbands. On the other stood Tchula Homa's grandmother, Lokana Tcheh; Tchula Homa's younger brother, Tathonoyo; and Kills Enemy's mother's brother, the king, Tinebe Mingo, whose other sister, now dead, had been Moon Behind Cloud's great-grandmother.

Moon Behind Cloud presented Tchula Homa with a bowl of hominy soup (without a rock in it), signifying that she was a woman and could provide vegetables. Tchula Homa in turn presented her with the deer, to show that he was a man and could bring meat. Tinebe Mingo pronounced them husband and wife, and they returned to Nonconnah.

One day, later that spring, Tchula Homa was just coming out of his house into the sunshine when he heard East Wind whinnying madly in the paddock. The stallion was racing up and down, rolling his eyes. Then Tchula Homa looked across the square and saw, or thought he saw, a ghost, dressed in the black suit and white shirt of a white man, walking straight towards him.

"Kills Enemy?" said Tchula Homa.

"Yes," said his uncle. "It is me."

"Shall I invite you into your own house?" said Tchula Homa, reaching for the eagle-feathered staff and holding it out to Kills Enemy.

Kills Enemy waved it away, and came in and warmed himself at Tchula Homa's fire. "This is a new house," he said.

"Yours was knocked down by the earthquake in February."

"Ah."

"Your pipe," said Tchula Homa, lighting it and passing it to his uncle.

"This is good. I'm glad to be home." He returned the pipe to Tchula Homa. "How is everything here?"

"My mother died in the earthquake. Do you have any idea what became of my father?"

"No. I will tell you all I know of what happened. He is probably dead."

"I have grieved for him."

"Tatholah ennobles the ancestors with whom he now sleeps," said Kills Enemy in the traditional formula of condolence. "And how is our dear village?"

"There's less illness now, but many have died. Game is scarce. You were presumed dead, and I was made chief. Of course now you'll take over again."

"Let that pass for now," said Kills Enemy. "I will tell you my story."

"Good," said Tchula Homa.

"It was night when the earthquake began, so I couldn't see anything. I reached for your father's hand, but he was already out of bed. I tried to climb up the bluff, but it was coming to pieces and falling on me. I found some other Chickasaws, and we prayed in the dark for a long time. When the sun rose, the river had turned black, and there were huge whirlpools and waterspouts. Whole trees shot out of the water.

"Then there was a great roaring from the north, and there were flashes of red light—not lightning; fire from the lower world, perhaps—and the river began to flow *backwards,* and a big wave came, and I was swept in. I clung to a cottonwood tree and rode it as far as the Forked Deer River, I think. When the backward current met more water coming from upstream, the river went all the way to the top of the sky, with no air in between, and I began to drown.

"The next thing I knew, I was looking into the face of a white man, on the biggest boat I have ever seen. He wrapped me in a blanket and took me inside a house that was built on top of the boat, where it was very warm, and I slept for a long time.

"When I awoke, there were white people all around. I couldn't talk to them, of course, but I did learn some of their names. The man in charge was called Nicholas Roosevelt. His wife was there, too, called Lydia, and their newborn baby, and their big black dog.

"Now, this boat, Tchula Homa, was the most amazing thing I have ever seen. It moves along at an incredible speed, *without human work.* It was as long as five houses, and wider than two. It made a noise like fifty thunderstorms. Inside the wooden house there was a small iron house, and in this there was a fire bigger than ten Green Corn bonfires, with two men feeding it logs all day and night. On top of the iron house was a great pipe like a hollow tree, with black smoke and sparks and burning coals pouring out of it. Every day they would cut up as many trees to feed that fire as our whole village uses in a winter!

"At the back of the boat, there was a huge sort of drum covered with paddles, which drove into the water endlessly, without ever tiring. And then one day, Nicholas Roosevelt spun the big wooden wheel that steered the boat, and we began to go *upstream!* Tchula Homa, I tell you, these white men know things beyond our conceiving.

"Whole islands had been scalped of their trees. At places the river was filled from bank to bank with dead animals and uprooted forests and the wreckage of flatboats and Indian canoes. Sometimes also there were dead men in the water, and then also Lydia cried.

"After a while we came to a white man city, named for our ancient kinsmen who have now disappeared—the Natchez.

"How can I describe it? Countless white men's houses, some of them as big as small villages, full of room after room! In these houses, everything is shining and very complicated, and you cannot find your way around. There are pictures on the walls so real you'd think you could walk into them. You sit on soft, high chairs, and drink a thing like black drink from tiny cups that gleam like mussel shells, with tiny handles. They showed me how to eat in their way, which is very difficult, with many metal tools. Their food is very strange. But it's good—look at me!" Kills Enemy laughed, and patted his belly.

"And these white people have dozens of Negro slaves, who do all the work. The white people just sit and drink their black drink. The women talk and sew, and the men talk and drink whiskey. They get drunk, but not like the ones at Fort Pickering: these white men laugh and tell stories, and I never once saw any of them get angry when they were drunk.

"Every night I would sleep between snow-white cloths in a bed high off the floor, softer than a dream. Frankly, sometimes I would feel sick and have to lie on the floor to sleep. And even on the floor there were soft rugs.

"There was another earthquake when I was in Natchez, but all that happened was that their lamps flickered, and the white women pulled their shawls more tightly around their shoulders, and the white men poured themselves another drink of whiskey. I'm sure that's because they've tamed earthquakes there as they've tamed everything else.

"They introduced me to many white people. Nicholas Roosevelt had this suit of white man clothes made for me. You see how perfectly it fits?" Kills Enemy rose and walked up and down, and bowed low, and grinned. "*How do you do?*" he said in English, his eyes glittering.

"Then one day when I was riding with the Roosevelts in their carriage pulled by two black horses, I saw some Choctaws, and I got down to say hello, and it was such a relief to be able to talk again that I didn't mind even when they mocked me in my white man suit. Later, I thought about how those Choctaws had laughed, and I began to realize that I was only a curiosity for these white people. And I realized how much I missed my village, and you, and all this world.

"So I went into the bottomlands and made a blowgun as Tinebe had taught me when I was a boy, and I lived on small game. I have been walking now for a long time. There was a third earthquake—very violent, too, no doubt because I was now outside the white man world—and it ripped the earth apart terribly. In many places the road was swallowed up, and there were big downfalls of timber. I am very tired, Tchula Homa," said Kills Enemy, and suddenly he was weeping.

"Uncle, sleep here," said Tchula Homa, indicating his own bed.

Tchula Homa went to find Moon Behind Cloud at the women's gathering-house. She came out, kissed him, and before he said a word asked, "Is it true that Kills Enemy has come back?"

"He's asleep in our bed."

"Will he be chief again?"

Tchula Homa frowned.

"Where has he been?"

"It's a long story," said Tchula Homa.

"Is he all right?" she asked.

"We must let him rest, and then we'll see. He's been among white people, and it may have affected his reason. I think they may have put him under some sort of spell."

"Have you talked to Tsatsemataha?"

"I will. I haven't talked to anybody."

Moon Behind Cloud took Tchula Homa's hand. "You love him very much," she said.

"Yes."

"What's the matter?"

"It's hard to express," said Tchula Homa. "We'll talk tonight."

"You don't include me in your thinking," said Moon Behind Cloud. "You always put me off until you've made up your mind."

He said nothing.

"I love you, Tchula Homa," she said.

"I want to be sure I'm right before I speak," he replied.

"It's easier for you to be alone in your thoughts."

"Yes, alas," said Tchula Homa. "Perhaps you don't want Kills Enemy to be back. I ask myself why it should be important to you if I'm chief or not. You've said that you want what will make me happy. Will the chiefship do that? Or does it just put me in a position to fail the more shamefully?—a higher spot, to fall farther from? The world moves one way while I lean against it, trying to push it back—back to where it was before I was born. Is that not a fool's idea? If I were to seek your counsel, wouldn't you advise me that I'm setting myself up for a fall? You see, my solitude protects my folly."

"What, in your view, is a wife for?" demanded Moon Behind Cloud, her tone more gentle than her words.

He did not speak for a long moment, then took her tiny frame in his long arms. "Ah, dear girl—"

She stiffened.

"Just now," he said, still holding her, "I did try to share my thinking with you, however clumsily."

"I'm still strange to you," said Moon Behind Cloud.

"Yes," said Tchula Homa.

"Shall we stay at Tathonoyo's house tonight," she suggested, "so that Kills Enemy can rest undisturbed?"

Kills Enemy slept through the day and all night and into the next morning. When he awoke, Tchula Homa and Tsatsemataha were at his side. The high priest began to chant a song of exorcism.

"This was just a precaution," said Tchula Homa. "You have been in the white man world."

"Yes, I have, and I have a few things to say about it. Will you kindly convene your council?"

Kills Enemy did not tire now, nor weep. There was lightning in the old man's eyes, thunder in his voice. As he finished the narrative of his journey, Kills Enemy's voice dropped to a grave and confidential softness that forced his listeners to lean forward to hear him. "Last night," he said, "I awoke from a vision, which stayed with me into my waking, as only the truest dreams do.

"Listen, old men! Listen, warriors! In Natchez, I have seen a future for us. It will enable us to stand against the white man, Tchula Homa, so you should like it. In a word, it is this: the Negro.

"With slaves, we too can plant cotton, and be rich. This cotton is the source of the miracle of white wealth and strength. Let us do as our king has so many times advised us—let us take from the white man only what can make us strong as Chickasaws.

"In my vision I saw our fields enlarged into the forest, which we have always had more of than we need, and hundreds of slaves raising cotton for us and our posterity. With cotton, we will have money, and it is clear that only money, in the end—not war, nor even our sacred purity—can protect us from the white man. He comes to us year after year, offering pittances for this, for that, for whatever he has lately set his mind on getting from the poor Indians, and many of our people have not the strength to resist. Even now, who among us has real power, and can stand up to the white man, and strike bargains with him? Only the Colberts and the other mixed bloods.

"And what is the source of their special ability? It is not English: we can always find interpreters. It is money. And how is it that they have so much money? Is it not their ownership of slaves, and the surplus of crops that those slaves produce in the fields of the capital?

"Brothers, listen. Let us start with a few, mainly women, and breed them. Have we not already bred the finest horse in the world? As the Colberts have shown, Negroes are even easier to keep than horses. They grow their own food!

"And here we are, much closer to the Fourth Bluff trading post than the Colberts, with a good road all the way. There is already booming trade on the Father of Waters. We too could sell cotton to the thousands of white men far away across the oceans.

"How many of you have seen cannons? We had one on the deck of Nicholas Roosevelt's boat, and, let me tell you, it is a weapon of unbelievable power. One cannon ball can blast a crater in a river bank as big as a house. Could we not have cannons, too? Could we not then, some day, regain our ancient supremacy?

"Brothers: I ask you only to think."

The words of Kills Enemy sank into Tchula Homa's heart in slow throbbings of sorrow. This was not madness which had entered his uncle; it was corruption.

Tchula Homa rose and moved slowly to the front of the room. "This staff," he said, raising it, "is my uncle's. He has returned to his village. He has traveled a long way, and seen a great deal, and he is very tired.

"Kills Enemy, welcome! You bring us a vision. We want this staff to be returned to you. As I understand you, for you to accept the staff would involve an exchange: the implementation of your vision, in return for your resumption of the Nonconnah chiefship.

"Brothers: this would be no small event. As Kills Enemy urges, we must think. For myself, I have been happy and honored to serve you this little while as chief, but now I would prefer that my uncle take back his staff. And yet against this preference I must weigh his vision. Tell me, Uncle: could you not take back your staff, and come back to us, and lead us all in the life we have always lived, the true Chickasaw life?"

Kills Enemy looked into Tchula Homa's eyes across the room, and said, "The life we have lived will make us weaker and weaker, until finally the white man consumes us." His voice dropped to an almost inaudible whisper. "I have seen the white man's strength, and it is greater than any of us have ever imagined."

"Old men," said Tchula Homa, "this is something we must discuss, and think about. I do not want to keep this staff. But I do not want to be a cotton farmer and an owner of Negro slaves. I do not want to be an imitation white man. I am a Chickasaw!"

For several days the council deliberated. In the end, as by tradition there always had to be, there was a unanimous declaration: Tchula Homa would be retained as chief, and cotton farming and slavery would be spurned.

Tchula Homa felt no pleasure in his victory.

Kills Enemy grew sick. The belief was general that the white man had worked some evil magic on him.

Each evening Lokana Tcheh would puff tobacco smoke into the setting sun, calling on the spirits of the dead to be ready to welcome her son. She bathed his brow with a cool cloth. She sang lullabies to him, and cradled his head in her arms, and fed him with the same cherrywood spoon from which he had eaten his first corn mush as a child.

Kills Enemy did not enjoy Tchula Homa's frequent visits to his bedside, but as his time came near the old chief reached out his hand to the young, and, taking it, Tchula Homa felt Kills Enemy's fear.

"I want you to have East Wind," said the old man.

"Yes. Yes! No. There. There. Yes. *Yes,*" whispered Moon Behind Cloud fiercely, her head thrashing. "No. No. Wait. No, I've lost it. I can't." She began to cry, hopelessly.

"Tell me what to do," said her husband.

"I don't *know,* my dearest."

"I'm sorry."

"So am I."

After many such failures, Moon Behind Cloud went to her mother at the capital. Both male and female orgasms being considered necessary to conception, there seemed little hope of her ever bearing a child. Moon Behind Cloud's mother agreed to ask her uncle the king to grant them an annulment, and at the Green Corn Festival, after a long talk between Tchula Homa and Tinebe Mingo, the marriage was dissolved.

Moon Behind Cloud moved back to the capital, and married her old lover Atchelata. By late fall she was pregnant.

Tchula Homa went to the sacred swamp. He sat in the circle of painted stones, surrounded by the earthquake-shattered forest, and swore never to touch a woman again.

1816

Tathonoyo came back from the Fourth Bluff with his pack horses bearing rifles, axes, saws, bright cloth, tin cooking pots, and many other white man luxuries.

"What are these?" demanded Tchula Homa, holding up a pair of heavy white man boots.

"Tushka Hopoyea, from the capital, wanted them. He's coming through next week."

"There are none for anyone in Nonconnah?"

"No," said Tathonoyo with an indulgent sigh. It was understood that such possessions were frowned on in Tchula Homa's village. "Listen. Our father is alive. I saw him at the race track. He was drunk. He didn't see me."

The two brothers bowed their heads and were silent for a long moment.

Tchula Homa went into his house and wept.

After a while, Tathonoyo came in and put his hand on his brother's shoulder. "Nonconnah is very quiet today," he said.

"You've been in a noisy and crowded place," said Tchula Homa.

"I remember," said Tathonoyo, "when it used to be noisy and crowded here."

The young men's long, lazy afternoons of jokes and old stories under the sycamore in the square were now only a bittersweet memory, their only vestige the exercise of hopeless nostalgia in the darkness around the fires, for most often now the hunters were out till nightfall.

These weary days of hunting were not, as the white man sometimes liked to insist, due to collapse of the game populations: although the hunting was harder, and the hunters had to travel farther to do it, the Fort Pickering trading post's own records showed that in the past year the Chickasaws had brought in thirty-six thousand deerskins alone, as well as pelts of wolf, elk, cougar, beaver, otter, fox, bear, and raccoon, and hundreds of gallons of tallow and beeswax. What kept the hunters so long in the field was the desire for money.

There were now as many whites as natives in the Chickasaws' ancestral hunting grounds. Although white occupancy of Chickasaw lands was forbidden by treaty and therefore illegal under United States law, settlers had razed great tracts of forest, planted thousands of acres in cotton, built houses and slave quarters, harassed and swindled and sometimes even killed the Chickasaws. The state of Tennessee and its most prominent chief, Andrew Jackson, actively albeit quietly encouraged this settlement. The Chickasaws' only hope of enforcement of the treaties guaranteeing the integrity of their nation, therefore, lay in faraway Washington. Time and time again, under such pressure as the Chickasaws could bring, the federal government had ordered the squatters to vacate their farms as soon as their crops were in in the fall, and spring after spring they were quietly back.

There were white men now even in the village of Nonconnah, although they lived with Chickasaw wives and tried to observe Chickasaw customs. Despite the village council's resolution of 1812, there were also a few Negro slaves. More and more of even the full-blood Chickasaw men—*warriors,* thought Tchula Homa bitterly—were devoting their time to the humiliating and effeminate task of farming. Already half-black children and half-white children joined in the games of the full bloods. Tchula Homa could not look at them without helpless rage mounting in his gorge, and he dreamed of a purging massacre in which every Chickasaw man, woman, and child polluted by blood or alcohol or money would be returned, in propitiation, to the earth.

At last the anger was alive that had lain so long inert. Now that I truly am a man, and own a warrior's righteous wrath, he mused, where do I find it directed? Against my own people, whom I tell myself I love? Against *children?* Oh, yes, also against the white man, as ever—but here Tchula Homa's thoughts sank into a wordless dejection, for he knew that so many of his people remained fascinated by the wealth and labor-saving tools of the whites, and were so delighted to be living near white settlement, that to try to expel the whites now would be to risk the fate of the Creeks. Three years ago, already weakened by factional struggle between the fiery Red Sticks and the appeasers, the Creek nation had been utterly crushed by Andrew Jackson and his warriors.

Would purification be worth such a cost? A civil war, and white invasion?

In any case, Tchula Homa knew, there was more to the Chickasaws' impurity than miscegenation and money. When even brief contact with the white man way of life could corrupt such men as Kills Enemy and Tatholah, was it not only a matter of time until temptation and corruption should infect all the nation?

Now it was autumn, and Tchula Homa had been called by the king to a meeting with the white man at the national council house. All the Chickasaw chiefs would be there, as well as chiefs of the Cherokee, Choctaw, and Creek nations.

Long before Tchula Homa could see the capital, he could hear the shouting and the singing and the drums, and he called on the spirits for courage.

The scene in the streets and the square was heart-breaking. A few old men in full dress stood here and there in solemn denial of it all, but they were tiny islands in a sea of riot and degradation.

One of Tchula Homa's cousins sat singing in a puddle, drunk. "Come here a second!" he called. The boy produced a bright silver pistol from within the layers of his white man clothes and leveled it at Tchula Homa. Terrified, Tchula Homa dove flat on his face—as his cousin cried "Bang!" and the pistol expelled a billowing red silk handkerchief. "Look at you," said the boy. "You've got yourself all muddy. Would you like to buy a nice officer's coat?"

There were a few comforts. Big Warrior and his delegation of inveterate trouble makers, for example, never showed up. And although the Cherokees were a week late—giving rise to deep suspicion on the part of Tchula Homa and the other traditionalist Chickasaws—when the Cherokee representatives did finally arrive they came with strict orders to hold tight to all their land no matter how splendid the offers of the white man. Tchula Homa was also relieved to see that a good number of his fellow Chickasaws were comporting themselves with some dignity. He allowed himself an anxious twinge of hope when George Colbert assured him that he and his brothers were determined to restore the nation's lands to full Chickasaw control.

Andrew Jackson strode into the council house and surveyed his adversaries with a grim, tight smile. He was tall, pale, stiff. "Red brothers," he said, "I am happy to see you." He worked his way among the Indian leaders, taking each by the hand and staring hard into his eyes. The white man's hand was thin and spotted, with long hard fingers; his eyes were pale, pale blue. He smelled of flowers.

The matters under consideration—principally involving ownership of the nations' ancestral hunting grounds—were exceedingly complex, and hard for the Indians, at least the full bloods, to understand, for possession did not describe their relationship to the land. The first two days of talk went by in confusion, without result.

The third day was devoted to discussion of a vast tract south of the Tennessee River, well to the west of the Cherokees' nexus of towns, well to the east of the Chickasaws, well north of the Creeks, yet hunted by all from time to time without conflict. It was true that the Creeks had used it most often, and after his victory over them Andrew Jackson had decreed it to be Creek land and had taken twenty million acres of it into the legal possession of the United States of America.

Why then, on the fourth morning, did Jackson announce that the Cherokees had signed a treaty ceding the same land? Didn't he own it already?

"My brothers," said Jackson, "your father in Washington wishes all hearts to be straight. Your Cherokee brothers had disputed the Creek claim to this land. It is far from your father's wishes to become embroiled in disputes among his red children."

And as for the express orders of the Cherokee people binding their representatives to an oath against any cession of land? The Cherokee negotiators were not even there to reply. They had fled in the night.

And what about the Chickasaws?

Why, certainly, Jackson wished to buy it from them too. Suddenly, Tchula Homa thought he understood. Only last spring, the four nations had agreed to use all lands between their centers of population *cooperatively,* and to spurn any efforts to divide them with firm boundaries. Once the Indians accepted the notion of national ownership, then the white man could play them off against one another and gradually buy his way amidst them—precisely what Jackson was doing today. This twenty million acres was surely only the beginning.

The Chickasaws withdrew. William Colbert said, "We have not used this land for generations. Even if we do not take the money, Jackson will send white men to settle the land. He has title to it from two nations."

"This is an old, old trick," said Tishomingo. "As he has done often in the north, soon the white man will be buying land that is truly important to the Chickasaws—but he will buy it from the Creeks, or the Choctaws. Then he will demand to buy a Choctaw hunting ground—from us. The red nations will hate one another, and squabble while the white men move in behind their backs. I have seen this before."

"It is worse than that," said William Colbert, flourishing a stack of papers. "These are deeds. Jackson has promised to destroy these documents as soon as we sign this treaty. Consider what will happen if we do not. This land," he said, waving a paper, "lies astride our northern trade road, and the deed is signed by the former councilors Maneke and Numinisah, who for good reason have left the nation. Here's another; this one entitles Andrew Jackson to possession of the sacred swamp near our village of Nonconnah. It is signed with the X mark of Tatholah. And this one—"

Tchula Homa did not hear the rest of William Colbert's recitation. What had his father done?

"One hundred thousand dollars is a great deal of money," Levi Colbert was saying. "Brothers, listen! Let us accept Jackson's offer, and get him out of our lives! Let us grant him his insistence on this idea of land ownership, because that will mean that the land can be legally established *as* our own. We can work out ownership within it according to our own lights. We lose nothing, and gain much: peace; perpetual sovereignty over our ancestral homeland, on terms the white man recognizes; protection by the white man government against intruders; and money for our poor. We can learn to read and write and cipher. We can do business, and hold our own. Our nation will be secure, its boundaries settled forever."

Tchula Homa shot a pleading look at Tinebe. Surely he would speak up! This went far beyond any of the accommodations the king had ever counseled. But he only looked away, and said nothing.

The majority favoring Levi Colbert's position was large, and it was traditional that the will of the nation be expressed as unanimous. Those, like Tchula Homa, who disagreed were expected to be silent and step aside. In the end, Tchula Homa was the only chief who did so. The twenty-three other Chickasaw chiefs signed the treaty ceding to the United States of America the ownership of the so-called Creek lands south of the Tennessee.

In return, the Chickasaw nation was to be paid twelve thousand dollars a year for ten years. There were to be grants of private land to George Colbert, for his ferry across the Tennessee; to the capital chief Appassantebe; and to the statesman Levi Colbert. Levi Colbert was also to receive forty-five hundred dollars in cash, "as a compensation for any improvements which individuals of the Chickasaw nation may have had on the lands surrendered." Andrew Jackson assured the Chickasaws that the deeds had now been burned.

The treaty also stipulated that white traders would henceforth be forbidden to do business in the Chickasaw nation except from the trading post at the Fourth Bluff. This last provision cemented the Colbert family's monopoly of the Chickasaw economy.

Tchula Homa did not go directly home. He rode instead to the Fourth Bluff—Fort Pickering—to try to find his father. From the pathetic trading post Indians there he learned that Tatholah had married a Negro woman, and that she was the chattel of a white man whose plantation was one of the most brazen encroachments yet on Chickasaw territory. The plantation stood directly astride the road that led from the Fourth Bluff and across Nonconnah Creek to Tchula Homa's village and, forking there, linked the Father of Waters with the centers of Chickasaw, Choctaw, and Creek population to the east and southeast. Indians traveling that route had now to ride through open fields in full view of the planter's house and slave quarters. It was likely, therefore, that Tatholah had watched his own villagers, and his own kinsmen, on their way to and from the trading post, and had never even come out to greet them.

Tchula Homa found his father sleeping under a tree just inside the plantation gate. Tatholah had difficulty waking up and getting his bearings, but when he did, he ran forward and embraced his son, and wept softly against his chest. He stank.

"I want to hear it all," said Tchula Homa. "Let's go into the woods and sit down."

Tatholah followed him meekly.

"You're wearing white man clothes," said Tchula Homa as they sat down facing each other.

"They're all I have," said his father.

"Now: tell me what's happened to you."

"Well," said Tatholah, "let's see. After we got to the bluff and set up camp, your uncle and I went to Rawlings's store with the pelts, but Mr. Ike said they didn't have any call for furs and hides just then. So we thought we'd stay around for a few days and see if some traders would come down the river. And they did come, but they said that the people across the ocean didn't want to buy furs any more, and of course we didn't have anything else to trade. So we really didn't know what we were going to do. All I knew was that I had to get that medicine for your mother somehow.

"Then one night, after we'd been there for about a week," he continued, "I got started drinking with some of my old friends from my warrior days who were up there racing horses, and they persuaded me that the only way I was going to get any money was to steal a horse for a certain white man who lived next to the race track, and who also spoke our language and so was a great favorite with all the Chickasaw people there. So, in the middle of the night I got up and climbed the bluff and went sneaking around the fort, and decided that the best place to get a horse was from the Army corral—an idea that gave me no little personal satisfaction, as you may imagine."

Tatholah cleared his throat, and for a moment there was almost a twinkle in his eye, but he looked away quickly and continued talking in his weary and dejected voice:

"So there I was, right in the paddock, picking a horse to steal, when the first shock of the earthquake hit, and suddenly there were soldiers pouring out of doors I didn't even know were there, screaming and crying and shooting off guns, and I was caught. They would have hanged me, of course, but the earthquake was so bad by the time it got light that they just forgot about me. Then when things calmed down, they decided to put me to work. They needed all the help they could get, including Indian horse thieves, I suppose, because that place was a mess—most of the buildings down, big cracks in the bluff. And then when they didn't have any more use for me, they locked me up for—a year.

"That's when things got really bad. I got sick, you see. They put me in a—in a hole." Tatholah's voice broke, and he paused. "And there was a soldier, a guard, who brought me whiskey. He was doing it to be nice to me. Medicine was scarce, but there was plenty of whiskey, and he was trying to help me. I stayed sick a long time, and this white man saved my life. The only problem was that after a while I couldn't do without the whiskey. And then when I finally got out, I was just ashamed to come home. I heard that your mother was dead, and Kills Enemy was dead, and you were chief—and I was just ashamed."

"I want to know about your selling the sacred swamp," said Tchula Homa.

"I knew the deed wouldn't be legal. That's how I justified it. I was hungry. I couldn't get anything to eat."

"You have not heard of hunting?" said Tchula Homa coldly.

"I didn't have a rifle."

"And you'd forgotten how to make a bow, or a blowgun? *You* taught *me*." He held up his knife. "A Chickasaw can get his food with no more than this, for a lifetime. You told me that, when I was a boy. I thought you were a Chickasaw."

"Perhaps I'm not, anymore," said Tatholah quietly.

"So," said Tchula Homa. "Gods, hear me! This man is not my father. My father is dead."

And after Tchula Homa had told the Nonconnah council about the meeting with Andrew Jackson and the other white men at the capital, he added that he had been to the Fourth Bluff to inquire about his father and had learned that he was dead.

The village gave Tatholah a magnificent funeral.

1818

In a cedar bottom in the headwaters of Nonconnah Creek, which in better times had been a rich hunting ground, Tchula Homa and four of his fellow villagers had hunted all morning and killed nothing. Four years now had passed since elk had been seen on their old winter range in the beech-forested breaks. Suddenly, this winter, deer too had grown scarce, and those few which remained were exceedingly cautious.

Stepping out of the broken ice and deep shadows of the cedars and into the arc of blazing day that was the road, the hunters started toward home. From eastward came the rumble of ironbound wheels and the jingle of harness. A wagon crested the rise into view, and then another, and another and another, all piled high with Indian belongings—blankets, baskets, painted gourd bowls, woven cane seats, fish traps, war clubs, blowguns, digging sticks, drums, pots—all decorated in the style of the Cherokees.

As the wagons came near, Tchula Homa and his companions lowered their muskets to the ground and raised their right hands in greeting. The white drivers looked away as though the Chickasaws were not there at all.

Later that day, the first of the Cherokees themselves came through, on foot. They had been walking for six weeks, they said. They had come nearly five hundred miles, and they still had far to go. Many had already died, of exposure, exhaustion, disease, starvation.

Tchula Homa ordered that the travelers be brought black drink and soup and cornbread, and many of them stayed overnight in tents they set up in the square. The leading men sat and smoked with the Nonconnah council, and told their story. In the Cherokees' honor, or in honor of their sorrow, great fires were built, to which some drew so near as to risk being burned.

The Cherokee elders explained that talks between Andrew Jackson and their now entirely corrupted chiefs had ended in a stipulation that some of their people must move to an unknown place, somewhere beyond the Father of Waters, where, some years ago, a few of their kinsmen had been induced by the white man to settle. The chiefs themselves and all the richer Cherokees were to stay in their ancestral homes in the east, in the ancient towns along the rivers: they had accumulated private property in those wide, rich valleys, and had white man deeds to their farms. These refugees huddling around the fires of Nonconnah were the poorest of their people, mountain villagers who until recently had been all but untouched by white man ideas and affairs. The rich and "civilized" members of the Cherokee nation had in effect traded their poor to the white man, in exchange for their own continued freedom.

Boats were waiting for the emigrants at the Fourth Bluff to take them to their new home, which was called Arkansas.

That winter, some four thousand Cherokee men, women, and children passed through Tchula Homa's village on their way west.

In March, there were earthquakes again.

Summer came, and plenty. The harvest was bountiful, and many whitetail does bore twin fawns. The people of Nonconnah traveled to the capital for what promised to be the grandest Green Corn Festival in years.

At the invitation of the king, Tchula Homa had come early. Today before dawn he had taken a canoe and paddled upstream to catch some fish as a present for his host, and now, at midmorning, returning, he heard the voices of women and girls bathing in the bayou ahead. This was not like him, not like him at all, to linger as he did now, to pull silently in to the bank beneath the overhanging vines, to stuff the ripe and unripe grapes alike into his mouth, not looking at what he picked, only spying through the sun-spattered shifting layers of leaves, but amidst the women's laughter he had heard the unmistakable soft laugh of Moon Behind Cloud.

And yes, there she was. She climbed out onto a grassy peninsula. Small, dark-skinned, she mounted the steps cut into a leaning sycamore, and with her arms extended for balance she walked, glistening, out on the foot-polished limb. She pushed her wet hair back from her face, and rose on her toes. She lifted her arms above her head. She took flight, arched, straightened, slipped into the water like a lance. Tchula Homa's eyes followed her otter-shape green growing brown growing gold till she exploded laughing in the midst of laughing friends.

He pushed the canoe back into the current and began to sing, to warn the women that a man was coming. They drew into a modest cluster in the pool and watched him skim past still singing at the top of his lungs. He lifted his paddle in greeting, and some of the women joined in on the chorus, " 'No, you won't,' said the beaver to the tree." For an instant his eyes met those of Moon Behind Cloud, and she smiled and then looked away.

This was the first time Tchula Homa had seen her since the annulment of their marriage. He missed her too painfully to admit it. But he had chosen solitude; it had not chosen him. Certainly it was painful sometimes, but was that not part of the bargain he had struck with himself?

After a late lunch of the bass he had caught, Tchula Homa sat and smoked with Tinebe Mingo on the king's balcony. Below them, in the capital square, the bustle of preparations raised a haze of dust which in the soft September sun shone gold. Tchula Homa took out his cane flute and played a slow and quiet tune. A V of whooping cranes, their long black-tipped white wings pounding slowly, their long black legs trailing out behind, their trumpeting loud, moved slowly across the western sky.

"One winter when I was a boy," said the king, "I went with my father to the great salt water, where the whooping cranes go. It's far, many weeks' ride. We were trading for shells and spices. A very lonely place it was, some of it the darkest, densest forest in the world, full of vines and moss and snakes, and the rest all open, water as far as you could see—frightening in a way, it made you feel so small. But, ah, Tchula Homa, the birds! Countless birds, of every kind we have in summer, and many others. Out in the marshes there would be long lines of cranes, spearing crabs in the mud. A couple of the local people took my father and me out fishing with them in a big sea canoe, around the mouths of the little creeks there, and we caught endless baskets of splendid green-and-blue crabs, which our friends boiled with hot peppers. That was delicious! I suppose you don't even know what a crab is, do you?"

Tchula Homa put down his flute. "No."

"And you're not curious."

"Curiosity can lead to envy, and dissatisfaction with one's place in the world."

"Ah," said the king wearily. "Here we go again."

"Would you wish to live in the south, Tinebe Mingo, on the great salt water?"

The king stared angrily at him and said nothing.

"I'm sorry," said Tchula Homa. "I mean no disrespect." This was a lie: Tinebe's collaboration with the white man had opened a chill distance between himself and Tchula Homa. Although the United States had failed to deliver on the treaty's guarantee of a personal annuity for the king, Tinebe had not protested, for he did not wish to offend the white man. Worse, he had also not protested the government's failure to pay the very large sums that had been promised the nation as a whole. But what mattered to Tchula Homa was not the question of any economic loss or gain due to Tinebe's timidity but the cost in honor and self-respect and that ineffable quality which the Chickasaws called purity, which included among many other ideas that of independence. As far as Tchula Homa was concerned, the king was in Andrew Jackson's pay, and pocket.

Yet in the unhappy gulf between the young man and the old an ember still glowed of the love that had been kindled on the day they had met, nine years before, and their distance was not so great that they could not still feel its warmth. Tinebe put his hand on Tchula

Homa's shoulder, and Tchula Homa covered Tinebe's hand with his.

As the afternoon faded to evening, fat old William Colbert labored up the ladder from beneath.

"There is whiskey in the warrior house," said Colbert with lugubrious gravity.

Tchula Homa passed him the pipe, and said, "I trust you got a good price for it."

"What evil inspiration comes into you, Tchula Homa, to make you say such things?" returned Colbert. "You know perfectly well I had nothing to do with it."

"Ah," said Tchula Homa. "Your white friend Isaac Rawlings, then, friend of the Chickasaws."

"This is intolerable!" said William Colbert to Tinebe.

"Tchula Homa," said the king sadly, as ever indulgent even when the young chief transgressed the most basic precepts of decorum, "Mr. Ike Rawlings has moved to Arkansas, to establish a trading post among the Cherokees there. And in any case William was never his partner in any enterprise. I believe you owe our brother an apology."

"And our king," added Colbert, "whom you interrupted."

"Tinebe Mingo, I regret very much having interrupted you. It is not our way, and I truly am sorry," said Tchula Homa. Then, rising, towering over William Colbert, he continued in a low, hard voice, "And to your brothers, too, *Tchushemataha*"—he spat out Colbert's dishonored Chickasaw name—"who have never been in league with the white man either, I should undoubtedly also apologize. Gods, hear me! To all those good Chickasaws who have cared only for their people's welfare and who have never done them harm, who have never brought whiskey among us and have never profited from trade in whiskey and whom I may have maligned, Tchula Homa sincerely apologizes. If Tchushemataha is in that category, he may consider his forgiveness to have been humbly begged."

"I would wring your neck, young man," said Colbert, now also rising, "if you weren't the size of a horse. I've got a mind to bring you before the council and demand that you be whipped."

In his anger Colbert let the pipe slip from his hands, and it fell through the balustrade and into the dust below, where it shattered.

Tinebe stood between them and looked down from the balcony at the broken pipe. "Brothers," he said quietly, "tomorrow is the first day of Green Corn. Peace. Reconciliation." He took Tchula Homa by the hand and said, "You have behaved very badly."

"The survival of our nation is at stake, and you worry about my *manners!*"

Still holding Tchula Homa's hand, the king took Colbert's as well, and joined the three of them. "Brothers," he pleaded, "we are of one fire forever."

"I'm sorry," said Tchula Homa, without feeling one bit so. He turned to descend from the balcony, and had barely set foot to the ladder when a woman's cry came up from the darkness of the house beneath.

"Tinebe," sobbed the voice, "my cousin, my king, please help me! Are you there? Are you there?"

Tinebe put his finger to his lips and in sign language told Tchula Homa to stay on the balcony, and Colbert to precede him down the ladder and depart. "Close your ears," signed Tinebe to the young man.

Tchula Homa truly wished to obey the king's admonition. But he could not keep from listening. He moved to the top of the ladder and looked down into the house.

Moon Behind Cloud was sobbing in Tinebe's arms, her head buried against his chest. When at last her weeping subsided, Tinebe lifted the young woman's face and looked at her. Her eyes were swollen nearly shut, her cheeks blackening with bruises.

"Who did this?" demanded the king.

"Atchelata!" she replied. "Who do you think?"

"What can have happened," said Tinebe, "that your husband would do such a thing?"

"I didn't do *anything,*" she cried in fury. "He's drunk! Tinebe Mingo, you've got to help me! He goes insane when he's this drunk. He could *kill* me. I took a nap this afternoon and had a dream and spoke the name of Tchula Homa in my sleep, and Atchelata started drinking and ranting and—then this. You've got to have him confined!"

"Tomorrow, you know, the Green Corn Festival begins," said Tinebe, "and all wrongs will be righted. Atchelata and all of us men will be purged, and all our sins forgiven. Don't worry, little cousin. Purity is always restored. This is much more effective than punishment. Sleep at your mother's tonight."

"You're going to forgive him?"

"Of course," said the king. "That is our way. It always has been."

Tchula Homa did not know what to think. Justice and custom seemed to be at odds. In the end he concluded that Tinebe was right. The old ways should be trusted to work their wisdom, which was far superior to that of any mere individual. Still, when he thought of Atchelata's wife he was troubled, and not only by questions of justice and tradition.

The Green Corn Festival began, the next day, in solemn hope and humble thanksgiving. Tinebe Mingo saw to it that Atchelata purged himself repeatedly with button snakeroot tea and ancient tobacco.

Three days later the ceremonies ended, as seemed now to have become traditional, in gambling, fighting, and alcoholic oblivion.

When the United States government requested another conference, the Chickasaw nation was in no position to refuse, for there was no other forum in which to press their grievances. This time, surely, Tinebe insisted, we will be paid what was promised us.

Major General Andrew Jackson of the United States Army and former governor Isaac Shelby of Kentucky had been appointed commissioners by the Secretary of War to treat with the Chickasaws at their former capital, known as the Old Town. Jackson was ill with jaundice, and in an exceptionally wrathful mood.

Negotiations were to have begun on the first day of October, but the Chickasaw council refused to begin until they had been paid what was owed them. Even then, they added, there would be no talk of further cessions of land.

On the twelfth of October, a flatboat docked at the Fourth Bluff containing seventeen large bundles of presents for the Chickasaws. The saddles, bridles, and horse blankets were of very inferior quality, and moreover had been damaged in transit; most of the cloth was stained and ruined; the thimbles, fish hooks, nails, scissors, and needles were rusted beyond recovery, as, worst of all, were the rifles; the gunpowder was wet; and all the mirrors were broken.

On the same day, a courier from Nashville arrived with thirty-seven thousand five hundred and fifty dollars in United States currency. After a solemn inspection of the money in its chest by the chiefs, all the Chickasaws present assembled to hear the speech of Andrew Jackson, rendered into Chickasaw by James Colbert:

"Friends and brothers,

"We have been chosen by your father the President of the United States to meet you in council, and brighten the chain of friendship, by shaking hands and greeting you as his children; we come to see that the sums due your nation be equally distributed among the poor and the rich to benefit all and make you happy. Your agent is prepared to pay you all that is due so soon as you can furnish him with the numbers of each chief's clan.

"Your father the President, always anxious to keep peace and friendship between his red and white children and do justice to all, has charged us again to bring to your view that neck of land lying in the states of Tennessee and Kentucky which was sold by North Carolina and Virginia about thirty-five years ago to pay the debt of the revolutionary war.

"Brothers,

"This piece of land is claimed by your nation, but our white people paid for it many years ago: and our father the President has kept them away from it, that his red children might hunt on it; but the game is now gone, and his white children claim it now from him.

"Brothers,

"Next year your white brethren will have nearly one hundred steam ships running up and down the Mississippi River, and they will want much wood for their fires that make them go on the water; and when a ship gets broke your white brethren want to be on the shore with their own people until it is mended; this helps to make your white brethren uneasy about their land.

"Brothers,

"Your father the President wants to have your lines finally settled, and he wants to give you as much land over the Mississippi, for this country which is granted to your white brethren, where there is no claim by any other state or people and where there is plenty of game and good land.

"Your father the President has told us, if you don't want to exchange land, to give you a fair and reasonable price in money for your claim to this tract of country which will not interfere with the settlement or arrangement of your nation. You will then have more land left than your nation can cultivate for six hundred years, and your father will feel happy in protecting and perpetuating your nation here.

"Friends and brothers,

"Listen. Your father the President has shown to you his care and justice by choosing us to come and give you a fair price for your claim to this land, and if you refuse to let him have it, and your white brethren go and settle on their land, which they are sure to do, you must not blame him, but your chiefs, if they refuse his friendly and just offer.

"Brothers, listen! The land we ask you for was granted by England almost two hundred years ago to the states of Virginia and North Carolina, and was conquered from England in the revolutionary war, when the Treaty of 1783 was made with England. She acknowledged the states to be the owners of all their land within their charter, to the great river Mississippi. Listen. These states, having spent all their money in carrying on the war, opened a land office and sold this land to their children to pay the debts which they owed when the war was ended; but to keep peace with your nation, and give you the benefit of the game, your white brothers have been kept off their land; but now the game is destroyed, your father the President is bound to give it to them and protect them in their possession.

"Friends and brothers,

"We have spoke plain and given you the truth, and we have yet one plain truth to tell you. Listen. As the states of North Carolina and Virginia owned this land about two hundred years ago, and before your nation was here, you having no claim to it but what the General Government chose to give you by permitting you to hunt on it, and from the Constitution of the United States, which admits no other sovereignty within her limits; all Indian claims are considered merely as a hunting privilege, subject to the will and pleasure of the General Government, and which you agreed to by the second, third, and eighth articles of your own treaty held at Hopewell in the year 1786.

"Listen well! When you sell your claim to this neck of land to your father the President, the rest of your large country lies in the lines chartered by England to the state of Georgia, and that state sold it to your father the President and Congress, who hold it fast for their red children to live on and be happy.

"Friends and brothers,

"We hear that bad men in your nation threaten your chiefs with death if they surrender this land to your father the President of the United States; if this is true, we call you all to listen well. If the bad men of your nation do any act of violence upon your chiefs for treating with your father the President, he will put them to death for it. Your nation has felt much of the bounty and care of your father the President, and he will not suffer such threats and insolent conduct to pass unpunished. Listen once more, for we must speak plain and tell you the truth: if you refuse the friendly offer of your father the President, the land will be taken possession of by your white brethren who have patents for it, and your father will look on your conduct as acts of ill will and ingratitude.

"Friends and brothers,

"We have given you our talk, and have nothing more to say until we get your answer; take our talk with you and think well, and let us have your answer as soon as you can."

All of western Tennessee, most of western Kentucky! Far from the capital, yes, but for untold generations the exclusive and uncontested and the richest hunting ground of the Chickasaws.

For three days, the leadership of the Chickasaw nation met in tumultuous council at the tall white white man house of George Colbert. While their attention was thus preoccupied, a party of Creeks burglarized several Chickasaw houses and made for the east with bedding, furniture, bolts of calico and homespun, and various articles of clothing including a richly decorated regimental coat.

On the third day of the council, it was unanimously resolved, again, that no land whatever would be ceded to their father the President. That evening, the warriors danced, singing the ancient song "We Will Never Be Defeated."

But no official reply was then prepared for the commissioners, and two more days went by while obscure private conferences among the Colberts and other chiefs were held in quiet corners of the town. Tchula Homa was deeply uneasy.

Again, the warriors danced and sang. Andrew Jackson stood at the edge of the Old Town square, watching.

On the morning of October eighteenth, Levi Colbert, Itawamba, dressed all in white buckskin and swan feathers, tall, silver-haired, the very type of Chickasaw dignity, rose to address the commissioners:

"White brothers,

"We have heard your talk, and we have discussed it at great length. As for your suggestion that we trade for lands far to the west, let us hear no more of such strange ideas. We were not born in that place. We are told there are warlike savages there, who would surely annihilate the peace-loving Chickasaws. To us, our homeland is the whole world. The Chickasaw does not travel here and there like the white man: where we are born, we live, and we die. Our land is a part of our very being, and can never be mere property. We could no more change land than we could change bodies.

"We have always loved our white brothers," continued Itawamba, "and have shown them the best of our friendship and hospitality. We know that our father the President is kind, and good, and keeps our well-being close to his heart. But there are real differences between our peoples, and one of the most profound is this matter of how we regard the earth. We do not say the white men are wrong to buy and sell it among themselves, but it would be wrong for us to do so. Please try to understand this."

Without even a word of reply to Itawamba's point, Jackson calmly offered the Chickasaw nation an annuity of twenty thousand dollars a year for twelve years for the cession of their lands in Kentucky and Tennessee.

Itawamba was silent, looking down at his feet.

"Two hundred forty thousand dollars! Are you deaf, Mr. Colbert?" shouted Shelby.

"Friends and brothers," replied Itawamba, "take my words into your hearts. It is out of the question."

"Two hundred fifty thousand, then, brothers," said Jackson without hesitation.

Tchula Homa rose and asked to speak. With a quick suspicious glance into the young chief's eyes, Jackson motioned him forward. Itawamba frowned—this was definitely out of order—but he stepped aside.

"As you have seen in the past," said Tchula Homa, "the Chickasaws love money. But you have heard today, and you will see henceforth as long as you shall look, that we love our land better. What good is your offer of money to us? You never pay! Do you really think us so stupid as to have forgotten about the money promised to our nation in the treaty signed two short years ago? And do you not realize that to most of us still, money is not good at all, but a white man's trap?"

Shelby jumped to his feet and interrupted Tchula Homa: "We've brought you your money, you jackass! Have you not seen it? General Jackson, show this rascal the valise. There! You will be paid."

Tchula Homa gazed coolly into Isaac Shelby's eyes and said, "Ah. Yes. Two years late. Now that it's worth your while to seem to honor your debts—hoping for further concessions, promising more money which you will not pay until the next time there is something you want to squeeze out of us. There may be fools among us, Shelby, and there may even be criminals, but we're just not that stupid. So I say to you, *Shelby*, white snake, and to you, *Jackson*, white tick, take your money and go home. Take it to our father the President in Washington city, and buy him rotten saddles with it, and wet flour, and rifles that jam after one shot!"

The Chickasaws were on their feet shouting for joy, tossing straw from the floor into the air. Even the Colberts and their clique felt obliged to join in the cheers. Tchula Homa looked around himself in a daze, and felt glory surging through his veins.

It was a short-lived glory. The Chickasaws fell silent, fearing what might come next. A stillness came over the white men, and for a long moment no one spoke.

Then, in a gentle tone, Jackson assured Tchula Homa and Levi Colbert of the United States' respect for Indian societies.

There would be no difficulties, Shelby concurred.

It was as if, somehow, Tchula Homa's speech of intransigence had meant not what he had said but rather its very opposite, as if somehow he had actually assured the commissioners of the Chickasaws' ultimate pliability. In confusion, Tchula Homa returned to his seat.

Jackson looked straight at Itawamba and, still in a soft, avuncular voice, proposed that the price be raised to twenty thousand dollars for each of thirteen years.

Itawamba rose. "We cannot trade for land," he said. But now there was something brittle and uncertain in his tone—something, perhaps, false.

"To make all hearts straight," said Jackson, "let us set the price at two hundred eighty thousand dollars, and be content, and say no more."

"Friend and brother," said Itawamba to Jackson, "forgive us, but your ways remain mysterious to us. Let us withdraw to our council, and consider how we might best reach some form of agreement with you; for it would be grievous to us to disappoint you and our father the President; but it would equally be injurious to ourselves to do as you would have us do. Pray excuse us. We will return to you in a little while."

The council house was chaos. Most of the Chickasaws jostled about aimlessly, shouting, laughing, sharing jokes, guesses, gossip. They had forgotten, as quickly as they had embraced it, the glory that Tchula Homa's oration had harkened them back to. Meanwhile the

Colberts and their allies withdrew to a corner of the room, talking quietly and rapidly among themselves. Tchula Homa began to shoulder his way toward them but was intercepted by Tinebe. "That was quite a speech," said the king.

"What's going on over there?" demanded Tchula Homa, pointing toward the Colberts.

"Very cogent, very eloquent. But out of line, you know. The kind of thing that brings trouble from the white man."

"It seemed to me to have no effect on them at all. No more than it's had on these fools here"—with a sweeping gesture he took in the whole houseful of milling, laughing Chickasaws. "Excuse me, Tinebe Mingo, but I want to hear what's being said over there."

Tinebe reached for Tchula Homa's hand and drew it to his chest. "Among the Colberts, you mean? I think that would be unwise. They have long experience in negotiating with General Jackson. Let's go outside and smoke a pipe, like old times."

Tchula Homa twisted roughly away and pushed forward through the crowd toward the Colberts. "Tchushemataha, excuse me," he called.

"Go away, Tchula Homa," returned William Colbert. "This is the business of national chiefs."

"Since when is a village chief not a councilor of the nation?" Tchula Homa demanded.

"I don't wish to argue with you. Tinebe Mingo has asked us to act on behalf of the nation."

"Only the council can appoint you to anything. The king has one vote, the same as you or I."

"Please, Tchula Homa." With a glance Tchushemataha summoned to his side a man with a rifle.

"Atchelata!" breathed Tchula Homa, shocked.

"I am sorry," said Atchelata.

"Full blood, fellow warrior," pleaded Tchula Homa to his ex-wife's husband.

"Go *away*, Tchula Homa," whispered Tchushemataha fiercely.

"I see I have no choice."

Atchelata took Tchula Homa by the arm and led him away. "I am sorry, brother," he said.

Tchula Homa found Tinebe and Tishomingo on a bench outside, smoking. The old king looked at him sadly, and said, "The moon has eaten the sun." Tishomingo sat staring into the trees, silent.

For several minutes, as the noise of pointless chatter poured from the council house, they sat and smoked in silence.

With the blowing of a conch-shell horn the council was called to order, and Tchula Homa, Tishomingo, and Tinebe Mingo went in and took their seats, ready for formal discussion to begin.

"Brothers, listen," said Itawamba. "It has been decided that if the nation can persuade the commissioners to agree to an extra year's annuity of twenty thousand dollars—making three hundred thousand in all—the treaty will be signed."

Has been decided? Tchula Homa felt as if he was losing his mind. He looked around him. Why was no one speaking up? The thrice proclaimed and "forever irrevocable" resolution to give up no land had apparently ceased to exist. Had the morning's great show of refusal, then, all been a sham—a ruse to raise the white man's offer? If so, when had it been agreed to, and by whom, and where had Tchula Homa been then? Surely the Chickasaws would not just accept a fiat from the Colberts without a word of discussion. Surely they would not abandon their time-honored ways of decision making—the elegant oratory, the elaborate courtesies, the probing of every last option, the final shout of unanimity. But still no one spoke. What was *happening* here?

Six and a half million acres! The patrimony of the great and ancient Chickasaw nation to be flung away! Tchula Homa still could not rouse himself to speech, struck dumb by the unimaginable acquiescence of the gullible fools all around him lost in—what? their dreams of riches? Alas, to protest was hopeless, for he would find no support. Even Tishomingo, even the king himself had no power now against the Colberts. Tinebe was king in name only. "Shall it be unanimous then?" boomed the Colberts' speaker.

"Yes!" roared the council as one, but for the few who were silent.

—•—

There were to be fifteen annual payments of twenty thousand dollars each, in cash, to the Chickasaw nation. In addition, there were to be various payments to a number of Chickasaw chiefs, including one of one thousand and eighty-nine dollars to James Colbert for his services as interpreter, "it being the sum of money taken from his pocket in the month of June, 1816, at the theatre in Baltimore." Further exclusive commercial concessions were granted to several other members of the Colbert family.

In return, the Chickasaw nation was to cede to the United States of America, in perpetuity, all their land within the states of Tennessee and Kentucky—an area bounded by the Tennessee and Mississippi rivers and, on the south, by the Thirty-fifth Parallel. The ceded lands included the four Chickasaw Bluffs that had always stood their people's guard over the Father of Waters.

Because the precise location of the Thirty-fifth Parallel was still to be determined by a white man survey, Tchula Homa did not know if the village of Nonconnah was in Tennessee or in the newly created state of Mississippi—whether it was now American or still the Chickasaws' own. And many of Nonconnah's warriors seemed barely to care.

Through vine-draped woodland, scratched and snagged by nettles, holly, wild rose, blackberry, devil's walking-stick, well off the packed clay road, determined to avoid all encounter with human beings of whatever color—for these days he abominated them all—Tchula Homa traveled to the sacred swamp once more.

One flank of the flat-topped earthen pyramid at the heart of the swamp, the center of the lost city of his ancestors, had caved in in last spring's earthquake. Many of the tall black oaks on the mound had fallen, their leaves still clinging to the splintered limbs, their roots clawing the air like corpses' hands. Fragments of ancient sculpture and pottery had been cast up by the earthquake, and at the head of what seemed perhaps to have been a brick stair there was a low opening from which cool air and grave-scent rose. This Tchula Homa would not go near, fearing the anger of the dead whom his people had betrayed. The cypresses and tupelo gums of the flood-lands leaned against each other, creaking in the wind.

The circle of painted stones had been swallowed up, and Tchula Homa could not find the place where his mother had returned to the earth.

And yet, he said to himself, I still know I am here. It is still itself. The essential is not altered. I will bring the high priest here with paints, and we will rebuild the circle.

In the night the ground shuddered feverishly, and Tchula Homa leaped to his feet in alarm. He had been dreaming that he was lost in the tunnels of an ancient tomb, among the smashed skulls and curled-up skeletons of murdered kings, and on his alarm relief quickly followed, merely to be awake and alive. Far away, a single white-throated sparrow was calling. The earth beneath his feet grew warm, and he knelt to kiss its soft, still heaving breast.

1819

A white man town, called Memphis, was founded at the Fourth Bluff. Its chiefs, John Overton, James Winchester, and Andrew Jackson, began to sell the land, parcel by parcel, to individual owners.

The United States government trading post at Fort Pickering was moved to Arkansas, where there were still plenty of Indians, and more on the way. The Chickasaws were glad to see it gone.

White settlers began to pour in to the rich and now unencumbered lands of western Tennessee. They cut down the trees, built log cabins, planted corn and cotton, erected fences, and sometimes, hunting in the forests to the south, passed through the village of Nonconnah. There they would peer into the houses and frighten the women, and cautiously raise their right hands to the men.

As Kills Enemy had foreseen, there were many paddle-wheeled steamboats now on the Father of Waters. The trade in cotton was brisk, the price rising. The Colberts and the other Chickasaw planters extended their holdings in the southern lands remaining to the nation. The numbers of their slaves multiplied.

Deer, browsing at the edges of the newly cleared fields, grew more plentiful, as did turkeys, passenger pigeons, and blackberries; with more to eat, wolves and cougars and bears also increased. A herd of elk was reported to have been seen in the bottomlands along the Father of Waters, the first to be heard of in some years.

In winter, many of the Chickasaws who had not adopted white

man clothing went about draped in extravagantly long trailing robes made all of wolves' tails. With the coming of spring, they put on flowing smocks and leggings of the finest, softest fawnskin. Calico turbans, the brighter the better, came into fashion. Some of the people wore arm bands and necklaces of silver and coral and colored glass. You could tell at a glance who was rich and who was poor.

With the passage by the United States Congress of the Indian Civilization Act, the Cumberland Presbyterian Church established a mission in the nation on the Tombigbee River, where modern agriculture and animal husbandry were to be taught to Chickasaw boys, and weaving, spinning, and household management to the girls. Both sexes were also to learn English, and to receive the Christian gospel. Luckily, this settlement was far from Tchula Homa's village.

Word came from the capital that Moon Behind Cloud had borne Atchelata a second child, another boy.

An old woman presented herself at Tchula Homa's door one day and said, "I am Hananata. A chief needs someone to look after him. And I need somewhere to live." One of Hananata's eyes had been put out in a war long ago. She had lived at the capital, but she disapproved of its modern ways; she had lived among the Creeks, but had found them too primitive; she had lived in the forest but grown lonely. Everywhere she had been, she had heard sooner or later of the Chickasaw chief who would not tolerate any white man ideas, and so she had come. She presented Tchula Homa with no choice in the matter.

Tchula Homa smiled indulgently and said, "Welcome, Hananata."

A few miles west of Colbert's Ferry on the Tennessee River, the chiefs James Colbert and Sam Seely joined the surveying party of General James Winchester, to observe the operation of his mysterious tools of reckoning.

General Winchester explained to them that the Thirty-fifth Parallel ran due west to the Father of Waters, and he showed them the indicator of that direction on his compass. At evening, James Colbert pointed out that the compass did not agree with the sunset.

"It is summer," replied General Winchester. "In summer, the sun does not set at true west."

In the morning, to prove his point, Winchester set his surveying instruments by the rising sun (then nearing its northernmost point of the year), and showed that if he were to use that as a reckoning of the east, and that if, as all agreed, west was exactly opposite to east, then a line thus drawn would cut deeply into the state of Mississippi, and lands the Chickasaws regarded as their own. "Likewise," he said, "if I were to run the line from here into the setting sun, that too would go far into your territory. The middle course, you see, is the true one, as the compass shows, and the best for you."

These ideas were strange to the Chickasaws. What if the instruments had been corrupted somehow, perhaps bewitched? And what of the Fourth Bluff? The new town of Memphis had been surveyed and laid out—also under the supervision of General Winchester—just in the month before this line had been drawn. A suspicious sequence. Perhaps, after all, the Fourth Bluff was rightly the Chickasaws' property too. If so, the white men might very well have falsified this survey to protect their investment there. The Chickasaws had no confidence in Winchester's enigmatic instruments, and they insisted that the line be run when the day and the night were of equal length, at summer's end.

Winchester *laughed.*

James Colbert and Sam Seely took their grievance to the national council, and the council in turn took it to the Agent of the United States, Mr. Sherburne, and he in turn lodged a formal appeal on the Chickasaws' behalf. After a lengthy delay in Washington, it was turned down.

But Tchula Homa did not care. The Thirty-fifth Parallel had been shown to lie just to the north of his village. Nonconnah would remain the Chickasaws' own!

1820

Tinebe Mingo called Tchula Homa to the capital and, dying, said, "The moon has eaten the sun."

Tchushemataha, William Colbert, became the first mixed-blood king of the Chickasaws.

1826

Along Daylight Bayou, the first pale green of sedge was pushing through the fallen silver stalks of last year's nutgrass. Tchula Homa's old stallion, East Wind, picked his way around the rushes and tight-curled ferns where the mud was deep, and came to the water's edge. He knocked a hole in the ice with a delicate hoof, and began to drink. His winter coat was falling from his flanks in tatters, and, beneath, the new black shone blue. He lifted his head and cleared his nose. The morning sun, rising above the underbrush and into the bare limbs of the oaks and hickories, brought fresh scent on a warm puff of breeze from the village. East Wind whinnied in recognition and stamped.

The answer came. East Wind danced an anxious circle, whinnied again, and snorted. Again the answering whicker came. Tchula Homa said, "All right, all right, let's go see who it is," and East Wind followed him back to the square, so close he had to tuck his head down tight to keep from bumping his master's back.

Five horses were tied outside the chief's house. Tchula Homa went in.

"Tchula Homa," said Levi Colbert, "this is Colonel John D. Terrell, special agent for the Bureau of Indian Affairs."

"Welcome," said Tchula Homa.

Terrell rose, bowed, took Tchula Homa's hand, and thanked him for his hospitality—in Chickasaw. His command of it was limited to a few polite rudiments, but Terrell was the first white government official who had ever even bothered to try.

"We have been at the Fourth Bluff," continued Itawamba, "to meet Colonel Terrell, who has come down the river from St. Louis to make our people's acquaintance. He brings us an interesting message, and, in light of your village's special standing and your well known views, I recommended to him especially a visit with you. I had the pleasure of meeting Colonel Terrell when I was in Washington two years ago, at the home of the Secretary of War, and I can tell you that he is an honest man."

Malcolm McGee, an old mixed blood who was the Colberts' longtime interpreter, translated for Terrell:

"The great general and explorer William Clark is now superintendent of Indian affairs for the United States. He is not a man like other white men you have known. He has known Indians all his life, and he knows them as brothers, not as children. The tribes of the great Northwest call him Red-headed Chief, and love him as one of their own. In the days of your fathers, as you may know, General Clark was instrumental in evicting Gayoso and the Spaniards from their occupation of the Fourth Chickasaw Bluff. Behind the scenes, he has worked diligently on behalf of many Indian nations, including your own, though admittedly not always with success. General Clark freely acknowledges that his red brothers have suffered at the hands of the United States, and he regrets it very much. He believes, however, that lasting peace and mutual respect are now possible among all the peoples of America. He is devoted in particular to the welfare of the Indians, and among them in particular to the great civilized tribes of the Southeast, and among them in particular to the Chickasaws. Let me read to you from a letter General Clark has written. Shall we sit down?"

Hananata came in and passed out bowls of black drink. Terrell lifted his bowl toward his companions and sipped at it noisily, like a Chickasaw.

When she had withdrawn, Tchula Homa said, "I would like my village council to hear this letter. We act together."

"Fine, fine," said Terrell. "All the better."

In the years since the land cessions, the village of Nonconnah had come to be the center and paragon of what remained of Chickasaw purity. Elsewhere, farming, slavery, commerce, and the white man's other innovations had reduced the Chickasaws' traditions to a vestige of their ancient ways; the substance of nearly all of the old rituals and observances had been forgotten, and their form alone survived, in the cant of ceremonies and festivals. Daily life at the capital and the other populous Chickasaw towns of the Tombigbee highlands had become a drudgery—of brutish labor, counterfeit style, and poverty both spiritual and economic—leavened only by binges of whiskey and dancing. But at Nonconnah Tchula Homa had determined to preserve the ancestral dignity of his people, and his determination had drawn hopeful immigrants from all over the nation.

Some came at first only because they had been uprooted from their lands by white settlers and were full of hate, and most of these did not last long. Depressingly many of them had long ago been too thoroughly polluted by white ways to be able to accept the stern decorum and prohibitions which the village of Nonconnah insisted on, and they would drift away to the capital region, where they soon found themselves engulfed in the swelling tide of the abjectly poor. The village council had decreed that once these wanderers had spurned Nonconnah, they were not welcome to return, and there was nowhere else for them to go.

Nonconnah had known poverty too, these recent years. Game had increased sharply at first after the opening of western Tennessee to white settlement, but more recently, as farmland ate away at the forests, and the settlers grossly overhunted what game remained, whole populations of animals had disappeared. The fur trade was dead. White men bred and traded their own Chickasaw horses.

Still Nonconnah, small and poor though it was, subsisted, and was proud. Ancient conventions ruled every aspect of the village's life. Not only coffee but whiskey and pork and all other white man foods were forbidden. The form of the town was rigidly modeled on the pattern of their ancestors' palisaded villages, with densely spaced rows of wattle-and-stucco thatch-roofed houses surrounding a large square lined with the principal buildings—the chief's white house at the head, the council house, the bright red warrior house, the priests' house, the women's gathering-house, the visitors' house. Language and religion were pure Chickasaw; teachers and missionaries were warned to ply their trade elsewhere. Old Negro slaves were permitted to stay, but no new ones could be brought in. Mixed bloods were not allowed to serve on the council. The old men of the village and the priests were restored to their place of honor. And as in the days of their ancestors, women were treated with reverence.

Tchula Homa had seen that it was not the mercurial and boastful warriors who were the strength of Chickasaw purity; it was the women. He had set out, therefore, to attract the most trustworthy and punctilious women of the nation to come to Nonconnah. He guaranteed each of them a traditional Chickasaw house, her own fields, and vigilant protection. And as the hotheads and drunkards and mixed bloods and slaves began to seep out of the village, a new male element had begun to appear, strong, good men. And now in Nonconnah there were, once again, beautiful full-blood Chickasaw children.

That evening after supper, the children and women stood in watchful silence in the square as the warriors and honored old men left their homes and began to gather outside the council house. Tchula Homa blew his conch-shell horn, and lifted his eagle-feathered staff of office, and all filed inside. He rose from his woven cane seat. "Brothers," he said, "Itawamba has come from the capital to bring a visitor before us."

Levi Colbert rose, his long silver hair shining gold in the lamplight, and lifted his hand to the assembled council. Tchula Homa called him Itawamba only out of politeness; for to Tchula Homa and all the other Chickasaws now except the very old folks like Hananata, he was properly known by his English name, Levi Colbert. His elder brother William was still nominally king, but the power of the nation was in Levi Colbert's hands. Levi's fluent English, his diplomatic wiles, his ruthless pragmatism, and the sheer cold force of his reason had made him not just the Chickasaws' leader but their ruler. What Levi Colbert had to say, therefore, even in this village that abhorred all he stood for, demanded hearing.

"Friends and brothers," he began, "Colonel John D. Terrell has come many days' travel down the Father of Waters to bring us the talk of General William Clark, superintendent of Indian affairs of the United States government. He presents himself as our advocate with that government, and tells me that General Clark is our friend."

Malcolm McGee came forward to translate. Terrell said that the letter he had brought would show clearly the goodness of General Clark's heart and the concern he bore for his red brothers. McGee began to read:

" 'The relative condition of the United States on the one side, and the Indian tribes on the other, is, in my opinion, perfectly correct; and the obligation which is imposed upon this government to save them from extinction is equally the dictate of magnanimity and justice. The events of the last two or three wars, from General Wayne's campaign, in 1794, to the end of the operations against the southern tribes, in 1818, have entirely changed our position with regard to the Indians. Before those events, the tribes nearest our settlements were a formidable and terrible enemy; since then, their power has been broken, their warlike spirit subdued, and themselves sunk into objects of pity and commiseration. While strong and hostile, it has been our obvious policy to weaken them; now that they are weak and harmless, and most of their lands fallen into our hands, justice and humanity require us to cherish and befriend them. To teach them to live in houses, to raise grain and stock, to plant orchards, to set up landmarks, to divide their possessions, to establish laws for their government, to get the rudiments of common learning, such as reading, writing, and ciphering, are the first steps towards improving their condition. But, to take these steps with effect, it is necessary that previous measures of great magnitude should be accomplished; that is, that the tribes now within the limits of the States and Territories should be removed to a country beyond those limits, where they could rest in peace, and enjoy in reality the perpetuity of the lands on which their buildings and improvements would be made.'

"That is the letter of General Clark."

The councilors looked at one another in speechless dismay. The high priest Tsatsemataha hawked and spat.

What was Levi Colbert up to? He could hardly have expected Terrell and this letter to get a sympathetic hearing here.

Colbert rose to speak. "There are forces in the white man world that bode us no good," he said, "but we cannot wish them away. If our nation is to stand against them, we must show the white man that we can be useful to him where we are—that we can be productive, and peaceful, and beneficent; that when called on we will fight side by side with him against his enemies, as we have done before; and that he can be proud to have us in his midst. We must also have the white man understand that if our nation were removed to a land we do not know and where we could not thrive, we would be a burden to him. And we must maintain our separateness and sovereignty, not only technically, by law, but spiritually. It is for its role as an exemplar of our spiritual sovereignty that the village of Nonconnah is so important. The Chickasaw nation must both advance and endure. Brothers, we must stand together."

Although it was cool in the council house, Colbert was sweating.

"Remember what division meant for the Creeks," he continued. "I do not know how to bring about reconciliation and unity among our people. We are weak, and poor. Some of us are striving for advancement and prosperity, while others seek a return to our forefathers' ancient, unchanging way of life. Can both factions go on and yet remain one people?" Colbert sat down abruptly.

On a sudden apprehension that Terrell might know more of the Chickasaw language than he revealed, Tchula Homa rose. "Let us thank Colonel Terrell and bid him return to the visitors' house."

When that had been done, Tchula Homa continued: "Itawamba, consider how our villagers hear whatever words the white man speaks, and the words of any member of the Colbert family. We live apart from you, far from the capital, for what we consider good reasons. We believe that our understanding of our people's history in this generation is a true understanding. We know that there are some who do not share it, and we believe that this failure to see our history in its true light has led many Chickasaws astray. There has been a great forgetting. Some have forgotten the truth on purpose. Others have been drawn into this forgetting without understanding, because of their trust in their leaders. Their trust has been betrayed. As time has gone by, some of us have been able to recognize that. This recognition has opened a breach between Nonconnah and the capital, as wide and as hard to cross as the Father of Waters. But as our ancestors once crossed that great river to come here and establish our nation, so too can those who do not see the truth now cross over the breach between us and come here where the truth is as clear as the stars. Or let them call to us, and we will cross to them and bring the truth with us, the most precious gift we can offer. But either crossing must be preceded by a knowledge of the distance between the two shores. Speaker?"

Old Pothanoa hobbled to the front of the council house and stood beside the chief.

"Speaker," said Tchula Homa, "tell us about the brother of General William Clark."

"In the year of the Black Flood," said Pothanoa, "the brother of William Clark, General George Rogers Clark, built a fort in the Chickasaw nation, far to the north. You old men will remember his deputy, Captain Richard Brashears, who came to the Fourth Bluff with a boatload of trade goods to stave off our wrath. You will also recall that the man who was one day to become our king, Tchushemataha, had been hiding in the mouth of the Wolf River in those days, and raiding the boats of the Spanish on the Father of Waters. Those goods brought by Captain Brashears had been meant for all our people, but you old men will remember that most of them fell into Tchushemataha's hands, and it was not long thereafter that Tchushemataha was assuring us of the good will of General George Rogers Clark towards our nation. Let it be particularly noted that our national council took no action against General George Rogers Clark for taking that land of ours for his fort. You old men will also recall that Captain Brashears was granted the right to trade in our nation and was among us many years, deceiving and despoiling the innocent people of the countryside, and ultimately fathering a number of mixed-blood children who carried on his tradition of cheating us."

"Thank you, speaker," said Tchula Homa. "Please, now, also tell us about Meriwether Lewis, the long-time partner of William Clark."

Pothanoa collected his thoughts for a few moments, and then spoke. "Some winters after the building of that northern fort—you old men will recall it well, and all Chickasaws know it as the first step of the Americans toward the heart of our nation—another American fort was built, at the Fourth Bluff. You will remember that it had come to be put there only after a long and angry dispute between the Americans and the Spanish as well as among the Chickasaws. There was Ugula Yacabe on one side, who favored the Spanish because he thought that they would soon leave; on the other side, favoring the Americans and the establishment of permanent trade, were Piomingo and Tchushemataha. There was very bad blood between these two factions. You old men will remember that one of the first commanders of the American fort was this Meriwether Lewis, who never tired of reminding us of the certificate of our first so-called father the President, General George Washington, the king of all white men, guaranteeing full Chickasaw sovereignty over all the land from the Ohio River south to the Choctaw country, and from the Tennessee River on the east to the Father of Waters on the west.

"When Fort Pickering was first established in our nation, William Clark was already Meriwether Lewis's great friend, and Clark visited his friend Lewis at the Fourth Bluff, and talked to our people and understood us well, and made us many extravagant promises—and did nothing to fulfill them, except perhaps to assist his government in its plots to deprive us of our lands. And you will remember that some winters later Meriwether Lewis was back among us, as governor of the entire Louisiana Territory, a land of unimaginable vastness, he told us, of which our whole nation, big though we may have thought it, formed but a tiny part, the size of a fly on a horse. As for our sovereignty over that tiny part, and its guarantee by our father the President George Washington, the king of all white men? Meriwether Lewis had forgotten it.

"Remember, old men, how much whiskey Meriwether Lewis drank that well known night at the Fourth Bluff, and how our people had to restrain him, in his delirium, from shooting himself. Remember that some white men blamed us when Meriwether Lewis finally succeeded in shooting himself some weeks later on the Natchez Trace, in the heart of our nation. They accused us of murder, who never shed the blood of one white man!

"These, then, are the closest known associates of General William Clark: his brother, who stole our land and corrupted Tchushemataha; and his partner, who could not remember the promises made by George Washington and who was insane and left his accursed suicidal blood in our soil." The speaker spread his hands before him.

Levi Colbert's eyes were shut tight, and a tear made a bright path down the braided channels of his cheek.

"Thank you, Pothanoa," said Tchula Homa. "And now, finally, if you please, recount to us briefly the history of the Colbert family in our nation, with particular emphasis on the trust we have been asked by the Colberts to place in the white man, and in themselves."

Coweamothlo, a Colbert cousin, stood up and cried out, "Tchula Homa, stop this!"

There was a long, uneasy silence in the council house.

Finally Levi Colbert took Coweamothlo's arm and rose. "Brothers, listen," he said, his voice hoarse. "You are right. Spare me the story of my family and what you will call our villainy. You know that I know it all, and more, and worse." He paused for a long moment, then went on. "Nevertheless we are who we are *now*—all of us. We are *where* we are. Not where we may have used to be. The white man is closing in on the Chickasaw nation. Hear what Terrell has said tonight! Do you not hear the threat in it? I don't like it either, and we shall not yield! *We shall not yield.*

"Brothers, listen. We must resist the white man together. Unless we stand together, we will fall. We may fall anyway. Remember Jackson's campaigns in Florida and against the Creeks. My brother Tchushemataha and two hundred Chickasaws fought beside him, and they have seen Andrew Jackson in his rage of destruction, as awesome as the Father of Waters in flood, sweeping away the lives of every red man, woman, and child in his path.

"Jackson was nearly elected President of the United States the year before last, and I am told he is likely to succeed at the next election, two years from now. We cannot wish him away.

"I am heartily sorry for my family's past involvement with Andrew Jackson, and my own. It was a terrible mistake."

Itawamba paused again, a long time, breathing hard, his eyes closed tight, an old man, sick. He opened his eyes, took a deep breath, and went on.

"You may not like it, but it will be to my family and me that Andrew Jackson will come with his next move. Kill me, kill all Colberts, it will do you no good. Jackson will find Chickasaws to his liking and will deal with no other. He will never treat with you, Tchula Homa, or any of your ilk. He would kill you like a mosquito, and burn Nonconnah to the ground. You must have me, and my family.

"And yet also we must have Nonconnah, as the emblem of our people's past greatness. And I must have you, you all—you honored old men, you priests, you young full-blood warriors, and you, Tchula Homa—in whom to seek atonement.

"Forgive me, then. Forgive me, all of you, I implore you. We must be of one fire forever. We must remain in our homeland forever. Tchula Homa, give me your hand."

Tchula Homa hesitated. But the old man's tears were real. And he was right. They needed him.

Tchula Homa sighed, and took Levi Colbert's hand. He had been down this road before, and seemed to be destined to go down it again and again, each time a little farther.

Colonel John D. Terrell spent the whole spring and summer working his way through the Chickasaw nation's chiefs and councilors. Bit by tantalizing bit, he let it be known that the Chickasaws could be the richest Indian nation of all if only they would agree to General William Clark's generous plan of removal. Life beyond the Father of Waters would be a paradise, he said. Herds of buffalo miles across. Beautiful fertile soil. No white men anywhere near. Independence, wealth, comfort, and sovereignty—forever.

No one believed him. No one was willing even to discuss removal. Serious consideration was given to killing Terrell, as an eloquent gesture of the nation's unanimity.

Terrell fell back on the inveterate strategy of his predecessors, the encouragement of large-scale farming. This was meant to entangle the farmers in debt, and to reduce wildlife habitat, and to support the same number of Chickasaws on less land than before, thus making more land available for sale to the white man.

Atchelata was easily inveigled. A determined if not an accomplished sycophant, he had at last become a councilor to the king—by this point in the nation's history a largely meaningless position, but one he was boastfully proud of. He would set an example to the backward, who could not accept progress.

When Tchula Homa rode into the capital square, Atchelata was sitting on the king's balcony with Tchushemataha and John D. Terrell. Atchelata waved blandly in Tchula Homa's direction, and went on talking. They were all three smoking cigars.

A long-haired boy wearing only deerskin pants and a mother-of-pearl medallion came running up to Tchula Homa and grasped his hand. "Tchula Homa! I am Atchekoyo," he panted. "My mother wants to see you. Come with me now." There was an urgency in the boy's eyes, and also a confident, trusting coolness. Tchula Homa let the boy lead him by the hand through the streets.

As it always did when he had not seen her for a long time, the sheer beauty of Moon Behind Cloud struck him like a blow to the chest. Atchekoyo stood behind Moon Behind Cloud's seat, shifting from foot to foot, now fingering his mother's hair, now tilting his head to the side to look out the front door at a horse and rider passing by, now studying Tchula Homa.

"Atchekoyo is quite the little man," said Tchula Homa.

"He is an excellent boy," said Moon Behind Cloud.

"How old is he now?"

"I'm thirteen, but I can outwrestle any boy fourteen and under in this town!" crowed Atchekoyo, puffing out his chest. "And throw a ball farther, and ride my horse Tornado faster, and, and—" Moon

Behind Cloud poked her finger in Atchekoyo's navel and tickled, and he fell backward, laughing, onto a stack of red blankets. "Stabbed to death by his own treacherous mother, the warrior falls," the boy chanted in the lilting story-telling voice of a speaker. "An ignominious death for the great Atchekoyo. A tragic loss to the Chickasaw nation."

"My son has a well developed sense of his great destiny," said Moon Behind Cloud.

"You have another son, I believe?"

"Look at you, Tchula Homa," laughed Moon Behind Cloud. "You need a haircut. Yes; Lakowea; he's outside somewhere. And that tunic is falling apart! Who takes care of you? If anybody."

"You remember Hananata."

"One-eyed old witch. I'm surprised you're not covered with warts by now, like her."

"Tchula Homa," said Wren, in greeting and judicious interruption, "my daughter's manners have never improved, alas."

Tchula Homa smiled sadly.

The expression on Moon Behind Cloud's face, as he remembered its so often having been, was divided: one side hopeful and affectionate, the other sad and fearful. "When are you going to go home, Tchula Homa?" she asked.

"Tomorrow," he replied, wondering what she was getting at. "I've only come to buy an axe. The Fourth Bluff is closer to Nonconnah, of course, but, as you may know, we don't go there. Tomorrow before first light." He summoned the courage to meet her gaze.

Her long hair fell forward over one shoulder. She shrugged it back.

Tchula Homa's heart was stirring, and he hated it.

"Good. We'll come with you," she said.

"To the bloody heart of nowhere," chanted Atchekoyo at the top of his lungs, leaping up from his blankets and striking a warrior's pose, his imaginary arrow drawn. "To the wolf's den and the bear's hollow sycamore and the sacred swamp of the ancients!"

"You remember Tsatsemataha, our high priest? He will want to know Atchekoyo," said Tchula Homa, his heart pounding.

Tsatsemataha did not like to ride. One misses too much, he said. He walked very slowly, and in perfect silence. As they moved into the flood plain of Nonconnah Creek he stopped short, one foot lifted; although he was very old now, Tsatsemataha's balance was still perfect. He pointed. An ivory-billed woodpecker flapped through the trees, its red crest flashing. Clinging to a dead cypress in full view, and ignoring its visitors, the woodpecker started hammering away. When it stopped for a moment, the sudden quiet was as loud as the noise had been. Finally Tsatsemataha turned to Tchula Homa and whispered, "The forest is at peace today." The woodpecker looked down now, cocking its head, listening. Tsatsemataha called to the bird in the bird's own tootling language, and after a startled pause the answer came, so little a tootle for such a big bird.

The old priest laughed. "You know what Ivory-billed Woodpecker says?"

"Yes, I remember. 'Persistence, persistence.' "

Tchula Homa always stowed his canoe beneath a canopy of muscadine on the shore of Nonconnah Creek just above the mouth of Daylight Bayou. When Tchula Homa turned the boat over this time, there was a litter of tiny opossums in a nest of straw. He knelt, put his hand down palm up, and one of them crawled into it. He held the creature close to his face, and it blinked sleepily at him.

"Here comes Mother," said Tsatsemataha.

She was ambling toward the nest, ignoring the men and her lost young one. "Fierce, isn't she?" Tchula Homa chuckled. The remaining babies climbed into her stringy fur, and she waddled away. "Wait!" called Tchula Homa, settling the lost one onto her back, which she seemed not to notice at all. "Good luck with Bobcat," he called after her. And then to Tsatsemataha: "She's going to need it."

The canoe sliced through the warm clear water, which was just high enough for easy travel and would not be too fast to paddle back against. Shoals of tiny silver fish swirled away in the bow wake.

"At first I thought it was for me that Moon Behind Cloud was coming back," Tchula Homa was saying, "and I could so easily picture her just hurling that in Atchelata's face, without thinking of the consequences for me. I spent that whole night at the capital in the visitors' house with my rifle in my hands, expecting Atchelata to burst in any moment and try to slit my throat. But I might have known: he was drunk, with our great benefactor Terrell and Tchushemataha Mingo. Then on the road the next morning she told me that Atchelata was actually glad to be rid of her, because now he gets her fields, and her mother's too, which are considerable. Atchelata's going to be a big cotton planter—a full-blood Colbert!" he laughed. "It turned out she had divorced him weeks ago, and was going to leave—and come to Nonconnah—whether I happened to be around to escort her or not. It's all been a great relief, after what I went through that night, worrying not only about my throat getting slit but also about what was going to happen at home with Moon Behind Cloud back."

"You really loved her, didn't you?" said the old man.

"I did, yes, Tsatsemataha."

"And now? You are comfortable?"

"I'll never be comfortable," said Tchula Homa. "But I'm reconciled. It doesn't trouble me."

"She is a very clever girl," said Tsatsemataha.

"That she is," Tchula Homa agreed.

"A beautiful woman."

"That too."

"She will be lonely in Nonconnah," said Tsatsemataha.

"She makes friends easily," said Tchula Homa, "and she still has friends from when she lived here before, when we were married." He paused. "And I hardly think she'll be wanting for male attention."

"She has no babies," the high priest observed. "Is she still fertile?"

"I don't know. I would guess so. I think it was just bad with her husband. For years."

"Her son Atchekoyo is quite a boy."

Tchula Homa smiled in assent.

"It will be well if she can bear us more such sons," said Tsatsemataha.

Rounding an oxbow, they came on a beaver house, and tails slapped the water like gunshots. Two alligators slid from a sand bar and sank. A flock of passenger pigeons swirled out of the laurels on the bank, which were in bloom.

Tsatsemataha took a fatty chunk of rabbit from the tip of Tchula Homa's knife, and held it out. Softly, he hissed into the darkness, and a porcupine shambled into the circle of firelight. It ate the meat from the old man's hand.

Tchula Homa played his cane flute.

Later, the high priest sang to the wolves, and from far off they sang back, amidst a yipping of pups.

The bullfrogs fell silent.

In the morning, Tsatsemataha took Tchula Homa by the hand and showed him, on a hummock forested with tall, widely spaced oaks and beeches, the twin scrapes and ammoniac leaf-litter pile that marked a corner of a cougar's domain. The pugmarks followed the water's edge, ending at a high tulip-tree. In sign language the old man said, "Somewhere up in that tree is Cougar." He began, very quietly, to sing to the cougar. The cougar, invisibly watching, did not reply.

"We won't shoot your deer," Tsatsemataha assured the great cat, in song. Then he said to Tchula Homa, "Cougar is not so many now. I remember when he was so bold, years ago, that he took meat from our camps, like a bear."

"I remember hearing Cougar screech in the big sycamore right there in the village square when I was a little boy," said Tchula Homa. "The dogs had run him up it. It was the most terrifying sound I'd ever heard."

"And I remember the next day telling you the story of the cougar called Warrior's Shadow," said Tsatsemataha.

"Bringing meat to the warrior's lost little boy," mused Tchula Homa, remembering. "And the boy promises never to shoot him. Which is why no warrior may ever kill Cougar."

"And no one ever need fear him."

The day was hot, the sky white. The forest edge glimmered with watching presences. Tchula Homa and Tsatsemataha, singing, dragged their net through a pool, and returned to the village with a gift of catfish for the honored old women.

Moon Behind Cloud and her boys came to the chief's house to invite Tchula Homa to dine with them. "Mother's going to make strawberry pudding," said Moon Behind Cloud.

Lakowea, who was seven, closed his eyes and rubbed his round dark belly in anticipation. "I hope Grandmother makes lots of strawberry pudding," he said.

"That depends on you, Lakowea," said his mother. She turned to Tchula Homa. "Will you come help us gather?"

There had been a time when no man would have gone out for berries—the warriors would have howled him out of the warrior house—but Tchula Homa no longer saw the sense in that prohibition. He was long past worrying about men's laughter.

Moon Behind Cloud, Atchekoyo, Lakowea, and Tchula Homa worked along in a line on their hands and knees, the spring sun beating down on their backs. From time to time, Moon Behind Cloud would look to the side at Tchula Homa, toss her long hair back over her shoulder, and smile.

After a cold lunch of cornbread and fried quail, the boys took a nap, nestled together like puppies. Soon Moon Behind Cloud was sleeping too, face to the midday sun, one arm flung back. Tchula Homa sat, cross-legged and erect, watching, hands clutching the grass as though he might float away.

He took up his cane flute and began to play.

Her outflung hand groped slowly across the grass.

Tchula Homa could not move.

But her hand found Atchekoyo's shoulder, and she sighed in her sleep and slept on.

Tchula Homa leaned back against a tree, and he too dozed off. Once, he woke briefly, and saw Lakowea wandering across the field, swinging his bucket. The boy knelt, and began looking under strawberry leaves for more berries.

Tchula Homa woke again. Moon Behind Cloud and Atchekoyo were still sleeping. Lakowea had reached the edge of the forest. Something was stirring in the trees. Then Tchula Homa heard the *whap! whap! whap!* of a bear's jaws popping in warning.

Then there was the bear.

Tchula Homa had already sprung to his feet and was running toward the little boy, calling out, "Go away, Bear! Go away!"

The bear just stood there, blinking, head low, hackles bristling. Tchula Homa scooped up Lakowea in his arms, repeating, "Go away, Bear! Go away!"

Every other bear he had ever seen had gone away if told to go away, but this one did not budge; merely turned its head and woofed back toward the forest. Two cubs appeared far up in a hickory tree and bawled down. A mother—that was why she was so brave. The bear woofed again, and the cubs shinnied rapidly farther up, swinging back and forth at the limit of the crown's ability to hold them. The bear turned her attention back to Tchula Homa and Lakowea. She growled softly. She has a day bed here, thought Tchula Homa, and maybe a carcass. He began to back off slowly, and with each step he took backward, the bear took one toward him.

"We mean you no harm, Mother," Tchula Homa told the bear. But she would not hear him. There must be another cub, he now realized. No matter which way I go, I may go toward that cub, and then she will attack.

From the corner of his eye he saw Moon Behind Cloud. She had risen to her knees and had her arms tight around Lakowea. Atchekoyo, standing next to her, was rocking on the balls of his feet and kneading his hands together. The bear growled again, and flattened her ears back, a bad sign.

Then Atchekoyo was off like an arrow down the road toward home. The bear started, woofed angrily, and peered after him, but she did not give chase. The last boy I would ever have expected cowardice of, Tchula Homa said to himself.

The stalemate dragged on, neither bear nor people moving a muscle. Then Lakowea began to whimper in fear. The bear popped her jaws and took a heavy step forward.

"Bear, Sister, please," Tchula Homa pleaded in an urgent whisper, "I'm going to take two steps back, and then you take two steps back, and then you'll understand that there is no reason for ill will between us."

The bear growled in answer, and her head sank still closer toward the earth. A mockingbird was singing loudly somewhere nearby. Lakowea could not get control of himself. Tchula Homa could feel the child stiffening in his arms, quivering, coming closer to panic.

Then Tchula Homa saw Atchekoyo inching toward him across the field, as flat to the ground as a lizard, Tchula Homa's long rifle in his hands. The bear also saw. Her hind legs began to crouch, the toes flexing into the earth for good purchase. She lifted one front paw as if to wave.

Then she hesitated, looking back and up toward her cubs in the hickory tree. Atchekoyo stood up, pulled back the hammer, took aim, and moved slowly toward Tchula Homa. The bear was still peering back at her cubs, and holding her ground. Atchekoyo came to Tchula Homa's side and looked up, for an instant, from the sights.

Tchula Homa whispered to him, "Give me the rifle, and take the child."

All in an instant little Lakowea and the rifle had changed places, Atchekoyo was racing across the grass with his brother in his arms, the bear was bounding after them, closing the gap fast, Tchula Homa aimed and fired, the bear's front legs were crumpling under her, the two cubs were wailing in the treetop, and the third cub, till now unseen, was running out of the woods toward its mother. The bear was coughing, tearing up clots of sod. Blood poured from her mouth and nose.

He had gotten her in the lungs: good. Atchekoyo was back at

Tchula Homa's side, with the kit bag, powder, pack, ball. The bear was still coughing, clawing the earth. He shot her again, in the head.

The third cub sniffed noisily, pushing at her with a paw, trying to nurse.

Tchula Homa drew his knife and killed the cub.

Now the second cub, in the tree. Tchula Homa reloaded, aimed, fired. The cub fell straight, snapping off limbs, and then lay still at the edge of the field. The first cub was still up there. He reloaded, and shot. The dark shape crashed down through snapping limbs. The cub was screaming. Tchula Homa raced through the forest, leaping deadfall, following the blood spoor. He found the cub on its side, hind legs still running, front legs twitching, little eyes wide, white patch on its neck. He drew his knife and cut the cub's throat.

Tchula Homa fell to his knees and sang to Bear's spirit and wept.

Moon Behind Cloud was at his side. He could not look up. "They couldn't have lived without their mother," he heard himself saying. "I had to kill them." But of course it had been blind killing—murder. Just like his dead brother Tchilatokowa, long ago, murdering Kills Enemy's son Hushta Hiete. At least Tchilatokowa had been drunk.

"Bless you, Tchula Homa," Moon Behind Cloud was saying, but he would not hear her, his whole soul clenching inward, shutting out the light.

Lakowea clung to his mother's buckskin skirt, eyes wide, uncomprehending. Atchekoyo came to Tchula Homa's side and peered up into his face.

Grinning that lopsided grin, Atchekoyo let out a whoop and started dancing, pounding the earth with his little brown feet. Ho-yo, hoy-ho, ha-hee-yo-hoh! Ho-yo, hoy-ho, ha-hee-yo-hoh *ha!* Yo-ye-*ha!* Yo-ye-*ha!*

Atchekoyo hurled himself into Tchula Homa's arms, still singing.

That night after dinner, the villagers gathered in the square around the carcasses of the cubs. Tsatsemataha called Wren forward, and she led the women in singing the song of triumph always sung by women when a bear had been killed. Then Tsatsemataha led the men in their song, of sorrow for the bear.

Lakowea and Atchekoyo threw the bodies of the cubs on the fire, in propitiatory sacrifice to All-Bear. Tchula Homa had skinned the mother's carcass, and the hide was curing on a frame behind his house; Tsatsemataha had decreed that because of this bear's extraordinary fearless character, her skin would be used as a priestly garment. Moon Behind Cloud and Tchula Homa together had butchered the meat, and it was boiling in a big pot outside the women's gathering-house. Tomorrow the women of Nonconnah would skim the fat from the broth, set strips of the meat out on racks to dry, polish the teeth for jewelry, and distribute the broth to the houses of the village, where it would be reverently sipped at dusk.

Bits of the liver were distributed to all the villagers. When they had eaten it, Tsatsemataha told the story of Atchekoyo's heroism. "A few years hence, when this boy becomes a man, he shall have a great name," the high priest boomed. "Tchula Homa, you, too, are a hero, and not just for saving this boy from the bear. Bless you both, in the names of Chickasaw womanhood, Chickasaw childhood, Chickasaw courage!"

All night, Tchula Homa drank bowl after bowl of ancient tobacco tea, to purge himself of his murderous rage and his sorrow.

"Like a kind and good parent, your father the President is ever mindful of the best interests and true happiness of his children," said the commissioner to the assembled leaders of the Chickasaw nation. "By his long experience and sound judgment, he knows what is best for all of us. When, therefore, he offers his advice and counsel, he expects all his children to receive them as coming from their father, their friend, and protector.

"It is the policy and interest of our Government to extinguish the Indian title to all lands on this side of the Mississippi. We must have a dense and strong population from the mouth to the head of this father of rivers."

The design of William Clark had come to pass: the United States of America was demanding that the Chickasaws leave their ancient home.

"You will then be enabled to live in peace and quietness," the commissioner said; "nor will you be ever asked for any portion of the lands which will be given to you. The Government will guarantee to you and your children forever the possession of your country, and will protect and defend you against all your enemies. Your father the President will also defray all expenses of removing you to the country on the west side of the Mississippi, and furnish you with all things necessary for your comfort and convenience."

Levi Colbert, this time, was true to his promise to resist. He likened the Chickasaw nation to an old tree, which if transplanted would wither and die.

"The trees of the forest," the commissioner replied drily, "and particularly the most useless trees, are most difficult of transplanting; but fruit trees, which are more particularly designated by the Great Spirit for the nourishment and comfort of man, require not only to be transplanted, but to be nourished, and cultivated, and even pruned, in order to bring forth good fruit."

The Chickasaws listened in stubborn silence.

The cloak of politeness and obliquity that had shrouded earlier talks between the white man and the Chickasaws had now fallen away, to reveal the naked threat: "Are you willing to sit down in delusive security," the commissioner continued, "and see your nation gradually diminish, and your people dwindle away, until the very name, and language, of Chickasaw is forever lost?"

The threat was that all the Indians east of the Mississippi would be brought under the white man's law, and lawlessness. They would be trampled, scattered, dispossessed.

"Here," said the commissioner, "you have a small country greatly too large for you, if you intend to depend upon the earth for a support, and entirely too small, if you intend to depend upon game for subsistence."

The Choctaws, the Cherokees, the Creeks all had reached agreement to remove, the commissioner said. Would you not wish to join with them and make a common cause and mutually defend one another against your enemies?

The Chickasaws' only remaining enemy, of course, stood now before them, and no force of Indians, however united, could conquer him. Nevertheless, Levi Colbert stood his ground. "It is true we are poor for money," he said, "but we love our lands better."

The white man scaled back his position, offering to buy a portion of the Chickasaws' lands. The Chickasaws refused. The commissioner then offered to take four leaders of the Chickasaws on a journey, at no obligation, to see the beautiful lands that were offered to them in the west. Again the Chickasaws refused. The Chickasaw leaders could also be taken to Washington city to meet their father the President in person. No.

"This is the most important subject ever presented to the consideration of the Chickasaws," the commissioner said. "Upon their decision hangs the destiny of their people to the latest generations. If calamity shall ever hereafter fall upon this people, let the blame also fall upon their own heads."

1828

The hunting party still had not returned. Tchula Homa paced up and down in front of his house. There had been white men seen lately nearby. The forest was not safe.

Atchekoyo strolled past, singing. He stopped, peering at Tchula Homa through the darkness. "Uncle"—for so the boy now honored his mentor—"the moon will be up soon, three-quarters, a good hunting moon."

"I instructed them specifically not to stay out late," grumbled Tchula Homa.

"Let's go and find them! They went to the east side of the cedar swamp, to hunt Squirrel Creek down to the slough."

"If they're not back tonight," said Tchula Homa, "we'll go at first light."

" 'We,' including me?"

"Yes, Atchekoyo. As you know, the age at which a boy customarily becomes a man is still some summers away from you, but exceptions are sometimes made. You show every sign of deserving such an exception. If you wish, then—"

"I wish, Uncle."

"Do you like the name Brings the Rifle?"

The boy bowed his head in mute pleasure.

Moon Behind Cloud was not pleased. "This is my eldest son!" she cried.

Lakowea stirred in his bed. Moon Behind Cloud's old mother went to him. "Sleep on, little Mouse, Fox too is asleep," she sang softly, kneeling at the little boy's bedside, "you are safe in your house, and the night is deep."

"He is soon going to be a Chickasaw warrior," whispered Tchula Homa, resting his hand on Atchekoyo's shoulder.

"Until then he's mine," insisted Moon Behind Cloud, pulling the boy back to herself. At fifteen, Atchekoyo was tall now; at his mother's touch he drooped like an obedient dog, and lost inches.

"Shall I bring Pothanoa to quote to you the laws of war?" demanded Tchula Homa. "As chief I may have any boy if I decree the village to be in danger of attack."

"Gods!" exclaimed Moon Behind Cloud. "Some hunters have stayed out all night, and you call that an attack? Besides, how many warriors do you need? You have at least a hundred sleeping here right now."

"They're not asleep," replied Tchula Homa. "We're on alert. The village may have to be defended."

"I think you have taken leave of your senses," said Moon Behind Cloud.

Tchula Homa said nothing.

She could see that Tchula Homa was not going to be moved. "Unreasonable, hopeless, impossible bear," she murmured.

How odd it was that she should most love him when he was most resistant to her, when indeed his stubbornness put the life of her son at risk. But so it was.

"Courage, then," she whispered, touching her fingertips to his chest.

Atchekoyo began to sing the song of bravery in battle.

Tsatsemataha called blessings down on Tchula Homa and Atchekoyo as they mounted their horses and rode east into the faint pink mists. Tchula Homa had given Atchekoyo a rifle this morning, and, grinning, the boy raised it in salute to the old high priest.

From a tree outside the village came three whippoorwill calls. East Wind's ears swiveled forward, and he gave a soft kick. Atchekoyo's mare, Tornado, rolled her eyes, shook her head, and snuffled. Tchula Homa called back three times in a whippoorwill's voice.

"Warrior?" inquired Atchekoyo.

"Yes. Horse Eater. His brother should be over here." Tchula Homa called again, and the calls came back. "Good."

"Uncle?"

"Yes, Brings the Rifle."

"I'm scared. Don't call me that."

"It's not wrong to be afraid," said Tchula Homa. "Fear keeps men alive."

When they came to the edge of the swamp that led through a maze of cypress and mudflat down to Nonconnah Creek, they tied the horses in a dark, damp grove of pines and proceeded on foot down Squirrel Creek.

The fog was burning off. They stopped at White Deer Spring, the last good water, drank deep, and moved on. Mosquitoes clustered on their necks; Tchula Homa and Atchekoyo, as rapt in their tracking as cougars, ignored them. To the left, in the swamp, bullfrogs were croaking. To the right, upland, cricket-racket grew irregular and died. A flock of turkeys ran across the path, flapping and muttering. A flame-yellow warbler spun through the cedars. Atchekoyo led the way, each step silent.

Ahead, the dense forest gave way to Old Beaver Meadow, where a pond had silted in a generation ago. The meadow was no longer quite meadow, but reverting to blackberries and other low brush. In another generation, Tchula Homa said to himself, when Brings the Rifle is chief (gods so grant), the trees will have claimed it again.

There was a cow in the brush.

Tchula Homa heard a hard thump behind him, something heavy from above. He whirled, to see the cool blue eyes of a white man with a long black beard, and a rifle butt coming through the air toward his forehead. Did he hear a shot? The pain was brief.

He came to in the noon sun. They were all sitting in a clearing stamped flat in the meadow, four white men facing Tchula Homa and Atchekoyo and the four Chickasaw hunters across a space of about twenty paces. The Chickasaws' hands were tied tight behind their backs, and their ankles were also bound, with leather thongs. The white men's horses were picketed amid willow stumps the beavers had made, where the edge of their pond had been. Scattered through the briars and tall grasses beyond were about a dozen clay-red cows with calves. Farther on, the Chickasaws' horses were tied to birches at the edge of the field. Harnessed to one of them was a makeshift travois loaded with fresh meat. The flies swarming around it were the only sound to be heard. "Are you all right?" Tchula Homa whispered to Atchekoyo.

This brought one of the white men to his feet. Atchekoyo nodded, and said something too softly for Tchula Homa to hear more than the boy's tone of hopeless desolation. The blue-eyed one snapped a leather quirt across Atchekoyo's cheek. Then he took Tchula Homa's face in one hand and lifted his eyelids with the other.

Tchula Homa drifted in and out of consciousness, tasting the blood on his lips. Eventually the pain in his forehead grew intense, and he knew then that he was not going to die. The white men began to talk among themselves, passing a jug of whiskey. The sun was white-hot. Why did they not sit in the shade? Occasionally one of them would come over and check the Chickasaws' bonds, and look down the trail behind them, which led north to the Squirrel Creek ford across Nonconnah Creek and on to the main east-west road.

One of the hunters, Kimmetehe, said quietly, "One of them rode away this morning. They seem to be waiting for him."

"What happened?" asked the chief.

"It was my fault, cousin," said Latse Ineshka. Latse Ineshka and his brother Nene Ineshka were Tchula Homa's only blood relatives left in Nonconnah. "We came across the cows, and I said to myself, 'In the Chickasaw nation, every animal not proscribed is game.' Kimmetehe and I were dressing the carcass, and Nene was making the travois, and Immayotutla went to get the horses, and the next thing I knew these five white men were marching into the meadow with a pistol to Immayotutla's head. It was just unforgivably stupid. And now we have the problem with the boy."

"What problem with the boy?" demanded Tchula Homa.

"When Blue Eyes jumped you, the boy tried to shoot him."

"I missed," whispered Atchekoyo bitterly, fighting back tears.

In the late afternoon, the fifth white man rode into the clearing. There was a long discussion among the white men, with much pointing of fingers at Atchekoyo.

Tchula Homa lost consciousness again. Once, he felt cold water splashing over his neck. It felt good, and only made him sleep the more deeply. Then he felt the point of a knife just below his ear, and climbed slowly out of his inner darkness. The sun was in his eyes.

The blue-eyed man with the long black beard advanced on Atchekoyo with his pistol leveled at a spot between the boy's eyes. He rested the muzzle on the bridge of Atchekoyo's nose and pulled back the hammer till it clicked and set. Atchekoyo stared straight ahead. The flies were still buzzing on the calf carcass. The man rubbed his thumb on the hammer, pulled it back past the click, and let it come slowly to rest. He stepped back and blew his nose, one nostril at a time, spraying the boy's face. Atchekoyo was looking into the man's eyes not angrily or with fear but with the perfection of Chickasaw resistance, the mild and neutral mien their warriors had been famous for for all the years of time, which gave the enemy not even the satisfaction of hate.

He slashed the boy's face with his quirt. Two others beat Atchekoyo with thick branches on the arms and back and legs. The fourth took the blue-eyed man's pistol and cracked it over Atchekoyo's shoulders. The fifth had a black club, a Chickasaw war club, of hickory. He started on the boy's neck, at first only tapping, the blows growing slowly harder. It was not going to end; Tchula Homa could see that now.

Atchekoyo spat in the man's face.

The man shoved the war club, big end first, against the boy's throat. Choking, Atchekoyo fell. They began to beat him on the back and head.

The Chickasaws watched, as time passed and Atchekoyo bled.

Then the white men mounted their horses and rode away.

It was dark by the time the Chickasaws got themselves untied. Atchekoyo was lying face down, silent. Both his arms were broken. They splinted them, and patched his cuts with moss, and packed mud on his bruises. He was still breathing, although poorly. He could not move his legs, and he could not speak.

Atchekoyo never spoke or walked again.

The nation was in tumult. A stern request, in the name of the Chickasaw king and people, to clear the land of squatters, poachers, and tradesmen was presented to the states of Mississippi and Alabama and to the President of the United States, along with a reminder of George Washington's guarantee of the Chickasaw nation's sovereignty. There were no replies.

Levi Colbert called a council of war.

The high priests confirmed that the spirits were calling for vengeance. Tchula Homa rode to the capital to deliver to the nation's elders an account of the beating of Atchekoyo. The war council stopped just short of a declaration, and decreed a state of preparedness: if the nation were to be provoked again, it would be ready to act. Guards were posted along the roads. The warriors danced in their rage late into the night, and slept with their rifles in their beds.

Tishomingo was named national war chief. Wearing an ancient belt festooned with enemy scalps, he walked three times around the warrior house at the capital, beating the war drum. The honored old warriors—including Tishomingo's father, who was now a hundred and twelve years old—joined him, singing, dancing around and around the warrior house. Tishomingo, ninety-two years old himself but never flagging, led the march to Nonconnah.

Latse Ineshka, named by Tchula Homa as Nonconnah's war chief, met the procession at the village gate and welcomed the men of the capital. For three days the warriors fasted, drinking button snakeroot tea. Stripped down to breechcloths and moccasins, they painted themselves black and red, the colors of blood and darkness. The war medicine bundle was placed at the center of the square and its wonders opened to view, beside a furious fire. The warriors from the capital smoked ancient tobacco with the warriors of Nonconnah in the firelight, and at dawn they moved into the forests to take their positions in the outlying war camps and await the beating of the drum.

Atchekoyo lay in his mother's house, his face blank with sorrow. When Tchula Homa came to visit him, as he did several times every day, Moon Behind Cloud would make it her business to be elsewhere, and usually she took Lakowea with her. Old Wren watched Tchula Homa from the shadows and would not speak to him. The boy, with inconsolable eyes, listened long to Tchula Homa's accounts of the nation's preparations for resistance and revenge.

At Atchekoyo's bedside, Tchula Homa began to sob. He felt comforting hands on his shoulders, but for a long time he could not bring himself to turn and see whose they could be. He sat cross-legged, the boy's wide eyes still fixed on his. A long time passed. The hands of Moon Behind Cloud still rested on his shoulders.

Their father the President dispatched to the Chickasaws a large force of his soldiers. The Chickasaw scouts reported that the advancing army was huge, with cannons and long rifles and an infinite number of horses. Levi Colbert persuaded Tishomingo to demobilize the Chickasaw forces.

That fall, Levi Colbert, his Negro manservant, and a party of eleven other Chickasaw chiefs rode to the new town of Memphis at the Fourth Bluff and journeyed then by boat up the Father of Waters to St. Louis, where, after joining a delegation of six Choctaws and four Creeks, and accompanied by a detachment of the United States Army, they set forth to explore the west.

1830

An Act to Provide for an Exchange of Lands with the Indians Residing in Any of the States or Territories, and for their Removal West of the River Mississippi became, on May 28, the law of the United States of America.

The legislature of the state of Mississippi voted that the laws of that state should now be extended to the Indians—except that Indians were denied the right to vote, to sue, or to testify in a court of law, and all public assembly of Indians was forbidden. The institution of an Indian tribe as a legal entity was abolished; it was now a crime for the Chickasaw nation to seek to govern the conduct of its own members, or for any Chickasaw to perform the functions of a chief. Anyone found guilty could be fined one thousand dollars and sentenced to a year in prison.

Indian lands were opened to white settlement. Squatters, traders, speculators, bootleggers, gamblers, and swindlers poured in.

The Chickasaws appealed once more to their father the President for relief.

The President—now Andrew Jackson—replied that in the lands they had been offered in the west, he would protect them and be their friend and father. Where they now were, they and the President's white children were too near to each other to live in harmony and peace.

Levi Colbert pointed out, as he had recently learned, that President Jackson was well known to be adamantly opposed to South Carolina's doctrine of nullification, which held state law to be superior to federal. The President's insistence on the central government's supreme authority seemed to the Chickasaws inescapably to oblige that government to enforce the treaties it had made guaranteeing the integrity, sovereignty, and protection of the Chickasaw nation. Was not their great father's arm, wrote Colbert, stronger than that of the governor of Mississippi?

Jackson's reply was in the vein the Chickasaws expected: an invitation to negotiate with him and his commissioners regarding the removal of the Chickasaw nation to the west.

It was now well known that their father the President was a partner in the real estate venture at Memphis which was the principal broker of the now unencumbered Chickasaw lands of north Mississippi. Indeed, the first parcel there had already been sold, to a white man from across the ocean. He himself did not occupy the property right away, but sent an overseer to buy slaves and clear the arable land of its trees. Thus, when Tchula Homa wished to go to the sacred swamp to meditate, he was obliged to travel under cover of night across long, flat fields of cotton.

Meanwhile, among the Choctaws a new generation of young and corrupt mixed-blood chiefs had come to power, and without the consent of the people they had signed the Treaty of Dancing Rabbit Creek, by which all remaining Choctaw land east of the Mississippi was ceded to the United States. The people, outraged, promptly voted these chiefs out of office and replaced them with full bloods who opposed removal. But the President refused to recognize the full-blood chiefs, and finally the Choctaws were induced, by bribery and threat and their own hopelessness, to accede.

The Treaty of Dancing Rabbit Creek provided that any Choctaw who wished to remain in Mississippi could do so by registering with the United States agent within six months of the treaty's ratification. But registrants were turned away on technicalities, names were erased from the rolls, delegations of applicants could not find the agent (who was usually drunk), chiefs' petitions for their villagers were rejected on the grounds that chiefship no longer had any legal standing, the registers were inexplicably closed for weeks at a time, and in the end only sixty-nine Choctaw families were granted permission to stay. Thousands of others made preparations to leave their native land.

Facing the unendurable laws of the state of Mississippi, and watching in horror as their brothers the Choctaws were crushed, the national council of the Chickasaws agreed at last to discuss the removal of their people beyond the Father of Waters.

No sooner had they done so than the United States army of occupation, no doubt in order to soften the negotiators' hearts, began to clear the countryside of white intruders. Several hundred squatters were expelled, and their houses and crops were burned. Particular attention was paid to expunging the nation of those few white men who were actually sympathetic to the Chickasaws' desire to remain in their homeland.

In late summer, Andrew Jackson himself arrived at Franklin, Tennessee, to treat with his red children. Though he was over six feet tall, Jackson weighed only a hundred and forty-five pounds. Two bullets he had received in battle were still festering in his body, leaching lead into his blood. Headaches often incapacitated him. An illness of the lungs caused mucus to clog constantly in his throat; sometimes he could not stop coughing. His kidneys were inflamed. He suffered from malaria, rheumatism, intermittent smallpox fevers, constipation, and chronic dysentery. His wife had just died. Grief and his ceaseless pain tried to drag him down, but hatred and the power of his will drove him on.

The weary leaders of the Chickasaws, sweating in their ill-fitting modern black suits, lined up outside the town hall to shake hands with their father the President. When Tchula Homa appeared for the negotiations, in his feathered headdress, his long beaded skirt, and a jeweled mantle that Tinebe Mingo had given him long ago, Tchula Homa was the only Chickasaw there in Chickasaw clothing.

The ringing of an iron gong called the chiefs and honored old men to the building that was to serve as council house, a white church with a high white pointed tower in which somewhere the gong was concealed. The councilors took their seats on gleaming wooden benches.

Jackson's cold blue eyes swept the crowd, lingered a moment on Tchula Homa, and fell to his text as a falcon falls from the treetop to a quail on the ground.

"Friends and brothers," he began:

"Your great father is rejoiced once again to meet you, and shake you by the hand, and to have it in his power to assure you of his continued friendship and good will. He can cherish none but the best feelings for his red brethren, many of whom, during our late war, fought with him in defense of our country.

"By an act of Congress, it was placed in his power to extend justice to the Indians; to pay the expenses of their removal; to support them for twelve months; and to give them a grant of lands, which should endure as long as 'the grass grows, or water runs.' A determination was taken immediately to advise his red children of the means which were thus placed at his disposal to render them happy, and preserve them as nations. It was for this he asked his Chickasaw friends to meet him here.

"Brothers:

"You have long dwelt upon the soil you occupy, and, in early times, before the white man kindled his fires too near you, and, by settling around, narrowed down the limits of the chase, you were, though uninstructed, yet a happy people. Now your white brothers compass you about everywhere. States have been created within your limits, which claim a right to govern and control your people as they do their own citizens. Your great father has not the authority to prevent this state of things; and he now asks you if you are prepared and ready to submit yourselves to the laws of Mississippi; make a surrender of your ancient laws and customs; and peaceably, and quietly, live under those of the white man?

"Brothers, listen:

"The laws to which you must be subjected are not oppressive, for they are those to which your white brothers conform, and are happy. Under them, you will not be permitted to seek private revenge, but in all cases where wrong may be done you, through them to demand redress. No taxes upon your property or yourselves, except such as may be imposed upon a white brother, will be assessed against you.

The courts will be open for the redress of wrongs, and bad men will be made answerable for whatever crimes or misdemeanors may be committed by any of your people or our own.

"Brothers, listen:

"To these laws, where you are, you must submit. There is no preventive, no alternative. Your great father cannot, nor can Congress, prevent it. What then? Do you believe that you can live under those laws? that you can surrender all your ancient habits, and the forms by which you have been so long controlled? If so, your great father has nothing to say or to advise. He has only to express a hope that you may find happiness in the determination you shall make, whatever it may be. His earnest desire is that you may be perpetuated and preserved as a nation; and this, he believes, can only be done and secured by your consent to remove to a country beyond the Mississippi, which, for the happiness of our red friends, was laid out by the Government a long time since, and to which it was expected, ere this, they would have gone.

"Brothers:

"There is no unkindness in the offers made to you. No intention or wish is had to force you from your lands, but rather to intimate to you what is for your own interest. The attachment which you feel for the soil which encompasses the bones of your ancestors is well known. Our forefathers had the same feeling, when, a long time ago, to obtain happiness, they left their lands beyond the great waters, and sought a new and quiet home in these distant and unexplored regions. If they had not done so, where would have been their children? And where the prosperity they now enjoy? The old world would scarcely have afforded support for a people who, by the change their fathers made, have become prosperous and happy. In future time, so will it be with your children. Old men! arouse to energy, and lead your children to a land of promise and of peace, before the Great Spirit shall call you to die. Young chiefs! forget the prejudices you feel for the soil of your birth, and go to a land where you can preserve your people as a nation. Peace invites you there. Annoyance will be left behind. Intruders, traders, and, above all, ardent spirits, so destructive to health and to morals, will be kept from you. And that the weak may not be assailed by their stronger and more powerful neighbors, care shall be taken, and stipulations made, that the United States, by arms if necessary, will maintain peace amongst the tribes, and guard them from assaults of enemies of every kind, whether white or red.

"Brothers, listen:

"These things are for your serious consideration, and it behooves you well to think of them. The present is the time you are asked to do so. Reject the opportunity which is now afforded to obtain comfortable homes, and the time may soon pass when such advantages as are now within your reach may never again be presented. If, from the course you now pursue, this should be the case, then call not upon your great father hereafter to relieve you of your troubles, but make up your minds conclusively to remain upon the lands you occupy, and be subject to the laws of the state where you now reside to the extent her own citizens are. In a few years, by becoming amalgamated with the whites, your national character will be lost; and then, like other tribes who have gone before you, you must disappear and be forgotten."

The Chickasaws deliberated into the night, and the next morning Levi Colbert said to Andrew Jackson:

"Father:

"You say that you have traveled a long ways to talk to your red children. We have listened, and your words have sunk deep into our hearts. And as you are about to set out for Washington city, before we shake our father's hand, perhaps with many of us the last time, we have requested this meeting to tell you that, after sleeping upon the talk you sent us, we are now ready to enter into a treaty based upon the principles communicated to us."

Jackson threw his head back, clasped his hands together over his chest, closed his eyes, and emitted a long and grateful sigh. "Brothers," he said, "let me shake each of you by the hand."

There followed three days and nights of hectic negotiations over financial arrangements and the scheduling of removal. Tchula Homa sat silent through it all.

The provisions of the treaty included an annuity of fifteen thousand dollars for twenty years; individual grants, in fee simple, of three hundred twenty acres of land in Mississippi for every warrior, widow with family, and white man with Indian family in the nation, to be sold upon emigration for a minimum of one dollar and a half per acre; one hundred sixty acres each for all other members of the nation, on the same terms; larger allotments to the honored old men of the nation, on the same terms; compensation for all costs of removal, including the value of possessions necessarily left behind; subsistence for one year after arrival in the new country; grants of axes, hoes, and plows; grants of spinning wheels, cards, and looms; grants of rifles, powder, lead, kettles, blankets, and tobacco; a new council house, two churches, and two thousand dollars per year for ten years to support Christian teachers in those churches; education in the United States for twenty Chickasaw boys of promise, for twenty years; for Levi Colbert's sons Abijah Jackson Colbert and Andrew Morgan Colbert and for George Colbert's grandson Andrew Jackson Frazier, education in the United States also, under the personal direction and care of the President of the United States; a blacksmith for twenty years, and a millwright for five; permission to remain on the land they now occupied for those Chickasaws who were willing to submit to the laws of Mississippi; and suspension of the operation of those laws until removal.

And so it was that on August 31, 1830, the Chickasaw nation ceded to the United States all the lands owned and possessed by them.

Within Article II of the treaty, however, occurred a phrase that was to be of great moment to the Chickasaws in the near future:

"If, after proper examination, a country suitable to their wants and condition cannot be found, then it is stipulated and agreed that this treaty and all its provisions shall be considered null and void."

After yet another expedition to the west, Levi Colbert reported to his great father that they had been unable to find a country suitable to their wants and condition.

On the morning after the winter solstice, Tsatsemataha led the people of Nonconnah in the annual Ceremony of the Day Returning. The honored women of the village, dressed all in white, sang the song of White-headed Eagle, great-grandfather of birds, who brings peace. Young men, in green, sang the song of Red-tailed Hawk, which tells of the heartache of love unfulfilled and ends in the lonely whistle of the soaring searcher. The warriors lined up to drink black drink and button snakeroot tea, and be purged of darkness.

Tsatsemataha slowly unwrapped a deerskin medicine bundle and produced from it a transparent crystal with a blood-red streak running through its center. "Sun," he sang, "shine through the crystal and tell us if all will be well." He rubbed the crystal with the mingled blood of Rabbit, Raccoon, Porcupine, and Wolf. He dipped it in water, held it high against the sun, frowned, and called Tchula Homa forward.

"Our future is clouded," the high priest declaimed. "But our chief is wise and good. Our chief, like this crystal, cannot know the future now, but the light of our history flashes through him, illumining the present. As he leads us in our living, let us lead our children, along the Chickasaw path, the path of purity, as long as the light returns from darkness."

Tchula Homa stood alone in the center of the square. He blew his conch-shell horn four times, to each of the cardinal directions, and stamped his eagle-feathered staff on the earth also four times. He smoked ancient tobacco in his soapstone pipe, and blew smoke to the four winds. Lifting the ancient red pot, full of spring water, toward the sun, he walked across the square to where Atchekoyo lay on his pallet, and moistened the boy's forehead with his fingers.

Tchula Homa returned to the center of the square. "I am the chief. I take you all by the hand," he sang. "Follow me to water; I will follow you to war. You are my wisdom; I only speak for you. Trust me as I trust you. Gods, hear me! Gods, hear me! I am the chief, the lowest man, heavily laden, a servant."

In the forest a bugle blew, and horsemen poured into the square, white men, all armed, in gray uniforms—Mississippi state militia, someone whispered.

A militiaman stood up in the brush at the edge of the square. A mixed-blood Choctaw rose beside him, and commanded the villagers not to move. The militiamen's rifles were trained on the honored old men and women; the white men must have been told, presumably by the Choctaw, that that would be the best way to subdue the people of Nonconnah.

Two white men seized Tchula Homa's arms, and manacled his hands behind his back.

The Treaty of Franklin having been declared null and void owing to the failure of the Chickasaws to choose a country in the west, the Choctaw explained, the laws of the state of Mississippi had been extended over them. Tchula Homa was under arrest for violation of the law against performing the functions of an Indian chief.

In a squatter's log cabin in the forest, Tchula Homa appeared before the county circuit court. He was sentenced to a year in prison and a fine of one thousand dollars.

Tchula Homa did not have any money. Therefore the judge added a second year to his term.

1832

In the dead-still forest, the only sounds were the buzzing of wasps and the occasional heart-stopping song of a mockingbird. Tchula Homa made his way slowly north, his leg muscles weak with disuse. He rested on a mossy bayou bank and drank long, cautious lungfuls of the hot, moist, delicious air. He was free.

He had been let out early; he did not yet know why. He did know that he might not have survived the remaining cold months of his sentence in the fetid log cellar that was his cell. Tishomingo had ridden all the way back to the prison himself to deliver the order for Tchula Homa's release.

Tchula Homa and Tishomingo had been cellmates, for five months, until a short time ago. It had seemed incredible, beneath every known or even imaginable indecency, that the white man would put a ninety-three-year-old man in jail, but one day the door in the ceiling had opened—Tchula Homa sitting dazed, blinking at the light—and the great old chief had hit the floor like a bag of grain. The next day, when he was at last able to speak, Tishomingo had explained that two white men had opened a store at a Chickasaw crossroads, and he had seized their goods, sold them, and delivered the proceeds to the nation's general fund. The traders had brought charges under Mississippi law, and Tishomingo had been arrested, convicted, fined five hundred dollars, and sentenced to six months in prison.

Unlike Tchula Homa, Tishomingo did not submit in silence to the beatings of the guards, the rancid food, the cold and the dark. He spoke a little English and could even write a little, and, shouting up at the trap door, he had demanded pen, ink, and paper, to write to his great father in Washington for deliverance from this unjust captivity. After several weeks of no more reply than laughter, the white men left the hatch open one day, and set the writing materials at the edge. As the old man reached for them, the oak door slammed shut on his hands. Tishomingo did not even cry out.

On the day of Tishomingo's release, the guards left the door of the little log prison open, and all day they did not return. Tchula Homa remembered being able, that day, to thrust his head through the open trap door and see into the street and the sunlight. White women and children were passing up and down. There were wagons, their wheels flashing. A group of slaves walked by, laughing, with scythes over their shoulders. Slowly the traffic ceased, and he could hear crows calling. The guards were nowhere to be seen. Presumably, they were tempting him to escape. He turned his back on the open door and tried to picture the face of Moon Behind Cloud, but it swam away, and he sank back into his cell.

Then, not two weeks later, Tishomingo had come back. The old chief's broken hands had not healed, and never would; he could barely hold the paper. When Tishomingo turned toward Tchula Homa to speak, the guard rapped his truncheon on the desk, but Tishomingo managed to shoot Tchula Homa a dour smile before they hurried him out and dropped Tchula Homa back into the cellar. And then a few mornings later they opened the trap door again.

They brought a Choctaw to tell him what the paper had meant, but Tchula Homa would not climb out. They came in and dragged him out. They threw him into the street.

He could not stand up straight, for the ceiling of the cellar had been a foot less high than himself. He tried to walk, but his legs gave way. When he collapsed for the third or fourth time, he stopped trying to get up. For a long time he just sat there, in the wagon ruts, in the heat of the August noon, with the townspeople going up and down. He imagined they were used to Indians in the street unable to get up; Chickasaw and Choctaw drunkards (and white ones as well) had been thrown into Tchula Homa's cellar from time to time.

Women hurried by with their faces averted. A little white boy with hair nearly white came haltingly up to him and said something and smiled. Tchula Homa raised his right hand to the boy in greeting and tried to speak but found he could not. An angry white man in buckskin swept the boy away.

Then Tchula Homa had begun walking slowly north in the white, consuming sun, every step a bolt of pain, through acrid, dusty fields where the mournful songs of the slaves hung in the air like smoke. Long rows of Negro men, women, and children, in ragged straw hats, moved down the rows of cotton, chopping out weeds with their hoes.

In the forest he came to a mean, trash-strewn crossroads where amidst the girdled and leafless trees a squatters' settlement had sprung up. Two white men were sitting whittling on the porch of a crude log store, silently watching him. Perhaps these were the men whose goods Tishomingo had seized.

Long ago the Chickasaws had had a little hunting camp here, just a cluster of low shelters, with a permanent population of two: old identical twin sisters who tended the fires and made black drink and cooked for hunters. He and his father had spent a night here once with a party of warriors from the Tennessee River country, and the warriors had taught him the right way to throw his knife. He remembered the slick skin of the Chickasaw warriors, greased with bear fat, and their hunting paint, streaks of green across their cheekbones. He remembered the wrinkled and elaborately tattooed old twins, with their pot of soup to which every hunter added a morsel of game. The same pot of soup had been cooking here, his father said, since before those old women were born. Tchula Homa remembered their cornbread baked in chestnut leaves, and the honey cakes they made just for him, "boy-cakes," they called them, "to make boys good killers," and how he had feared that the boy-cakes were actually made with the meat of little boys, and the old women were cannibal witches. His father had laughed and eaten the first boy-cake to show him it was all right.

Tchula Homa was hungry. He hobbled toward the white men with his right hand raised. They stopped whittling, and at first just stared at him, chewing their tobacco, but after he had stood there awhile with his hand in the air, they looked at each other, shrugged, and raised their right hands too. Tchula Homa rubbed his stomach and made eating motions. In answer the white men laughed, and spat tobacco juice at his feet.

He had learned in prison that white men clasped their hands together to beg. He tried that. The white men laughed harder.

Tchula Homa decided to sit down, facing them, and wait. It was not, perhaps, a decision as such—he was too weak to keep standing. Again he rubbed his belly and clasped his hands and looked at the men. One of them, at last, sighed, pushed himself slowly out of his chair, went into the store, and came back with a piece of bread. He tossed it into the dirt in front of Tchula Homa. It was soft, and white, and wonderful.

When he had gained enough strength to rise again, he went forward to shake the white men's hands in thanks. They waved him away, and he resumed his slow journey toward home.

There were new, small farms carved out of the forest here and there all along the way, some of them Chickasaw, some of them white—indistinguishable, in their filth and disorder, until the dogs came: the Chickasaw dogs greeted him avidly, the white ones barked at him or slunk away.

Juncos chattered in the honeysuckle thickets. The trees and climbing vines, black in the gold light of unclouded sunset, blurred in the deepening green. He knew this place; a sad, fierce love for it came over him.

He arrived at Nonconnah after midnight, beneath a single icy star. The village was asleep. His house swam to him through the darkness and swallowed him into its soft light. A lamp was burning in the corner, his bed ready. He blew out the lamp, lay down, and slept.

A scent from long ago, something sweet, woodsmoke, and a certain slant of light—he woke with a start. Hananata was sitting at his bedside with a bowl of black drink. "Do you have any idea what time it is?" she demanded, gesturing brusquely toward the midmorning sun streaming in through the door.

Tchula Homa could not stop weeping. Old Hananata stroked his hair.

Later, she led him down to Daylight Bayou and gave him a bath. Then she fed him cornmeal mush and red beans, and then he slept again, the rest of the day and all night.

In the morning, Tsatsemataha came to him and chanted the blessing of Red Fox. Together they went outside. It was a typical late-summer morning, dew heavy on the grass, the sun still yolk-yellow in the oaks eastward. In front of the women's gathering-house, smoke was rising from the wash fire. Nearby, a group of little girls sat in a circle, quietly mending. Tsatsemataha's hand rested on Tchula Homa's shoulder. As they drew nearer, Tchula Homa looked again at the little girls, and his heart shrank in his breast.

They were too thin. As the chief and the high priest came among them, the children's eyes rose round and sad not to the men's faces but to their hands—looking to see if they had brought them something to eat.

The women looked on shyly and sadly, murmuring among themselves. Moon Behind Cloud was not among them.

"Come and see Atchekoyo," said Tsatsemataha. "I've told him you're back."

Old Wren was outside the house, sweeping the foreyard. Tchula Homa raised his hand in greeting.

"Welcome home, Tchula Homa," she replied listlessly. She peered into the house and called, "Atchekoyo, wake up. Look who's here."

Tchula Homa ducked his head and went in. The crippled boy opened his eyes and smiled weakly.

"Brings the Rifle," said Tchula Homa, kneeling and taking his hand. Atchekoyo clutched back hard. His arms were unspeakably thin, his whole body covered with sores. "You have smallpox?"

The boy nodded, still clinging to Tchula Homa's hand, his eyes imploring.

"Where are Lakowea and Moon Behind Cloud?" blurted Tchula Homa.

Tsatsemataha and Wren brought him a woven cane guest seat and sat with him at Atchekoyo's bedside. "Lakowea is with the other sick children in the sick house," said the old man. "They have smallpox too."

Tsatsemataha gripped Tchula Homa's shoulder. "Moon Behind Cloud has died," he said, "also of smallpox. Only last week."

"The fever came quickly," said Wren, "and took her away in peace. She blessed you with her dying breath, Tchula Homa."

"She enobles the ancestors with whom she now sleeps," said Tsatsemataha.

The old sycamore's roots crept across a little creviced world of ants, spiders, shaded passages, polished surfaces, feathers, potshards, flecks of flint, bowls of dust, moist nests of moss, twined tendrils of the hundreds of plants that lived in the tree's manifold grasp of the earth. Tchula Homa's hands sought through the crevices to the cool soil beneath. He buried his face in the bare-worn hollow where she had sat one day looking up at him. Sunshine bore down on his back as heavy as stone. A sob tore its way out of his heart, and another, and another, until his heart was cold at last.

In the place inside him where his soul, in the dark, had dreamed of deliverance, now an emptiness dozed like a dog in the sun.

Tchula Homa sat in the circle of painted stones, remembering everything he could of Moon Behind Cloud, every moment they had ever spent together. A windy day, the black twigs haloed blue, the sweet scent of leaf mold in the curling hairs at the nape of her neck. The cool scrutiny of her eyes; that crooked smile, one side happy, one side sad. Her craving; the vastness of his regret.

He tried to picture all he had not seen. Moon Behind Cloud making love to Atchelata, giving birth to her sons, dying. Her burial: sitting upright, facing east, her long hair shining with oil, her face painted bright red, her dead eyes wide, her jewelry, her beaded white dress, the grave covered with thick logs and layers of cypress bark and the mound of red clay. The darkness of the lower world, the swirling winds, the deep blue light drifting away down the caverns.

A sob tore its way out of his heart, and another and another. He was not dead inside after all, alas.

When Tchula Homa returned to Nonconnah he went straight to Tsatsemataha. "Atchekoyo is now nineteen years old," he said. "It is time for him to become a man and warrior."

Tsatsemataha's heavy-lidded eyes told it all. Atchekoyo had died.

"Being ignorant of the laws of the white man, the Chickasaws cannot understand or obey them. They prefer to seek a home in the west, where they may live and be governed by their own laws," read the preamble to the Treaty of Pontotoc Creek. Levi Colbert, the nation's only really effective negotiator, had been confined to his bed by illness throughout the discussions, and it was not clear if he understood the document they carried him out in a litter to sign.

There was to be a grant of land in fee simple to every member of the nation who wanted one; the Chickasaws might either stay on the land and submit to the laws of Mississippi, or sell it and remove to the west. Aware that this might be their last chance to amass the resources necessary to sustain them through their removal, more than half of the people of Nonconnah drifted away. Hungry, sick, and exhausted, they camped in groves of tall, straight relict forest trees amidst the cotton fields on the outskirts of the capital, awaiting the distribution of lands. Tchula Homa's younger brother Tathonoyo was among them, bargaining for a new brood of pigs.

Lakowea had survived the smallpox epidemic, and his grandmother took him home with her to her old fields at the capital. His father Atchelata and his slaves were teaching him to plow, and plant, and fertilize, and weed, and harvest cotton.

Tchula Homa stayed in his house. Hananata brought him black drink and corn mush. Old Tsatsemataha sat with him in the evenings, drumming softly as Tchula Homa played his cane flute in the starlight.

The first contingent of their brothers the Choctaws began their forced march west. Several thousand of them, caught in a snowstorm, died of exposure. In the fall, the next wave of Choctaw emigrants, denied blankets and provisions by the white contractors entrusted with managing their removal, were struck down by cholera. The six thousand Choctaws remaining in the state of Mississippi, unwilling to follow their brethren in the path of doom but now uprooted from their ancient villages, wandered through the countryside, slowly starving to death.

On the streets of the white man town called Columbus, Georgia, members of the once fierce Red Sticks of the Creek nation were begging for food. The city of Mobile, Alabama, passed a law authorizing its justices of the peace to seize any wild game found in the possession of an Indian; there was little opportunity for such seizures, however, for most of the game was gone and most of the Creeks were too much weakened by hunger to hunt.

The Creeks signed the Treaty of Washington, which guaranteed each member of the nation an individual grant of land and ceded all the rest to the United States, on condition of an orderly removal. As soon as the ink was dry, white men overran the lands reserved to the Creeks, burning Creek towns, looting Creek storehouses, raping Creek women and girls, and murdering Creek men, women, and children.

A white man named Henry Clay, decrying the suffering of the American Indians, ran for the presidency of the United States but was overwhelmingly defeated by the incumbent, Andrew Jackson.

An ice storm. Rattling, shivering, shimmering silver trees bending earthward and broken. A deep stillness, the villagers in their houses close to their fires. A slow crunch, crunch, and thump of footsteps and a walking stick, approaching. Pothanoa at the door, wrapped in his old fur-trimmed red blanket.

"Speaker!" called Tchula Homa. "Come in and warm yourself. It's not safe for an old man to be walking around on that ice."

Another crunch, crunch, and thump. Tsatsemataha came in now, laid his stick against the wall next to Pothanoa's, and sat down. He had brought a pipe, and ancient tobacco and dried sumac to smoke in it, but he set it aside. Tsatsemataha unwrapped his medicine bundle, and spread seven beads on the hearth, three black, three white, one red. He picked up the red bead, rubbed it between his fingers, and closed his eyes—looking into the future. He opened his eyes, and nodded to Pothanoa.

The speaker, turning toward Tchula Homa, said, "A dead man has come to us. That is, we thought he was dead, and we addressed him as such. But he insisted he was not. Then Tsatsemataha looked at him through the crystal, and saw that he is alive after all. And the red bead tells us—?"

The high priest nodded a second time.

Pothanoa continued, "He will live a long time still."

"Is this some sort of riddle," demanded Tchula Homa irritably, "or have you come here with something to say?"

"Tatholah is alive," said Pothanoa.

"And here?"

"In my house," said Pothanoa.

Tsatsemataha's eyes were fixed on Tchula Homa, who he now knew had lied, long ago, when he said that his father was dead.

Hananata passed out bowls of spicebush tea, and all four sipped at it quietly, showing their recognition of the moment's gravity.

"He was dead to me and to our people," murmured Tchula Homa, half to himself. "He signed a paper to give the sacred swamp to Andrew Jackson. But I shouldn't have lied."

Tsatsemataha took Tchula Homa by the hand. "It was a long time ago," he said. "We in Nonconnah are of one fire forever. Pothanoa?" The speaker added his hand. "Hananata?" And she hers. Tchula Homa was forgiven.

Tsatsemataha took fire from the hearth, lit his pipe, puffed four times to the winds, and passed the pipe to Tchula Homa. The high priest nodded again to the speaker, and Pothanoa said, "You will forgive your father now."

—·ɛ·—

The two old men walked very slowly, steadying themselves on their sticks, across the patches of ice in the square. Tchula Homa followed, two steps behind. Those houses which were still inhabited had heavy rugs drawn tight across the doors, and smoke curling from the tops of their steep thatched roofs; many others stood open, their hearths cold, empty.

Tchula Homa's father was pacing up and down outside the speaker's house, wrapped in a heavy black white man cloak and wearing a white man raccoon-skin cap. Only when the three had stopped before him did Tatholah look up, and then he did not seek his son's eyes. The white lace of the clicking ice-covered trees, when the wind gusted, shed crystals on Tatholah's stooped shoulders. The wind did not stir the greasy matted fur of his cap.

"Father," said Tchula Homa, coolly.

"Tchula Homa," wept Tatholah.

He was thin, in his big black cloak. His skin was drawn tight across his sharp cheekbones, and his eyes had sunk deep into dark sockets. His face was an archive of sadness, but as of a sadness long ago passed through, weathered into obscurity, and now overlain by a strange blankness, a smoothness, a softness. Tatholah stepped back and wiped his eyes. He reached out both his hands, and Tchula Homa gave him his.

"Good," grunted Pothanoa and Tsatsemataha together.

"Shall we go to my house and sit down and smoke?" asked Tchula Homa. "Just the two of us?"

Tatholah declined Tsatsemataha's offer of his walking stick, and walked stiffly across the frozen square on his own. His heavy black hobnailed boots, too big, shuffled clumsily in the fallen split cylinders of ice that had encased the twigs above.

Tatholah drew close to his son's fire. "I've heard about your troubles, son, and I'm sorry, though now we may again have some common ground."

Tchula Homa said nothing.

"Things have gotten much better for me in the last few years," his father went on. "My wife was bought, seven winters ago, by a white lady from across the ocean named Fanny Wright, and we went with her to a sort of community she owned called Nashoba. You've heard of it?"

"No."

"Well, it was a community of Negroes, where everyone was equal. A school, too. Miss Fanny would buy young slaves, and when they finished their schooling they would be set free. It was an extraordinary place."

"Ah, yes. The place of fornication."

"Oh, people exaggerate. Well, Miss Fanny Wright got sick, and she had to go back across the ocean to her friend Lafayette. Do you know his name, the great hero of the American revolution?"

"No," said Tchula Homa.

"Anyway, she went away for a long time, and Nashoba began to run down. Finally she returned with a husband, and saw the mess that had been made of Nashoba, and she said that it had failed. She said she was going to close Nashoba down and take all the people there who were still slaves to a place far away across the southern ocean, called Haiti, and set them free, and then they would all found a new community together. But Glory said she wouldn't leave her home country of America."

"Glory?"

"My wife. And then—the great lover of Negroes!—Miss Fanny tried to get hold of Glory and lock her up. She said Glory didn't know what was good for her. Did she want to run around loose with nowhere to go, starving to death, like a wild Indian? Obviously I did not appreciate that expression. Miss Fanny never liked me. But bless my Glory—we escaped from Miss Fanny! We hid for a while in the sacred swamp, but we got caught—you're aware that the swamp is part of that new plantation, very near here?"

Tchula Homa did not know this. He might have known that Jackson would not have burned the deed.

"And they marched us in to the planter," his father continued, "and Glory started talking as fast as she could. He couldn't understand her at first, because he's from far away across the ocean and doesn't know English very well, but finally he said we were not to worry, he would take care of everything. Then he sent Miss Fanny Wright a pledge to set Glory free, and Miss Fanny sold Glory to him, and now she's free! And both of us are working there on his plantation. And guess what, son? I'm a father again."

Tchula Homa said nothing.

"Quite a man, this white man," continued Tatholah, oblivious. "He makes pictures, with paint on a board, amazing pictures, of people's faces, and flowers, and the landscape, and just about anything. Mostly pictures of people. They're so real they'd make you jump out of your skin."

"How does he do that?" asked Tchula Homa, who had once heard of such a thing from Kills Enemy, when he came back from Natchez in the white man's spell.

"How do white men do anything? I don't know! But you ought to see these pictures, son."

"I've vowed never to leave this village, Father, if I can possibly help it."

"He'll come here. Listen. He's very interested in our people, and he wants to paint a picture of a Chickasaw chief, in real Chickasaw clothes. Naturally I thought of you. I knew you'd be right back here, living the old way. He'll pay you well."

"We need some corn. There aren't many children left now, but the ones we have are hungry. And I need a new rifle."

"Then you'll do it?"

Tchula Homa sighed from the dull, encrusted depths of his resignation, and nodded.

"You'll like him, son."

Tchula Homa closed his eyes and waited for his father to leave. The villagers who recognized the old man shouted in amazement. Boys were sliding on the ice all around him, asking him about the land of the dead, and he told them there were horses there twenty feet high, lakes of honey, and no white men.

You must be patient, the white man seemed to say with his hands on Tchula Homa's shoulders. This will take a while.

Corelli stood behind the board he was painting and stared at it for a long moment. Sometimes he would approach Tchula Homa and gently lift his hand and examine it, or run his hand down Tchula Homa's cheek, or turn his face toward the light. Then, for a while, he would paint.

With his gift for stillness, Tchula Homa sat easily all day long, day after day. Corelli would talk steadily to him in a dusty half-whisper.

One day, as he posed, Tchula Homa found himself meditating on the manifold varieties of his shame—his failure to keep the wife he had loved, his murder of the bear cubs, his father's disgrace, his people's degradation and dispossession. Unconsciously he slipped his old knife from its sheath and ran a hard-callused finger along its sharp edge. At that instant Corelli began to gesticulate and shout. He wiggled his fingers at Tchula Homa in a gesture of beckoning, as if to be saying, Yes, this is how I wish you to look—whatever you're thinking, keep thinking it.

Corelli's face always seemed full of emotion, but Tchula Homa could not make much sense of his expressions because they were so foreign. He had never really studied a white man's face before. Today, nonetheless, he felt sure that he saw in Corelli an overflowing of sadness which, inexplicably, the white man seemed in some way to be enjoying.

Angelo Corelli was an old man, and feeble, but when their rest periods came he would always shuffle over to Tchula Homa and lay an affectionate hand on his shoulder, or shake his hand vigorously, and smile at Tchula Homa with frank admiration. At the end of the day he would be very tired, and soon Tchula Homa, in sign language, invited him to sleep in his house. Late at night, when the fire died and only a silver-blue softness of starlight remained, Tchula Homa would talk to Corelli—about Moon Behind Cloud, Atchekoyo, Andrew Jackson, Kills Enemy, days long ago. He knew that the white man could not understand him.

By gestures, Corelli had made clear that Tchula Homa was not to look at the picture until it was finished, and now, as Corelli gazed at him for long moments, adding only a stroke here and there, Tchula Homa sensed that the moment was near.

In the golden light of a warm December day, the painting was unveiled. Tchula Homa stood before it unable at first to open his eyes. Corelli, he knew, was watching him hard.

He opened his eyes.

He stared for long minutes, barely blinking, barely breathing.

Then a spasm began to move up his spine, and, as though the earth was quaking, he pitched forward onto his face in front of the picture, and from deep inside him there came a long, low moan. Corelli had taken Tchula Homa's sorrow and given it concrete and permanent form. Not even death now could end it.

He managed somehow to get to his house and his bed, and, as he wept on, night fell. Hananata came with something for him to eat, but he motioned to her to leave. Then Corelli came, and took Tchula Homa in his arms like a child. Each sob came now as though wrenched from tangled roots, and still he could not stop. Corelli held Tchula Homa's head against his chest and rocked gently back and forth, and said nothing.

When Tchula Homa woke in the night, Corelli was there beside him, watching, close.

Morning came. Corelli was still with him. Tchula Homa searched in the white man's face for the cruelty that must have inspired the picture—the delight he had seemed to take in sadness—but he could not find it.

Let me see the picture again, he said in sign language.

But Corelli replied, by gesture, that he had thrown it on the fire yesterday.

1837

The red fox, his namesake, came to Tchula Homa in the circle of painted stones and lay down and slept beneath a lightning-splintered tupelo. In meditation Tchula Homa chanted the fox's name, and the soft tail quivered as the fox dreamed on.

Tchula Homa bade the swamp, the circle of stones, the lost city farewell. To the bear; to the wolves and the death and life of the deer they killed and loved; to the oaks and tulip-trees and their song of time; to the muscadine and its music of victory; to the great blue heron and its patience; to the white-headed eagle and its courage and the limitlessness of possibility; to the dreaming red fox and hence to himself, Tchula Homa bade farewell. To Ivory-billed Woodpecker's persistence, persistence; to irresponsible mother Opossum, and to Bobcat, who ate Opossum and her young; to Catfish and Bass, in the dark water; to irrepressible Beaver; to hungry, stupid, trusting Porcupine; to Cougar, watching, not speaking, whom no one may ever kill; to Elk, exterminated, never again to whistle and roar in the pumpkin moon; to All-Bear, who will never forgive me; to White-tailed Deer, who gave me my wife and my love—to all these, farewell. To my mother Tahanata, to my brother Tchilatokowa, to my uncle Kills Enemy, to Lokana Tcheh his mother my grandmother, to my king and mentor Tinebe Mingo, to my darling, my darling, Moon Behind Cloud, and my soul-son, Atchekoyo, Brings the Rifle, beneath the earth, goodbye.

—·ɛ·—

As the years had passed, Chickasaw delegations had visited Washington, Chickasaw diplomats had temporized, Chickasaw expeditions had explored the west and returned unsatisfied, Chickasaw children had sickened and starved in the states of Mississippi and Alabama, the Choctaws had left their homeland, the Cherokees had left their homeland, the Creeks had begun to leave their homeland, the forests had been settled and cleared, and still the sacred swamp remained; and Tchula Homa remained, in the village of Nonconnah, waiting.

Now the waiting was over. The Chickasaw nation, by signing the treaty of Doaksville, had agreed to accept a corner of the Choctaws' grant as their new home in the west. This Green Corn Festival, therefore, was to be the Chickasaws' last in their native land.

Tsatsemataha, in his tattered white moccasins, white vest, white shawl, and turban of white swan feathers, took the mother wood of oak and the father wood of pine into his house, and with them engendered new fire. Pothanoa walked through the village calling the few remaining women out of their houses. Hananata brought green corn ears and persimmons to the square. The high priest did not throw them into the flames this year; food was too precious to be sacrificed. There had been no fasting either, by Tchula Homa's decree; the old men were too weak to endure it.

The women took fire to their homes, and the people of Nonconnah gathered around a pot of corn and beans with squirrel, leaning into the smoke to catch the meat-fragrance. The seven warriors of the village danced. The people painted themselves white with clay, walked down to Daylight Bayou, and were purified.

That night, the villagers sat in the square and talked about times gone by.

The moment that was always going to come, the moment that had been coming since first a Chickasaw raised his right hand in peace to a white man, had come: the soldier in the doorway with a rifle.

Tchula Homa rose from sleep and raised his right hand. He took his knife and wrapped it in cloth and put it into a red clay ceremonial pitcher. He nestled the pitcher carefully in the corner of his house. This he would leave behind him in Nonconnah, in the ancient land of the Chickasaws. The white man beckoned with his bayonet.

The soldiers loaded the women and children and old men onto wagons, tied the able-bodied men's hands behind their backs, and set fire to the houses.

Late that afternoon, they came to a stockade. Within it and three others like it, the Chickasaw people were to be concentrated to await the completion of arrangements for their transportation.

Summer passed.

One morning in late October, the Indian camp was awakened by a brass band. Many soldiers had arrived in the night. A long line of wagons stretched far down the road. Near the stockade gate Tchula Homa saw his father standing watching, with a half-Negro boy at his side. When Tatholah saw Tchula Homa, he took the boy's little brown hand in his own and waved. "Your brother!" called Tatholah before the soldiers pushed him outside.

Tchula Homa joined Tsatsemataha and Pothanoa sitting silent and unseeing on the Army buckboard. The gates were opened, a bugle blew, the flag of the United States was raised at the head of the column, and the last of the Chickasaw nation began their long journey west.

Part Two

1860

Giovanni Corelli had just received a new dove-gray worsted suit from his tailor in Rome. Of Caleb, his long, tall, white-bearded valet, he demanded, "It is not splendid?"

"You a fine-looking gentleman all right," said Caleb. "No doubt about that. No, sir."

"Eh! See if the carriage is ready."

Caleb walked to the window. Below, sprawled on the roof of the carriage in a pool of warm spring sun, lay Sylvester, a stable boy.

Caleb commandeered a broom from a housemaid and hurried downstairs and out. "You just be glad I ain't calling Mr. B. on you, that's all," said Caleb, whaling Sylvester with the broom.

Corelli appeared on the front steps, pink and dewy as a peach. Instantly Caleb pretended to be sweeping. "Yes, sir, Mr. Joe, yes, sir," he was saying. "Beautiful morning, everything fine."

Sylvester and his friend Aaron, also a stable boy, helped maneuver the master into the carriage; Corelli was very fat. Uncle Duncan, the old stable boss, seemed to be asleep on the box until he heard the three walking-stick knocks beneath him.

Surveying the long rows of his cotton, Corelli cracked his knuckles slowly in contentment. Farther on, where his field hands rose from their sowing of cowpeas amidst the corn and doffed their hats to him, he issued a dim smile.

Soon the trees closed in on both sides; here the road was corduroyed with cedar logs fighting a losing battle with the gumbo mud.

Beneath an unsteady bridge flowed a bayou that drained a wild, dark swamp in the heart of the forest. Giovanni Corelli owned this swamp, but he had never seen it. It was a place of bears, and snakes, and fevers.

The sky was darkening fast. Soon the rain was hammering on the roof, slashing at the isinglass, brimming the ruts in the road. The carriage lurched, and sank to its axles in mud. The long, gloomy face of Uncle Dunc appeared in the window. "We stuck, marse," he said.

"So get not stuck! I have appointment."

"You got to get out."

"But my new suit!"

"I can't help that, boss."

Corelli stood panting, ankle-deep in mud. As suddenly as it had begun, the rain ceased. There was a rustling up ahead: a whitetail buck with a broken hind ankle limped across the road, splashed through a beaver slough, and disappeared into the willows beyond. A minute behind the deer, trotting in single file along the edge of the water, came a pack of seven wolves, the first and largest of which turned toward the horses and men with a yellow-eyed stare before moving on into the forest.

The Gayoso House in Memphis was always a splendid luxuriance. Corelli took a long, hot soak in a marble tub, had a massage, smoked a cigar, and ordered in a supper of turtle soup, raw oysters, quenelles de brochet, roast capon with peanut stuffing, Swiss cheese, strawberry fool, and a bottle of Chambertin. When he came downstairs the next morning, his new friend Nathan Bedford Forrest was there waiting.

"I have come," said Corelli, shooting his lace cuffs, "to accept your offer."

They walked together to Forrest's depot. From within came the sound of dozens of Negroes singing, first the thin and lonely melody of the call and then the roar of the mass response.

A detail of men awaiting auction were painting the high brick wall of the depot and singing along with their brethren inside. At the appearance of Forrest they stopped and fell silent.

"Good morning, boys," said Forrest.

"Good morning, master," chorused the men, hats in hand.

"Come on in the back, Giovanni. I got her her own little room back here. I keep a nice little old room for the likes of this one."

Forrest picked a key from a huge iron ring and unlocked the door. The room was all in white: lace curtains, a big white bed, white doilies and antimacassars on white stuffed chairs.

"Come here, sweet thing," said Forrest as the woman rose from the chair where she had been reading.

Corelli stared at the woman a long moment, and then he said, "Comme elle est belle!"

"Would you listen at that!" exclaimed Forrest. "I sure didn't know you spoke French, Giovanni. She speaks it too! She can even read it. Can't nothing beat your New Orleans high yellow."

The woman looked Corelli straight in the eye. Unlike any other Negro whose purchase he had ever contemplated, she showed no sign of fear. She was a pale caramel in color, with emerald-green eyes; she was tall, slim, a little angular, but soft and round where it counted.

Forrest stood at her side and ran his hand up her back, and she wriggled away, smiling shyly. "Ain't this the primest of the prime? I declare. Name Félice."

Félice curtsied, and Corelli bowed. Then he and Forrest withdrew to Forrest's office, where Corelli learned that the price of the woman was seven thousand dollars.

"You joke?"

"That gal come from the Quadroon Ball, Giovanni," said Forrest patiently. "You know about the Quadroon Ball, don't you?"

"No, my friend."

"Well, it's like this, Giovanni. Down in New Orleans, every spring, all these free colored mamas that have been messing with the white man—and most of them does—they bring their prettiest daughters to these dancing balls, all done up like a princess in a fairy tale, and they march them up and down, and the young men come in there and pick theirselves out a mistress. It's a beautiful thing to see, Giovanni! And it ain't been but two years since a friend of mine downriver, name of Duquesne, picked out this here one. Lord, Giovanni, that old boy paid six thousand for her! And a virgin then still needing to be broke. Now you figure in the wardrobe and the shipping and the room and board, and I barely get clear. I'm doing you a favor, Giovanni—friend to friend."

"I am sorry," Corelli moaned, his indignation displaced by embarrassment. "I do not know these things."

"You are definitely getting your money's worth, Giovanni. That there is the single best piece of tail ever been through this depot."

Corelli gave Forrest a wide-eyed look.

"All merchandise guaranteed," chuckled Forrest, "by the proprietor. What the hell you expect?"

As they passed out of town and into the fields, she said, in French, "It is quite different here from Louisiana. You have neither live oaks nor Spanish moss."

"Yes. That is to say, no," mumbled Corelli, trying to think of something worth saying but unable to.

"The cotton market, it is good?" she asked.

"Ah, ah, so-so," said Corelli, wiping his brow. Florid Italian phrases raced through his head, but they would not cross into French. He cleared his throat, and she sat forward to listen, but still he could not speak.

"Once, with my mother and her master, I went to Paris," she said, "and there we bought such lace as cannot be found even in New Orleans. This is all that's left of it." She spread her hand between her breasts. "Do you like it?"

"Very much," he stammered, watching her chest rise and fall.

Finally he gave up. He turned to look out the window at the passing scene, the deep forest, the rain. This was how it was when he was six, in Jamaica, watching the rain on the cane fields from his sick bed or the hammock on the sleeping porch while the servants never came with the cool drink they knew he needed. This was how it was when he was twelve, in Rome, home from school to his stiff-necked aunts lifting pink tea cups with pinkies outstretched, and the lisping, nodding priests across the high-vaulted room. This was how it was when he was twenty-one, thirty, forty, still in Rome, marrying, fathering, dithering as his father endured uprisings in Haiti, emancipation in Jamaica, the American wilderness—hero to his sisters, fool to his son. Even after his father's death and his own assumption of the sole command of this vast plantation, Giovanni had never known how to assert his so evident supremacy; he did not know what to say. Yet at the briefest thought of the stench and stridor of the Roman streets he was filled with loathing. He would never go back to those priest-ridden, aunt-ridden parlors! Give me hurricanes, and wilderness!

Behind his back, Félice smiled.

At the house, Sylvester opened the carriage door and extended his hand to help her down. As she alighted, she brushed his cheek with her fingertips and looked into his eyes and briefly, sweetly, smiled.

Sylvester's head was engorged with fire.

"I surely would like to get a little bit of that yellow mud on *my* turtle," said Aaron.

"You shut you filthy mouth," said Sylvester.

"You is getting so *housey* we going to have to get you a little calico apron, Sylvester, and a little old headrag to match."

Sylvester swung wild, and soon the two young men were wrestling wildly in the dirt.

As Hattie came puffing down the marble steps in all her grandeur, Aaron danced away. Sylvester, always the plodder, caught a long-handled broom full in the tailquarters for the second time in two days. "I going to put Mr. B. on you sure as Christmas come," cried Hattie. "Fighting on the manor house steps like some wild Indian!"

Aaron crept up behind Hattie while she was busy assuring Sylvester that if he still had such notions as coming to work in the house she would just as soon allow a blind mule in there as the likes of him. Aaron got down on all fours behind her. She was now poking Sylvester in the chest with a finger that felt like a sharpened stick.

Sylvester could restrain himself no longer. Grinning evilly, he took a step toward Hattie. She shrank back—just enough—and came crashing down. Sylvester and Aaron lit out across the back pasture and into the woods.

"Like to broke my back," said Aaron between sobs of laughter.

Sylvester had already recovered his usual somber mien. "If that ain't the dumbest thing I ever done, Aaron, I don't know what is. Now I never going to get near that yellow gal."

"And law, here come Mr. B. come to tan us."

"Goodbye, house," grieved Sylvester. "Goodbye, yellow gal."

Benedict O'Connell, the plantation overseer, came into the clearing laughing. The young men waited with bowed heads to be thrashed. Sylvester could not take his eyes off the quirt in Mr. B.'s hand. The customary indication of the coming punishment was for Mr. B. to remove his gold ring and button it into his breast pocket, but all he did was sit down between them, still laughing, turning the ring slowly on his finger. "I'm supposed to whip y'all's tails, of course," he said, "but that there was one of the funniest things I ever seen in my natural-born life. I was a-watching from down by the clothesline."

Aaron and Sylvester looked at each other in astonishment.

"Don't y'all tell nobody I let you off, you hear? Just go on to bed and act like you been whipped. You hear?"

"Yes, sir, boss," said Aaron. "We surely won't. We surely will. Thank you, boss."

The next day, Corelli plantation underwent a visit from Miles Glory, a free person of color.

"How y'all black niggers getting along?" Miles inquired unctuously.

The people in the slave quarters endured Miles because he was always full of news of their families and friends around the countryside, and because he always had plenty of money, and he loved to shoot dice, and sometimes he lost.

Sylvester fell into step with Miles, who was strolling briskly around the packed clay courtyard, rattling his dice. "Where you get so much money at, Miles? How you like to buy me free? I pay you back."

Miles coughed in disdain. "Where you going to get money at to pay me back with, little black nigger?"

Sylvester was indeed very black, and little, but he did not like this form of address. "You got money, ain't you?"

"I ain't no little black nigger, neither." This was also true enough. Miles was tall, and reddish brown.

"Where you get that money at? How you get it?"

"Don't you be studying my money too hard, Sylvester. I gets it because my womens gives it to me. There ain't nothing a little nigger girl love better than a wild Indian, and I is half wild Indian. So they gives me money."

"*Gives* it to you."

"That's right, boy. You want to shoot some dice?"

"I ain't got no money," said Sylvester.

"Well," scoffed Miles, "I reckon you just can't play then, can you? And talking about buy me free, Miles. What you going do if you free? These niggers! I swear to God."

"You mama was a nigger!" cried Sylvester.

"My mama was a *free Negro,* direct descended from the king of Africa."

Miles Glory hung around the big house waiting for a look at the girl, but for five long days neither she nor Giovanni Corelli even came downstairs, much less outdoors.

Hattie was on her way out into the swamp to collect herbs for her asphidity bags by the light of the full moon when she saw a ladder thrown up against the side of the house and an unmistakable stick-legged figure climbing toward the master's window. Skirts flying, she bustled to the foot of the ladder. "Take one last look, Mister Smarty-breeches," she hissed up at Miles, and yanked the ladder away.

Hattie lifted him ear first and marched him to the plantation gate, and dropped him in the mud.

The first thing she saw the next morning from the kitchen window, however, was Miles Glory sauntering past, picking his teeth and grinning.

"You got to do something about that man!" she cried to Luigi.

Luigi Carbone had come from Rome to Corelli plantation in 1836, after Giovanni Corelli's father Angelo had for six years tried alternately to stomach the indigenous cuisine and to teach Italian cooking to Hattie. In the ensuing twenty-four years, Luigi had grown from a fat and foolish youth of two hundred and fifty pounds to a gargantuan oaf of three hundred and seventy-five.

"What you expect me to do?" demanded Luigi. "He is one of yours."

"But he messing with one of *yours*. I cotched him last evening spying in on the master room, and I throwed him straight out the gate, and now look here today he right back."

"Animal!" cried Luigi. "I kill him!" Luigi's character was not uniformly swaddled in appetite and vanity; there were a few scattered spots of honor, and Hattie seemed at long last to have found one.

Luigi was roaming the lawn with a pistol in his hand.

Miles appeared casually from behind a sweetgum tree. "What you want, white nigger?"

Luigi didn't hesitate to pull the trigger, but he did miss. Miles high-tailed it for the swamp, with Luigi close behind. Hattie ran out into the fields hollering for Mr. B.

When Mr. B. found Miles and Luigi, deep in the swamp, Miles was lying on a mossy bank, picking his teeth and grinning as Luigi, waving his pistol and hopelessly threatening to murder Miles, sank slowly into a pool of quicksand.

Mr. B. told Miles to hold him by the belt with one hand and hold to a tree with the other and to consider his life finished if he should slip. Mr. B. leaned out steeply over the mire. He could just reach the pistol barrel, and began to work Luigi loose.

With a great sucking noise from the morass, Luigi surged forward, and the pistol went off. The ball passed through Mr. B.'s heart, and he fell dead on the bank.

Perceiving immediately the awkwardness of his position, Miles was gone like a ghost through the tangled woodland.

Luigi writhed and flailed until he could move no more—and, thus, at last, discovered that stillness made him buoyant. Stretching hard, he was now able to reach the roots on the bank, and inch by inch he began to haul himself out.

When he awoke it was in moonlight. Beside him, swarming with insects, lay the corpse of Benedict O'Connell. Luigi rolled the body down the bank, and with one hungry slurp from the quicksand it sank.

All that night he heard the hounds baying, but no one heard his cries. Luckily the night was warm, and the moss was soft, and he slept.

Luigi awoke in daylight, with a blue tick dog licking his face. Aaron and Sylvester and four other boys rolled him up in a blanket and struggled home with him through the swamp and the woods and the fields and across the wide lawn, gathering more dogs all along the way.

The nearer they came to the house, the louder Luigi moaned. The dogs could not resist joining in. Finally the boys got their cargo into the house and unrolled him at Hattie's feet.

"Get them dogs out my kitchen before I—"

"Dogs just loves Mr. Louie," said Aaron. "Loves how he sing."

"Bad dogs, bad boys, filth, racket, botherment, and disrespect all *out* this kitchen now this instant!" cried Hattie. "You, Sylvester, carry me one of them big bristle brush from the stable." She regarded Luigi sitting dazed on the floor. "Won't no regular wash rag do you, Mr. Louie. We got to scrub you down. Master want to see you." She began to peel Luigi's mud-caked clothes away.

"Draw me hot bath."

"You don't have no time for no hot bath," said Hattie. "Just step on in that tub."

"Is cold!"

"Warm right up, you in it."

"Is *freezing!*" Rivulets of mud oozed down the tortuous landscape of Luigi.

At the kitchen door stood the master, pale, unsteady, and not amused. It was the first time Giovanni Corelli had been downstairs since the day Félice arrived, one week ago today. "When you are decent, come to my office," he said in curt Italian, pointedly foregoing the Roman dialect in which he usually addressed his chef.

Luigi dressed, stood outside the office door awhile, knocked, and entered.

The master glared at him from the shadows. "Where is Benedict?"

"I don't know, boss," whined Luigi. "I never seen him."

"And Miles?"

At this Luigi perked up. "Gone, boss! I kill him, I think, maybe. He was spying on you, he climbs the ladder to spy on you in your bedroom. I pursue him! He throws me in the quicksand! But I escape his diabolical clutches! I throw *him* in the quicksand, and down he goes! Incredible!" Luigi was a very incompetent liar.

"Incredible is the word," said Giovanni Corelli. "The best overseer in America is gone, who knows, maybe dead, thanks to you, you cockroach, and a delightful zambo—maybe he was a bad boy, but he grew up in this house, he ate in your kitchen—you try to murder him and expect me to praise you? Idiot! I am going to hang you."

"No! Please don't hang me, boss," moaned Luigi. "It was self-defense! I didn't know what I was doing! Please!" He fell to his knees, sobbing. "Maybe Miles is not dead anyway. Maybe he only ran away."

"I'm too upset to look at you, you parasite. Come here in the morning, and then I will hang you."

"What he say?" demanded Hattie when Luigi, head in hands, had reappeared in the kitchen.

"He is going to hang me," wept Luigi, "when I should get medals."

That night, with his prayer book, his rosary beads, and his red silk Bersagliere sash in a pillow case, Luigi set forth through the swamp, hoping to come out on the other side and find his way along back roads to Memphis. There he would book passage for New Orleans and, thence, for Italy and freedom.

Corelli and Sylvester and the dogs treed Luigi next morning about half a mile from the house.

"Go ahead and shoot me, boss!" he cried. "I will never be captured alive."

"Come down, you fungus, or shall I shoot you there?"

"Go ahead and shoot me! Why should I come down only to be hanged?"

"All right, I won't hang you. Now come down, cretin."

"I'm stuck, boss."

"Come, Sylvester, we go home," said Corelli in English, turning his horse. "I learn to eat corn pone."

Luigi got himself unstuck somehow and was home in time to make supper, which at last the master took in the dining room—tonnarelli alla papalina, roast guinea hen, black-eyed peas with bacon, sweet muscadine wine, and Hattie's pecan pie. Félice's supper was to be sent up to her on a tray.

At this last instruction Hattie gave Corelli a questioning look.

"The new girl," he said, "she is going to help you in the kitchen, starting tomorrow."

"That's real kind, Mr. Joe," replied Hattie, "but you know with me and Mr. Louie we gots too many cooks right now."

"Well, now you got another one."

The master looked so miserable that Hattie didn't pursue the matter. "Yes, sir."

"And tell Uncle Duncan please to have the big carriage ready for to drive to Memphis in the morning."

"Yes, sir," said Hattie. "Mr. Joe?"

"Yes, Hattie," he sighed.

"You needs to get out with peoples more, Mr. Joe. Mix and mingle, mix and mingle. How come we don't have us a ball? Everybody in town say all the white folks there be wondering, wondering, how come that nice gentleman don't socialize. You daddy he had some beautiful soirées in this house, all the fancy white folks coming in from Mississippi, Tennessee, Memphis, I don't know where all. Pasture full of horses, house full of peoples, quarters full of visiting kinfolk. One of them soirées, I fix you daddy a raised peach cobbler that was two foot long. And brandy punch, ham biscuits, cheese straws, ice cream—all such as that. Mr. Louie fix about a ton of spaghetti, in the wash kettle out in the kitchen yard, and you ought to seen them white folks sucking up them noodles and *laughing?*

None of them ever heared of no spaghetti, you understand. Had us our own ball down in the quarters too. Fiddler come all the way from Holly Springs—Caleb first cousin Cato, childhood friend my own daddy in Virginia. Everybody have so much fun!"

"Now I see. You want to have big darky ball, that's all."

"Mr. Joe! Shame on you!"

"You no sass me in my house!" barked Corelli.

"No, sir," muttered Hattie, and withdrew.

Sylvester contemplated with pleasure the prospect of a found free day. Mr. B. was still missing, Miles Glory was missing, maybe even dead, Mr. Joe was gone to town, the cotton was all chopped, his stable chores were done, and the sun was shining bright. Tonight, he was thinking, I going to borrow me a gig and torch and go find Mr. Bullfrog and fry him up sweet, and then me and Aaron is going to eat frog legs till we pops. Ham sam bone jury!

Something tickled his foot, shattering his reverie.

With the sun in his eyes, Sylvester could see only a dark hulking shape, and hear a deep voice droning, "For Satan finds some mischief still/ For idle hands to do." It was the Reverend Augustus T. Lowdermilk come to call.

"Morning, Preacher."

"Get up, boy, and put my mule in the barn. We going to have us a prayer meeting."

This man's prayer meetings could last all of a day and well into the night. "I ain't feeling too good, Preacher," said Sylvester, holding his stomach.

"Nothing the matter with you a little gospel won't cure."

"Yes, sir."

Sylvester pushed the tack shed door open and sighed. "Hey, knucklehead," whispered Aaron from behind the saddle racks, brandishing two fishing poles.

Sylvester and Aaron slipped through the stable yard and out the back gate, past the privies and the trash heaps and the beehives and the gardens, and into the woods. They did not slacken pace until they reached the old Indian town.

The very air was different here, stiller, cooler. "This place give me the creeping crawl," whispered Aaron. His round, beardless face shone with sweat.

Rows of ruined Indian houses lined the weed-grown streets, their charred roof frames clumped with moss, the fire-blackened wattle walls alive with spiders. In a few of the houses, low chairs still sat on woven cane mats around a fire pit. Scraps of blankets hung from shelves. At the bottom of a painted clay pot Sylvester found the jawbone of an animal.

"Look like Indians ate coon too," he grinned, waving the bone at Aaron.

"How can you even touch that thing?" said Aaron with a shudder, from the door.

"Oh, man," breathed Sylvester, staring into a still intact red pitcher. From it Sylvester drew a slim, horn-handled knife trailing strips of rotten cloth. "Oh, man."

"Put it back, Sylvester. This a graveyard. It ain't right."

"I *owns* this knife now, brother." He had never owned anything before, except his miserable clothes.

A broad and still bare path led from the Indian town to a bend in Daylight Bayou where the channel narrowed and the foliage closed in overhead. Here the trees were draped with vines, the banks thickly willowed, the sky only a winking and dappled absence in the forest canopy—the whole waterscape like a huge green room. On a grassy peninsula, an old sycamore leaned out over the pool. There were steps cut into the tree, leading up to a wide limb from which you could dive into the shimmering depths.

Sylvester was busy trying to catch a cricket in his bait bucket when Aaron nudged him in the ribs and pointed upstream.

There was Félice—standing at the base of the sycamore tree in her long white dress.

For a while she just stood there, unmoving, looking into the clear green water. Then she undid the top two buttons of her dress.

"Now this what I call *fishing,*" whispered Aaron.

"You shut you dirty mouth," replied Sylvester, without taking his eyes off her. She undid two more, three, four.

She ran a finger down the opened V, and slowly unbuttoned the rest. She slipped out of her dress, out of her shift, out of her bloomers, hanging each on a willow branch.

She climbed to the diving limb. She lifted her arms above her head and slipped into the water. The boys' eyes followed her shape till she burst from the surface much nearer than they had anticipated, beads of water sparkling in her hair. But she did not see them crouched in the willows, holding their breath for dear life.

She breast-stroked back up the pool, with each frog-kick opening a view of her black pubic hair. "Go ahead stob me, Sylvester," whispered Aaron, "I ready to die."

She lay on her back on the grass and threw one arm across her brow. Inch by inch her knees were rising, and parting, as her hand slid down her belly. It came to rest between her thighs, and then was moving. Her breath came faster. Her head was tossing side to side, her back arching. She bared her teeth. Then suddenly she cried out softly, "Whoo, *diable!*" Her whole body went limp, and her eyes half opened, staring vaguely into the shifting leaves high above.

"You please tell me what the hell be *that* all about?" demanded Sylvester.

"You ain't never beat you meat, I suppose," said Aaron.

"You trying to tell me womens beat they meats?" said Sylvester. "They ain't even got no meats."

"Hush, Sylvester," whispered Aaron. Félice was sitting up now, legs drawn up against her chest, arms wrapped tight around them; fear in her eyes, looking in their direction.

A long minute passed. At last she snatched her bloomers down from the willow, dressed hastily, and fled into the forest.

"I does love this *fishing,*" said Aaron.

"I *sees* a *land* of *milk* and *honey,*" the Preacher was roaring. "I *hears* the *voice* of *angels,* I *feels* the *glory* of the *Holy Ghost breathing* down my *neck* like the stalking *panther* of the *forest!*"

Occasional shouts broke in: "Yes, *honey!*" "Yes, *angels!*" "Yes, *glory!*"

As the panther of the Holy Ghost stalked Augustus T. Lowdermilk through the forest of sin, Aaron and Sylvester slipped into the back of the congregation.

Aaron nudged Sylvester and pointed up the hill toward the big house. Walking up and down on the veranda, hands clasped behind her back, was Félice. She paused and peered down toward the crowd in the quarters court, and then turned away.

An hour later, the Preacher was still preaching hard. The children of Israel were dwelling in Beulah Land, drinking from the fountain that never will run dry, feasting on the manna from a bountiful supply. Sinners were grinding their teeth in Hell, and devils were poking them with red-hot pitchforks.

The evening sounds had struck up along the bayou and back in the woods. "Listen them bullfrog," whispered Sylvester.

"I don't know about no manna," said Aaron. "I ain't never ate none."

"Done ate frog legs, though, ain't you?" said Sylvester.

"Oh, man."

"How long you reckon he going to preach?" asked Sylvester.

"Let's light," said Aaron.

Sylvester and Aaron were just moseying quietly along toward the cookhouse to borrow out a bucket of grease when a cold hand fell on Sylvester's shoulder, and squeezed, hard.

Might have known. It was Uncle Dunc. Next thing they knew, they were standing captive in the Preacher's circle of lamplight and the Preacher was waving their frog gigs over them like the devils' own pitchforks and the whole congregation was staring them out of countenance and the Preacher's hot blast of rhetorical fire was scorching the sin clean out of their benighted souls.

"Bedford, my friend, you must tell me what to do," said Corelli, draining his glass.

"Well, I don't hardly know what to do my own self, but I do know a thing or two about the niggers. You got to learn how to deal with your niggers. And you know that gal's just a nigger like the rest of them, and you got to deal with her accordingly. She won't understand nothing else. She wasn't brought up to no fancy Italian manners. I ain't suggesting you whip her. Not yet."

Corelli's eyes opened but did not focus. "She does not fear me. She laughs at me. Already I tell her she must work in the kitchen, and she just looks at me. It is terrible, Bedford, how she looks at me!"

"I'll tell you something that will help you, Giovanni. You just ask that yellow bitch if she wants to go back to Monsieur Duquesne. Tell her N. B. Forrest got a offer from Duquesne to take her back down the river. You just tell her that and see if she don't come around."

"All right, my friend. I try." Forrest poured them another round, and Corelli raised his glass. "*Cent'anni!* One hundred years! To the finest gentleman in the South!"

Angry tears came to Forrest's eyes. "Then how come these high-and-mighty grandees won't have me in the house? They buy the niggers and I sell them. It's two halves of the same proposition, ain't it? How come their half is clean and mine is dirty? I'm the richest son of a bitch in Memphis. I been the best kind of citizen, the most charitable, the most friendliest—and they treat me like a damn river rat."

"It is certainly not fair, Bedford."

"And look at you, Giovanni, a damn Catholic, if you don't mind me saying so, and a foreigner, and you don't care nothing about them, you don't give a plug nickel for their balls and soirées, and all they talk about is let's get that nice Mr. Corelli in here to meet my daughter, my cousin, my niece—"

"I am married, my friend," said Corelli quietly, darkly. "My wife lives in Italy. And children."

"Well, dog my bones, Giovanni! You ain't never said nothing about no family."

"My son is at the university at Rome. And my baby, my Annamaria, she writes me letters every week, from the convent of Siena."

"How come you don't bring them here? Big beautiful plantation like you got?"

"Alexander, he come when I come, eighteen and fifty-six, but he gets the yellow fever, and I send him in Europe again. Now he is cured. Only small scars. But I am afraid always." There was more to it than that, and in time, perhaps, Corelli would explain.

"Damn that yellowjacket, Giovanni! Just you keep out of that swamp down there."

"Not to worry about me, Bedford. I am strong like a mule. Except maybe"—here suddenly he was thinking of Félice, standing by the bed in white, her acrid laughter; and of his wife. "Except maybe in my heart. Anyway, you help me, I help you too. I give a ball for you, my friend, with everybody of Memphis and all the countryside! Yes?"

"That's mighty considerate of you, Giovanni, but wouldn't none of them come if they knowed it was for me."

"They will come for Giovanni Corelli! I will sing for them!" He strained upward to strike an operatic pose, but toppled back onto the settee, and began, recumbent, to sing, "*Una furtiva lagrima negl'occhi suoi spunto—*"

Forrest's valet came rushing in. "Hoo," he said, "I thought Judgment Day done come. Mr. Bedford, you go on to bed. It's after midnight. Miss Mary be worrying. Come on, finish your drink."

"Jerome's the only nigger in the United States ain't afraid of me," said Forrest. "Ain't that right, Jerome?"

"You just a old white hound dog likes a scratch on the head like any of them, that's all," said Jerome, wagging a finger at Forrest.

"I ought to whip him. Insubordination, Jerome—you know what that means?"

"If it mean taking good care of a no-count master, I is guilty as charged. Get on with you now."

Forrest gave Jerome a dismissive wave, but the valet stayed put, tapping his foot impatiently.

"Did you mean that, Giovanni, what you said about that ball?"

But Corelli was out cold.

"You get Mr. Corelli back to the Gayoso, you hear? And look sharp," Forrest barked at Jerome.

"Me and what five roustabout, marse?"

"All right, all right, let's put him out on the damn porch."

"Oof, Lord have mercy, this man fat!" They dropped Corelli into the bed, and Jerome stumbled forward, brushing against Forrest and then steadying himself with a lingering hand on his master's arm.

"Boy, you getting too sassy for your own good." Forrest swayed back on his heels, drunker now with the exertion. He was clenching his left hand, and his left eyelid was twitching, both bad signs.

"Yes, sir, marse."

"I don't want to hit you."

"No, sir, marse."

"But I will."

"I knows that."

"I'll knock your god-damned teeth out, nigger."

"Yes, sir."

"We understand each other."

"Yes, sir."

"I'm going to bed."

"Yes, sir."

"Help me upstairs, and keep your god-damned hands to yourself."

"Yes, sir."

Caleb's cousin Cato, too old to walk, arrived in a donkey cart. He drove through the gate and up the drive and down the lane to the quarters playing his fiddle the whole way. Children clapped and laughed and danced in his wake.

From the Delta came field hand families dressed in rags, trudging along behind their masters' gleaming carriages. The Corelli plantation workers lined the freshly whitewashed fence, waving bandannas and whooping, rushing into the highway as they spotted their kin. From time to time the babble of festivity would be split by a woman's wail at the news of a death or disaster.

Hattie's was one such voice, as she learned that her son Joe John had run away to the North, been caught and returned for bounty, and been beaten with an axe handle by his master's slave driver. Joe John was blind now, and had been sold for a pittance to a factory in a big city somewhere far away, no one knew quite where.

There was quilting for the girls and wrestling for the boys and trading and story telling for the men and cooking and gossiping for the women. And there was dancing.

Sylvester whirled around the court with Aaron's mama Bess. "Sylvester," she cried, "if you ain't a caution! I got to catch my breath, boy, let me go." She stood puffing, leaning back against a cabin wall, watching Aaron do-si-do with a plump and pretty girl wearing white ribbons in her hair. Aaron's papa, Aaron Senior, danced over to his wife, clapping in time to the music, doing a little jig step that raised an ochre billow of dust around his bare feet. "Senior, I swan," hooted Bess, "you in you second childhood!"

"That's right, old woman!" he hooted back, still dancing. "Next thing, I be playing with dolls."

"Just don't you be playing with no *living* dolls, that's all," called Bess as he cake-walked into the midst of the dancing. Senior took Aaron's giggling partner by the hand, and spun her away.

As the Turkey Trot gave way to a Buzzard Lope, Aaron sidled off to the sidelines to join his mama and Sylvester. "That gal just getting sweet on me," Aaron panted, "then come the boogie man put the evil eye on her."

Here came the boogie man now, with the girl. She was sashaying, swinging her wide hips, pretty as a peach.

"You got to wrastle me for this one," cried Senior over the girl's shoulder at Aaron.

"You got to wrastle *me* first, old goat," boomed Bess. "What you name, gal?"

"My name Charity, but they calls me Cherry."

"You know my boy Aaron?"

"Does now, kind of like."

"Where you stay at, child?" demanded Bess.

"Mr. Forrest depot," said the girl.

"So you in transit."

The girl looked away darkly, eyes clouding. "Yes'm." Aaron was biting his lower lip.

"Likes to dance, don't you?" Bess went on, trying to change the subject. "Why don't y'all children go back dance?"

"Yes'm," said Aaron and Cherry at once, with a quick eager glance at each other.

"Senior," said Bess, "help me get this foot out my mouth. Sylvester, you got kin coming to the ball?"

"No'm," said Sylvester. "I ain't got no kin."

"Senior, help me, it's plumb down my throat!"

"I mean, I don't got no papa," said Sylvester, "and I don't know where my mama at. I comed from Georgia, over the mountains."

"You meet any girls today?" asked Bess.

"No'm." Félice had not appeared, and was not expected to.

"Don't you want to meet girls?"

"No'm."

"Well, I swan. You want to dance with old me again?"

"Yes'm, in a little more while, if you please."

"Well, I swan. Senior, you want to dance with you wife?"

"Do I gots to?" said Senior.

"Yes, baby," said Bess.

"All right then, great-grammaw, let's cut."

Sylvester walked the outer edges of the crowd, kicking up dirt with his too-big brogans. Every so often he would look up toward the house hoping for a glimpse of Félice.

All the while, the revelers were dancing and whooping and hollering, and the band was pounding away—Cato's long tall drink-of-water brother Atticus plunking the washtub bass, Cato sawing at his fiddle, two Memphis slicks playing the spoons, a knob-headed blacksmith from east Shelby County pounding on an army drum with a knob-headed cane, various field boys hamboning, and old Uncle Dunc strumming on the banjo for all he was worth, with a face of solid stone.

There was a sudden slowing of the tempo, a quiet in the dancers.

Nathan Bedford Forrest and Giovanni Corelli had entered the quarters gate.

Forrest knew them all. "Y'all having fun, Bessie?"

"Yes, sir, Mr. Bedford. Plenty fun."

"Everything all right, Senior?"

"Yes, sir, Mr. Bedford. Everything fine."

"Hey, Jonah Johnson, you come to the ball all the way from Arkansas?"

"Yes, sir, Mr. Bedford. All the way."

Forrest grinned. "You swim that big Mississippi River, Jonah?"

"No, sir, I can't swim a lick."

"Then what was you doing that day my boy Jerome catched you halfway out to Arkansas already?"

"I wasn't but just chasing my hat where some fool throw it, and that's a fact."

"They broke the mold after they made Jonah Johnson, Giovanni. He's the slickest nigger I ever saw. Ain't you?"

"Just didn't want to lose my hat, that's all," said Jonah.

"Hey, Cherry," boomed Forrest, "you getting in a dance or two?"

"Yes, sir."

"You look mighty pretty today."

Cherry did not answer, but only looked uneasily at the ground. Aaron stood at her side, staring a hole in Forrest's gleaming boots.

"With all them ribbons in your hair," continued Forrest, fingering one, pointedly blind to Aaron. "We got to find you a real nice home. Though I will admit I'll hate to see you go."

"Borry me that Indian knife, Sylvester," said Aaron when the white men had gone. "I got somebody need killing."

"Hush," whispered Sylvester, crooking his head slightly. Aaron followed the line indicated, to Jerome, who was watching them hard.

"That's all right," said Aaron, "I kill that sister too."

But when the band struck up a reel, and Cherry took his hands in hers and tugged him into the dance, Aaron soon forgot his anger and the girl's uncertain fate. He had learned early not to look too far beyond the here and now.

Society's curiosity about Giovanni Corelli had overcome its distaste for Nathan Bedford Forrest. Some older Memphians had seen the splendid manor house in the days of Angelo Corelli—with its long double parlors mirrored and Corinthian-columned, draped in silk velvet, ablaze with crystal chandeliers, hung with his own paintings—and most of the newer arrivals had heard, and wanted to see.

Corelli plantation was indeed splendid today. Every surface had been polished to a fare-thee-well, every servant freshly outfitted in European livery. A French string quartet, imported from New Orleans, played all afternoon in the gazebo on the lawn; in the front parlor, as evening fell, Herman Frank Arnold and his orchestra of Memphis Prussians performed a serenade. There was champagne punch in chased silver bowls, and no end to the ice.

Luigi's whole roast lambs and rococo pièces montées of candied fruit dazzled the pork-and-hominy tastes of the guests. Corelli kissed the ladies' hands. Forrest, with his cool gray eyes and his long black hair, struck awe into discomfited hearts wherever he moved through the glittering rooms.

The orchestra struck up a waltz, and with a bow Giovanni Corelli took the hand of Mary Montgomery Forrest. "Signora," he purred, "the pleasure."

"I truly ain't much of a dancer, sir."

Nor was her corpulent host, nor could he, after so much punch, have cared less. He whirled her across the room in a blur, and slammed her headlong into the wall. The diminutive Mrs. Forrest slid to the floor and sat there blinking, legs outstretched. Trying to scoop her up in one arm as a preux chevalier surely ought, Giovanni Corelli pitched forward on top of her, and the last of Mrs. Forrest's breath was forced from her narrow chest in a scream of mortal terror.

Forrest and his valet Jerome, with a quick grin between them, hoisted the floundering chevalier from his flattened princess. Smelling salts were called for, the goggling Germans bidden to resume.

Maestro Carlo Patti, newly come to town to superintend the newly formed Philharmonic Society, looked on Memphis's only other gentleman of Italian extraction and shuddered. Corelli's valet Caleb opened an ivory fan and tried to cool the master's glistening brow. The stiff-collared and stiffer-necked old gentry ("old" meaning that their families had been in Tennessee long enough to have sired a second generation here; "gentry" meaning that they owned a dozen or more Negroes) turned away in urbane delicacy. The younger swells—most of them the cadet offspring of Virginia and Carolina families, come west to make fortunes commensurate to their station—put no premium on such primness; as far as they were concerned, this was still the frontier, and laughable barbarity was altogether to be expected. Sylvester passed into a raucous gang of them to offer up his tray of oysters, but they were laughing too hard to eat, and waved him on.

Félice emerged from the kitchen and moved among the guests with a silver tray of canapés, expressionless—until she lifted the tray to Nathan Bedford Forrest, and met his eyes.

"Still here, I see," said Forrest, baring his teeth.

"Yes, monsieur," said Félice, smiling back coolly.

Forrest guessed in that instant that she was still defying Corelli. Had the damned fool not even threatened her? "Duquesne's back on his feet, I hear," he said. "*Big* old plantation. *Lots* of money."

"Yes, monsieur."

So Corelli *had* made his threat as planned, and still she'd stood up to him. Félice must have known that for Corelli letting her go would mean admitting total defeat. Forrest leaned forward and said, "I sure would have fancied having you pass back through my depot."

Félice gave Forrest a clear, level, studiously neutral look, and said nothing. She turned to move into the crowd.

Forrest leaned down just behind her ear. "Sassy, ain't you?" he whispered. "I like a sassy yellow gal."

Aaron and Sylvester stood watching this exchange across the room. "That white man do got a nerve," said Aaron. "I heared him my own self telling the master how all the black folks just *loves* him—'Sell me at Forrest mart, marse,' he say they say. Uh *huh*."

Caleb materialized behind the two young men. "Every nigger in the world know that gentleman, and scared of him."

"Not Félice!" crowed Sylvester.

"You don't know nothing," said Caleb.

"I knows enough," replied Sylvester. "I know she don't take no botheration from no white man."

"You want trouble, don't you, boy," said Caleb.

"You going to give it to him, Caleb?" laughed Aaron.

"I don't take no insults to my master," Caleb solemnly declared.

"I thought we was talking about Mr. Bedford," said Sylvester.

"Oh, *that's* right," said Aaron. "Mr. *Joe* get everything he *want* from that gal. *Don't* he, Caleb."

"You strutting close to the edge there, Aaron," Caleb said hotly.

"Then it's true, Sylvester!" cried Aaron triumphantly. "That's how come she working in the house like just a servant. Because just like you say, she don't take no botheration from no white man."

"Boy, I is warning you," whispered Caleb, hotter than ever.

"I still don't understand," complained Sylvester.

"Your Félice she won't put *out!*" cried Aaron in exasperation. "Mr. Joe buy her to put out, didn't he? But she won't even do it. Ain't that right, Caleb? I bet you dicking her yourself, you old stallion."

Caleb had his razor out. And in an instant Aaron had feinted left, feinted right, kicked Caleb hard in the wrist, and knocked the razor to the floor. Sylvester snatched it up.

From then on it was just a plain old fist fight. Old Caleb may have been skin and bones, but he was still remarkably spry.

The white folks gathered around enthusiastically, most of them cheering for Caleb.

There was a hand on Sylvester's neck. He bowed his head at once and waited passively for the pain he remembered so well from his sojourn in the marketplace, but it did not come. "Give me the razor," said Forrest quietly.

Sylvester complied.

Forrest pocketed it and waded into the fray. He lifted Aaron by the collar and marched him roughly toward the kitchen. Corelli wrung his hands and then, in imitation, took Caleb by the collar and followed. The white folks crowded in behind.

Sylvester wandered through the now nearly empty parlors, into the front hall and to the open door. He peered out into the darkness, inhaling the scent of honeysuckle. He could hear the snuffling and whinnying of horses at the high heaps of hay in the pasture, the racket of locusts in the big oaks. There was a ring around the moon; black clouds were moving in from the south; it was going to rain. He heard a soft footfall behind him, and turned. It was Félice.

She just stood there, smiling serenely, one hand drumming her fingers on her hip. Sylvester started to giggle, and couldn't stop. He had no idea what he was laughing about. Then she was laughing too. Abruptly, they both stopped and looked around. Not a soul.

Sylvester and Félice stepped into the locust-loud darkness of the long front porch, and then they were kissing. Minutes passed.

Suddenly Forrest was there—one hand in his famous nerve-lock on Sylvester's neck, the other, more gently, on Félice's. Through a long, eerie passage of white faces Sylvester and Félice were marched to the kitchen.

"Looks like a regular nigger fighting jubilee tonight!" one of the young Virginians exclaimed as they passed.

Aaron and Caleb were still in the kitchen, stripped to the waist, eyes downcast. From the way they sat out from the backs of their chairs, Sylvester surmised that they had been whipped. Yes, there, on Hattie's marble pastry board, beside Caleb's razor, lay Forrest's black quirt.

Hattie stood at the stove frying up crawfish fritters, head down, trying to seem oblivious. The two young kitchen maids Mattie and Isabel cowered together in a corner. Luigi was presumably still outside, cooking his spaghetti in a wash pot.

Forrest closed the door against the curious horde.

Sylvester looked around in a daze. Both Forrest and the master wanted Félice, but she wanted *him*—him only, Sylvester. She loved him! And the white men seemed, to Sylvester, to know it.

She had been staring blankly at Forrest, in a way slaves were not supposed to do. Now Forrest was glaring back at her, his gray eyes cold. Well, *he* knew, for sure. And still she would not drop her gaze. Forrest's left fist was clenching, his left eyelid twitching; his eyes flickered to the quirt and then back to Félice. If Forrest so much as touched that quirt, Sylvester was going to pick up the razor and cut his throat. But Forrest unclenched his fist and turned away.

For a long moment, Forrest stared hard at the wall. Then he came over to Sylvester and said, "Open your mouth." He jerked Sylvester's mouth this way and that to catch the light, inspecting his teeth.

"Giovanni," said Forrest, "let's you and me have a word."

"Watch out, Sylvester," whispered Aaron when they had withdrawn. "These white mens crazy tonight."

"They whipped you, didn't they?" asked Sylvester.

"*He* did, surely," said Aaron.

"It wasn't so bad," said Caleb. "We had it coming."

Aaron looked ready to resume their fight, but the latch was lifting.

Forrest and Corelli stood facing the slaves. Forrest stared at Sylvester until Sylvester raised his eyes, and only then did he speak:

"Now, it ain't no need to look so scared, son," said Forrest to Sylvester. "You just going to come with me down to my new plantation down Coahoma County, Mississippi. You appear like basically a good boy, that got into something you ain't got no business in, that's all. We'll find out anyhow. Sylvester—that's your name, ain't it, son?"

"Yes, sir," said Sylvester.

"Sylvester, we going to get you straightened out, don't you worry. Everything be fine. You pack up tonight, you hear?"

"Yes, sir," Sylvester mumbled disconsolately.

Toward dawn, Aaron reached over from his bed and touched Sylvester's shoulder.

There was a tall, slim shape in the cabin's open door.

The locusts and the crickets and the frogs had quit for the night, and the silence was immense. At the far horizon above the cotton fields, low clouds were turning the color of hot coals.

She had a lantern. They hurried through the woods to the old

Indian town. She led him down the path to the bayou and around the bend to the soft-mossed peninsula beneath the sycamore.

The light was all dark silver; day would bring hard rain. An owl called, muffled in the thickening mists.

Félice loved Sylvester; he loved her. For a brief moment, all the hardness of the world dissolved in that simplicity.

Neither Aaron nor Sylvester spoke as they worked together to secure a tarpaulin over the load of cottonseed bound for Nathan Bedford Forrest's Greengrove plantation. Then Sylvester pulled his hat over his ears and climbed up top, and the driver clicked his tongue at the mules, and the wagon rolled out into the rain and down toward the gate.

1861

Night after night, that January in Memphis, there were torchlight parades, some urging and the others opposing the secession of Tennessee from the United States of America. Because most of the booming young city's trade was with the cities and farmlands upriver, there were strong arguments for alliance with the North. But abolition of slavery seemed now to be the price of union—a higher price than just the loss of trade—and so with the coming of each blazing night more and more of the white men of Memphis were marching for secession.

The council of aldermen voted an appropriation of sixty thousand dollars for a rampart of cotton bales to be built along the top of the Chickasaw bluff. The Memphis Arsenal, employing some two hundred and fifty women, was turning out fifty-five thousand bullets a day. Three foundries had converted their production to cannon. Hardly a white man had not joined a new militia.

In February, in Montgomery, at the inauguration of Jefferson Davis as president of the Confederate States of America, Herman Frank Arnold's Prussian Orchestra, of Memphis, introduced his new orchestration of the anthem "Dixie."

In March, in Washington, Abraham Lincoln took office as president of the United States, vowing to preserve the union.

Only two military installations in the South had not been seized by the Confederacy. In April, as a United States supply mission approached one of them—Fort Sumter, at Charleston—secessionist cannons opened fire. Civil war had begun.

A Garibaldi Brigade was formed in Memphis, and called on Giovanni Corelli to be its general. Corelli replied that he had not taken American citizenship and therefore was not now a Confederate citizen, and, therefore, could not serve.

In May, the Tennessee legislature enacted an ordinance of secession, and in June the people ratified it. The vote in Shelby County, of which Memphis was the seat, was seven thousand to five.

The planter elite—now the military elite as well—did not consider Nathan Bedford Forrest to be officer material. It was, thus, as a private that Forrest enlisted in the Tennessee Mounted Rifles Company.

Private Forrest promptly set about raising his own cavalry. He ran newspaper advertisements for volunteers, and sent recruiting agents throughout Tennessee, Alabama, and Mississippi. He would soon lead an expedition to Kentucky, where, in secret, he would raise Rebel troops and, with his own money, lay in supplies of blankets, ammunition, and horses, to be brought south, by night, along back roads, to Memphis.

Life at Greengrove Plantation was not so bad at first. Forrest had promised Giovanni Corelli to keep Sylvester under close observation, and Sylvester was assigned, as at home, to the house and stable. It was easy labor, and, moreover, soon after Sylvester's arrival, Aaron's new sweetheart Charity had come to work as a parlor maid, and she was good company.

Cherry was virtually Félice's opposite. Whereas Félice smiled hardly ever and with conscious meaning, Cherry seemed to smile all the time and indiscriminately. Félice was cool and slim and hard, Cherry warm and round and soft.

In springtime Cherry had learned to sew, and was often now confined for days at a time with the other seamstresses, working on the master's new military uniforms and banners and flags. When Forrest thudded down the bare oak floors upstairs in his hobnailed boots, Sylvester grew uneasy for her.

Preparing for war had made Forrest as springy and sudden as a cat. When the overseer Sweeney's dog barked all one night beneath the full moon, Forrest threw off the covers, grabbed a shotgun, stalked to the front porch of Sweeney's cabin, and, without a word, blew the dog's head off. Mary Forrest, at this, had gone to stay with her sister in town. Sometimes now Forrest would stare for minutes on end at Cherry bent over her sewing.

Jerome teased Cherry cruelly, but she seemed not to care—until one morning when he went mercilessly on and on, calling her the master's night dream, chocolate pudding, sweet jelly roll, and at last drove her to tears. "He coming to get you," said Jerome, curling out his long pink tongue, "sneak up in you bed in the night, but don't worry, pudding, I knows what to do with that white man. Then you going to owe me some plenty."

Cherry looked up from her tear-spotted work and past the leering visage of the valet to see the master himself leaning against the door frame in his stocking feet, stroking his black beard with one hand and rattling the ice in his crystal glass with the other. Jerome whirled, and stood stock-still, watching the twitching of Forrest's left eyelid, a sign he knew all too well.

"He teasing you, gal?" demanded Forrest thickly. No doubt, he was drunk, at ten o'clock in the morning.

"Just funning, that's all," said Jerome.

"Shut up. Jerome teasing you, Cherry?"

"He make me laugh, sir."

"I won't have this, Jerome," said Forrest.

"But Mr. Bedford—"

Forrest's fist flew backhand into Jerome's cheek. Jerome merely bowed his head. Forrest caught him by the placket of his shirt as he tried to sidle toward the door. "I am leaving this place in the *morning,*" he yelled in Jerome's face, hardly an inch away. "I don't *know* for how long. There is going to be a god-damned *war,* and I am going to be a god-damned *general* in it, and this place has got to run *without* me, and one thing it can*not* tolerate is nigger discord. There has got to be *discipline.* You understand that word, boy?"

"Yes, sir," said Jerome meekly.

"Get out of my god-damned sight." Forrest shoved Jerome out and closed the door. "Now, sweet darling," he said softly to Cherry, "we can't let a thing like this trouble you. Come here a minute."

She stood before him.

"Pull up that shift, child."

"No, sir. I can't do that."

"I am your master."

"Yes, sir, but no, sir, I can't do that."

"Don't rile me, girl. Don't perturb my feelings. I ain't been sleeping but poorly. My feelings are easily perturbed."

"Yes, sir."

There was a knock at the door, and Sylvester came bustling in without waiting for an answer. He was bearing a tray with a crystal decanter of whiskey and a crystal bowl of ice on it.

"What the devil *you* want?" roared Forrest.

"Well, um, see, Mr. Bedford," stammered Sylvester, "I were just wondering if you would be happening to be wanting me go fetch that little paint mare, little paint mare name Daisy, up from down where she been at, down by the cow pond, where she been at with that roan stallion, name Star, in the south paddock, down by the cow pond, you remember old Star, that roan stallion with the blaze? She been kicking and biting that stallion, she won't stand for him nohow, seem like, and I just wondered, and also Jerome he say carry you this?"

Forrest stared at Sylvester. "Jerome?"

"Yes, sir. Jerome he say he don't feel good, going to lay down, and would I do this something for him, carry you this here tray, and then I thinks, well, Mr. Bedford fixing to leave out for the war and I better hurry up and ask him about that little paint mare, name Daisy, in the south paddock, down by the cow pond, because she been kicking and fighting fit to kill, down where she been at with that—"

"—Roan stallion, Star, with the blaze, yes, I think I got that, much obliged, Sylvester." Forrest thought for a few moments, sucking on a piece of ice. He spat it back into his glass. "You take a interest in the gals, don't you, son?"

"No, sir. No, sir."

"Specially somehow when they in the proximity of the white man. Somehow."

"No, sir."

Forrest poured himself a drink. "You going to have to go to work in the fields, boy. It'll do you a sight of good."

"But Mr. Bedford, I don't know nothing about no field work. I wasn't doing nothing—I just—"

"I'll talk to Sweeney—Sweeney's my overseer—and he'll talk to Theo—Theo's my field driver—and Theo'll get you a bunk in the quarters. I don't know how the hell I'm ever going to get out of here tomorrow. Christ almighty."

Queen, Forrest's seamstress, came waddling in, took a sharp look at Sylvester and the whiskey and the master sweating and staring and the terrified girl, and sat down in judicious smiling oblivion. "That real pretty work you been doing, Miss Charity. She catch right on, Mr. Bedford. Such a good girl. So sweet."

"Well, that's fine, Queen, that's fine. Christ almighty damn. Go on, Sylvester, get out of the house, I seen enough of you rolling your damn yellow eyes. *Damn* your eyes. We don't keep no girls down in the field quarters, son. Not a damn one. You going to be lonesome."

Elmo, Jackson, and Drury held Sylvester down while Ice Pick pawed through Sylvester's meager bundle.

"Wool jacket," said Ice Pick.

"That *my* jacket!" Sylvester protested, thrashing.

"Fit me just right," said Ice Pick, trying it on. "Too big for you, runt."

"Pair brogans," said Ice Pick. "Too small. Jackson, you feet ain't so big."

"I don't need no shoes," said Jackson.

"Trade with them," Ice Pick advised him.

"What I supposed to do come the winter?" cried Sylvester.

"Winter long ways off, runt," said Ice Pick. "You might not make it so long a ways. Other hand, you might just already be back in the house, warm as fresh bread. Wool weskit—Drury. Indian arrowhead."

"Give me that arrowhead," growled Elmo.

"Rabbit foot," Ice Pick continued. "Rubber ball. Fish hook, line, bobber. Penny. Oh, now *now,* ain't this something? Where you get such a knife, boy?"

Sylvester closed his eyes.

"This a Indian knife, ain't it? With a nice new leather scabbard. Sharp, too." Ice Pick flung Sylvester's knife into the wall with a thunk and a quivering whir. "Throws real nice."

"Imbecile, go!" cried Luigi. "Gee! Avanti! Haw! Andiamo!" But the buggy only sank deeper, and the mule stood immobile in the traces. He found a stout limb, and shook it in the mule's face. The mule, however, was no longer paying attention. Luigi gave the mule's forehead a gingerly tap, and then a sharper one. The mule stared dully straight ahead, and did not move. Wild animals were making noises in the swamp.

Once again Luigi had traveled to Memphis in vain. Shipments from Europe, the postmaster had told him, were no longer to be expected. No more pasta asciutta, no decent wine, no olive oil. And now this. Luigi clubbed the mule between the ears. The beast grunted once, and sank to its knees; its hindquarters heavily followed, splush in the mud. "Aigh, madonna! Stand up, my friend!" begged Luigi. "I give you oats!" But it was too late. With a long, low moan the mule stretched out its head across the mud and died.

Luigi waited for hours, but the road remained empty, and night closed in. Snakes and spiders crept into his mind and made nests. He would try to make it home on foot. The moon was new, the sky overcast, the road invisible. Luigi crashed into trees, fell into the borrow pit, and prayed for a miracle.

And one appeared: far behind him, back down the road toward town, he heard the creak of harness, and then the rumble of ironbound wheels, and singing. A lantern swung in the blackness. Luigi cried out, "Help me, help me!" The singing stopped, and a second lantern flared. Luigi struggled to his feet and ran toward the light.

"That there a ghost?" called the voice behind the lanterns. A Negro. "Oh, my mercy sakes alive! Mr. Louie his own self!"

"Who you? How you know me? Why you out in the middle of midnight? Ah? You answer me, you."

"You know, I could have swore I just hear a man in distress and crying for help—and now he address me in this disrespectful fashion?"

The light caught the side of the speaker's face and confirmed, as Luigi had soon guessed, who the Negro on the buckboard was. Was there still a chance—Luigi was trying to think quickly—that Miles could be blamed for the disappearance of Benedict O'Connell? Or might Miles go now to the master and accuse Luigi of murdering Mr. B.? Miles did know where the body was, after all. Or would quicksand not give back corpses it had taken? Perhaps they floated away into the underworld. Perhaps Luigi should try to murder Miles Glory. But Miles was pretty big, and young, and fast. This was too much to think about in such a hurry. "You go south, to the Corelli plantation, yes?" demanded Luigi.

"With a real heavy load and real crowded, Mr. Louie," said Miles, "and way farther still to go this night."

"You will take me home."

"Might. Might not. Let's us talk a minute."

"Help me up," commanded Luigi.

"Seat real narrow, Mr. Louie," Miles replied. "You be ever so much more comfortabler in the back." Miles reached down with both hands, and hauled Luigi in. "And please don't set on the merchandise. It's fragile."

Luigi was ensconced amidst wooden crates all angles and rough rope and splinters. Farther forward, however, he could make out a big soft-looking heap beneath a tarpaulin. As Miles clicked his teeth at the two big Percherons and the wagon clanked into motion, Luigi tumbled into the heap.

It was not as soft as it had looked. And then from the midst of it came a baleful groan. The canvas began to move beneath Luigi, and he found himself suddenly endowed with the gift of flight. He landed behind the driver, upright but swaying dangerously, only his hands clutching the cloth on Miles's shoulders keeping him standing, while the horrible something beneath the tarpaulin continued to writhe and groan between his feet. "Aw, now, Mr. Louie," Miles was hollering, twisting away, "didn't I done *told* you—"

The wagon lurched. Luigi lost his grip on Miles and grabbed for the light pole, and the lantern spilled into the cargo, and in an instant the canvas was in flames. Leaping for his life, Luigi knocked half a dozen boxes off the back of the wagon and plunged headlong after them. By the firelight, Luigi could see ranged topsy-turvy round him in the mud the contents of the shattered crates: two stuffed owls, a stuffed eagle, a stuffed skunk, a stuffed weasel stalking a stuffed passenger pigeon across a landscape of papier-mâché, and a stuffed red fox, all glaring at him with flame-flickering glass eyes.

"Aigh," moaned Luigi.

Luigi struggled to his feet. Miles was standing beside the buckboard holding a lantern turned low. "Hush, now, darling," Miles was whispering into the wagon bed, "you going to be just fine. Hush, now."

In the dim light, as his dizziness cleared, Luigi was at last able to discern the object of Miles's consolations.

An alligator. Ten feet long if an inch. Writhing, groaning, tied at tail and nose and all four feet to the wagon bed.

"Aigh," repeated Luigi.

"Shush, Mr. Louie," whispered Miles. "She just quietening down."

She? wondered Luigi. How he knows?

"Cherry all right?" were the first words out of Aaron's mouth as Miles Glory's buckboard rolled into the quarters, after midnight.

There rose from the charred canvas the unmistakable pear shape of Luigi, scratching his head and yawning. "Can't never tell what you might find in them Nonconnah bottoms," observed Miles as Luigi stumbled groggily up toward the house. "Not a word of thanks too. Damn fool killed you master blue mule."

"Cherry all right?" repeated Aaron impatiently.

"You got my peckerwood?" demanded Miles, turning up his lantern wick.

"I got him." Aaron reached into a croker sack and held up the big dead bird, its ivory bill bright in the lamplight.

"I don't know what in Lucifer name that Yankee want with with all such as this," mused Miles, "but business be business. I done drove halfways down through Mississippi, I done prowled all out in Tennessee clear up to the Forked Deer River for them owls, I done sneak around Memphis in the middle of the night with this damn white taxidermyist charging me double. I is just plumb wore out. Let me smell of him, Aaron."

"He clean, Miles, all scrape and salt up just like you say. But come on, tell me about my sweetheart."

"She couldn't hardly be better, and that's a fact, with old Forrest gone off up north somewheres and Sylvester out in the fields. Want to see my alligator?"

"I done seen considerable too many right out here in that swamp. What she say? And what you mean, Sylvester in the fields? He ain't no field hand."

"*Live* alligator, that Yankee want, and female. Old Ice Pick down Forrest plantation, he say, 'Sure'—just like that. And just like that, one night on the bayou and he get me my gator. Plumb full of eggs too—he just push on her, kind of down here like, and out one pop."

"What she *say,* Miles?"

"You chucklehead friend Sylvester done got in *all* kind of trouble down there. Old Forrest don't like nobody get in he way, and he do like the colored girls. Sylvester getting in the way of some business of mine too. Which remind me. Who watching the cotton storehouse hereabouts these days?"

"Master keep the key his own self. What you mean about that white man and the colored girls? What she *say,* Miles?"

"Who, that gal? Cherry? She say how do."

Aaron paused and looked away, and muttered, "That all?"

"May hap she get sweet on old Forrest, I don't know. May hap Sylvester get sweet on *her.* Sound like a real good recipe for trouble. Just about perfect." Miles was laughing hard now.

Aaron folded up the woodpecker cape and slid it back into the croker sack. "This ain't half worth the effort," he said. "Reckon I just gots to wait for the next Yankee that wants him a ivy-bill peckerwood."

Miles laughed again. "You gots you one long wait, boy. Oh, and damn if I ain't almost forgot—that gal say give you this."

Aaron reached to take it.

"I wants my bird," said Miles, snatching Cherry's paper-wrapped parcel back out of Aaron's reach.

"You ain't no kind of Christian," said Aaron.

Miles tossed Aaron the package. "Nor makes no such claim. Listen, I gots to get down to the river before daylight, all through them swamps, get this cargo on the boat, and they got every kind of white trash think they soldiers, going up and down that river looking for contraband and Yankees and runaway colored folk and I don't even know what all, so I can't set around passing pleasantries with no-account niggers all night. Give me that croker sack, boy."

Aaron handed the sack up to him, and, surfeited with Miles Glory's company, made for the cabin.

"Turn that damn light off," came the sleepy voices. The wrapping paper crackled loud. "God almighty."

"Y'all hush," said Aaron, "just give me a minute." And there it was: a rectangle of linen stiff with ornate embroidery, leaves and blossoms entwining a heart of gold. Pale green blades of grass, each a single strand of stitches, rose from the bottom edge. The sun shone down from above through scalloped clouds. Bluebirds sang in the corners. In the distant background, on the horizon, Cherry had embroidered a tiny white house with a smoking red chimney. Two tiny stick figures stood before the house, holding hands.

—1—

Sylvester lay on his pallet watching a big mosquito pump itself full on his arm. The sun was hours down, and a light rain was falling, but the heat, for the seventh night straight, was like noon in the sun. Out in the fields, in weather like this, weeds pushed up thick and fibrous overnight in the rows the hands had chopped the day before.

Drury's dark bass came from down the bunkhouse aisle:

> *"When I die, please bury me deep.*
> *Yes, men, when I die, please bury me deep.*
> *I don't want to hear my woman weep.*
>
> *Don't want to hear my woman weep,"*

sang the other men in reply.

> *"Children, don't weep, no, children, don't moan.*
> *Children, don't you weep, no no no, don't you moan.*
> *It's just another nobody gone."*
>
> *"Just another nobody gone,"*

came the chorus.

A wagon rattled into the courtyard. No one stirred; the only sound was the click of the dice in Elmo's cupped hand. Miles Glory appeared in the bunkhouse doorway, raindrops glistening in his long wavy hair. From the game several chins tipped up in his direction.

"What y'all playing for?" demanded Miles. "Where the money at?"

"Ain't no damn money," said Elmo. "We playing for credit."

"Say *what?*" Miles laughed.

"Master ain't paying no spending money while he gone up north," Elmo explained. "Going to pay us a big bonus when he get back. Each one of them matchstick worth a penny."

"I swear to God. Y'all all going be rich, ain't you," Miles mocked.

"Soon's emancipation come, y'all going to buy riverboats, factories, cotton plantations."

"Emancipation, *huh*," said Drury.

"Y'all dumb country niggers ain't heard about the war, I suppose," said Miles.

"We done heard about you war," said Drury. "Master say if he don't kill the Yankees they going to come get us all. Say the Yankees going to take all the colored folk prisoner."

"It's so lucky y'all got such a nice master to tell y'all all about everything," said Miles. "And out there risking his life just to defend y'all? It move me. It do."

"You want to quit flapping your lip and play?" suggested Ice Pick.

"Ain't got no matches," said Miles. "Unless you can change a twenty-dollar gold piece."

Every eye was on the coin Miles slapped down. None of them had ever seen a double eagle before.

"Where you get that kind of money, man?" demanded Elmo.

"Business," said Miles, showing his teeth.

"What kind of business?" asked Drury.

"General merchandise, wholesale, retail."

"Alligator business," said Ice Pick.

"Man know his market, he can turn a penny on a alligator, that's true," said Miles.

"You got my dollar?" asked Ice Pick.

"Surely I do," said Miles, flipping it to him.

Ice Pick snatched it out of the air and looked at it hard, front and back. "Yankee dollar," he said.

"You prefers Rebel? I got that, too." Miles produced a thick roll of bank notes.

"Naw, naw," said Ice Pick, "I ain't studying no folding money."

"Wise man. Now, how I get me some of this credit?"

"One dollar buy you one hundred matchstick," said Ice Pick. "Silver dollar."

"Ain't I done told y'all I ain't got no small change?" said Miles. "Oops, now, wait a minute, what's this here?" He fished up another silver dollar. "All right, boys? Let's us roll." Miles leaned back, picking his teeth with his first matchstick and watching as Drury, with frequent reference to his fingers, painstakingly counted out the rest.

By midnight Miles had won back his dollar credit from Ice Pick and was fifty matchsticks up besides. Ice Pick saw Sylvester looking on in mild contentment and barked, "Get away, runt! You trying to hex me or what?"

Sylvester was glad to oblige, and went out for a stroll. The rain had stopped, and in the thinning overcast a three-quarter moon was skimming the cypresses. He could feel every beat of his heart in the stillness, every blade of the wet grass beneath his bare feet. He walked toward the old oak whose tangled roots made a comfortable chair. He stretched back and looked up into the stars. His foot nudged something soft, dry, somehow both metallic and fleshlike. There was a quick hard prick at his ankle, and a rush of fire. As he lost consciousness he saw the moon-white of the snake's still open mouth.

"Damnation," said Ice Pick, spitting out blood. "Drinking poison out this fool's leg. Somehow this just ain't my night."

"I be taking that knife, Mr. Doctor," said Miles.

"Shit fire," said Ice Pick, handing it over, "if I ain't hex."

"I won that knife fair and square," Miles reminded him.

"That *my* knife," cried Sylvester weakly.

"You still alive?" Ice Pick inquired.

"Looky here, gentlemens," called Jackson from the door, grinning. He had a squirming water moccasin by the neck, thick as his arm. Jackson squeezed, and the snake opened its mouth wide, hissing. "Live, Miles, just like you say."

"Ten cent," said Miles. "Coin, not no matchsticks. On the barrelhead."

"Give me my knife," mumbled Sylvester, trying to get up. "Let me at that snake."

"I swear to God," said Ice Pick, pushing him roughly back down.

Sylvester drifted in and out of consciousness, reviewing his situation. I don't got no mama nor papa. I do got a cruel master, that make me do work I ain't fit for. I been bullied and chivvied and robbed. No way possible to even see the girl I loves. And now, snakebit. "I could use me some luck," he heard himself saying out loud. "I ain't had much."

For two more days and nights Sylvester slept.

"Ain't this fine!" Miles Glory was saying, lifting a green wool weskit from a paper parcel.

"That my weskit," mumbled Sylvester, struggling up through shifting mists. "Félice done make it for me."

"You reckon?" Miles was grinning, but he handed it over.

"Listen, Miles," said Sylvester. "I needs to talk to you."

"That's a particular coincidence," said Miles. "I wants to talk to you too. Don't even tell me. You wants to go up Corelli plantation and see her."

"Also I wants my knife back."

"I done already turn down a dollar for it this morning in Tutwiler. And I suppose you about as rich as usual." Miles slid the knife back into the scabbard.

"What you want, Miles?"

"You too ignorant to understand, but I going to tell you anyways. Yankee got what they call the Anaconda. That's a type of a snake."

"I don't need to hear about no snakes," said Sylvester.

"They got this Anaconda way down the Gulf of Mexico, where the river go in the ocean, and it stop all the Rebel boats, so they ain't no more cotton on the market over yonder in England and France and Europe. Now you mind last year cotton crop, how big it was?"

"Lord, yes," said Sylvester. "Work everybody to the bone. Biggest crop ever was."

"You getting less ignorant by the second," said Miles. "This here Greengrove plantation done growed so much cotton that Mr. Bedford he keep a bunch of it back. You know that warehouse with the lock and key, don't you?"

"Sure," said Sylvester. "Full of cotton up to the brim."

"And now to make room for this year crop, they going to move up a whole bunch of them cotton bale up to Corelli plantation. Mr. Joe got him a big new warehouse. The Anaconda done made cotton right dear over in England and France and Europe. You following me yet?"

"No, Miles, I ain't."

"I ain't surprise. Well, the long and the short of it is this. They going to need drivers to drive that cotton up the road. And one of them drivers going to get rob of one cotton bale. That's all; just one. And he going to go in the big house at Corelli plantation to tell what happen to him, all about them four white mens wearing masks that done hold him up. And he going to make him five dollar silver cash."

"And what about my knife?"

Miles slipped it off his belt and handed it to Sylvester. "This what you call a earnest."

"We going to take that cotton to England and France?" wondered Sylvester.

"I ain't going no further than the damn Mississippi River, Sylvester. You know how far it is just to New Orleans, curling in and out and all round about?—three, four mile of river for every mile the crow fly? And then you got that Anaconda to get past of, and the Gulf of Mexico, and the ocean sea. All told, it must be a thousand mile."

"I ain't never been in no boat," said Sylvester longingly.

Returning to Memphis in the first week of August with a hundred Kentuckians and a long wagon train of supplies, Nathan Bedford Forrest found several hundred more men waiting, drawn by his advertising and his traveling touts. One company had already chosen to call themselves the Forrest Rangers. Private Forrest had amassed six hundred and fifty fighting men—a battalion. They elected him Lieutenant Colonel.

"I tell you, Giovanni, them Yankees is already half whipped. They can't fight. They're cowards. Turned tail at Bull Run like a damn flock of hens, what I hear. Half my boys ain't got but shotguns, but I'll put them up against twice that many Blues."

"I have seen civil war," said Corelli. "Even now, there is blood in the streets of Rome."

Forrest gave Corelli a long, appraising look. "We all got our contributions to make, I reckon. Somebody got to grow the damn cotton. Don't know how much good it would do us if we was under the Yankees' heel—can't hardly grow cotton without niggers, can you?"

"You have seen the new warehouse?"

"We about ready down home to get a-moving. You and me got to talk about your cut, Giovanni."

Corelli raised a hand. "Please, my friend. Think of it as my contribution, to the war."

"Soon as this thing break, going to be big money made in cotton, Giovanni. Small commission might be big money."

"Please," said Corelli. "I insist."

"You a fine gentleman, Giovanni," said Forrest, coming as near as he ever came to smiling. "Well, Sweeney and them is all set. We got us a heap of wagons down from Kentuck and ready to roll."

"I am at your service. You will take coffee?" Corelli rang.

"Still got coffee! I sure would love me a cup. Getting right scarce, you know."

It was Félice who brought the tray. "Well, hey there, cutie pie," said Forrest heartily.

"Good morning, monsieur," said Félice with a coquettish bob.

"So, uh, Giovanni," began Forrest when she had withdrawn—

Corelli's shy half-smile gave him his answer.

"Another satisfied customer," Forrest chuckled.

"Yes and no," said Corelli softly. "It is not so simple."

Sylvester and the other wagoneers set off in fog. By noon it had burned off, and the horizon shimmered dusty blue across the flat green miles of the Delta. The sky was as white as the cotton bolls. There was not a breath of breeze.

They stopped for dinner in a stand of bottomland woods. With every step the snakebite pain shot up through Sylvester's leg like a wire of hot steel. Deer flies buzzed in manic circles around his head; one cut a plug from his earlobe, and the blood down his neck felt cool.

These cotton-country bayous, their headwaters shorn of timber, now ran thick with silt. A beaver broke the milky surface, stared at his visitors, and slapped the water hard with his tail. A canebrake rustled, and Sylvester, thinking snake, froze. But it was only a possum, with her babies riding on her back. She squinted at the men, and waddled fearlessly into their midst. Without even getting up, Ice Pick took a fallen limb and smashed her skull. He shook the babies from the possum's stringy fur into the water.

"Borrow me that nice sharp knife, Sylvester," said Ice Pick.

"You gots a knife," said Sylvester.

"Don't you like possum, Sylvester? Going to be nice smother possum tomorrow night. All cook up with green onion, garlic, maybe some side meat?"

"That's all right," said Sylvester.

"I save you god-damn *life,* little nigger."

Sylvester, not knowing what to say, said nothing. He didn't remember it clearly, but he believed that what Ice Pick said was true.

"I save you life," warned Ice Pick, "I can take it back."

"Don't try, brother," said Sylvester quietly.

Ice Pick went to work skinning the possum with his own knife.

The baby possums swirled slowly on an eddy and into a backwater slough, where, one by one, with little sharp splashes, they were snatched down by the snapping turtles.

The wagon train camped that night beneath the high bank of a long-ago Mississippi River channel. Sylvester said he was going to go out for a walk to stretch his snakebit leg. He lashed the Indian knife to a length of greenwood in case of cottonmouths, copperheads, diamondbacks—the very names made him shudder.

Careful that no one was watching him, he unhobbled his black jenny mule, led her into the woods upstream, tied her to a poplar, and limped on. The bluff grew steeper as he walked along its base till at last it was an overhang, from which, silver in the moonlight, there trailed the naked roots of the trees above. Scattered all around were bones.

And arrowheads! And spear points, and little carved human figures. Sylvester had often wondered about the Indians who had lived in this country not so long ago. The closest thing to an Indian he'd ever known was Miles, who hardly comported with what folks said Indians were like—silent hunters, violent savages, magicians, painted, feathered, wild. Whatever they had been was gone. Well, them Indians had everything to lose; I don't got nothing. What I got is everything to gain. They wanted to stay like they was. What I want is change. Everything changing these days, and I going to change with it. That's my advantage.

Sylvester stuffed his pockets with artifacts and tiptoed back through the camp. With some wire and a croker sack he secured his booty under the wagon bed. Who knew what these treasures might be worth in trade? Something, surely. A nest egg, perhaps, for when emancipation should come, when the white folks' war was over. For when he and Félice would go to France, or even have a little farm of their own. Chickens, ducks on a pond, big fat brown milk cow. Little cabin with a porch, all painted nice. Flower bed. Long winter nights beneath a quilt, white sheets like the master's. Such dreams crowded Sylvester's sleep that night, crowding out the fear that all that day had seized him like a claw whenever he thought of tomorrow.

"Sylvester, you damn fool," said Theo, "I might just have thunk that a damn *stable boy* would have enough brain to hobble his damn mules, in the middle of nowhere like this here."

"Yes, sir," said Sylvester, head bowed. "She ain't never run off like that before, but you right, Theo, and I is just as sorry as I can be. Can you just only borrow me a bucket of oats? I know she ain't but done run back in them woods."

"Whole damn wagon train waiting, Sylvester."

"Y'all run on," said Sylvester, "I catch you right up."

"God almighty damn," said Theo, swabbing the sweat off his shiny bald head with a red bandanna. It was already getting hot. "Sylvester? You wouldn't be thinking about lighting out, would you, son?"

"No, sir! No, sir!" Not as long as Félice remained in bondage.

"You knows Mr. Bedford hunt you down like a rat."

Sylvester holed up in a honeysuckle thicket and waited for the shouting and rattling and eventual departure of the wagon train. Then he found his jenny and gave her the oats she so well deserved, having refrained all night from braying and betraying him.

An hour passed, and another, as Sylvester lay back in the soft grass going over his story. Finally he led the jenny back to the clearing where they had camped, harnessed her and the white mule up, tied his Indian knife safe beneath the wagon bed next to his croker sack of treasures, and drove into the rutted road north.

It was full dark by the time Sylvester reached the corduroy road through the swamp. At the plank bridge over Daylight Bayou, three masked men rode up beside his mules. "All right," said one, whose voice Sylvester recognized as Miles's. "Whoa now. Put up them hands, little nigger."

Laughing nervously, he did so.

"Move, and get you head blow off," said one of the other masked men—Drury? It was dark as tar.

Sylvester didn't laugh now. He could not be sure how much the others understood of the hoax.

A buckboard, driven by a fourth masked man, squeezed up beside Sylvester's wagon. The masked men and Sylvester struggled to shove one of Sylvester's cotton bales across onto the buckboard. The driver took the reins, clicked his tongue at the two big Percherons, and started back north. Miles, still masked, clapped Sylvester on the back and, without a word, counted out five dollars, one soft slap on his palm and four following chinks. His future. Freedom, a farm, and Félice.

"We ought to beat the stew out of you a little bit," whispered Miles, "just to make extra sure it look like real robbery."

"That's all right," said Sylvester.

"Least you can do be roll in the mud and tear up you clothes."

"You ain't touching this weskit. Rest these here clothes get any more tore up than they is, they going to fall off my back."

"Don't want just a mite of mud and a black eye?"

"Much oblige," said Sylvester, "but no thank ye."

"All right, then, boy," said Miles, "you luck is you own. Long you stick to the story everything be fine."

"I is sticking like glue."

The masked men rode away into the dark.

Sylvester added the five coins to his arrowheads and spear points and figurines in the croker sack, and tied his accumulated wealth back tight beneath the wagon bed.

"If you ain't the chuckleheadedest baboon," growled Theo. "Didn't I *told* you you oughtn't not hang back like that?"

Uncle Dunc slowly shook his head, his lower lip tucked back behind his front teeth. "Come on, fool," he said, clamping Sylvester's arm in his bony fingers.

Down the long dark-paneled depth of the plantation office, Sylvester saw, in the lamplight, not only the round red face of Giovanni Corelli but also, half hidden in shadow but unmistakable, the sleek black hair of Nathan Bedford Forrest.

Now was the moment for Sylvester's imagination to take wing, and it did not fail him. He took a deep breath and started lying, and ten minutes later he was still lying. His heart was pounding, his breath was short, he was in a kind of transport—lying on so magnificent a scale was like having a happy dream! He could *see* those white robbers, feel the dagger the tall one had held to his ribs, smell the whiskey on their breaths. It was all Sylvester could do to keep from acting out the parts. "So, Mr. Joe, see," he wound up, nearly out of breath, "I is just as awful sorry as I can be, but it wasn't no kind of my fault."

The master said nothing; only sighed.

Forrest was smiling—an ice-cold, death's-head grin. But what at? Sudden fear froze solid in Sylvester's belly.

"Ring, Giovanni," said Forrest, teeth shining through his black beard.

Corelli rang.

It was Luigi who responded. He puffed out his chest, planted his feet wide apart, and leveled a quivering finger at Sylvester. "Liar!" he roared. "Every one word, by the bridge, I hear! Lies! Liar and robber! I see you help them. I see you take money. I see you hide it under wagon. Every one thing, I see! Signori, come, I show you."

In the stable yard, amidst a curious crowd, Luigi shone a lantern beneath the wagon. "*Eccolo qua,*" he grunted in triumph, pulling down the croker sack and spilling forth Sylvester's treasure.

Giovanni Corelli threw the arrowheads and spear points and figurines into the garbage heap, and gave the five silver dollars to Luigi as his reward.

Forrest, Corelli, Luigi, and Sylvester reentered the house through the kitchen. Sitting at the work table, picking his teeth and grinning, was Miles Glory.

Félice was standing by the stove staring at Sylvester, her face blank with shock.

"So, Mr. Louie," said Miles, "you done cotch them robbers?"

"What the hell's all this?" demanded Nathan Bedford Forrest. "What you know about this thievery, Miles?"

"Just something I heared about up in town, some white trash talking. Thought y'all gentlemens might want to know."

"You ought to came to Mr. Giovanni, buck!" said Forrest. "Don't you know that? We might could have caught them."

"Mr. Louie wouldn't let me in the house, Colonel Bedford," said Miles. "Say he going to cotch them his own self."

Corelli glared at Luigi. "Eh! Hero! Where is the cotton of Colonel Forrest? Where are the robbers? Moron!"

"I no can help, boss," whined Luigi pitifully. "Pistol she no shoot. Otherwise, I capture them all! And this one too, maybe even I shoot"—with a finger aimed at Sylvester. "And him!"—the finger now wagging in Miles Glory's face—Luigi had been going to improvise his way through a story pinning the death of Benedict O'Connell on Miles, but, seeing Miles so serenely sitting there, and fearing that Miles might know something he didn't, he suddenly lost his nerve. "And him, him I—"

"Hero," sighed Giovanni Corelli. "Moron. Buffoon." He breathed whiskey and garlic in Sylvester's face. "And you. What we will do with you?" he wondered aloud. "Bedford?"

Forrest's leer was horrible, but the chill and distant pity in Félice's eyes was worse. Miles touched her arm, and she gave him a sad smile; he had accomplished his every object.

And so Sylvester was returned to Greengrove plantation, in chains, and there, by Lieutenant Colonel Nathan Bedford Forrest himself, was whipped until the world went dark.

1862

"Shoot any man who won't fight!" thundered Nathan Bedford Forrest. He drew his sabre—ground to a razor edge, in violation of military rules—and sighted down it into the doubting eyes of a young, tow-headed lieutenant he had chosen at random from the front row. "War means fighting," roared Forrest. "Fighting means killing. Let's do us some."

Forrest was among the few who knew how overwhelmingly outnumbered the Southern forces were, here, in the defense of Fort Donelson—the only bulwark left between the Yankees and the center of military supply for the entire Southern midcontinent, Nashville. Fort Henry, hardly a dozen miles overland from Donelson, had just last week been cannonaded to rubble by the fearsome new Federal ironclads. From Henry the ironclads had pushed up the Tennessee to Muscle Shoals, Alabama, destroying railroad bridges all along the way. The South's very heart now lay exposed.

Forrest stood watching the black ships belching fire from the river, and the timbers of Fort Donelson splintering. The Southern generals faced a simple choice: either surrender their seventeen thousand men to the naval force on the river or fight their way through twenty-seven thousand Yankees in the woods.

But then, as the ironclads closed in, the Confederate guns, high on the bluff, were landing their fire squarely on the invaders' armor, and the shells were piercing it! One ironclad took a hit to the pilot house, another to the tiller, and both were drifting downstream. Another! and now the whole flotilla was in headlong flight.

Nevertheless the army of Ulysses Grant remained between the Rebels and anywhere. Their best hope, a very poor one, was to smash a way through Grant and retreat to Nashville.

Forrest's horse was shot from beneath him, and then a second mount. The snow throughout the shattered forest was spattered with Rebel blood.

The young tow-headed lieutenant sat with his gut bulging out of a gaping wound, and started pulling it further out. Now he had a loop of it out, swagged across his lap. He held it up to Forrest and said, "Look, Colonel. Look at this," and Forrest saw it but kept walking. Then he paused. Only hours ago, when the lieutenant had refused to lead his men across a waist-deep ice-choked creek to try—suicidally—to take the Yankee sharpshooters' trench, Forrest had called him a coward. The young man was still pulling, pulling till he had his whole bowel out. The smell was dense and foul. He said again, "Look, Colonel. Look." Forrest turned and, faintly, grimly, smiled. "You was a good boy after all," he said. "I was wrong about you."

Perhaps two thousand Confederates made it out of Donelson, but two thousand more were wounded, a thousand lay dead, and over twelve thousand Southern men were now prisoners of war.

Nashville was in panic. The depot of supply for the entire Confederate war effort west of the Appalachians was being looted in broad daylight. Enterprising traders (Miles Glory among them) led long lines of wagons into the countryside, heavily laden with plunder. The government of Tennessee was hastily evacuated—governor, archives, and all—to Memphis. What remained in Nashville were thousands of the poor and desperate, imagining or unable to imagine their fate as the first Confederate citizenry to see its city fall into invaders' hands.

When the looters jeered at Forrest's order to disperse, he and his men plunged mounted into their midst, slamming them with the flat of their sabres. The apparent leader received the butt of Forrest's revolver square on the top of his head, which split open like a melon.

The mayor rowed across the Cumberland to the small advance guard of Yankees and, much to their surprise, relinquished the city.

And now the very backbone of the South—the railroad from Memphis and the Mississippi east to Savannah, Charleston, and Richmond—lay open to the Northern hordes.

"So these Rebel be needing them some help," grinned Miles Glory, "even from the likes of freeman zambos. Y'all master done ask me personal to carry him that sissy up in the house, so he mens can all fight and don't got to wait on him."

"How you know all this here?" demanded Ice Pick. "All this here battles and generals and *ironclad* and all such white men talk?"

"When you in business, you got to keep *inform,*" replied Miles evenly.

"Yankee going to kill us?" wondered Drury.

"Lots of peoples tells me they going to set all the slave free," said Miles. "But I can't believe that."

"Don't got no slave up in Yankee land," said Ice Pick. "Lots of colored folk heading up there every day."

"Lots of them colored folk shot down cold too, brother," replied Miles. "Them soldier all along that river kills them just for the fun. Yankee soldier, Rebel soldier, don't matter. Don't give them no proper Christian burial neither. Leave them lay rot, eat up by the skunk and the coon and the crow."

"Lot of mens dying in this war, ain't it, Miles?" said Sylvester quietly, from deep in the bunk room shadows where no one had noticed him till now. "White or colored, zambo or what, and don't nobody know how, and all them white mens too busy or too scared to worry about it. Ain't that so, Miles. Ain't that so."

"Boy?" said Miles, his voice high and tense. "You better watch you neck."

"And *you* better keep you filthy hand off my woman," shouted Sylvester, losing composure, "or you might just, *might just* have one of them accident don't nobody worry about."

"*You* woman, huh. How come you don't ask her you own self who she belong to? Ain't she somebody? Can't she make up her own mind? You makes me laugh, always steaming up like this. Don't you understand you just going to keep getting deeper and deeper in trouble?"

Miles was right, which made Sylvester all the madder. He trudged out into the raw March night, the chain between his ankles clanking.

Nathan Bedford Forrest was a full colonel now, with a regiment under his command. The Yankees were coming on—not twenty miles north of the Mississippi-Tennessee line, just below which, outside Corinth, the Rebel army was encamped.

Jerome bounded down from Miles Glory's buckboard. "Colonel Bedford!" he cried out. "But don't you look peaked! Let me get you a drink, sir."

"Jerome," said Nathan Bedford Forrest, "if you ain't a no-good lying piece of carrion I ain't never seen one. God almighty. For empty gum flappery there ain't your damn like."

"I brung a jug or two."

"You know I done wiped it out long since, boy. Sent home for it special. You can't brought no whiskey."

"Thinks you just knows everything, don't you?" teased Jerome, reaching under the tarp.

"That's a Yankee jug!" Forrest exclaimed. "Where the hell you get this at?"

"We has our ways, sir."

Forrest's left hand alone, clutching the valet's shirt, nearly lifted him off the ground. "I ain't fooling with you no more, Jerome. Tell me where you got the damn jug at."

"From the *Yankees,* Colonel Bedford—where you think? We done pass through they camp. Ain't but just up yonder a little ways."

Jerome was pointing northeast; the Yankee encampment Forrest knew about—Grant's—lay due north. Neither, in any case, would have been anywhere near the line of travel from Greengrove plantation: Miles had clearly taken an excursion in order to trade with the enemy.

"How far a ways, boy?"

"I couldn't rightly say that, sir, but not but thirty mile or so, and they was moving, too. Thisaway like, round in them breaks toward Tennessee River," said Jerome. "Look, there go Miles! Miles Glory! come you here."

Miles confirmed Forrest's fear that the camp to the northeast was not Grant's but Buell's: thirty thousand combat-seasoned troops reinforcing Grant's forty thousand—against a total forty thousand Rebs, most of them green as the new spring grass.

The peaches were blooming along the hedgerows, bright warblers darting through the cedars, soft breezes luffing out of the south. Flocks of hen turkeys ran across the road, flapping and muttering, with amorous gobblers in hot pursuit. It seemed a perfect day to go to war, but soon the wind swung around to the north, black clouds rushed in, and a torrential rain began to fall.

The convoys sank in the mud. Creeks cut gullies across the roads. What was to have been a one-day march of twenty miles took two and a half.

So much for surprise attack.

Brass bands, presumably serenading Buell's arrival, could be heard in the night, punctuated by Yankee hurrahs.

Spatter of first fire. Waves of gray in ragged lines up the thorn-thick hillside, falling. Heaps of dead and worse. Of the first Confederate charge of four hundred twenty-five men, one hundred reached the ridge they had sought to attain.

The sky was blue now above the black smoke, the day warm.

A little log Methodist meeting-house called Shiloh Chapel had been serving as the Yankees' field headquarters, but now the Rebels had captured it. A guard outside the chapel felt a sudden touch of cold metal behind his ear and then nothing more, ever.

It was Confederate doctrine to keep the soldiers hungry, in order to make them mean. The Yankees had been having Sunday breakfast when the Rebels arrived. Coffee! White bread! A good many Southern boys sat down and feasted at the Union tables, reading the girl-scented letters they'd found in the tents.

The smoke grew thicker, confusion more contagious. Many of this morning's bold grew prudent in the afternoon.

Fire, smoke, cacophony. Men killing one another in blind terror, blind fury, blind obedience.

Every fifteen minutes, all night, the Federal gunboats sent shell fire screaming into the Southern encampments.

Thousands of men on both sides deserted in the night. Among them Miles Glory found the sales of whiskey and rations brisk; the price of travel directions was one dollar, silver only.

Carnage, horror.

Forrest and three hundred and fifty cavalrymen were to guard the rear of the Confederate retreat. Five times that number, in blue, appeared on the ridge behind. Between the two forces lay a half mile of swampy woodlot, cut over and abandoned some years ago and now a tangle of fallen timber, thorn scrub, and stumps. The Yankees, popping casual fire across it, began to thread their way through. Some lost their way; many stumbled, or mired.

"Charge!" Forrest cried, and led the way—bellowing, "Charge, boys, charge! Let's do us some killing!"—galloping into the midst of hundreds of Yankees, laying about him left and right.

And now why was one Yankee son of a bitch *grinning?* Forrest looked behind him. His men had refused to follow him.

A Yankee rode close and stuck his musket into Forrest's side and fired.

With one swing Forrest cut half through the neck of the nearest Yankee horseman. He reached down and grabbed a wounded foot soldier by the collar and swung him up across his horse's rump to serve as a shield against the fire spewing from behind, and fled to, through, and past his gaping troops, and somehow was not shot again.

Of the hundred thousand men who had fought at Shiloh Chapel, twenty-five thousand were now wounded, captive, or dead—more American casualties in this one battle than there had been in the

Mexican War, the War of 1812, and the American Revolution combined.

"Caleb, make ready!" cried Giovanni Corelli, hearing the bugle call from the road. The Forrest Rangers trotted up the drive in close formation, every man on a tall roan thoroughbred, followed by the ambulance wagon.

"Much—obliged—for—your hospitality," croaked Forrest, still breathless with the exertion of moving. "Be more nearer—to my men—here—Giovanni. Going to be—back up—and—in the fight—right soon. This ain't—nothing."

The Yankee ball had lodged against his spine. When the fevers came, Félice mopped his brow with a moistened towel, of Italian linen, edged in lace.

But today Forrest was sitting up in bed, reading a telegram, and he said, "Jerome, I want you to go on down to Greengrove and tell Theo to round him up a couple dozen of them good-for-nothing niggers and send them up to Memphis to Mr. Towery to work on the ramparts. And carry me back them new uniforms Queen's been making me up. I got to get back in this damn war! Félice, honey, do you know?—I think I'm hungry this morning."

"Oh, monsieur!" she cried softly. "You will have a *bouillon,* a milk toast, and then, maybe, then something solid."

"Hell, I want me some *eggs,* gal. Get me some eggs."

An hour later, he was doubled over a bucket choking up eggs and blood, as Félice held his head and kept his long hair from falling in.

Meanwhile, Jerome and Uncle Dunc drove south in uncongenial silence, till Greengrove plantation hove into view, white-columned, red-bricked, green-garlanded.

"Look all them nigger flat asleep on the ground," observed Uncle Dunc.

"Mr. Bedford got him some skinning to do, look like sure enough," agreed Jerome.

For indeed Greengrove was in rapidly advancing decay. The overseer Sweeney had gone off to war and left the plantation in the hands of the head slave driver Theo, and Theo had taken an interest in whiskey, spending most days now in the ice house with Ice Pick and Drury while the ground went unbroken and the rain kept falling and the weeds came surging up and the cotton seed rotted, and, as Uncle Dunc had noted, the field hands napped on the lawn.

"Hey," said Uncle Dunc, prodding Sylvester's back with a long bony finger. "Hey. Boy."

Sylvester did not even look around.

"Sylvester, hey, looky here, son." The old man dangled a little drawstring bag.

At last the boy turned and raised his heavy-lidded eyes.

"She done sent you these here sugar tit, boy," said Uncle Dunc. "Go on now and eat you one. We ain't even planting no sugar this year, account of the war."

Had she forgiven him his folly? "You want one?" Sylvester asked, sucking, warmth flowing into his heart.

"They for you," the old man insisted.

"Go ahead on," said Sylvester.

"Mighty fine," mumbled Uncle Dunc, his fat lower lip stuck out in satisfaction as he gummed at the candy.

At length, Sylvester hazarded, "She waiting for me?"

Uncle Dunc nodded overemphatically yes, eyes wide, a hopeless liar. "She nursing Mr. Bedford," he added. "Yankee shot him."

"That so," said Sylvester flatly.

Uncle Dunc put his hand on Sylvester's shoulder. It was the first soft touch he had felt in a considerable while. "You want to go to Memphis, boy? Mr. Bedford need mens to work on that pile of bale on the bluff, stop the Yankee cannonball."

"My, oh, my," breathed Sylvester. "I ain't been thinking I would ever see the outside this here fence."

"We got to get Theo to send you," said Uncle Dunc.

"Aw, he send me all right. Them boys don't like seeing me around." He gave his chain a weak shake. "Remind them too hard how they be *slave*."

Uncle Dunc looked down and frowned. Sylvester's legs were festering where the iron cuffs rubbed. "Can you work, boy?"

"You get me out these here irons, Uncle Dunc, and I could near about fly."

"Oh, and—shoot! If I ain't near forgot! Aaron done sent you something too." Slowly, lower lip pendulous in his version of a smile, he opened his canvas valise, took out a ball of string, and set it at his feet. Then he took out the package, put down the package, put down the valise, picked the package back up, turned it this way and that, and began to unwrap it, carefully folding the paper, stowing it in the valise, adding the string to his ball. At long last he presented the scrap of croker sack.

Aaron had saved Sylvester's Indian knife!

"I don't know what to say, Uncle Dunc," said Sylvester, fighting down tears.

"You don't got to say nothing, boy."

"I don't suppose Aaron be coming to Memphis," said Sylvester.

"No, son."

"You expect he might be going to light a rag out?"

"Aaron going to light, he ain't going to be talking about it," said Uncle Dunc. "He just go. But ain't nobody on the place lit out yet. Say the Yankees worse than our own white mens."

"Who you think want you thinking that?" snapped Sylvester.

"I ain't studying no subtlety and guile, Sylvester."

"You just can't tell, can you? I mean, can us—us colored," mused Sylvester. "I mean, what happening out there. In the war. Off the place. Other side the Mexican-Dixican. Can't nobody tell, except buckra. Nigger just don't know nothing." Sylvester took another piece of candy.

"That's a fact, son," Uncle Dunc agreed.

"That smart-britches Miles come down here time to time," said Sylvester, "be telling us this and that and the other about artillery cannon and ironclad boat and general and colonel and all such as that, but you can't believe but half what that man say, and half ain't no better than none when you don't know which half." Sylvester was feeling brave enough now to ask, "He ain't been messing with Félice?"

"I ain't hardly seen that rascal," lied Uncle Dunc. "He too busy getting rich."

"Mm-mm-mm," came the voice of Jerome from the bunkhouse doorway. "How my little jailbird is?"

Sylvester just sighed.

Jerome went heedlessly on. "You wrong, you know, about usns not knowing nothing. I knows *everything* about this war."

It struck Sylvester that Jerome might in fact know more than the rest of them did. "What going happen to the black folk when the Yankee take over?" Sylvester asked him.

"You think the Yankee going to win, do you? Just like that. You *is* a ignorant child."

"What *you* think, Jerome?" Sylvester demanded.

"They ain't done yet, neither Yankee nor Rebel. They just killing and killing, and then killing. You couldn't believe it, such as I done seen." Jerome's voice had lost its affectation; he seemed almost to be talking to himself. "And mercy Lord but they a lot of them Yankee. Rebel done kill more of them than they kill Rebel, by half, but they just keeps coming. Near about every day some soldier ride down from town with a message for my master, and he keep he own counsel but he don't look like jumping."

"He going to die?" asked Sylvester, trying to suppress a hopeful tone.

"He right sick, and no mistake."

So, indeed, was the Confederacy. The coast was being cut to pieces by the Union's naval artillery. Under relentless cannonade, New Orleans fell. Baton Rouge was next to be crushed. Natchez gave up without a fight, and now the enemy fleet was moving upriver to take Vicksburg and, thence, to push north, toward Memphis.

The vast Confederate host encamped at Corinth junction, facing the prospect of an insuperable siege, was evacuated southward, into the bleak hardscrabble of the Mississippi hill country. The

Union's even vaster Grand Army moved in immediately and severed there all Southern railway transport to the four points of the compass, and would soon march along the captured line west, toward Memphis.

The last Confederate defenses on the Mississippi River to the north, Fort Pillow and Fort Randolph, were abandoned. Nine new Union warships—battering rams, capable of fifteen knots, the fastest craft ever seen on the river—joined the ironclads and older rams above Pillow, and the Yankee armada started south, toward Memphis.

The city was full of wounded Confederate soldiers. They died so fast the grave diggers could not keep up, and the stink of the dead hung thick in the heavy riverside air.

The sixth of June dawned mild and fine, and most of Memphis turned out for the battle. By the time the sun was well up, thousands of spectators thronged the river front—ladies with little dogs, stiff-collared merchants, roving bands of boys, wounded Rebs, skulking deserters, circumspect loyalists, uproarious rivermen passing jugs and calling sarcastic encouragement to their defenders. There were also great numbers of watchful Negroes, of indeterminate provenance and inscrutable allegiance.

General Jeff Thompson, in full dress uniform and purple-plumed cockaded hat, rode back and forth on his white stallion, trying to look imperious while wondering what had become of his militia.

At a commanding height on the bluff, where his cotton factor maintained an elegant iron-fenced lawn, Giovanni Corelli was directing the disposition of a splendid picnic breakfast. Beneath a yellow awning, catfish and sturgeon and chicken were frying, risotti of morels and marrow were bubbling, a big pot of turnip greens steamed; a great silver tray displayed long rows of the season's first bright tomatoes, sprinkled with spring onions and the last of the best olive oil.

The hundreds of roustabouts were singing, as they had sung through the long driven weeks of their labor on the rampart of three hundred thousand cotton bales which was to have protected the business district from bombardment (and which, in these last frantic days, so that the Yankees might not have Southern cotton, Towery had ordered burned); they were singing all the harder today, now that their work was behind them, now that an epoch was past. Many of the roustabouts had linked arms in a long spiral chain, and Sylvester found it slow going getting to the outside of the singing, laughing, jostling crowd.

He saw Uncle Dunc at a gate of iron filigree, and beyond him a crowd of dressed-up white folks drinking and laughing, and behind them a yellow awning, and beneath that Luigi waving his arms, and Hattie with her hands on her hips giving Aaron a piece of her mind, and the master tasting something from a pot and smacking his lips and patting his big belly, while Mattie and Isabel looked on grinning proudly. And, then, appearing amidst them, in a white dress, twirling a white parasol, Félice.

She saw him, and her eyes grew wide, and she smiled.

"Mr. Joe," Sylvester said softly over the iron fence, "Mr. Joe, sir, please, sir, excuse me, sir."

"Eh! Sylvester? *Ecco* you *qua!*" boomed Giovanni Corelli. "You okay, boy?"

"They whips me, Mr. Joe," said Sylvester. "And I ain't eat no meat since the day I left Greengrove. I been sick, too, real sick, half about to die, and that Colonel Towery he just keep working you. Don't nobody look out for us colored folk here on this bluff. You gots to live in a shed don't got no windows, not fit for pig, all crowd up like bullfrog egg. Roustabout overseer going to tan me if he don't no more than see me over here. Now they says we going to all go back to Greengrove, and you know they going to put me in chain and manacle down yonder again just like they done before, and I get a infection in my leg and I can't even walk, and when Mr. Bedford go back to the war them colored folk down there they just goes wild. This life just ain't no good for me. No kind of good at all, marse."

"I am very sorry, Sylvester," said Corelli.

Sylvester sank to his knees and began weeping pitifully, his hands gripping the uprights of the iron fence like the bars of a jail, his close-cropped head bowed so Corelli could see the line of the scar the overseer had put there with a blow of a hammer handle. "I can't stand it, marse! Won't you bring me back on home? Please, sir. Please. Please."

A great cheer rose from the crowd as what remained of the Confederate river force moved out into the channel—a grand total of eight gunships, each no more than an old riverboat that had been swaddled in cotton bales and patched over its vulnerable parts with salvaged railroad iron. Each wore a modest ram on its prow and carried two puny artillery pieces.

The Yankees were coming around the bend, past the islands known as Paddy's Hen and Chickens—backwards, so they could steam back upstream if the going got too tough. There were five huge and ponderous ironclads, each bearing thirteen heavy cannon; nineteen of the new low, fast, and nimble battering-ram boats; troop transports and supply vessels; and, bringing up the rear, a motley flotilla of Yankee merchants, bankers, and speculators, ready to set up shop the moment Memphis should fall.

A pungent smell hung heavy in the air—molasses. The city's thousands of stored barrels of it had been smashed with axes, to keep it out of Yankee cakes and candy. Half the bluff was slick with its ooze. Glutinous rafts of it shone black on the tan backwaters.

A hundred and thirty million dollars' worth of goods had been destroyed in Memphis in the last few days. Even the mighty ironclad *Tennessee,* lying half finished at the quay, had been burned. The harbor was clotted with barrel staves, timbers, bolts of charred cloth.

The Rebel guns opened fire. The Memphians waved white handkerchiefs, and cried out hurrah, and laughed.

A close rank of four Yankee ironclads chugged toward the city, still backwards, in a swirl of black smoke. Two sudden spaces opened among them, and from the rear two of the dreaded battering rams rushed forward. One of them bore down full steam on the Confederate flagship, the *Colonel Lovell,* as though to ram her head on. The *Lovell* continued straight ahead, and then at last her captain lost his nerve and tried to turn aside—too late. The ram struck her amidships, and she sank like a brick. The crowd shook their heads in woe.

The *General Price* and the *General Beauregard* moved in together on the other little Yankee ram, one from the left, one from the right, cannons blazing. But the ram boat poured on the steam and squirted between them, and the two lumbering iron-plated riverboats helplessly converged. There was a hideous grinding of armor as the *Price*'s starboard paddle wheel sheared off, swirled on an eddy, and was gone. She struggled toward the far shore and went aground on a bar of mud.

Meanwhile the *Beauregard* took a shell through her boiler on one side and a battering ram through her hull on the other, and hastily pulled down her flag.

Groans, whistles, Rebel yells, outraged exhortations to courage, contemptuous moans at cowardice—at each successive exchange the multitude roared. All that could be seen from the bluff now were shapes in a soot-dark haze, and the Confederate ships' high twin stacks. Ducks and geese flew in terrified circles over the clamor and smoke. A spiteful Southern sailor turned his rifle on an eagle, and now it floated away with wings outspread on the flotsam-choked current.

The *Sumter* and then the *Bragg* were smashed amidships by the Yankee rams and crippled. The *Little Rebel,* her engine blown to bits by Yankee projectiles, drifted to the far bank; her crew ran helter-skelter into the Arkansas woods. The *Jeff Thompson* was in flames. Only the *General Van Dorn* escaped, fleeing ignominiously south.

As for General Jeff Thompson himself, looking on from the heights, he gave his white charger a flick of his spurs and hot-footed it out of town.

The river was quiet. The city was quiet. A rowboat came to the foot of the bluff.

Three sailors and a medical cadet—the Yankee ram commander's nineteen-year-old son—debarked. They marched through the molasses-caked weeds, through the black and still-smoldering remains of the cotton-bale rampart, and through the goggling spectators, who closed in behind them in a mass of speechless consternation. When the four Yankees came to the post office, they struck the Stars and Bars, raised the Stars and Stripes, and saluted. The Battle of Memphis was over.

It was all of seven-thirty in the morning.

A Rebel yell—a shot—a spray of splinters bursting from the flag pole. The occupation force and most of the onlookers hit the dirt.

A tall, skinny, wavy-haired Negro in an ill-fitting Confederate uniform stood on the seat of a buckboard with a smoking pistol in his hand. "Look out, Yankees!" he hollered. "Long as Miles Glory round y'all ain't whip us yet." He clicked his tongue at his pair of Percherons, and the wagon clattered away through the parting crowd.

"Sylvester!" barked Giovanni Corelli. "Eh! Come you here, boy. Go to get Aaron and please to take all the things from the picnic and load them up. Quick, quick! We got to get out of here before these Yankees put us in the prison."

"Thank you, Mr. Joe!" yelled Sylvester. "Thank you most kindly, *sir!* Hey, Aaron!"

The two young men threw their arms around each other and laughed. Then Sylvester shook hands with all the other servants in turn, ending with Félice.

Sylvester and Félice looked for a long moment into each other's eyes, and Sylvester felt certain that everything was still as it had been before.

Miles Glory, with a Yankee price on his head now, hid out for the next several weeks in the slave quarters at Corelli plantation—much to the discomfiture of Sylvester, who could not consider Félice's virtue safe as long as Miles was around.

One day, an ancient, stooped, rheum-eyed Indian appeared in the courtyard and asked to see Miles.

When Uncle Dunc saw the old Indian, he cried out, "Tatholah! Man, you still alive? I can't believe my eyes. You must be a hundred year old!"

"Very old, yes," said Tatholah.

"Glory, she dead?" asked Uncle Dunc.

"Dead, yes, three winter."

"Bless her soul," said Uncle Dunc. "Come to see your boy, did you? Here come he now."

Uncle Dunc modestly withdrew.

"My son," said Tatholah in Chickasaw.

"I done forgot my Indian talk, Paw," said Miles Glory, wringing his hands and looking at the old man's bare feet.

"Yes," said Tatholah, in English. "You not know your brother Tchula Homa. Once only, you see him, when my people go to the west. You are little boy then. My son Tchula Homa is dead, one moon, at Oklahoma. They send me letter."

The old man turned and trudged back toward the plantation gate.

Miles Glory just blinked and shrugged and walked the other way.

"Who that old Indian was?" demanded Sylvester, knowing damned well who. "I is interested in Indians."

"I ain't got no time to be jawing with the like of you, Sylvester," sneered Miles. "I got to go curry my horses. I got to get back in this war. There money out yonder not doing nothing but waiting to jump in Miles Glory pocket."

The weather turned cruel—brutally hot, and brutally dry. The well at Corelli plantation dried up. Daylight Bayou by August was a broken chain of fetid mudholes, no longer flowing at all; the stagnant water had to be strained and boiled. Turtles, beavers, and alligators roamed the fields of scorched cotton in futile search of new homes.

Memphis, meanwhile, with its infusion of Yankee merchants and refugee slaves, was booming. The runaways were paid by the United States Army in food and clothing, plus a full-pound plug of Connecticut chewing tobacco monthly. Cash wages were supposedly being reserved for their masters, but nobody expected much to come of that. By October, there were six thousand Negroes at work on the fortification south of the city, to be called, as its forerunner had been, Fort Pickering.

Businesses were seized from their owners and rented to the new arrivals. Most of those displaced went underground—generously abetted by their Northern suppliers—and thus it was that through occupied Memphis many tons of Union supplies passed into Confederate hands, and many tons of Southern cotton to Northern mills.

The city teemed with rivermen, moonshiners, gamblers, prostitutes, pawnbrokers, publicans, cat burglars, confidence artists, smugglers, itinerant musicians, idled railroaders, muleteers with gold teeth, preachers of implausible denomination, one-horse financiers with impossible propositions, drunken Rebel deserters, legions of Yankee heroes stump-legged, bandaged, swollen, oozing, syphilitic, gutshot, blinded, malarial, dying, in the hot dense clouds of yellow dust. Ladies, respectable old men, and children stayed at home, peeping out now and then from behind drawn curtains.

But for the fact that he had over and over to exhibit his frayed certificate of manumission to the Yankee soldiers, Miles Glory was very comfortable in Memphis. Under unknown but imaginable circumstances, the warrant for his arrest for the attempted murder of the Yankee occupation party at the Memphis post office had been withdrawn; this was the last time Miles would ever act on so disinterested a motive as sheer fun.

From a Cincinnati Jew (who had come to it in trade for a boxcar load of Enfield rifles purchased from Miles himself) Miles Glory bought a grandly gabled tall brick house—none other than the confiscated city residence of Nathan Bedford Forrest. From a polished cherry chair behind a leather-topped immensity of desk, he oversaw proliferating enterprises in shipping, sales, and capital investment. Driving decrepit wagons, dressed in rags, singing spirituals at the top of their lungs, his operatives carted mule carcasses out of Memphis to an abandoned barn in the country, each dead mule stuffed with gold.

—·Ɖ·—

Forrest himself had tried twice to return to active duty. The first time, in May, after he had jumped his horse over a split rail fence in the Confederate encampment at Holly Springs, the ball still jammed against his vertebrae had become infected, and he had undergone its surgical removal (in characteristic fashion, spurning anesthesia). By July, now promoted to the rank of brigadier general, he was at last in action, blowing up railroad bridges by the dozen, burning hundreds of thousands of dollars' worth of cotton, seizing tons of ammunition, capturing astonished Yankees at four in the morning, and raising fearsome hell all over middle Tennessee and even into Kentucky as far as the outskirts of Louisville.

Everything Forrest destroyed, of course, was made useless not only to the Yankees but to any future Southern reoccupation as well.

"I sure do wish I had me a pork chop," said Aaron. "Or a big fat sausage. Or some side meat with scramble egg."

"Shut up, Aaron," said Sylvester. The moss on the bank of the old swimming hole crumbled between his toes and wafted away like thistledown.

"Or a beefsteak," continued Aaron, "smothered in onions. Pot of chitlins. Turtle gumbo. Neck bone stew. Everything cover with salt a inch thick. Ham sam bone jury!"

"Frog leg. Fried chicken wings. Boil catfish with hot pepper and hushpuppies," said Sylvester, catching the spirit.

"I needs *meat,* knucklehead," said Aaron. "Barbecue rib. Hell, I settle for some Mr. Louie spaghetti with possum meatball. Lo, there she come."

Lifting her white skirts daintily, Félice picked her way along the path that followed upstream from the old Indian town. "No swimming no more," she laughed softly, wiggling her long fingers over the cracked and crazed mud beneath the diving tree.

"I be going," said Aaron glumly.

"Do not hurry," said Félice, reaching to touch Aaron's arm. "The master goes today all day to see the officers at Hernando. They want to take him in the army. But he has more than twenty slaves, and by the law one white man with twenty slave does not have to serve. Also he tells them he is no citizen. Maybe on the route a Yankee will find him," she sighed, "and seize him prisoner."

"Say a passel of them out there, roaming round," said Aaron.

"I know! They find the Preacher," said Félice. "He has no paper and they seize him."

"I likes these Yankee better and better," laughed Aaron.

"They put him to working at Memphis, at the fort," said Félice. "Him, so old! And a free man, legally."

"May be old, but he strong," said Aaron, recalling the iron talons of Augustus T. Lowdermilk.

"How you know where they take the Preacher?" demanded Sylvester.

"Miles Glory has come," replied Félice.

Sylvester kicked at the moss and said nothing.

"Always he bothers me!" cried Félice, bowing her head softly to Sylvester's shoulder.

Aaron's face showed his distrust, and Sylvester looked away from it. "Y'all don't do nothing I wouldn't do," said Aaron, rising to go.

Sylvester looked into Félice's eyes.

She touched him—and instantly Miles, master, war, poverty, ignorance, bondage, and dread all were lost, swept away in the hurricane of his love.

Up inside a hollow beech tree in the Indian ghost town, Sylvester kept a saddle blanket. He smoothed it over the crackling leaves, fallen early this drought year.

"I am animal for you today," she whispered, clinging to him, soft, sweat-sticky. "Crazy with this thing."

On September 22, a proclamation was issued by President Abraham Lincoln of the United States, "That on the first day of January, in the year of our Lord one thousand eight hundred and sixty-three, all persons held as slaves within any state or designated part of a state, the people whereof shall then be in rebellion against the United States, shall be then, thenceforward, and forever, free;

and the Executive Government of the United States, including the military and naval authority thereof, will recognize and maintain the freedom of such persons, or any of them, in any efforts they may make for their actual freedom."

"Aigh, madonna!" cried Giovanni Corelli. "These rascal blackamoors will murder us in our bed!"

Accordingly a search was undertaken of the slave quarters, and once more Sylvester was obliged to surrender his Indian knife.

1863

By the light of the moon Sylvester could see a figure crouched in the garden snatching up carrots. Then he heard the back door creak.

"Hoo! You, man!" hollered Hattie from the kitchen steps. "You better get out my vegetable patch before I shoots!"

The man scuttled past the trash heaps and into the woods.

The next day, when Sylvester went to the old Indian town to wait for Félice, his horse blanket was gone from the hollow beech tree.

"The moss is soft," said Félice.

"Full of chigger, too," said Sylvester. "Climb up in you knicker and *bite.*" He kneeled, stuck his head up under her skirts, and nipped at the inside of her thigh.

Félice danced away, giggling. She slipped out of her white dress and climbed to the diving limb above the pool, enjoying watching him watching her.

Soon they were writhing on a mud flat upstream, coated, ochre, slick. Afterwards, they floated together in the warm brown water of the pool below. "Félice," said Sylvester, "how come you takes such a chance for me? Master cotch you he skin you live."

"I love you," she said simply.

"You ever think about the future?"

"There are other worlds. In them one can be happy," she said.

"You ain't talking about heaven, is you?"

"No, my dear. Other worlds on earth. I dream we will go to them, some day. I dream we will have a child."

"I can't figure this, Félice."

"After the liberation of the South," she said, "when we will be free."

"I mean, what I can't figure is why me," said Sylvester.

"Who knows?" said Félice, with a soft laugh. "I do not understand, myself. You are an innocent boy. I have seen too much. You and I, we can have a simple life, clean, far away. I wish to be better. You can help me."

"I going to take care of you," said Sylvester solemnly.

"First, one must live," said Félice. "Me, I see the future only very near."

"But you dreams," Sylvester reminded her.

"Yes. I cannot help that. In the day—I must live as I am." she said. "I must go now." She climbed out on the mossy peninsula and began to dry herself.

Sylvester never understood her—her distractions, reluctances, abrupt departures. It may have been this sense of inner complexities someday to be understood that sustained his fascination. "Master ain't bothering you, is he?"

"The same. I live." She gave him a melancholy smile, and turned, and strode up the path toward home.

Sylvester sat on a log and watched the afternoon turn gold.

"Don't move, nigger." A white man's voice.

Sylvester raised his hands high and, without even looking around, said, "I ain't done nothing, sir."

"Not unless you count fucking your master's bitch as nothing. Turn around, sambo. I ain't going to kill ye."

In fact, as Sylvester turned to face him, the white man did not look particularly lethal. He was brandishing a thick hickory limb, but it was half rotten and the man was shaking so hard he could barely keep his grip.

"But what I *mought* do," the white man said, "is *get* you killed. How bad you think that man want to know you porking his private property? Bad enough to kill you? Henh?"

"Pardon me, sir, but is you a Yankee?"

"Fuck, boy, I'm your god-dang *neighbor.* You know that little track south off of Capleville road come off by that chinaberry tree, don't ye? You know it, don't ye?"

"No, sir, I can't rightly say I does. I ain't been out that way in some little time. There Yankees out yonder, folk says."

"Piss on the Yankees. Piss on Johnny Reb. Piss on the niggers too, and that mean piss on *you,* boy."

"Yes, sir."

"What's your name, boy?"

"Sylvester."

The man took a carrot from the pocket of his ragged overalls and started wolfing it down. "Sylvester," he sputtered through a mouthful, "you got to get me something to eat. Y'all got everything under the sun up there at that damn plantation, ain't ye? I'm about sick and tired of carrots and raw taters, and that mammy up there she like to shot me last night."

Sylvester felt like laughing. Hattie's shotgun had neither hammer nor trigger.

"And I tell you what I'm going to do, Sylvester," said the white man. "I'm going to make it worth your while. I ain't going to tell on you about that high-yellow piece of pussy you was eating—just long as you keep the vittles coming."

"There ain't so much as you might think, Mr.—"

"Andrew Jackson Wordlaw is my name."

"Mr. Wordlaw."

"Shit. Ain't nobody never called me Mr. Wordlaw."

"Mr. Andrew?"

"Ain't nobody never called me mister neither. Call me A. J., that's all." To Sylvester's astonishment, the white man stuck out his hand. It was missing the index finger and the tip of the thumb, but his grip was ferocious. "How d'ye do."

"I does all right," replied Sylvester, "thanky kindly. But see, master still want to grow cotton, and the foodstuffs suffers, and us folk suffers. Ain't got but broody hens and work horses."

"Don't play no game with me, Sylvester. I pop you like a tick."

"No, sir, Mr. A. J.—I mean A. J. No, sir. I just telling you it hard, but I going to try, definitely."

"And you ain't going to tell nary soul about me neither," said A. J. "I done about had it with that piece-of-shit war. Rich gentleman on a horse tell me to run straight in the mouth of a god-dang Yankee cannon? Well, fuck them gentlemen. I'm about tired of getting shot at. Not to mention lousy, flea-bit, sick, hungry, and cold."

"So you be living here in this here mansion," laughed Sylvester, with a wave at the roofless ruin of an Indian house where A. J. Wordlaw had strung up a piece of tattered canvas and stowed Sylvester's horse blanket. "Right cozy."

"Uppity little son of a bitch, ain't ye?"

"I wasn't but just funning," said Sylvester.

"You sleep under a roof out of the rain, don't ye, boy? You got a mite of meat on your damn bones, don't ye? And ain't no Yankees been shooting at you neither. Am I correct?"

"Yes, sir," said Sylvester.

"I want some eggs, Sylvester."

"I can't do that, A. J. They cotch me."

"Well, then, you got the choice of getting catched for stealing nigger slaves' eggs or getting catched for stealing white gentleman's poontang."

"That ain't half fair!" protested Sylvester.

"It ain't a half fair world, you wool-head piece of shit," snarled A. J., showing his sparse brown teeth.

"Just one question, please, sir, A. J.," said Sylvester. "Me and my gal—where we going to go now?"

"You expect me to bury my head under some cocklebur bush while you getting your stick dipped? You do got a notion."

Sylvester waited.

Finally A. J. exhaled a soft percussive "Pah!" Then he said, "I don't give a rat's ass where you fuck her."

Sylvester waited some more.

A. J. went "Pah!" again. "All right, all right," he said. "I'll take a powder when y'all come out here for your god-dang low animal doings. All right? Just get me something to eat."

Sylvester figured he might himself now offer his hand.

A. J. looked at it, snorted, and extended his own. "If my maw could see this," he said, "she would just abso-god-damn-tutely shit a brick. Rest her soul in peace."

"Rest in peace, amen," said Sylvester.

"Yes, sir, yes, sir, yes, sir," puffed Caleb, coming at last through the office door.

"Five times I ring!" complained Giovanni Corelli.

"I ain't but just been down to the quarters. What can I do for you, marse?"

"Give me a cigar," said Corelli. "The people are quiet?"

"Oh, yes, sir. Everybody just biding peaceful. Done had they supper. Singing a bit. Preacher come by this evening—Yankees done let him out—and we cook him up some cow pea with side meat."

"Eh! You watch this bacon meat. Not much remains us. The preacher brings news?"

"He say the black folk going plumb crazy some places. Down Walls a bunch of them done light a rag out. White folk ride out in the night with bloodhound dog and all such as that—cotch eight and hang four. Brung all the black folk on the place out and make them watch. Childrens and all. Preacher done bury them four men he own self. But our folk they just be quiet and peaceful as you might please."

"They don't want to be free, emancipated?" said Corelli.

"They don't be want to get kill," said the valet.

"Some day, they will be free," said Corelli, blowing a smoke ring. "You, Caleb, also you will be emancipated."

"What us going to do, marse?"

"Maybe you kill us," said Corelli. "I don't know."

"No, sir, marse," said Caleb.

"General Forrest, he say, 'Giovanni! We lick these Yankees! You see!' But Caleb, he dreams, this I say."

"Mr. Bedford done kill him a heap of Yankees, everybody know that," said Caleb. "Preacher say Mr. Bedford been in and out down Coahoma County and don't seem too much scared."

"Brave, yes," said Corelli, "he is that. But all the planters up and down the road here, they all say the big generals cannot win the victory. Because always it is politics, ambition, division. I study this in university. I see it in my fatherland. They do not listen to Forrest. So—the South loses—emancipation comes—poof!"

"Take a little more toddy, marse?"

"Thank you, my friend."

"It can't be so hard!" Aaron was insisting. "Straight north from where you setting right now, knucklehead, Yankee soldier got they camp—hop, skip, and jump across them Nonconnah bottoms—and right in yonder across that creek a whole big bunch of black folk got they own camp. Every last one of them *free.* Emancipated-proclamated *free.*"

"I don't fancy no rope on my neck, Aaron."

"You just pussy-whip," scoffed Aaron.

"It's a fact I ain't studying leaving Félice. And it's a fact she ain't studying no lighting out. She been places where she seen what happen. She seen a man swing. Seen him shit his britches, eyes pop out, buzzard eat him where the white mens leave him hang."

"You scared of snakes, ain't you?"

"Scared of ropes, scared of snakes. That's a fact, too," said Sylvester. "Got my good reason. Aaron, listen at me. Don't do it. There going to come a time to do it, but this ain't it. What happen if the Rebel get Memphis back, and you setting there a runaway slave? Huh? You think they just going to say, 'That's all right, Aaron, you just go on home now'? Rebel got a hundred thousand men just down the road one day ride. They got spies going in and out and round about, come right up this road here. Rebel ain't whip yet. But the time going to come."

"How you going to know *when,* knucklehead?"

"You got to *listen* to the damn *news,* Aaron," said Sylvester, exasperated.

"And you the one always be bitching how we don't know nothing," said Aaron.

"When the time come, brother, we going to know enough."

"How?"

"Damn," cried Sylvester. "Félice tell me. She find out things. Listen to the white folk that comes by, I reckon."

"Huh," said Aaron. But he was unwilling to tell Sylvester that he had now seen Félice twice disappearing with Miles Glory into the forest.

Amidst a tumble of white lace and pillows, behind the misty scrim of mosquito netting, Félice lay, naked, reading.

Giovanni Corelli sat in his deep armchair between her bed and the window. He leaned forward as far as he could, but he still could not reach the bell cord. "I am too fat," he said in French.

Without a word, Félice reached through the bed curtains and pulled it for him.

Caleb appeared, and bowed.

Corelli tapped the empty pitcher. Caleb took it, withdrew, and after a moment returned it replenished. Corelli nodded thanks and dismissal.

"You would like a taste?" he asked.

"You are kind, but no, thank you," she replied—calling him *tu*. Félice addressed her master in the familiar only after they had made love, and therefore infrequently. He did not know whether to like or to resent it. "You drink too much tonight," she said.

"Yes, too much," said Corelli.

"You are unhappy?"

"I am sad."

"For what? Tell me."

"I am thinking. I will be alone," said Corelli. "You will leave me. Which I will accept. I will want what is best for you. And then I will be alone."

"But your family," said Félice—"will they not come to America when the war is over?"

"You accept then that the South will lose."

"Ah!" she shrugged, with an ambiguous smile. "Your wife, at least?"

"My wife makes love to the cardinal," said Corelli bitterly.

Félice laughed. "In New Orleans, always, the cardinal is a pederast."

"My *son* is a pederast."

"Oh, blue heaven!" cried Félice, laughing harder. "And your daughter, she is a, a—"

"Annamaria is a nun."

"Marvelous!" cried Félice, and after a moment of consultation with his outraged dignity, Giovanni Corelli was laughing too. He laughed until he cried.

Félice slipped down from the bed and curled up in his lap. She kissed the tears on his cheek. Unlacing his night shirt, she kissed the gray hair on his chest, and down the long curve of his belly.

"I can't," he said, the tears starting again. "It's too soon. I drink too much. I am too old."

"That's all right," she said. "It feels good in any case, no?"

"I don't know. No. I'm embarrassed. Please, Félice, stop."

But she would not stop.

As the Yankees continued to pour into Tennessee, Forrest's strategic wizardry served him well. Horse after horse was shot from beneath him, but he never showed fear. He was toasted, whispered after, a legend all over the South. When it was rumored that he was going to come home to recapture Memphis, the citizens passed one another in the streets with secret smiles. Children played king-of-the-hill and proclaimed themselves General Forrest. But by his military superiors Forrest's advice remained largely unheeded, and his status among them remained, at best, that of an admired eccentric.

By the fourth of July, Vicksburg had fallen, and the Mississippi River was now under Union control from source to mouth. The South was broken in two. Federal troops began massing in eastern Tennessee to drive into Georgia and thus to break the Confederacy in three.

At Chickamauga the Union dead lay thicker on the ground than at any other battle of the war. Over six thousand Yankee soldiers died in two days. So did four thousand Southerners, but the Confederacy was now so beleaguered that that grisly slaughter was widely considered a Rebel victory.

Meanwhile, Forrest came home to Mississippi and began to recruit, from scratch, still another command. His plan was to get across the railroad east of Memphis and prowl around in occupied territory gathering up the oppressed and defiant. What he found were mostly deserters, more scared and hungry than defiant. He also decided, for the first time, to recruit Negroes, not as fighters—that would have been too much—but to serve his men and free them for fighting. Forrest's parties offered every able-bodied man they came across, white or black, the choice of volunteering for service or being involuntarily conscripted. Pretty soon he had five thousand men.

The Union authorities got wind of all this and sent out expeditions from the north, south, east, and west to chase down Forrest and his sorry new lot, most of them still unarmed. The first waves of Yankees were small, and Forrest's encounters with them not over-costly, but he knew that serious trouble was not far behind. He was going to have to make a run for it.

Federal troops slept all night on the cars of the Memphis and Charleston railroad, ready at a moment's notice to race toward the point where Forrest and his men should try to pass. But the Rebels found a bridge over the Wolf River only half burned, and across it in the middle of a freezing, rainy night, with some forty wagon-loads of commandeered supplies, two hundred beef cattle, and three hundred hogs, the Forrest brigade made its escape into Mississippi.

"I tell you, Giovanni," said Forrest, "I done had me some close calls lately. But you know, I enjoy it. I hate these god-damned muckamuck gentlemen generals worse than ever, but the son of a bitches can't keep me down. President Jeff Davis, his own self, he just made me a major general, Giovanni. How about that?"

"I drink you, my friend!" cried Corelli. "One hundred years!"

"In a hundred years, Giovanni, the niggers is going to be digging up our bones and pissing in the grave hole."

Sylvester found A. J. Wordlaw shuffling back and forth in front of his shanty in the woods, smoking a fat cigar and wearing a dove-gray tail coat that looked distinctly like the master's. It was seven o'clock in the morning, just getting light, and well below freezing, but A. J.'s face was red and sweating. Unmistakably, he was drunk.

"So, Sylvester, old buddy, what's for breakfast?"

"Got one egg, A. J., and a apple."

A. J. snatched the egg, cracked it deftly, and sucked it down raw. Then he reached back into the shanty and pulled out a jug of whiskey, with the initials "G. C." painted on it in blue. He took a hard pull and dangled the jug at Sylvester. "Want drink?"

Sylvester shook his head no. "Thanky kindly."

"Haw!" snorted A. J. "I wasn't going to give you none nohow. You think I want to drink after the like of you? Let me have that apple." From beneath Giovanni Corelli's gray coat A. J. produced a knife—Sylvester's Indian knife!—and began to peel the apple. There was a smear, surely of blood, on the blade.

"You in trouble, ain't you," said Sylvester.

"Fuck. Got to get my ass out of here," said A. J. "See my woman and kids. Getting too damn cold, Sylvester. Six months living like a animal about enough."

"How you get in that manor house?" Sylvester demanded.

"A. J. Wordlaw gets around, boy!" said A. J., sweat pouring down his flaming face, his eyes jerking wildly. "I been looking in them windows for months. I growed up hunting, Sylvester. You got to just lay quiet and wait for your shot. Last evening, I seen your piece-of-shit old fat dago in there with that ugly-looking black-haired sumbitch that was visiting, both of them drunk as a cooter duck. Your yellow gal goes on to bed, off down that long hall nice and out the way. Then sure enough, after while they pass out. That's my shot."

"You knows who that white man be, don't you?" said Sylvester. "That General Nathan Bedford Forrest."

"Naw!" gasped A. J.

"Yes, *sir*," Sylvester assured him.

"Christ almighty on a hickory crutch."

"What about the house servant folk?" said Sylvester. "House full of them."

"Hell, I know who all of them is. That old mammy, she sleeps like a dead rock. That string bean old darky that waits on your master, he's deaf. Them two little kitchen maids was down in the quarters with their menfolk—getting cornholed, I expect. That big fat old white boy sleep next the kitchen, he was snoring so loud he couldn't heared a bomb go off. Only trouble come right at the end, some damn nigger I ain't never seen before. Come busting out of nowheres hollering like a damn woman."

"That were General Forrest own valet."

"Fuck if it was! Well, I didn't hurt him. I just had to *discourage* him. Had me all my supplies laid in." A. J. started walking back and forth again, wringing his hands.

Sylvester pondered the situation for a moment in silence.

A. J. sectioned the apple, and took another pull on the whiskey jug. "I'm going to be moving on today," he said, sputtering apple bits. "I'm much obliged to ye, Sylvester. You done kept me from starving." He offered Sylvester his filthy, sticky, trembling hand.

"A. J.," said Sylvester, "I is going to ask you for something now. That my knife you got. Master stoled it from me. I wants it back."

"The hell you say," said A. J. blandly.

"When you finded me, here, that day, with my sweetheart, you had me in trouble, and you taken advantage of me. Now appear like I might be have you in trouble. I mean, you is a deserter, and now you is a robber too, and I don't even know what else but I bet it *something* else."

"Mought just sooner stick you too," muttered A. J., fumbling at the tail coat.

A. J. was too drunk to react when Sylvester sprang forward and wrenched his arm up behind him. "I wants that knife, white man."

"Shit fire! Let go, Sylvester! Damn. All right, all right. Take the sumbitch. Just don't break my damn arm. I need that arm." Sylvester released him with a shove.

"Thanky kindly, A. J.," said Sylvester.

"We got us a deal, ain't we?" panted A. J. "You don't know nothing, all right? Just like I don't know nothing. All right?"

"All right."

"Nathan Bedford Forrest?"

"He own self," said Sylvester. "Where you going to go?"

"Dog if I know. Keep out of that maniac's way, for one. Reckon I ain't going home no more. Mought just slide on up in Tennessee somewhere where it's more peacefuller."

A. J. Wordlaw gathered up his croker sack—clanking and bulging with God knew what—and staggered off into the forest.

By the time Sylvester reached home, Corelli plantation was in an uproar. "Damn, brother," whispered Aaron, "if you ain't just in time. Mr. Joe say Mr. Bedford want to see everybody on the place. We got to go up in the front yard. Say somebody done been stob."

"I know," said Sylvester.

Aaron's eyes were bugging out. Sylvester looked down, and realized that Aaron was staring at his Indian knife, in its scabbard on his belt. "You better put that thing *away,*" said Aaron.

"Yeah," said Sylvester with a quick sly grin, slipping the knife into its old hiding place behind a loose wall board. "I got it back. But no, Aaron, I ain't stob nobody."

Forrest appeared on the front gallery, and the crowd below fell silent. Then came Giovanni Corelli, pale and solemn. "My valet Jerome has been stabbed," said Forrest, "and he's hurt right bad. Any of y'all done this," he roared, "come forward now and take your punishment. Fail to come forward, and I will hunt you down and nail you to a wall and peel off your skin like the Indians use to done. Doubt me? Try me." He said no more, but his terrible eyes searched from face to brown face.

The little kitchen maid named Mattie half raised her hand. "Mr. Bedford, Mr. Bedford," she cried softly.

"Speak up, child," boomed Forrest.

Isabel came up the steps with Mattie, holding her hand. At first neither of them could speak.

"We seen somebody, Mr. Bedford, leaving out last night," said Mattie hesitantly. "Please don't whip us, marse—we wasn't where we supposed to be."

"I ain't going to whip you," said Forrest.

"We seen a white man with a big croker sack," said Mattie.

"Leave out the house and run in the woods," added Isabel.

"White man," repeated Forrest. "You wouldn't be covering up for your buck, now, would you, child?"

"No, *sir*, *no*, sir," said the girls in canon.

"Any of y'all know who that white man was," said Forrest to the assembled slaves, "come forward now and I give you twenty dollars gold." He held up a U.S. double eagle.

"*Damn*, Sylvester," hissed Aaron.

"Hush," said Sylvester through his teeth.

Mary Montgomery Forrest, though she had managed to get out of Memphis before the Yankee conquest, still declined to reside in what her husband insisted was her proper home, and the overseer had gone to war, so there was not one white person in residence at Greengrove plantation. Theo lurched down the lawn on unsteady legs, a week's white stubble frosting his jowls, a surmise of terror in his bloodshot eyes. "Mr. Bedford? Is that you?"

"Who the hell you think it is?" replied the general. "Santy Claus?"

"Didn't nobody tell us you was coming."

"That's right, Theo. I wanted to see for myself how y'all was getting along."

"Yes, sir. We all right."

"Reckon not doing no work agrees with you," said Forrest. "God almighty. Look at this place."

"We been waiting for the weather to warm up before we paints the house," said Theo, wringing his hat.

"Wasn't warm enough all summer and fall?"

"We was making cotton, Mr. Bedford," pleaded Theo.

"Huh," said Forrest. "I seen the factor's accounts. You made damn little."

"Yes, sir. Them boys we sended up to Memphis last year, most of them stay up there when the Yankee come."

"Well, we going to get them back this year. We going to go round them up ourselves. You coming too, Theo. Listen. We going to just shut this place down. Y'all ain't exactly accomplishing too much nohow. Get you some boys and board the house and buildings up. Just leave enough for the women and the children. Herd up the livestock, and get me all your able-bodied men ready to travel. I got colored soldiers now."

Theo looked as if his hair, if he'd had any, would have straightened out and stood on end. "Is that a fact!"

"That's a actual fact, my friend," said Forrest. "They don't fight. They serve. And we're right proud to have them. Now. Where's that girl Cherry?"

"She up in the house, I reckon," said Theo, rubbing his hat back and forth across his pate. "Colored soldiers. My, oh, my."

Forrest found Charity asleep, with one arm thrown back over her head, her mouth slightly open. Hearing the door but not waking, she tucked her chin down toward her shoulder, smiled, and sighed. Forrest took a stool and sat beside her cot to watch her, a portrait of calm and contentment. After a few minutes he gave a gentle cough.

Charity twitched, gasped, opened her eyes on him, and—screamed.

He took her hands, and softly said, "Hush, gal. Hush. You all right. It's only me—Mr. Bedford."

"Yes, sir," said Charity, trembling. "Just you give me a fright."

"You all right, child? Them wild niggers down the quarters ain't giving you no trouble?"

"Yes, sir, I mean, no, sir," stammered Charity. "Us house folk just stays up here in the house, quiet as a mouse. Everything fine."

"Cherry, listen," said Forrest. "We going to close up the house. You going to come with me. I need somebody to take care of me.

Jerome got stabbed. He ain't dead, but he's septic, so he can't travel."

"Lord have mercy!" she gasped.

"I wish he did, but he don't. I can guarantee you that. Listen, Cherry—naw, now, don't cry." It did not occur to Forrest that what Charity was crying about was having to go away with him.

There was consternation in the quarters, too. "Huh!" grunted Ice Pick. "Want us to come and fight for the sake of him owning *slaves?* We suppose to go *die* for our *right* to be *chattel?*"

Elmo, Drury, and Jackson all nodded agreement, but none of them had anything to suggest. Sissy, the upstairs maid and Drury's sweetheart, came rushing in, crying. It wasn't just losing Drury that had her upset; the master was taking away her best friend, Cherry.

"That do it!" bellowed Ice Pick. "We got to light. Going to get that sweet gal and light."

"Can I bring Sissy?" asked Drury sheepishly.

"Hell, yes!" cried Ice Pick. "We going to Memphis! Going to be free! Jackson?" Jackson was Drury's brother.

"Right here with you, bud," he replied.

"Last chance, Elmo," said Ice Pick. "We got to move."

"Shit," drawled Elmo. "Choice of shot by a Yankee or shot by my own master. Might as well get shot by the one that's again me."

"Sissy?" said Ice Pick. "Can you get Cherry out the house?"

"I try, Ice," she said, "but I scared."

"I know you is, baby. Go on."

Sissy returned quickly. Charity had left two hours ago, in the company of Forrest, who was headed for Seven Pines plantation to round up more Negro recruits.

"Well, childrens," said Ice Pick, "look like we got to go get her."

"You *crazy!*" cried Elmo.

"He didn't bring no soldiers, did he? It ain't but him. Four to one? That ain't good enough odds for you?"

"Don't he got a gun?" asked Drury.

"I bet he don't got he house pistol," said Ice Pick.

"Theo got the house pistol," said Sissy. "Down by the gate."

"I ain't scared of that nigger," proclaimed Ice Pick. "Listen. Y'all stuff you a blanket and all what you think you can carry fast in a poke and be back here in two shake."

Through the mobilization's hurly-burly of hammering, sawing, mule shoeing, packing, and tearful goodbyes, Ice Pick, Drury, Jackson, Elmo, and Sissy moved in an intent phalanx.

"Give me that pistol, Theo," Ice Pick said when they reached the gate and its guardian.

"You know I can't do that," said Theo. "Y'all get on back."

"We lighting, man," said Ice Pick. "You want to come with us?"

"Don't come no closer, Ice."

"Give me that pistol, Theo."

Theo raised it with both hands.

"You ain't going to shoot me," said Ice Pick.

"Don't try—"

Theo never finished his sentence. Ice Pick had feinted right, fallen to his knees, and jammed his ice pick upward beneath Theo's rib cage.

"Oh, shit," said Elmo. "I knowed there was trouble going to happen, but I surely didn't think it were going to be so soon. We ain't even out the gate, and you go killing peoples."

"Got us a pistol!" cried Ice Pick, his eyes aflame. "Now let's go get Cherry. Come on, childrens. We going to Memphis."

Theo lay dying on the ground, blood bubbling through his lips.

They spent the night in a bayou bottom, hard by the bridge that Forrest would have to cross on his way back to Oxford. The rain and the cold and their mounting fear discouraged everyone except Ice Pick, whom they merely made mad.

The morning passed very slowly.

"Yonder they come," whispered Jackson. "Just the two."

They waited until Forrest's horse clattered onto the bridge. Then Sissy sprang out of the canebrake back down the road to seize Charity's reins while Jackson blocked the bridge and grabbed Forrest's bridle. Drury, because he was the biggest, raced up behind and pulled Forrest's foot out of the stirrup, gave it a violent wrench, and hurled him into the water. Elmo got Forrest's arms pinned back while Ice

Pick waded in after them and set the pistol just below the point of Forrest's chin.

Charity was screaming. Forrest made not a sound but his stertorous breathing.

They tied him tight to a tree on the side of the road where his troops could not fail to see him when they came.

"All we wants is the gal, marse," said Ice Pick. "I ain't going to kill you."

"You going to wish you had," said Forrest.

Ice Pick, Elmo, Jackson, Drury, Sissy, and Charity waded deep into the cypress swamp so that no one could track them. There they waited until late that night, after the moon had set. Then—Ice Pick and Cherry on Forrest's charger, Drury and Sissy on the other horse, Jackson and Elmo on foot—they hurried across the fields toward the long narrow strip of woodland that clung to the ancient and now inland east bank of the Mississippi. It was going to be thorn-choked, mud-slick going, but these densely forested cliffs and ravines provided the only unbroken cover all the fifty miles north to Memphis.

When the refugees reached the Union fortifications at the state line, the Yankees were much amused to be presented with Nathan Bedford Forrest's own horse as well as a map and several military telegrams from his saddle bags. The refugees' firearms—the Greengrove house pistol, Forrest's revolver, and his silver derringer—were seized, and each of the six ex-slaves was presented with a certificate of manumission. Then they were marched to a vast shanty town stinking of human waste and surrounded by a high palisade. Soldiers pushed them through the gate and locked it behind them.

1864

"Let's us see now, Mr. Louie," said Miles Glory. "Two sack flour. Five tub lard. Two side of bacon. Sixteen gallon lamp oil. Master still want that pound of coffee? She don't come cheap, Mr. Louie, but I got her, come all the way from Brazil South America. I don't do this kind of personal traveling and deliverance much no more, you know. I is a boxcar-load-at-the-time man now. I just comes here for the sentimental pleasurement, visiting the humble scene of my youth. Does you know that President Abraham Lincoln hisself growed up in a log cabin? That's a natural fact. Oh, and dog if I ain't almost forgot! Looky here, Mr. Louie. I done brung you a lagniappe."

Miles reached into the box and came up with a bottle of golden-green—could it be?—*olive oil!* And before Luigi could expel the deep gasp which the mere sight of that elixir had caused him to draw, Miles had reached in again and come up with a five-pound pine-wood box of genuine Italian macaroni.

"Abraham Lincoln is Yankee," whined Luigi.

"Let me write that down," said Miles, examining the ruby-studded head of his gold toothpick and not quite grinning. "You is so right, Mr. Louie."

"*You* no can write, you."

"Modern man like me full of surprises," said Miles, replacing his toothpick in his mouth and mildly regarding the ceiling. "World is changing. I might can write better than you think, Mr. Louie."

"How much then this oil and pasta?" demanded Luigi.

"Comes right dear, I gots to confess," said Miles. "Them noodle done took six month coming here, Mr. Louie, cross the ocean sea."

Although both Yankees and Rebels continued to die in gruesome thousands, the war seemed to have reached a stalemate. It was certain now that the South would not win, but what might come of its defeat Sylvester could not begin to foresee. Even at the best—freedom, self-sufficiency, a farm of his own, a whole new life—his prospects filled him with unease. Free, like a wild bird at last uncaged, would Félice not fly away from him?

He was building her a rocking chair. When he imagined her sitting in it on the front porch of the little cabin he would build for her, looking out across the little farm he would work for her, and himself in a chair identical, rocking in time with her own, Sylvester felt self-contempt rising from somewhere dark within him. Who you think you fooling? this inner voice demanded. She ain't studying no dirt farm. She studying Paris France.

"You keep bearing down on that lathe like that there, Sylvester," said Uncle Dunc, his big lower lip stuck out wryly, "you ain't going to have a damn toothpick left."

"Yonder go Drury," said Miles Glory. "Ice Pick friend Drury."

"Where go he?" demanded Aaron. The minute Aaron had heard of Charity's escape to freedom, he had lit out for Memphis himself, without even telling Sylvester. Grim weeks had passed. He was very tired, and hungry.

"That big ugly blue-black nigger limping yonder."

"Say!" called Aaron, pushing toward the big man. "You, hey, there, Mr. Drury! Say!"

"What you want with Drury, boy?" said Drury, suspicious. Memphis was not a safe place.

"Yes, sir, I don't want but to visit with you one little minute. I is looking for a girl name Charity. Cherry, they calls her."

"She ain't here," grunted Drury. "I don't know her."

"You friend they calls Ice Pick, sir, from down Greengrove plantation? You think Mr. Ice Pick might know where she at?"

"That man you say, he ain't no friend of mine," said Drury. "He in the stockade block. You go ahead on try talk to him—buckra Yank going to arrest you for conspiracy, robbery, rape, and botherment. Ain't but walk down the street mind my own business, go down talk to that man you say, next thing I know my head stove in and my leg broke, bunch of white mens standing round laughing. Go ahead on try talk to that man you say. Never mind find no gal."

"I can't understand what you saying," said Aaron.

"You Ice Pick friend, Yankee don't care to know nothing else. They going to take you and they going to break you, and that's the end of you talking and the end of you finding no gal."

"Ice Pick he didn't say nothing about Miss Charity? Please, sir. I been looking for her ever so long."

"All kind of peoples looking for some gal. Some says the Yankee done took a bunch of them Mississippi country gal up the river where that fort be at—Pillow," said Drury. "Army camp. All kind of nigger up yonder."

"How you get there?" demanded Aaron, his heart surging.

"Boy, how you get anywheres if you black? Try walk down the street, Yankee going to cobble you up. Never mind no Fort Pillow. They's some us goes in the Yankee army, folks says. That's what up yonder, country boys from all round about, fighting in the army. Least that what some folks says. You can't trust nothing nor nobody here."

"Ain't but other day, I walk up Beale Street with this here tar crew the Yankee been working me on?" said Aaron, "and two white ladies *spit* on me. Memphis Reb white ladies, all dress up like go to church. They wasn't no Yankee."

"Can you kill, boy?"

"I don't know, Mr. Drury. Ain't never yet."

"You didn't never know a gal name Sissy, come up from Greengrove with the rest of us. She was my gal. White man took her."

"Yank or Reb?" asked Aaron.

"I can't tell the difference."

"I going to join that Yankee army, Mr. Drury," said Aaron, "and go on up to that Fort Pillow, and find me my sweetheart gal, and get me a repeat rifle."

"And can't even get down Beale Street without they spit on you," said Drury. *"Huh."*

"You watch. Miles Glory he going to fix it for me right up brown. Miles know every Yankee in Memphis."

"Miles Glory, *huh.*"

"That's all right," said Aaron. "I know he ain't no prize for decent, but say what you want, that's a man that know freedom."

"Time going to come," said Drury. "Black folk going to rise. Ain't going to need no zambo slick."

"I about tired of this sure enough," said Aaron. "I been looking for freedom, and they ain't give me but emancipation, that look about like slavery."

"Emancipation, *huh*," said Drury.

"Just like you says, sir," said Aaron. "Time going to come."

But Charity was not at Fort Pillow. And once he'd gotten in, and been issued not a repeating rifle but a pitchfork, Aaron could not get out.

One sultry April evening early, Andrew Jackson Wordlaw was strolling toward the village of Brownsville, Tennessee, minding his own business and whistling a little tune, not more than half drunk, when the thunder of hundreds of hooves began to shake the mud beneath his feet. He stood stock-still and bug-eyed, squishing gumbo up between his toes, as a torrent of Confederate cavalrymen came pouring over the rise and engulfed him.

A big, bad-looking Rebel with a thick black beard, long black hair, and cold gray eyes pulled up in front of A. J. Wordlaw and got down from his big black horse. "Your drinking days is over, bubba," the man said. "You in the army now."

"The hell you say," said A. J. This Reb didn't look like much—uniform filthy and torn, boot soles flapping. "I am official exempt by reason of personal injury, gained in service to the Confederacy." A. J. exhibited his mangled forefinger and thumb. "Who the hell you think you are?"

Quicker than a frog's tongue the big Reb's left hand flew out and snatched a hard hold of A. J. Wordlaw's shirt and, pulling him close, ripped it wide open. "I am General Nathan Bedford Forrest, bubba."

"Naw."

"And you have just joint my cavalry."

"Naw."

"And you going to start by shoveling shit for my niggers."

"I'm going to start by going home to bed and trying to wake up from this here bad dream," retorted Wordlaw.

Forrest's hand seized A. J. Wordlaw's shoulder in his famous nerve-lock. Pain of an intensity A. J. had never before experienced radiated through his body, and he fell to the ground. "Sergeant Riley," said Forrest, "take this buzzard bait and sign him in and give him a shovel, and put him digging the nigger latrines, and watch him close. If he keeps on having these here kind of problems with his mouth, just go on and shoot him and we'll feed him to them Mississippi River gar fish when we get to Pillow. And once we do get there, if you ain't shot him yet, give him a shotgun and put him in the front wave."

At Fort Pillow there were garrisoned some five hundred fifty Union troops—a few real Yankee officers, and the rest roughly equally divided between locally conscripted whites and refugee Negroes like Aaron. There were also a number of civilians in service there, both black and white, mostly women, some with children.

Sergeant Otto Riley could hardly wait to get hold of the white Tennesseeans. "Them kind of white men," he snarled, "they wouldn't hardly be worth the powder but for the pleasure it's going to give me to kill them."

Riley was an old hand, a hard-core Reb, but A. J. Wordlaw knew perfectly well that but for the random depredations of Forrest's "recruiting" squads in West Tennessee, many of Forrest's men might just as readily have wound up inside the ramparts at Pillow in service to the Yankees. A. J. himself had barely eluded half a dozen of their conscription sweeps around Brownsville. Thus the enthusiasm of his fellows-in-arms mystified A. J. Wordlaw.

"How many boys we got, Mr. Riley?" he asked, trying to figure how easily he could get lost in the crowd once the shooting started.

"Time General Forrest and his bunch catch us up, we going to have fifteen hundred," declared the sergeant. "We going to do us some *killing* tomorrow morning."

"Daff Godth own troof, tharge," put in a toothless Reb nearby.

"Y'all got your loads right, ain't ye?" demanded Riley.

"Thee buck and a ball, juff like you fay," said the private—three buckshot and a minie ball, a combination that produced a wound so jagged and gaping it looked more like the work of an axe.

"Going to kill us some *niggers,*" said Otto Riley in glee.

These here sumbitches are insane, said A. J. Wordlaw to himself.

The sharpshooter teams left camp before dawn. By the time the regulars brought up the rear, the riflemen had chased the first line of Yankee defenders from the outlying sapper pits, and Rebel cannon fire had demolished most of the barracks and storehouses outside the fortifications.

By midmorning the fort was already surrounded on the north, east, and south. On the west side, in the river, lay a mighty Union gunboat, but it couldn't seem to shoot straight. For the decisive attack now, Forrest hatched a typically original plan. A wave of men were to run flat out across the open ground while the artillery and sharpshooters kept the Yankees busy, and then, without firing a shot, they were to dive into a ditch at the base of a defensive earthwork—so close that they would be out of the line of all possible fire. At a signal, then, they were to storm the fort, over the top of the rampart, and to take it by sudden assault and hand-to-hand fighting.

Forrest believed that such an assault needed only to be threatened, not carried out, because once the Rebel troops had taken the ditch the Yankees' position would be so utterly hopeless that they would have no choice but surrender.

Sergeant Riley thrust a decrepit shotgun into A. J.'s hands as the bugles blew, and pushed him into the charge.

Somehow—mainly by crouching low and keeping close behind big men (two of whom were shot dead within their first couple of seconds out of the trees), and astonishing himself by keeping his pants dry—A. J. Wordlaw survived his sixty-yard journey to the wall of Fort Pillow. And sure enough, the earthwork was so broad at the top that the Yankee cannons couldn't tip down far enough to shoot at the Rebels in the ditch. Nor could the Federal riflemen shoot downward without exposing themselves to Confederate fire.

When the ammunition wagons arrived from the rear, there was going to be a white flag raised, and under its protection General Forrest was going to send a demand for surrender, and then pretty soon they could all go back to camp.

There was another volley of Southern artillery, and a peppering of rifle fire. A dozen mounted Rebel troops—Forrest Rangers, their best and bravest—swept past the last barracks row that remained undestroyed outside the fort walls, shooting into the windows. The few Yankees hidden within raced for the trees, and the horsemen ran them down, slashing them with their sabres or shooting them in the back. Not one made it to cover.

Big guns boomed from the Yankee boat beyond the fort in the river, and still the shells fell wide. One Union soldier atop the rampart braved the Rebel rifle coverage and put a ball straight into the face of a Forrest Ranger, and the trooper's head blew up like a dropped watermelon, spewing gore in all directions. The headless body somersaulted backward off its galloping gray horse. A piece of hot slop hit A. J. Wordlaw square in the face.

Again the countryside was silent, and the waiting resumed.

I be dog if I'm going to set in here all day like a damn puddle duck waiting for some dumb piece of shit to get smart and drop a brick on my head, thought A. J. Wordlaw. The nearest of the shot-out barracks, well outside the fort walls, was only a short sprint away, and before Riley could notice, A. J. was out of the ditch, across the grass, and in the door.

And oh, Lord God! A dead nigger. Grinning like a fool, still sitting upright on a stool at the window, with a neat black hole in his forehead.

The problem for A. J. now was deciding whether the man had been drinking from the jug that stood uncorked on the bench next to him, and if so whether he could bring himself to drink after a dead nigger.

"How many Reb you reckon down in that ditch?" wondered the big man at Aaron's side.

"More them than us," said Aaron quietly. There were also Rebel cannons visible among the trees on the high ground, and lines of Rebel sharpshooters. The gunboat in the river had spent nearly all its ammunition. Aaron had gotten his repeating rifle at last, this morning, but now he wished he hadn't. He wished he was back home in Mississippi, in bondage.

"Say ain't nobody seen Mr. Bedford yet," said the big man.

"Why you calls that man so familiar?" asked Aaron.

"I done work that man farm near about ten year. Lit out from Greengrove ain't but six month back."

"*Greengrove* you say!" exclaimed Aaron. "What you name, brother?"

"Name Andrew Jackson, but they always calls me Jackson."

"You know that man Ice Pick, and that man Drury? You know that gal Charity, that they calls Cherry?"

"Know them? Hell, boy, they's who I lit out with. Me and Drury is brothers."

"You knows Cherry! You know where she at? My name Aaron."

"No, son, she was here, but I think she goed back to Memphis. Heared tell a white man got her down yonder."

"I been looking for her."

"I don't reckon you going to be doing much more looking after today," said Jackson, "less you lucky enough to be looking at the paling of the Reb prison camp. More likely all us be dead."

—·❧·—

A party of Confederate soldiers under a white flag marched to the gate of Fort Pillow and handed over an envelope containing Forrest's demand for unconditional surrender.

The Union commander turned to his aide-de-camp and said, "I don't care if the last man jack of us dies. I'm going to kill that son of a bitch. Break out the whiskey." He wrote out his reply to Forrest: "I will not surrender."

"Well," said Forrest, "I guess we got to kill us some Yanks."

Many of the black soldiers had had little experience of liquor; Aaron had had none at all. But they found that it did serve to fortify their courage. When the Rebs came pouring over the wall, most of the defenders of Fort Pillow surged forward to meet them.

Aaron's rifle jammed at the first shot. He threw it down and took cover behind a water barrel.

Individual shots could not be discerned: the sound of rifle fire was a continuous roar. The Rebs kept coming, climbing up on the backs of their fellows below. Within two minutes a hundred Union men were dead, and still the Confederates came over the wall.

In panic the Federals turned and ran for the river, screaming for the gunboat to drive the onslaught back. But the Rebels were already in amidst them, and the cannons, therefore, were useless.

Drunk, without hope, men threw up their hands and begged for mercy, and, with rifles, shotguns, pistols, swords, bayonets, and knives, the Rebels cut them down.

The door of the barracks house flew open. "I just mought a knowed," said Sergeant Otto Riley. He took the jug and threw it against the wall, where it shattered, drenching the grinning face of the dead Negro. Riley picked up A. J. Wordlaw's shotgun and knocked the dirt out of the barrels.

"Afternoon, Sergeant," said A. J. "That's a waste of good whiskey."

"You was a waste of good vittles," said Riley, propelling him outside.

Men were still going over the wall, and the racket from within the fort was fearful.

"You ready to die, bubba?" asked Riley.

"Shit," said A. J. Wordlaw, with a grin. "I reckon so."

Riley grinned back, and handed him the shotgun.

Men in the ditch grabbed A. J. and boosted him to the top of the parapet. What he saw from there brought back his wooziness. It wasn't the heaps of the dead that were so bad, it was the injured—bleeding, moaning, pleading, reaching out toward him.

He had two shots in the breech and five more shells in his pocket. No sense wasting good ammunition on sumbitches that can't shoot back, A. J. Wordlaw said to himself, and so took his shotgun by the barrel and started smashing in the wounded men's heads with the steel-clad butt.

Aaron and Jackson were among the mass of men who fled in panic toward the river. The rear of the fort was crowded with the tents of the Negro troops, and the avenues of escape between them were narrow. As the Union men jostled through, the Confederate sharpshooters on the ramparts were able to bring down at least half of them. The bluff was thick with stumps and down trees—left there in a tangle intentionally, to obstruct possible attack from the river—and here, too, many men fell. Most of the Federal soldiers who made it alive down the bluff just kept running, into the water, and were swept away on the churning spring current, and many of these were shot, and many drowned. Aaron and Jackson and others who could not swim tried to make an escape upstream along the bank at the foot of the bluff, but as they neared the mouth of Coal Creek and what they hoped would be cover there, they ran straight into a horde of Rebels, who gave a yell and opened fire. Somehow Aaron was not shot, but he did not see Jackson any more. Someone shouted that there was a swamp below the fort, so Aaron and the others still ambulatory ran back downstream, but again they met Rebels, and another fusillade. Again Aaron, somehow, survived.

The two armies were now so thoroughly mingled along the riverside that the fighting was all hand-to-hand. Aaron stumbled through the midst of it, crying, half blinded, up the blood-slick bluff through the stumps and the corpses and back into the fort. He saw a hospital tent not burning, and plunged inside.

The six sick or wounded men there had been killed, and still lay in their beds. Aaron pulled a blood-soaked blue blanket off one body, rolled up in it, and took refuge under a bunk.

"In here, in here," he heard a white man's voice saying, and then he heard something fall heavily into the tent, and footsteps behind it. He held his breath. "Give me one of them nails," said the white man's voice.

Aaron peeked—and beheld the swollen face of Jackson on the floor. His left eye had been gouged out, and blood was oozing from the socket. A white man was driving a nail through Jackson's hand. Another white man held a bayonet to the back of his neck, and a third was sloshing coal oil from a bucket onto the beds. Jackson gave a soft groan then, and died.

It was quiet now. Aaron rolled out of the bloody blue blanket and out from under the far side of the bed. He could see the feet of the three white men gathered around Jackson's body, none of them saying anything. Two of them turned and left. Aaron peeked over the naked corpse in the bed and saw the remaining white man, with the hammer still in his hand. It was the same man he had seen a half-dozen times raiding the garden at Corelli plantation. His shotgun was leaning against the bed. In one motion Aaron seized it, stuck the barrel into the white man's face, and blew his head to pieces.

I can kill now, Mr. Drury. I can kill now.

From beneath the heap of corpses at the river bank where he found shelter until nightfall, Aaron could feel the heat of the burning tents, and smell the roasting of human flesh.

———

The Northern press went wild with news of the carnage at Fort Pillow. In the transcripts of the Congressional hearings that followed, illiterate soldiers seemed to have been speaking in long, ornate, grammatically perfect sentences, so the testimony was certainly less than reliable, but forty thousand copies of the committee's report were distributed, and in the mind of the Union public the name of Nathan Bedford Forrest was thenceforth indissolubly linked with what was now known as the Fort Pillow Massacre.

As far as Forrest himself was concerned, there had been no massacre; this had been merely an exceptionally bloody battle. Its bloodiness, moreover, he maintained, had been provoked by the enemy. As soon as he had mounted the wall of Fort Pillow and seen the slaughter before him, and the Union defenders swarming into the river, Forrest had called out for his troops to cease firing, and, with allowance for an understandable delay in the dissemination of his order amidst the confusion, the Confederates' arms had duly fallen silent. Owing to a leg injury he had received when his horse had been shot, Forrest had left the field early, but he retained full confidence in his officers' report of their subsequent clean-up operations. There were many Union dead, certainly, and it was true that their numbers were very unequally divided between black and white, but Forrest attributed that fact to the inebriation and inexperience of the Negro soldiers. Furthermore, the behavior of both the white and the black Union troops—their weeks of pillaging the countryside, of scaring local womenfolk, their baiting of Forrest's men while the white flag was flying, and, yes, damn it, their *treason* to the Confederacy—had quite naturally invigorated his men's zeal.

Aaron knew perfectly well that there *had* been a massacre at Fort Pillow. He had seen Union soldiers give themselves up to the Rebs, arms raised high, only to be shot down. He had seen civilians—women, children, all but a few of them colored—harried into the river and, as they floundered there, shot. He had seen Jackson mutilated and crucified. He had seen a Yankee officer nailed to the wall of a barracks house, and the building then set afire. He had seen the hospital tents doused with coal oil, and heard the cries of the sick and wounded burning in their beds. He had seen Negroes buried alive.

Jackson's brother Drury found Aaron a place to hide in Memphis.

"Come you out here, Sylvester," called Uncle Dunc softly from the doorway. "Look at this here."

In the velvet black of the mist on the bayou, through the indigo shadows of the oaks along the drive, and even into the stars above the dark shape of the manor house, an infinity of fireflies swirled. "Mercy me," said Sylvester.

"Eighty-some year and I ain't never saw so many lightning bug," said the old man.

"Make me feel strange inside, Uncle Dunc," said Sylvester. "Soft in my heart, like."

"Old folks says back in Africa this a sign and a portent good time coming."

"I don't believe in no sign and portents," said Sylvester.

"That's all right," said Uncle Dunc. "They don't care whether you believe in them or not."

The moon swelled green through the cypress tops, and a whip-poorwill called.

"That's all right," Uncle Dunc repeated in a whisper, peering into the darkness.

Horses snuffled and stirred in the corner of their pasture down by the plantation gate, and the little dog who liked to stay with them, Pearly Bell, gave a single sharp bark, her greeting call. A figure of a man appeared amidst the fireflies, hobbling up the drive step by slow step through dim pools of moonlight, leaning on a stick, with Pearly Bell frisking around his feet.

"Damn if that don't look like that old Indian man Tatholah," said Uncle Dunc. "Miles Glory daddy, don't you know."

"How you know who that be?" demanded Sylvester. "It dark as coal down yonder."

"Sylvester, you learns to see things with another kind of sight when you gets old like me. Plus I eats lots of carrot. Carrot make you see good in the dark."

"I ain't never heared such a bunch of hooraw as I done hear from you tonight, old man. Sign and portents, seeing in the dark, Africa, I don't know what all."

"That's all right," said Uncle Dunc. "Just bide till that old man get up here."

"Hello," said Tatholah, raising his right hand.

"Howdy do," said Sylvester.

"Old man," said Uncle Dunc, "you going to outlive us all."

"No. I come die," said Tatholah.

"Miles Glory ain't here," said Uncle Dunc. "We ain't see him since the winter time."

"I no look him."

And without further parley the Indian trudged toward the path that led upstream into the heart of the forest.

"Pearly Bell, you stay here," said Uncle Dunc. "You go in that swamp, old bear going to eat you up." She cast a longing look at the receding old Indian, but stayed dutifully put.

With Aaron gone and Félice less free, it seemed, to come to their meeting place on Daylight Bayou, Sylvester had recently been spending a lot of time there alone, and he had been thinking about the Indians.

The next morning, Sylvester found Tatholah, as he thought he might, at the old Indian village, sitting stiffly in a corner of a ruined house, with his arms crossed over his chest.

"Morning," said Sylvester, raising his right hand Indian-style.

The old man just stared at him blankly.

"What you doing?" asked Sylvester.

Again, a stare and silence.

"One time, I finded a knife here. Indian knife. You want to see it? I brung it out special this morning."

"This my house," said Tatholah at last.

Sylvester unwrapped the knife and proffered it.

Tatholah looked at it a long time. "This my son knife," he said finally. "One time my knife. I give him. Son kill snake with it, save my life. My son great chief. Many long time ago."

"Is that right? Tell me about that," said Sylvester.

But all the old man replied, turning the knife in his leathery, knobbly hands, was, "You give me."

"Naw, naw, now, I can't do that," said Sylvester. "I finded that knife outright. Tell me about you boy, that chief, all such as that."

"My knife," said Tatholah stubbornly.

"Ain't no such a thing! You better give me my knife back right now."

Tatholah sighed, and handed the knife over, and closed his eyes until Sylvester went away.

The image of Tatholah's ancient, sad eyes closing against him burned through Sylvester's dreams that night amid whirling galaxies of fireflies, shutting Sylvester out of his sight, depriving Sylvester of his only chance to find out what had happened to the Indians and so to know how to keep it from happening to him.

These were glorious days for Nathan Bedford Forrest. His army raged through west Tennessee and up into Kentucky as far as the Ohio River, capturing horses and mules and food, thrilling the white folks, terrifying the Negroes, and scattering flummoxed Yankees in their wake.

The Union command was not amused. Forrest was now in a position to sever the supply lines to Sherman's march on Georgia—a campaign of destruction and terror, with no less an object than to smash the South into final submission.

Again and again, with bigger and bigger forces, the Yankees tried to run Forrest to ground, and again and again he eluded them.

This time they sent eighteen thousand men after him. Forrest was down to five thousand. Leaving half of them at Oxford to give the impression that they were ready to fight, he took the other half around behind the Yankees, north, toward Memphis.

Most of the city's defenders, after all, were down in Mississippi looking for him. It shouldn't be that hard, he reasoned, to get into town and raise a little hell.

It was three o'clock in the morning when Forrest hobbled up the marble steps at Corelli plantation and pounded on the door.

No one answered. He pounded again, long and hard.

Forrest pushed on through and lit the lamp on the mail table. "God almighty, Hattie," he roared, "put that shotgun down!"

"Whoo! Mr. Bedford!" she cried. "You done scare me all to pieces!"

From the shadows emerged Mattie and Isabel, each with a butcher knife, Luigi with a rolling pin, and old Caleb with Giovanni Corelli's derringer.

"Lord have mercy, white man," said Caleb, "we thunk the Yankee done come. You lucky I ain't shot you."

Forrest laughed heartily. "Wouldn't that be honor and glory, though! Where's your master at, old monkey?"

"He sleep in the bed, where you think?" said Caleb.

"I need me a toddy," said Forrest. "You reckon you can rustle something up, governor?"

"I reckon." Caleb shuffled off down the hall.

"You don't look so good, Mr. Bedford," said Hattie. "You all *yellow,* like. You got the jaundice?"

"Lord, what ain't I got, Hattie. Jaundice, boils, toothache, headache, night sweats, shot in the foot. About the onliest relief I can find is putting the scare on some Yanks."

"I can't give you no Yankees, but I can draw you a bath."

"Just a quick one. I'm going to Memphis this morning, Hattie."

Hattie was sponging Forrest's inflamed back while he sipped at a hot tea-and-brandy when Corelli, in a purple silk dressing gown, came waddling in. "Damn, Giovanni, look at you!" boomed Forrest. "You don't watch out, old bud, you going to get fat."

"Bedford, my friend! Eh! It is true, now sometimes we have good oil, and beef—you know the very clever Miles Glory. Garden full of tomatoes, peppers, onions, beans. Eh? I cannot complain."

"Mighty smooth whiskey, too," said Forrest.

"Whiskey, no! *Cognac!*"

"Miss Félice keeping you passable content?"

"Yes," said Corelli shyly. "She sleeps now."

"That's right," returned Forrest with a mirthless smile. "Wouldn't want to disturb the lady. Setting right pretty, ain't you, Giovanni. You know something? I can't even imagine this no more. Well, never mind that. Listen, friend. I need to ask you a favor. Me and my boys are fixing to hit Memphis. If the Yankees kill me, I want you to get Miles Glory to steal my bones and bury them at Greengrove plantation. I want to lay in Mississippi. Rebel ground."

"The Yankees cannot kill you!" cried Corelli.

Forrest ignored this. "I swear that slippery sumbitch could steal the lightning out from underneath the thunder," he said. "Dead Reb oughtn't to trouble him much, in betwixt the Yankees all the time like he is, smuggling out liquor and luxuries. Promise me, Giovanni."

"But, but," sputtered Corelli—

"Listen, man," said Forrest coldly. "Look to me like you done got off pretty light in this war. I'm asking you this one damn thing."

"Yes, my friend," said Corelli, abashed. "I make sure."

"All right then," said Forrest.

"Y'all ready to whip some Yankee butt?" demanded Forrest.

By way of reply his men waved their hats above their heads and gave their fiercest "Yeee-ha!"

Dense fog cloaked the Rebels' approach toward the state line.

"Who goes there?" demanded a Yankee voice.

"A detachment of the Twelfth Missouri Cavalry," came the answer, "with Rebel prisoners."

The Confederate captain's Mississippi drawl sounded distinctly wrong to the Yankee, who replied, "Dismount, and come forward alone on foot."

Instead, the Reb gave his mount a hard spur and charged, leaning down from the saddle, and with his heavy pistol cracked the Yankee over the head.

Waking to see the Rebels bearing down on him, one of the Yankee pickets was quick enough to fire a single shot and alert his comrades.

Now the second line of guards, asleep farther back, were aroused.

With his plan to slip an advance by in silence thus thwarted, the general signaled for his whole force to head north en masse, still as quietly as possible. But the tension and excitement were too much for Forrest's men, and soon the city of Memphis was awakening to Rebel yells and pistol fire.

Forty Rebs rode straight through the front door of the Gayoso House, hollering and laughing and rearing their horses. But General Hurlbut, it seemed, had been sleeping elsewhere that night.

"I reckon there's a sight too many whorehouses in this town to chase the sumbitch down," said the captain.

"I don't mind starting," said one of his boys.

The rest of them were content to parade around the lobby rotunda smashing up the Chinese vases and leaving mud and horse shit on the Persian carpets.

Meanwhile, General Washburn—the capture of whom was to be this mission's grand prize—was warned in the nick of time: as two hundred screaming Rebel troopers poured through his front door, Washburn scrambled out the back, making his escape down the alleyway to Fort Pickering in his underwear.

Soon the third detachment rode in with their report that General Buckland too had slipped the noose, and that the whole Union garrison was now awake and taking up arms. Moreover, several small groups of Rebels had been caught and detained. "Shit fire," said Forrest. "Let's go home."

There were Memphians cheering and waving handkerchiefs all along their line of retreat, but soon there were Yankee troops too, and Forrest's army had to fight hard to reach and cross Nonconnah Creek.

For all their failure to capture the generals, Forrest's Rangers had succeeded in taking a number of other Yankee prisoners, many of them unclothed. They had also taken care to cut the telegraph lines into Mississippi, and so his eighteen thousand Yankee pursuers remained entirely unaware of what had become of their quarry. The best that they had been able to do was chase the remaining half of

Forrest's army out of Oxford and then, to vent their frustration, burn the town.

Under a white flag, Forrest sent back to Washburn a proposal for the exchange of prisoners, a request for clothing for the unclad captives, and a neat package containing the general's purloined dress uniform and Forrest's calling card, inscribed, "With my personal compliments."

Washburn declined the prisoner exchange. He did, however, send the clothes for his men, and within a week he had also dispatched a courier to Forrest bearing a new gray uniform made by Forrest's own tailor in Memphis. It fit perfectly.

Meanwhile the Mississippi expedition, its object gone, withdrew in dismay to Memphis.

And yet had it not, strategically speaking, succeeded? After all, Forrest was not in Alabama, and the Yankee supplies were flowing smoothly toward the annihilation of Georgia.

"The oftener Forrest runs his head against Memphis," Sherman wired Washburn, "the better."

Forrest scored victory after pointless victory as the Confederacy sank toward defeat. But officers rankled under his hard-edged will, and the soldiers never had quite enough to eat, and Forrest's famous daring was, of course, predicated on the death or crippling or disfigurement of many of his own men. Increasingly, his officers protested his orders, second-guessed his strategies, complained to his superiors, talked behind his back. He would turn and see them fall awkwardly silent.

He knew that he should have a bigger command, but Jefferson Davis and the other muckamucks were still prejudiced against him for his coarse English, his slave-dealing past, his low birth.

Worst of all, he could not shake his illness. His foot wound was slowly healing, but the skin infection would not go away. Fever would wash over him in his bed and leave him shivering. His muscles were wasting; his face was skin on skull, yellow, pitted, aflame with boils.

Women could not bear to look at him. His own wife would not come near him.

He requested a leave of absence, and withdrew to Corelli plantation to try to rethink his life. After a long struggle against infection, Jerome had died, but Forrest was well looked after. Hattie made him herbal voodoo poultices, Luigi fed him spaghetti and beefsteaks slathered with olive oil, Giovanni poured him cognac. Félice would stand behind him on the porch and massage his aching shoulders, his neck, the back of his head. Her hard slim fingers raked his hair till he laughed for the pure pleasure of it.

He turned around and looked into her level gaze. "I don't understand you, gal. Time was, not so long ago, you was looking at me like I was a turd in the punchbowl."

"Often I am confused," said Félice softly, looking down across the lawn. Sylvester was bringing the gig up from the stables, and looking hard at her with her hands on Forrest's shoulders.

At the sound of the gig's arrival out front, Caleb appeared on the front porch and, with a quick cool glance at Forrest and Félice, called down to Sylvester, "Boy? You call that gig polished?" By now Félice had taken her hands from the general's shoulders, but she still stood close behind him, uncertain how next to move.

"Ain't no more wax," replied Sylvester dully, not looking at Félice although she vividly felt his attention.

Giovanni Corelli appeared, twirling his gold-headed walking stick. Sylvester helped the master into the buggy and handed him up the reins.

"Bedford," called Corelli, "I go to Horn Lake, to look some mules. You want that I bring you anything I can find there?"

"You find a army, I'll take that," said Forrest grimly. Corelli left, Caleb went back in the house, Sylvester had gone back to the stable yard, and Forrest was alone again with Félice. "The look of that boy don't set right with me," he said.

"He is a very good boy!" Félice protested, warmly, but knew to go no further. "Excuse me, monsieur, but I must go in the kitchen."

Forrest sat frowning for a long while. Finally he rang, mostly just to see who would come.

It was Hattie. He told her to bring him a bottle of cognac.

"Naw, now, Mr. Bedford, you know you don't want no liquor so early in the day."

"I'm in pain, God damn it!"

Meanwhile, seeing Hattie and Forrest occupied there on the front porch, Sylvester slipped around to the kitchen door and softly called Félice to the screen.

"Yes, my love," she said.

"I got to see you," whispered Sylvester. "Today. At the Indian town."

"But Sylvester—"

"Master ain't going to be back till tomorrow. You knows that."

She looked back over her shoulder, to where Mattie and Isabel were craning their necks intently. "It is Forrest—he watches me," she whispered.

"*Please,*" Sylvester hissed through his teeth.

With an impatient sigh she closed her eyes, and said hurriedly, "When he has his supper."

Sylvester watched Félice's lantern dip and flicker through the half bare trees. She nestled familiarly in his embrace, and kissed his neck. "I cannot stay very long," she said, pulling up the now tattered green weskit.

Sylvester stayed her hands. "I just want to know why you all over that nigger-hating white man," he said.

"He tells me," she said simply.

"Bedford Forrest ain't you master. Matter fact, I wonder what you master think about how you treats that man."

"He understands so little," said Félice with a smile. "But who am I to say this? I too understand almost nothing. Do you love me?"

"What the hell you think we talking about, Félice?"

"Make love to me now, Sylvester," she pleaded, brushing his ear with her lips.

In a fury of possession he complied.

And not two hours later Sylvester looked in at the manor house window and saw Félice in the arms of Nathan Bedford Forrest.

—•—

He waited for Forrest in the white folks' outhouse.

Footsteps on the brick walk. Lantern light around the door.

Sylvester sat in the dark holding his Indian knife in both hands, braced against his stomach, ready to plunge forward and up.

The door opened. It was Luigi.

For a long, long moment, panting like an animal at bay, Luigi stared at Sylvester, and Sylvester stared back, stunned, the knife quivering in his hands.

At last Luigi found voice. "*Assassinio!*" he bellowed. "*Omicidio! Uccisione! Aiuto, aiuto, aiutarmi!* Help me! Help me!" The lantern swung wildly in Luigi's upraised hand, but his feet seemed glued to the floor. He all but filled the doorway.

Lights were coming on in the house. Sylvester charged head-on into Luigi, who reeled into the nandina hedge and toppled backward. Sylvester scrambled over him, but Luigi caught at his overalls and he fell. The knife flew into the darkness.

Sylvester looked up to see the unmistakable silhouette of Nathan Bedford Forrest limping hard down the walk, a glittering sabre in his left hand.

With a sharp kick of his free foot into Luigi's groin Sylvester was free. He tore through the blackberry thorns behind the privy, his feet found the path, and, with Pearly Bell yapping happily at his heels, he raced for the swamp.

By blind reckoning he made it to the Indian town and there waded into frigid Daylight Bayou, leaving the little dog whining on the bank.

He knew that the bayou flowed generally north to Nonconnah Creek and that across Nonconnah lay Yankee territory and freedom. But as it curled into the trackless depths of the swamp, Daylight Bayou divided, looped back on itself, spread out in shallow willow-choked ponds, dropped into bottomless kettles, sank through gravel and percolated under quicksand and oozed forth in green-scummed sloughs without discernible current. Streamside briars raked Sylvester's face and fumbling hands. Leeches clung to his ankles. He tripped on a cypress knee and smashed his nose on an overhanging limb.

When dry land came at last, it came so suddenly that Sylvester fell. It was a little crooked hill, four-sided, flat at the top. There was a sickening stench in the air. Too tired even to stand, he crawled to the dry height, curled his body up in a ball, and cried himself to sleep.

When he woke, freezing, at dawn, the first thing Sylvester realized was that he had slept in a circle of stones that bore faint traces of bright-colored paint. The second was that the nauseous smell in the air was that of the corpse of Tatholah, which sat at the head of what seemed to be a ruined brick stairway, leaning back against one side of a low opening into the hillside and staring out at Sylvester from eyeless sockets.

Sylvester slept again. When he woke, he did not move, but only opened one eye to see if this all was really real. The sky was darkening rapidly. The cypresses and tupelo gums of the floodlands leaned against each other, creaking softly in the wind. A great blue heron stalked through the shallows below, and with a sudden dart speared a frog.

It's always some little *detail* that you forget, he mused in dejection. That damn Luigi been there ever since *was,* and I go thinking Bedford Forrest the only white man on the place. Why I go for Mr. Bedford anyways? Félice the one I should have stob. And then myself and let that be that.

How come then I don't just go on get down in that cold water and drown? How come I knock myself to pieces in this swamp? What *for?* Go get free and then live all alone and poor and don't know nobody? That what freedom be—being alone? That what I staying alive for?

Out in the swamp he saw a half-sunk log sink from sight, and then another. Then another slithered down the bank below him and into the slough. Alligators.

At the top of a tree just a few feet out there was a flash of lightning, and Sylvester watched the fire shoot down the trunk and on into the still water and boil and hiss and then fall silent. Fat raindrops began to slap in the mud.

Time going to come, I recollect saying. Well, time done come. He waded carefully into the cold, dark water and pushed on toward Memphis.

Giovanni Corelli identified the knife as that which he had seized from Sylvester after the Emancipation Proclamation and which had been stolen from the house on the night when Jerome had been stabbed.

"You know anybody hereabouts can write good?" asked Forrest.

"There is the freeman preacher Augustus Lowdermilk. Félice writes very well French."

"I don't fancy no nigger scribes," said Forrest, "and I think a letter from me might be took kind of odd coming in French."

"Eh!" cried Corelli. "I remember! One very nice Miss McCracken, school teacher, two-three miles only. She writes beautiful."

"Let's call on her, Giovanni."

In Miss McCracken's ladylike hand, on her own pale blue stationery, that very day, a letter was dispatched from General Nathan Bedford Forrest, C.S.A., to General Cadwallader C. Washburn, U.S.A., at Memphis, respectfully requesting that a young Negro named Sylvester, five feet six inches tall, one hundred twenty-five pounds, medium complexion, missing one upper front incisor, be apprehended and extradited for prosecution by the State of Mississippi on a charge of murder.

"That son of a bitch certainly doesn't lack nerve, I'll say that. As if all I had to do was round up his runaway slaves! Put this in my Forrest file, lieutenant. One of these days someone's going to look at it and wonder. Wait a moment—give it back. I've got to smell it one more time," said Washburn, reaching for the letter and quaking with laughter.

It was raining hard now, and Sylvester was cold. The bottom here had frequent deep holes, and with each step he had to grope for something to stand on. Often he found a footing only to feel it give way under him. Several times he gave himself over to being eaten by alligators. He had lost all sense of direction. Still he struggled on.

Late that afternoon he came at last to Nonconnah Creek. A bitter wind was blowing now, and the creek was boiling, in full flood. But he was too cold to stop now. He would have to try to swim it.

The current swept him far downstream. The water was very cold. He swam for a long time.

He slammed into something hard—a bridge piling. He pushed off it to the next one, from it to the next, and then to a pile of garbage on the bank. Everything turned a beautiful, icy blue.

The first thing Sylvester saw when he awoke was a grinning, toothless white man in a blue uniform. The man had a piece of smoking punk in his hand and was burning leeches off Sylvester's legs.

"How you feel, nigger?" inquired the white man.

"Is you a Yankee, sir?" asked Sylvester.

"I sure am, son. Surely I am."

"Is you going to kill me, sir?"

"No, I ain't," said the Yankee.

"You going to put me in one them prison camps?"

"No, son, we filled up them camps long since with real prisoners—Rebs. I'm going to take you to the field hospital right over there and clean you up, give you one night of sleep in the dispensary tent, and then cut you loose to be a free man."

The next day, in the dazzling after-storm sunshine, along the endless rows of makeshift shanties, through the dice games and prayer meetings and countless jubilant song-singings of his emancipated brethren, Sylvester wandered the streets of Memphis.

I ain't a slave no more, he reminded himself over and over, in a daze of astonishment. I ain't somebody property.

That night, drunk for the first time in his life, Sylvester slept under a shack, in the mud, cold.

1865

Miles Glory sat with his feet up on the wide mahogany desk, admiring his alligator shoes, picking his teeth with his ruby-headed toothpick, and grinning.

His butler, Ice Pick Lincoln, announced a caller, but Miles had already looked out the window and seen who it was, which was why he was grinning.

"You let that man *see* you?" demanded Miles.

"Shit, no, boss, I be bold but I ain't crazy," said Ice Pick. "Had Drury let him in."

"I bet he don't much like the look of Drury neither. Well, I reckon he done cool he heel long enough," said Miles, still grinning. "Tell Drury go get him."

Drury, in his stiff new uniform, showed the visitor in, receiving a cold stare for his courtly bow.

Miles did swing his feet to the floor, but he did not rise. "Have a seat, sir," he said.

"I'll stand," said Nathan Bedford Forrest.

"What brings yourself to Memphis, sir?"

"I'm trying to round up some colored folks to come down to Greengrove and do some honest work. I come to see if you knowed any that doesn't prefer drinking and dice and the Yankee grubstake. Five dollar commission per nigger."

Miles shook his head. "Thanky kindly, sir, but I don't believe I knows too many so likely to be willing."

There was a long silence. At last Forrest said, "This is my house, boy."

"Use to was," said Miles Glory, not grinning.

"I want that big sumbitch you got in the white coat out there. Drury's his name, ain't it? He ain't no house servant. That nigger's a cotton picker. I want him back."

"Mr. Bedford. I want to put this delicate. You can't just do like that no more."

Forrest's left eye started twitching. He turned, slammed the door hard into Drury's face, strode past a very startled Ice Pick without even a sidewise glance.

"He didn't see me," said Ice Pick hopefully. "Did he?"

"Shit, naw, he was gone like a jack rabbit," said Drury, rubbing his nose. "He couldn't a saw you."

That night, Ice Pick put on his new apple-green tail coat with white-piped lapels and went out to pay a call on Charity, who he had heard was living in a white man's house on Market Street, but before he got there his head was cleft down to the spine by an axe.

"If you don't look like a damn fool I don't know what do," said Sylvester.

"Least I don't look like no damn ragamuffin," said Aaron. "Least I gets enough to damn eat. And Drury say Miles going to help me find Cherry."

"*Oh,* yeah. Miles Glory the good Samaritan," said Sylvester. "How he *love* to help the colored folk. He done so good by Ice Pick. Tell me, Aaron. How do being the slave of a black man compare to being the slave of a white man?"

"I ain't no slave," muttered Aaron sullenly, jingling the change in the pocket of his scarlet livery. "I be saving up buy me a dairy farm. Going marry my gal and raise me some milk cow."

"You a damn fool," said Sylvester. "That's all."

"You the fool. Get out the way," said Aaron, pushing Sylvester, a little harder than he'd quite intended. "I got business to do."

Sylvester pushed Aaron back, harder. "Go to hell," he said. "Run out on you best friend."

"I see how good you done staying back there to get Félice away from Mr. Joe or Mr. Bedford or whoever the hell she rubbing fur up against at the time," said Aaron.

"We going to see how good you do getting Cherry away from that white man *she* rubbing up against," said Sylvester.

There was a stunned pause before Aaron spoke. "What you talking about, Sylvester?"

"What you think?" Sylvester jeered. "I seen her."

"You lie. You *lie!*" cried Aaron. "What white man?"

"How I suppose to know he name, Aaron? Little fat ugly white man, that's all. Market Street."

Aaron's features were clenching. "She—all right—then?"

"I can't say this no way good," said Sylvester. "I sorry, brother. She were laughing. Patting him, like."

Aaron's eyes wandered, and fell on the figure of a blind man down the street who was leaning on a broom handle. The man wore only a pair of ancient knee-breeches, held up by a rope over one shoulder. Tapping his stick, he began to move toward Aaron and Sylvester. He looked starved. His back, shoulders, and face were spider-webbed with cat scars, his eyes milk-white and oozing. "Somebody help me," he was bawling softly. "Please, somebody."

"Joe John?" said Sylvester. "Is that you, Joe John?"

The blind man fell to his knees. He was so emaciated that Sylvester was reluctant at first to touch him, afraid that the skin might split.

"It's Sylvester," said Sylvester. "And Aaron. You mama looking for you, brother."

"I going go get him something to eat," said Aaron. "You hungry, Joe John?" he shouted.

"He blind, Aaron," said Sylvester, "not deaf."

Aaron whirled and raced up the street toward Miles's house. Cutting the corner short, he nearly collided with an old white lady, who took fright and flung her basket of eggs beneath the wheels of a passing wagon.

The driver, a toothless young white man, pulled his mule up and retrieved the basket. Eggs were dripping through it. "I'd a kilt that black nigger for ye if he wasn't so goldang fast," the young man said.

"Wouldn't been no point in it," replied the old lady. "They is done got thicker than flies."

Joe John sucked back some phlegm and croaked, "My mama—"

"That's all right, I going to take you to you mama," said Sylvester. "She right there, Corelli plantation, just like always. I were going that way anyhow. Got me a errand to do."

Aaron reappeared, with a whole iron skillet of corn bread, which Joe John wolfed down noisily.

"Hot out the oven," panted Aaron. "Miles like to skin me, he cotch me with that bread."

"I done walk from Mobile, Alabama," said Joe John through a mouthful of crumbs. "All the way."

"How you do that?" demanded Aaron.

"Just did," said Joe John.

"Bet you done took you a wrong turn or two," said Sylvester.

Joe John laughed, stood up, and found Sylvester's hand.

"So I was trying to round me up some deserters, at least," said Forrest, "but our horses was all so beat they was dying wholesale. Meanwhile the traitors and renegades and all the other no-counts was forming little piss-ant cavalries of their own, with the sole purpose of stealing horses, robbing womenfolk, and plundering the abandoned farms. All saying they was Forrest Rangers, and so I got the blame. I was down to three thousand men, half of them plain skunks, and the muckamucks in Richmond wouldn't send me no more. Wilson was up on the Tennessee with thirty thousand Yankees fixing to come down and kick my ass, and them yellow-gut peckerwoods of mine was leaking out by the dozens every night. I shot me a bunch of them, but it didn't seem to have no effect no more. I was losing my mind, Giovanni. Miss Mary wouldn't answer my letters. My temper was getting the best of me. I was sick, and I couldn't sleep. Couple fellers under me, they'd try to calm me down, but I wouldn't listen to them. Getting stomped on at Selma didn't help none, and what's more I got shot again. Finally one morning I come out the tent and looked around at that pitiful camp, all them spavined and broke-backed horses and them pitiful-looking froze-to-death sumbitches too wore out to even build a fire to get warm by, and I says, 'Bedford, old bud—you—are—whipped.' Took three weeks till I even heared about Appomattox, but I'd done quit fighting long before that."

There was a long silence before Giovanni Corelli spoke. "Everyone in town, they say, 'Forrest, he is coming, he will lead us, we will have a small confederacy just here, at Memphis.' "

Forrest snorted and said nothing.

"No?" said Corelli.

"No," said Forrest softly.

The manor house stood at the top of the only hill in that part of the countryside. It wasn't much of a hill, but to Sylvester the ascent of it had always been long and laborious. Tonight, with the parlor chandeliers flickering in the gusts of an incipient storm, nimbuses boiling above the horizon and lightning veining the blood-red light between them, the house loomed over him like the great mountain of the Book of Revelation that the Preacher said was to be cast burning into the sea and turn it to blood on the day of judgment. Sylvester had never seen a mountain, nor a sea, and this was not the end of days, but when he had crept to the house and looked in at the window—of the little room on the ground floor which he thought to be Félice's but where, since the incapacitation of his foot, Nathan Bedford Forrest had lodged when visiting—Sylvester wished that all the evil world might be cast into the sea.

Forrest lay naked on the bed, spread-eagled on his back, each limb bound with a length of rope to a bed post. Félice was stalking up and down beside the bed, also naked but for her white high-buttoned boots, snapping Forrest's own black quirt against the palm of her hand.

"You think I laugh!" she was snarling. "You think I make a joke! Ah?"

"Please, baby, please," Forrest cried hoarsely. "I know I ain't no good. I deserve to be punished."

"You deserve to *die,*" sneered Félice, reaching to the bureau and now brandishing something shiny—Sylvester's knife! She leaned over the bed with her legs spread wide and held the knife to Forrest's throat.

"I know," he said. "I know, baby. Kill me. I deserve it."

Then, suddenly, Félice was laughing, and, still through tears, so was Forrest. She set the knife on the linen-covered bedside table and blew out the lamp. Sylvester could see nothing now.

"Untie me, you devil," said Forrest in a new, thick, urgent tone. "Untie me, Félice."

"I think not," said Félice in a whisper. "Not yet."

"Where's that grease at, baby?" demanded Forrest.

"You want *that?*" she whispered.

"I want it," said Forrest. "God damn me, I want it."

"Ooh," she purred, "you are not nice, monsieur."

"That's a fact, you filthy bitch."

Sylvester heard Forrest sigh, and Félice groan.

Head bowed, Joe John sat on the kitchen steps with Hattie's fat arms wrapped around his skeletal hulk. She was singing him a hymn, but at Sylvester's passing he lifted his head. "Thank you, Sylvester," he called softly. "Mama say don't worry, won't nobody know you been here." Joe John waited to speak again until he had heard Sylvester walk slowly down the gravel drive and close the plantation gate. "He didn't have that woman with him when he left out, did he?"

"Naw, son, I didn't think he would," said Hattie. "That woman way too much for the like of that boy to handle. She been waiting, waiting for something, but that something ain't no kind of Sylvester."

"But he say he were going take her no matter what."

"Son, that woman be in the back of the house with General Nathan Bedford Forrest he own self. Ain't no little nigger going to just run in on that white man and say, 'Give me the gal, marse,' "

"But you master—I thought he—ain't he here? And ain't she—"

"Yes, Joe John, Mr. Joe be here," said Hattie. "Things done pass in this house the devil he self would not believe."

An owl began to call, low, from the edge of the forest.

"How you feel, son?"

"I feel all right, Mama."

"You hungry?"

"No, ma'am. I is so full of that peach cobbler I could bust."

That same night—not knowing that Sylvester had set out on a parallel enterprise—Aaron went to Market Street with a mind to try to rescue Charity, and no clear notion of how. He found her sitting in a rocking chair on the front porch of a tall skinny white house talking to a short fat white man sitting on a glider. Aaron stood beneath a street lamp till Cherry saw him. When she did, her hands flew to her mouth and her eyes went wide. The white man stood up and called out, "You, boy! Come here!"

Aaron opened the wrought-iron gate and sidled up to the porch, hat in hand. "Yes, sir?" he said to the bottom step.

"What you doing out in that street, young feller?" demanded the white man.

"Nothing," said Aaron.

"Staring a damn hole in a man setting on his own front porch."

"No, sir."

"Then what was you looking at, boy?"

"I were looking at Cherry."

"Hush, Aaron!" cried Cherry.

"I see," said the white man. "You want to talk to this boy, Charity?"

"Yes, sir, if you please," she said, sniffling.

"Well, if y'all will excuse me I'm going to go inside," said the white man, and did so.

"You got to come with me," said Aaron. "We going to get married. You forget, or what?"

"I sorry, Aaron," said Cherry. "I don't know."

"What the hell all this is?"

"It's hard to explain, Aaron. I was going to come find you, when things get settle down some. I knowed you was in Memphis. But then after Mr. Abraham Lincoln got kill, Dr. Beau—Dr. Beau*mont* be he right name, Dr. Christopher Columbus Beaumont—Dr. Beau goed all to pieces. He what they call a Tennessee Tory? You know? Memphis man, but he love Mr. Lincoln?"

"Is that a fact," said Aaron.

"He a real abolitionist, Aaron. He was right here all through the war, helping the Yankees. He want us to be free. He say I can do what I wants."

"Does you want to come with me? You got to say."

"He so sweet to me, Aaron," she said.

"You gots to say tonight. You gots to say now."

"Oh, honey, let me think."

"No thinking. Yes or no," said Aaron.

Cherry looked over her shoulder into the house, and then back at Aaron. "I been through so much."

"Is that a fact."

"I miss you, Aaron. I thinks about you every day."

"Huh. You missing me while I standing here, I suppose."

"Kind of like, yes," she said. "Seem like you was so long of a time ago."

"This is me right here right now, Cherry."

"I know, Aaron."

"Come with me, baby. We can get married legal now. We free."

She looked at Aaron for a long, long moment. "I gots to talk to Dr. Beau," she said. "Will you wait while I goes and does that?"

"You expect me to set out in the street and twiddle my thumb while you goes in and makes up you mind?" demanded Aaron, his voice rising.

"I done made up my mind, Aaron," she said.

She rose, turned, and went in.

A long time passed, in which the only sound seemed to be the heavy collisions of June bugs against the windowpanes. Then there came the long, low call of a steamboat from the river.

The door flew open and Dr. Beaumont plunged past Aaron without seeing him. He strode rapidly down the walk, through the gate, and into the street as if purposefully, but within a minute he was in sight again, pacing up and down and muttering to himself beneath the street lamp. Every so often he would raise his hand in a furious gesture, and then look at it, and lower it to his side. Finally he came back, and noticed Aaron on the porch.

"Well, you might as well come in and wait out of the damn mosquitoes."

"Yes, sir."

"Take a seat," said the white man, flinging his hand toward a chair in the parlor.

The chair was soft, feathers and silk. Aaron could hear clearly down the hall as Charity said, "I is so sorry, Dr. Beau."

"You can change your mind," came Dr. Beaumont's hoarse reply. "You *could.* Listen to me, Charity. You know I'll always take care of you. Go out there amongst those Negroes, and who knows what can happen? There's a lot of Rebs out there got grievances against your people. I hear talk about night riding, run them all out of town, *burn* them out. And hasn't none of them hardly got any money. You think that boy got any damn money? Don't do this to me, Charity. Please."

"You say I can do what I wants."

"You can, you can. I just—I just don't want you to want this."

"I will always be so much oblige to you, Dr. Beau," she said.

"This is final, then?"

"Yes, sir."

In a moment Dr. Beau was back in the parlor, walking back and forth aimlessly. He stopped, and glared at Aaron. His eyes were wild, his lips moving but not speaking. He walked down the hall again.

Fear washed over Aaron in a wave; the man had looked insane. He ran into the back of the house. Charity was pushing something into a valise. Then Aaron saw that the doctor had a pistol in his hand.

Aaron ran to Charity and put his arms around her. The white man lifted the gun in both hands and pointed it at them. The barrel swung wildly up and down. Tears were pouring down his fat pink cheeks. "Get away from her!" he shouted.

"I suppose to stand back and let you shoot me?" asked Aaron.

"I'm going to shoot *her*, you damn fool," cried Dr. Beaumont.

"I can't let you do that, sir," said Aaron.

"I'm going to kill y'all both!" yelled the white man.

"Don't do that," said Aaron very softly, beginning to surmise that the threat was quite real. "I is leaving out. I is fixing to leave out right now. Just only don't kill us. And don't kill Cherry when I gone. All right? Please, sir. Promise."

Dr. Beaumont sighed, lowered the gun, and put it on the dresser. He covered his face with his speckled hands, and began to weep, his big belly heaving.

"You got to promise me. Promise you ain't going to hurt nobody."

"I won't hurt nobody except maybe me," sobbed the white man.

"No!" exclaimed Charity, running to him, stroking his wet cheeks with her fingertips. "No, Dr. Beau. No, honey." She shot a look at Aaron, of infinite sadness, and he knew in that instant that she had changed her mind.

Aaron took from his pocket the linen handkerchief on which she had depicted her dream of their future together, so long ago. It was dense with ornate embroidery, leaves and blossoms entwining a heart of gold.

He held the handkerchief out, knowing she would not take it, and let it float to the floor.

Now Charity was crying too.

"Did you even know I come looking for you all the way to Fort Pillow?" demanded Aaron. "Did you know I was in that massacre?"

She lowered her head to the white man's chest.

"This what I been living for?" demanded Aaron. "All this war and running and hiding and hoping and waiting I done count the every minute of till I finds my gal? I done stay so *true* to you, Cherry. I ain't never thought of nothing but you since the year 1860. Now come to find out I had the wrong idea altogether. I been thinking all this time you was something you ain't. It wonders me, now I study it. What made me reckon you was going to wait and not change just because I ain't change? Folks change, don't they?" Aaron paused, fixing this moment in his mind. "What I suppose to do now, Cherry?" he said at last. "What I suppose to do?"

She had no answer for Aaron but these tears running down the white man's lapels.

He looked at the pistol on the dresser top. With one lunge he could have it.

But Aaron still preferred to see what freedom was going to be like.

Félice pulled on the heavy boots and stood up, stamping. "I will make them return to you very soon," she said.

Uncle Dunc eyed the shoes doubtfully. Even with Félice's feet wrapped thick in rags, they were much too loose. "Well, you can't go barefoot, not you nohow, and you sure as Christmas can't wear *them* things out in that gumbo"—sliding his eyes toward the white calfskin pearl-buttoned boots paired neatly on the clay floor—"so I reckon these here going to have to do you. You got anything to eat?"

"When I will come to the town, in the morning, then I will eat."

"You got any money?"

"No, my uncle. But don't worry."

"Mercy, child," said Uncle Dunc, turning up the lamp and reaching for his cigar box, "seem like it ain't no limit to what-all you don't know." He untied the frayed lavender silk ribbon and counted out fifteen cents—most of what he had. He wrapped the money in a scrap of calico rag and stuffed it deep inside Félice's bundle.

"No, my uncle," she said, "I cannot take this from you."

"You give it Sylvester, then. Tell him it my present to y'all."

"Oh, sir," said Félice, "you are so good!" She threw her arms around the old man before he could duck away, and kissed him hard.

"Law!" gasped Uncle Dunc.

"I swear to God," said Miles.

"You will help me?" asked Félice.

"Look what I got for you, baby. Been just a-waiting for the right time." He produced a long, fringed, flowing, crimson silk scarf.

She could not resist trying it on, however much her purpose might appear to falter in the act. Wrapped twice round her neck, the scarf hung nearly to the floor. The fabric was so delicate that her slightest movement set it swirling into the air.

Miles had a new front tooth—gold, with an inlaid ivory heart. "Come here, sweet thing," he said, grinning. "Come and give you sweet daddy a tickle."

Félice pursed her lips and sighed. She took off the scarf, folded it up neatly, and set it on the leather-topped desk. She feared the likely consequence of resisting his advances, so she did not speak right away; she thought awhile, and then said, "Remember: two years ago you telled me that you would buy my manumission. Remember? You did not do nothing, then. Now I am a free woman. Still I have need of your assistance. You want to make love—yes? If I will do this with you, you will assist me to find Sylvester."

"I ain't never saw the like for sass," Miles observed. "Listen, Phyllis. I couldn't a bought you free long as Mr. Joe didn't want to sell. And as long as you was keeping his flagpole good and greased, he wasn't going to be too eager to do no selling. Now, was he? You didn't play you cards right, baby."

As long as she had met the master's demands she had insured that she would remain his property. But if she had refused him, he might well have sold her into some situation far worse. Could she ever have trusted that Miles would make good on his promise, and buy her manumission? Even if he had tried, his bid might not have been the highest. The master and Forrest could even have bypassed the open market and sold her straight back to Duquesne. Or Forrest might have bought her himself, and dragged her from camp to camp all across the South, in the midst of the war, living in tents, cold, dirty, terrified, miserable.

For she did hate Forrest. She did not understand why she always had yielded to him. Something about him was simply irresistible—perhaps it was that air of latent violence—and God! he did know how to make love. Afterwards she would feel soiled, bitter, ashamed, but as long as he was in the house it did not take long before she was ready once again to be seduced. It was shame that fed on shame; it may have been not so much the arousal as the humiliation that she craved. Somehow, now, nevertheless, with a conviction slowly growing since the end of her legal bondage this past spring, Félice had decided to put an end as well to her psychological bondage to Forrest. That, vaguely, not well understood but at least resolute, had been her purpose in the bizarre scene that Sylvester had witnessed through the window—one last humiliation in farewell. Then Hattie's sullen silence had at length given way—she had told Félice that Sylvester had seen it all—and Félice had learned how much more horrible than she could have dreamed her last humiliation had been. In her mind she saw, again and again, Sylvester at that window.

Let Corelli and even Forrest hunt her down. She was free.

She began to unbutton her blouse.

"You reckon I is going to help you," said Miles.

Félice sank to her knees and began to unbutton Miles Glory's fly. She lifted her long-lashed eyes and gave him her boldest smile.

"You wrong, baby," said Miles, stepping away. "You wrong again."

Félice wandered through Memphis for days, but no one knew what had become of Sylvester, nor of Aaron. She slept in an encampment of other homeless refugees, beneath a filthy tarpaulin. She was hungry. White and black men whistled as she passed, and grabbed their crotches, and pawed at her.

Then one day she saw the old Preacher. He was looking fat and prosperous.

"Please, monsieur," she said, "do you remember me? Félice, of Corelli plantation?"

Augustus T. Lowdermilk gave her a long, cool look, and said, "I remember you."

"I search Sylvester," she said, "but I cannot find him. I wish to marry him."

The Preacher's eyebrows met in the middle. "I never taken you for the marrying kind, somehow," he said. "Leastwise with that shiftless little knucklehead."

"I have changed," she said simply. "Sylvester has loved me for a long time. I wish to be his wife, on a small farm. I do not wish to be as I have been. Is it possible, sir, to find innocence after one has lost it?"

" 'Her sins, which are many, are forgiven; for she loved much.' That's in the gospels, child. Lord Jesus forgiving the harlot that anointed his feets with oil."

"You help me to find Sylvester?"

"I believe I knows where you can find that rascal."

"You know what, old woman?" said Senior. "This here about the best mess of chitlins I ever eat."

"Got them sherry pepper in it," said Bess. "Them as Aaron brung us out from town."

"You hear that, son?" said Senior. "This you pepper sauce in here. Sure is good. Sure is good."

Aaron nodded but had nothing to say.

"Yes, sir," said Sylvester quietly. "Sure is good, Aaron."

This was the first time Sylvester had been able to rouse himself to an initiative of speech in the whole two weeks the two young men had been with Aaron's family. Even more deeply than Aaron, Sylvester had seemed sunk in disillusionment and despair. A slow, sad smile spread across Aaron's face.

In return Sylvester gave him a weak and brave and not nearly sincere smile.

Then someone was knocking sharply at the door.

How Félice had found him she did not say. Aaron's mother and father laid her a pallet on their cabin floor, but she was not ready to sleep yet. The old folks withdrew to the sleeping loft, and Aaron hung up his hammock.

"You will come to walk with me a little?" asked Félice.

"I reckon it don't much signify what I does," said Sylvester. "Walk, run, sleep, or shit a brick."

"Oh, my dearest, let me talk to you!" said Félice in a rush as soon as they were outside and away. She took Sylvester's hand, but after a moment's reflection he took it back.

Katydids were screeching in the treetops. Through blue-white strata of fog the big house of Bess and Senior's former master and mistress cast gold rays.

Félice poured out her heart. "I love you," she pleaded. "I will always love you. I will love you forever."

"Is that a fact," said Sylvester. "Seem like I heared that before."

"Come with me," she begged, laying her head softly against his chest. "Now we begin. Now we are free. We love each other!"

"*Huh,*" said Sylvester, pushing her away.

After Félice had left, he burned up his tattered green weskit in the stove.

Meanwhile, Drury was riding as hard as he could to the Chickasaw Siding railroad station. The stationmaster's wife informed him coldly that her husband was eating his supper.

"Please, ma'am," pleaded Drury. "It's a emergency." Exactly as Miles had instructed him to do, Drury took the thick wad of bank notes from his pocket and pretended to be counting.

"What in the hell's all this?" muttered the stationmaster as he came to the door, wiping his mouth on his sleeve.

"Yes, sir," said Drury, still fingering the money, "I knows this a real inconvenience to you, sir, but I just gots to send a telegram to Memphis, and my boss he say there should ought to be special consideration for the telegraph man."

"Niggers sending telegrams," said the stationmaster, shaking his head. "What in the hell is next?"

"Yes, sir," said Drury.

"You can't write, neither, can ye, boy?"

"No, sir."

"So you want me to write the dang thing for ye too."

"I sure would be much oblige if you would do that, sir," said Drury, peeling off five dollars.

On receiving Drury's telegram—specifying that Sylvester had been located inside the state of Mississippi—Miles sent his own telegram, to Sheriff Otto Riley of De Soto County, along with a money order for ten dollars in the name of the Riley for Sheriff Reelection Committee.

Late that night, after sending Félice sobbing on her way, Sylvester Woodson was arrested for the murder of Jerome Forrest, Negro, at Corelli Plantation, De Soto County, Mississippi, December 2, 1863. Aaron Corelli, Jr., was charged with aiding and abetting the concealment of evidence of a felony, entering the state of Mississippi for the purpose of evading legally obligated labor (that is, running out on his job at Miles's house after Charity had broken his heart), and resisting arrest. Aaron Corelli, Sr., and his wife Elizabeth were also detained, for harboring a fugitive. Félice Renard had already been picked up on the Hernando Road and returned to Corelli plantation.

Because the De Soto County jail was overflowing with recently freed Mississippians of color and a new interstate memorandum of understanding was now in force, the custody of the four prisoners awaiting trial was to be transferred to the Shelby County Penal Farm, situated on Governors Island, in the Mississippi River, at the city of Memphis, Tennessee.

Bess and Senior were sent first, but they were returned to Mississippi the next day and promptly released: the private contractor who operated the penal farm for Shelby County had known the two old folks for years, and he knew damn well, he said, that they would not have been involved in any such kind of monkeyshines. He had sent a letter with them addressed to Sheriff Riley, who had served under him during the war.

Bess and Senior begged the sheriff also to release their son and his friend.

"Now, y'all know I can't do that," said Riley. "Papers all signed, sealed, and delivered. Them boys going up to Memphis today."

As Aaron and Sylvester, with their hands and feet heavily shackled, came down the gangway from the ferry boat, the operator of the penal farm was there to greet them, his gray eyes glittering.

"Well, well, well," said Nathan Bedford Forrest.

1866

Giovanni Corelli pulled the velvet cord again, again without effect. Félice, in her white flannel nightgown, lay reading. Corelli sank into his armchair between her bed and the window, and lit a cigar. He watched the smoke twist in the lamplight. Félice looked briefly at him and then back into her book.

"I pay him only that he may loaf, nap, and drink my whiskey?" Corelli demanded, in French.

"Always have you complained of this, let him be slave or free," said Félice mildly, using the formal *vous*.

Caleb appeared, and did not bow. "Yes, sir?"

"Eh!" Corelli grunted. "I see this Preacher going up and down here today. Now he has a new suit, he looks like a big black crow!" Corelli gave a sharp bark of laughter. "He brings news?"

"Well, sir," said Caleb reluctantly, "You knows as how some of them colored folk in town comed out to start in farming together, yonder on Tchulahoma Road? Making them a little settlement and all?"

"How I know this? No."

"Well, sir, they a whole bunch of nigger down that way, on that abandon land the bureau say what they can have?"

"Freedmen's Bureau. Pah!"

"Well, Mr. Joe, these nigger down yonder they had them a old white preacher come a-visiting. Old Yankee man. Say he going to fetch them a teacher, learn them all how to read, write, and cipher.

And sure enough, by and by, come this little white lady. Miss McCracken—don't but live right up the road."

"I am amaze."

"And Miss McCracken, see, she set up right there, schoolhouse and all such as that, just out in the quarters that's laying empty. Got her a childrens class, and then at night a adults class."

"Very bad idea," observed Corelli.

"Well, sir," continued Caleb, "evening before yesterday, the adults class was setting in there looking at books. Then come them white mens in the hoods. Night riders. Burnt everybody smack out."

"They are—hurted?" asked Corelli, shocked.

"Two old mens they couldn't get them out. Burnt up."

"Who these men are, these night riders?" demanded Giovanni Corelli. "And Miss McCracken—she is all right?"

"They whipped her, Mr. Joe."

"*Whip?* A white lady? Aigh! This is no good, my friend. Bring me paper and pen. I write to Bedford Forrest."

Caleb rubbed his head harder. He looked at Félice, and she, through narrowed, astonished, unwilling eyes, looked back at him.

The front door bell rang, and Caleb shuffled out.

"I don't like this at all," said Corelli, first in Italian, to himself, and again, in French, to Félice. "You see how much better is slavery than this so-called freedom?"

"Yes, monsieur," said Félice quietly, avoiding his eyes.

Caleb knocked and reentered. "Sheriff here. Want to see you. I got him waiting on the porch. I ain't going to have no trash like that in the house."

"Idiot!" cried Corelli, heaving himself out of his chair. "Bring him in the front parlor! You bring him whiskey!"

When Corelli entered, Sheriff Otto Riley was bowing over the cuspidor, lopping off a long brown drool of tobacco juice.

"Sir," said Corelli, clicking his heels together.

"Yes, sir, yes, sir," said Riley thickly. "How d'ye do, sir." As Caleb poured the whiskey, the sheriff looked around for a place to park his plug, finally choosing a silver bonbon dish. Caleb bore it in dignity out. "I wasn't quit with that chew," Riley remarked.

"I bring him back," offered Corelli.

"Naw, forget it. Much obliged, though. Yes, sir. Now. I am sorry to be bothering you in the evening, but we got us some serious nigger trouble in this county, Mr. Corelli. And I got reason to believe there's some fugitives from justice somewheres round about. May be some of them done gone in that swamp of yourn. I just come by out of courtesy to let you know as how if you hear some hound dogs making music, that's just my boys rounding up niggers. What's worrying me, sir, is it looks like they's a whole bunch of these jigaboos acting in a conspiracy. Might be some real innocent-seeming ones be harboring some of them fugitives I made reference to. So with your permission, sir, me and my boys would like to take us a little gander round your nigger quarters."

Caleb came rushing in. "Mr. Joe, Mr. Joe," he said urgently. "They trouble down the cabins. Peoples be yelling, torches burning, I don't know what all."

"That'd just be my boys looking around, Mr. Corelli. I wouldn't worry none about it."

"You come! You ask my permission! I don't give it yet! I don't give you permission! You take these men and go away!"

"Little late for that now, sir," said the sheriff.

"I speak to General Forrest!"

"You do that, sir. You just do that. Evening to you, sir." Riley turned and shambled out.

Corelli followed. There was already one captive in shackles—a big, burly, clay-colored man. Two deputies chained him to the fence and headed back into the quarters with their blazing lanterns.

Uncle Duncan sought out Corelli. The old stable boss was trembling. "That be Elmo, boss," he said. "Use to was Mr. Bedford field hand. Can't you help him?"

Corelli and Duncan continued down the lawn toward the prisoner. Félice appeared, barefoot, shivering in her nightgown, and tiptoed to Corelli's side. Joe John stood at the head of the kitchen steps holding his mother's hand, listening.

Elmo was bleeding from cuts above both eyes. "Uncle Dunc," he said, "this is them. These the same mens that got us in the school.

That sheriff, he was there. I can tell by how he walk, rolling-like."

"These mens be going to kill him, boss," whispered Uncle Dunc to Giovanni Corelli.

"Please, monsieur," added Félice, her fingertips urgent on Corelli's arm.

"I will send to Bedford Forrest tonight," said Corelli.

Elmo cried out, "No, sir! Mr. Bedford he one of them too!"

"You know nothing, you!" snapped Corelli. "Duncan, you go now to Memphis. What a thing, eh? To accuse the General Forrest of this."

"Going to be too late, marse," said Uncle Dunc.

"I cannot get involved in this, Duncan. I don't want no trouble. You go."

The sheriff's men were gathered near the quarters gate muttering among themselves, having found no other fugitives.

Corelli lumbered back toward the house and drank himself to sleep.

When he awoke, Félice was gone.

And that afternoon the Preacher arrived to announce that when he had gone to the burying ground in the morning, the corpse of Elmo had been hanging from a tall beech tree there, except for the feet, which stood side by side on the ground six feet below the stumps of his legs, in warning to all who might fancy outrunning their fate.

Four thousand Federal troops were still garrisoned at Fort Pickering. All of them were black, nearly all former slaves from Memphis and its hinterlands. They were not popular with the white people of the town. A few of the soldiers openly taunted the vanquished and their womenfolk. But mostly they were hated simply for what they were: black, free, victorious, glad, and armed.

Four important things were happening in Memphis at once:

In their freedom and gladness, black people were behaving in new ways. Often they no longer stepped off the sidewalk as a white person approached. They no longer automatically tipped their hats to whites. They no longer averted their eyes when addressed. (The stare of a

Negro was intolerable to nearly every white man in Memphis, and terrifying to nearly every white woman.) There had been a widespread rumor among the whites that there was going to be a mass uprising of Negroes on Christmas Day of 1865, and although that had not come to pass, the fear had had its effects on both black and white: many whites remained afraid, and many blacks felt an irresistible thrill at the whites' intimidation. The powers of the Freedmen's Bureau had just been extended by the U.S. Congress: another increment in Negro power. A new civil rights act had been passed: another. In the belief that forty acres and a mule would soon be provided to every ex-slave, many were doing little more in Memphis than biding their time until they could return to the countryside, and with continued subsidy from the Freedmen's Bureau many were able to get by without gainful employment. This rankled the white poor extremely.

The second big change was that, in part owing to the federal government's financial aid, and in part to their inurement to poverty, Negroes took work at lower rates of remuneration than even the poorest whites would accept. Those most affected by the entry of blacks into the labor market, ironically, were the people who were least likely to have fought for the Confederacy: the Irish. It also happened that the neighborhood in which Fort Pickering was situated was largely Irish, and it was therefore the Irish who most often came into contact with the black soldiers quartered there. Sooner or later these four thousand men would be mustered out—more competitors for jobs.

Moreover, Memphis was in the grip of a crime wave. Robbery, burglary, bribery, blackmail, arson, assault, and even murder were commonplace. Some of the criminals were black, and many others were Irish. But the Irish miscreants tended to have advantageous connections: of the Memphis police force (in which ex-Confederates were forbidden to serve) nearly every member was Irish. Thus while Irish criminals went free, the jails and Forrest's penal farm were overflowing with Negroes. White fear of crime came to hatred of blacks.

These three changes led to the fourth: hatred of blacks was taking concrete form. A secret society of former Confederate soldiers had been formed which devoted itself to the twin ideals of upholding white Southern honor and suppressing black impudence. Its members rode at night, wearing white robes and conical white masks, wreaking their idea of justice on Negroes who tried to learn to read, or called for black suffrage, or dared to look a white woman in the eye. This society's name was Ku-Klux Klan. Its first leader, known as the Grand Wizard, was Nathan Bedford Forrest.

In early April, the troops at Fort Pickering were demobilized, and four thousand jubilant black men, their pockets jingling with pay, many still bearing arms, poured into the streets of Memphis.

The charge against Aaron of concealment of evidence of a felony was postponed until such time as the commission of a felony should be proved. Because Sheriff Otto Riley had overslept that morning and therefore was unable to testify, the charge of resisting arrest was dismissed. The court ruled that Aaron had in fact entered the state of Mississippi for the purpose of evading legally obligated labor, but, this being far too common a crime for its violators to be imprisoned, the sentence was suspended on the condition that Aaron return to his previous post of employment, namely, the household, at Memphis, Tennessee, of Miles Glory, Negro.

Miles shot out of his seat at the back of the courtroom. "Objection, you honor!" he cried. "I don't want this no-count nigger back. Not nohow!"

"That's your problem," said the judge, and blew his nose. "What in the hell time is it getting to be, anyhow? All right, let's have some dinner. Court'll reconvene at two o'clock." He rapped his gavel on the bench and said to the bailiff, "I haven't been able to think about anything for the last two hours but the smell of that mulligan out back."

Aaron stood looking around dimly, not knowing what came next.

The judge paused at the door, turned around, gave a short laugh, and called to Aaron, "You're free to go, son."

Miles was waiting for Aaron in the corridor. Aaron gave him a wide mocking smile, and opened his arms as though to say, Here I am.

"You fired, nigger," said Miles. "Go starve."

Luigi emerged from Strozzi's bakery with a hot loaf of sesame-seeded semolina bread, a dozen assorted pastries, and a sweet potato pie. He stopped next at Stern's butcher shop for a salami and some hot peppers. At Dickerson's dairy he bought a sheep cheese, a half-dozen pickled eggs, and a pound of butter. He had brought a bottle of wine from home. Struggling with his overflowing baskets, he waddled to Market Square, spread a white tablecloth on the lawn, and started making sandwiches. The boss and Mr. Forrest were talking business today, and Luigi was going to make the most of his day in town.

Drury mounted quickly and galloped to Miles Glory's house. Miles was already seated in his carriage out front, wearing his new suit, of dove-gray Italian worsted, just delivered that morning from the best black tailor in Memphis. There was no need for either to speak. Drury gave Miles a nod, and Miles gave him back a flash of gold and white teeth. Miles walked to the square.

"My, my, my, Mr. Louie," said Miles, "if that don't look like a good mess of eatments."

"Mmph," said Luigi, sputtering crumbs. "What you want?"

"Matter of mutual interest, Mr. Louie," said Miles. "One of my boys been out in the swamps, running a trap line along Nonconnah Creek and up Daylight Bayou a ways? And he finded something so interesting I goed down yonder my own self and taken me a look-see? Some bones is what. Human skull and what-all."

"Eh! So?" Luigi pushed a whole pickled egg into his mouth.

"They was something on the finger bone *extra* interesting," said Miles. "Looky here, Mr. Louie." Miles held out his smooth brown palm, cradling the gold ring of Benedict O'Connell. In all the years of war, and of Luigi's and Miles's mutually advantageous silence on the question, Mr. B. had been assumed simply to have wandered away, as plantation overseers so often did.

Luigi's mouth was open, displaying chewed egg.

"They was a eyewitness to that crime," added Miles, grinning. "Kind what they didn't use to have in no court, but's all legal now."

"Why in the hell can't he come to us?" demanded Forrest.

"He say they no let nigger in Gayoso House," said Luigi miserably. "He say nigger hotel not enough private, too many ears."

"How we know this matter is so important?" asked Corelli.

"He say tell you he got the girl Félice."

Corelli and Forrest looked at each other sharply. Forrest pushed out of his chair and was flooded with the pain of his unhealing wounds.

Félice, reclining on the chaise longue in Miles Glory's parlor, did no more than languidly raise her eyes when the white men came in.

"Afternoon, sirs," said Miles, bowing slightly. "I appreciate y'all coming. Phyllis, go tell Drury get us a pot of coffee, and then if you'll excuse us awhile?" She rose and drifted airily out. "Won't y'all set down?"

Forrest and Corelli took their seats on straight-backed chairs facing Miles, who settled into the down-pillowed sofa, clasped his hands behind his neck, and put his alligator shoes up on the walnut tea table that Forrest's father had made. "I ain't going to waste y'all gentlemens' time," he said. "I'll get right to business."

As Drury served the coffee, he gave his former master a hard, cold stare.

"All right," said Miles when Drury at last had withdrawn. "Y'all knows that boy Sylvester. He coming to trial next week. Y'all knows the freeman courts been turning niggers loose left and right. Y'all knows what Phyllis going to do soon's that boy go free. Y'all knows what she were doing down in the country that night the sheriff cotch him. Y'all both knows she ain't runned off but for the one reason of finding that little nigger and marrying him."

All of this, in fact, was news to both Corelli and Forrest.

"What you want, eh?" demanded Corelli.

"Well, Mr. Joe, you daddy were good to me, and I gots respect for you family, and now I is in a position as I can do you a favor."

Forrest was tempted to demand, What in the hell's this got to do with me? but forbore.

It seemed as if Miles Glory had read Forrest's mind. "It were Sylvester that stob you personal servant Jerome, Mr. Bedford. He was in there stealing out that knife. Jerome cotch Sylvester cold, and he stob Jerome. Y'all knows the proof is him having that knife, that time when he jump Mr. Louie and drop it."

"Hell, boy, we know that," barked Forrest. "Mr. Giovanni's going to testify."

"But this here court ain't like they use to was. You can't just say let's hang the nigger and that's that no more. You can't make no case without a eyewitness," said Miles. "And I got you one."

"Them girls," said Forrest, "them two kitchen maids, what's their names—"

"Mattie and Isabel," said Corelli.

"Them girls seen a white man," said Forrest.

Miles shrugged, and grinned. "Empty-head little nigger girls. They don't gots to testify nohow. Does they, Mr. Joe?"

Corelli said nothing, frowning.

"Y'all got every kind of reason to see that little nigger hang," Miles reminded them softly.

Forrest's eyes narrowed. "What's *your* reason, Miles?"

"Now we comes to business. I understand y'all wants to build a little railroad."

"God almighty damn," said Forrest.

"Yes, sir," said Miles. "Y'all knows they ain't that much capital round about Memphis. Ain't much capital raising nowheres in the South. But y'all knows they's Yankees wants to help the South rebuild. As a matter fact, they is a Jewish gentleman come all the way down from New York City want to help. Banker. But you know what he say? He say the South ain't going to rise back up without they is colored people working in industry. Like railroad building, for instance. This banker he thinking about a bond issue. New kind of bond, back up with cotton."

"Niggers talking *bond issues*," said Nathan Bedford Forrest.

"Yes, sir," said Miles meekly. "This here bond issue could be where that railroad get the money to build all the way to Selma. All the way to Mobile, even. They going to gots to be colored workers on that railroad line, if we gets that bond issue, and I is dabbling in the business of providing workers. Mr. Joe, you in the cotton business—still got you all that cotton in that warehouse down yonder, don't you? Mr. Bedford, you in the cotton business too. And both y'all wants to be in the railroad business. Ain't that so? This Jewish gentleman he in the money business. Then you got me, in the labor business. Seem like we all ought to could do business together. Course I wouldn't be but way back on the sideline, where couldn't nobody even see me. Y'all wouldn't have to pay me no mind at all, once I collects my fee on them labor contracts."

"Shit fire," said Forrest, rising.

"I is much oblige for y'all dropping by," said Miles. "Y'all gentlemens *is* going to think about it?"

"Who is eyewitness?" demanded Corelli.

"Why, it's you own Mr. Louie," said Miles, grinning. "I reckon Sylvester had him so scared he couldn't say nothing."

"How come he change?"

"Sylvester in the penal farm, and then he going to hang. Can't hurt Mr. Louie no more now."

"Why we need you then? I tell him to tell the truth, he will tell it."

"Y'all *needs* me for y'all's *railroad*," Miles reminded him.

"Hell, Giovanni, we can just dig up this Jew our own selfs," said Forrest.

"Mr. Bedford," said Miles, "with all due respect, I don't think that Jewish gentleman be want to deal direct with no Grand Wizard of no Ku-Klux Klan."

Corelli pondered a moment, and then said, "And Félice?"

"Well, sir, I reckon Phyllis going to miss that there trial."

"And then? And then after?"

"Well, sir, I reckon she come on back home to Corelli plantation."

As soon as the white men were out the door, Miles rang for Drury and told him to give the girl another dose of laudanum.

Drury's mournful bass came down the alley:

"Troubles don't come single, troubles comes like rain.
Lord, troubles don't come single, naw, they comes like rain.
Ever since my baby die, I don't know nothing but pain.

"Church bell ringing, won't stop, church bell ringing in my head.
Church bell ringing, keep ringing, church bell ringing in my head.
I don't hear nothing but the funeral bell, now my baby dead.

"Blues in the morning, blues all night long.
Blues in the morning, I got the blues all night long.
I can't do nothing but sing this song."

"Can't do nothing but sing this song,"

sang Aaron in soft reply.

"Who that go there?" barked Drury into the darkness.

"Ain't but me. Aaron."

"You like to scared me to death," gasped Drury. "I been looking all over this town for you, boy. I got some things to tell you. You got you ears on?"

"I reckon," said Aaron.

"You know, Aaron, I never had no call to do much thinking, and I still ain't use to it. I ain't clever like Miles, but it appear to me Miles done got *too* clever. He done got y'all's old boy Mr. Louie to testify that it was Sylvester that done that stobbing that he didn't do. He got Mr. Joe to keep them two girl home so they can't testify they seen that white man that night, that really done it and kilt my brother too, just like you told me about—but Mr. Joe and Mr. Bedford don't know the half of it. They thinks Sylvester really done it, and Miles got both them white mens thinking they going to get

Phyllis back, plus they all kind of money business in it. But I knows Miles. He going to keep Phyllis, prisoner-like, all drug up with laudanum so she can't hardly move."

"We got to *stop* that man."

"Don't interrupt me, boy! I got enough trouble keeping all this straight. Now, listen at me, Aaron. I been involve in all this plumb up to my neck. And it ain't right. It just ain't no kind of right. And so like I says, I been thinking. And by and by, I had me a idea. Listen at me, Aaron—"

"What the hell you think I'm doing?"

"—because I is talking—"

"I is *listening,* Drury. Lord have mercy!"

"—because I needs your help if we going to save Sylvester. And you can just leave the good Lord out of it, Aaron, because he don't have nothing to do with it. Now, I believe you knows a white man call Christopher Columbus Beaumont?"

"Oyez, oyez, oyez! The criminal court of the United States Bureau of Refugees, Freedmen, and Abandoned Lands is now in session, the Honorable Justice Augustus T. Lowdermilk presiding. Order in the court! All rise."

Justice Augustus T. Lowdermilk? Sylvester, standing manacled in the dock, swiveled his head back towards Aaron with a look of purest bafflement.

Sitting next to Aaron was, amazingly, Charity. Next to her sat a short, fat white man. A cautious distance down the bench, gawking and fidgeting, sat old Bess and Senior. Behind them sat Uncle Dunc, Caleb, Hattie, Mattie, and Isabel. Across the aisle sat Giovanni Corelli, Nathan Bedford Forrest, and, down front, Sheriff Otto Riley. In the last row, picking his teeth and grinning, sat Miles Glory.

"You gots a lawyer, son?" asked the Preacher.

Another short, fat white man stood up and said, "Simon Bolivar Beaumont, your honor." He was the spitting image of the one sitting with Aaron and Cherry.

"Mr. Beaumont," said the Preacher, looking perplexed, "is you not the chief of police of the city of Memphis, Tennessee?"

"Yes, sir, that's right, but I am a member of the bar of the state of Mississippi too, and I did not serve in no military capacity in the late rebellion."

"Well, if the defendant's agreeable, I don't have no objection. That's you, boy," he said to Sylvester. "You the defendant."

"Yes, sir," said Sylvester.

The first witness for the prosecution was Luigi Carbone, who testified that on the night of December 2, 1863, at Corelli plantation, he had been awakened by screams, and had run down the hall to the house servants' wing, and there had seen Sylvester Woodson stabbing Jerome Forrest with the Indian knife.

Sylvester leaped to his feet, hollering, "Why you lie like that, Mr. Louie? What that man say just ain't so, Preacher, not none of it!"

"Set down, boy!" cried the judge. "You going to get you chance. And you suppose to call me You Honor."

Luigi went on to recount Sylvester's ludicrous assault on Hattie in 1860—

"Objection!" boomed Simon Bolivar Beaumont. "He ain't on trial for that."

"That's right," said the Preacher.

—and his attempted dalliance with Giovanni Corelli's mistress the same year—

"Objection!" hollered Beaumont again.

"It ain't relevant," said the judge. "Objection sustain."

—his robbery of the cotton shipment in 1861 (which he, Luigi, had heroically thwarted)—

"Objection!"

"I am *trying* to establish that this young man is a practiced criminal," pleaded the prosecutor.

"All right, all right. Overrule."

—his illegal possession of the Indian knife in 1862, and his attempt to murder Luigi in 1864 with the selfsame knife again—

"Objection!"

"Naw, now, Mr. Beaumont, we gots to look into this here knife. Overrule."

The prosecutor called for the production of Exhibit A, the murder weapon, so that the witness might identify it for the record.

It was not there.

Sylvester shot a look at Aaron, who was looking at the ceiling and wearing a very faint smile.

S. B. Beaumont said he wished to postpone his cross-examination of Luigi Carbone until later in the trial.

Giovanni Corelli was called to the stand.

"Now, that knife that was stolen from your house on the night of the murder, Mr. Corelli," said the prosecutor, "was the same which was subsequently known to be in the possession of Sylvester Woodson when he assaulted your employee Luigi Carbone in 1864, was it not?"

"I did not see. I was at Horn Lake."

With that, the case for the prosecution ended.

The defense began to call its witnesses. Mattie the kitchen maid testified that she had seen a white man fleeing from the manor house on the night of the crime, whom she had previously seen stealing vegetables from the garden. Isabel corroborated this, and added that from that night forward that white man had never been seen there again.

Uncle Dunc said he usually looked in on his boys during the night, and had seen Sylvester asleep at the time of the stabbing; the lights had all gone on in the big house just after that.

Hattie and old Caleb, astonishingly, both testified to Sylvester's good character.

Drury was called, and he materialized in the courtroom door next to Miles, whose ruby-headed toothpick fell from his lips. Drury explained that Sylvester had been an unwitting pawn in the cotton robbery.

Aaron testified that during the battle of Fort Pillow, in 1864, he had killed a white Confederate soldier engaged in the torture of United States Army troops who had already surrendered, and that the man he had killed was unquestionably the same white man who had been stealing vegetables at Corelli plantation in 1863.

Sylvester Woodson was called, and his lawyer asked him only one question: "Who stabbed Jerome Forrest?"

"I didn't see him do it, marse, but he told me he had him a tangle with Jerome. I taken my knife back, because it mine, and it did have blood on it. Like they says, he'd done been raiding the garden, and then he goed up there to rob out the house. I use to talk to him, but I didn't have nothing to do with no crime, not never. He name were A. J. Wordlaw."

The prosecutor declined to cross-examine the defendant.

De Soto County Sheriff Otto Riley, formerly Sergeant Otto Riley, C.S.A., sweating copiously, confirmed that one Andrew Jackson Wordlaw had been among the Confederate dead at Fort Pillow.

Nathan Bedford Forrest asserted that the testimony of Luigi Carbone had been suborned.

Luigi was recalled to the stand, and, blubbering, admitted it. Unprompted, growing hysterical, he also confessed to killing Benedict O'Connell. "But it was accident!" he wailed. "I was sinking in the quicksand—I reach to him but I cannot reach—"

"Order! Order!" roared the Preacher. "You *hush,* Mr. Louie! That don't have *nothing* to do with the price of these here beans. The witness is excuse. Lord, give me strength!"

The case against Sylvester was dismissed.

Giovanni Corelli shook hands with Aaron and Sylvester, and gave each of them a dollar. "The slavery, truly, is finished," he said. "I see this now."

Meanwhile Miles Glory fled furiously across the courthouse lawn. Forrest intercepted him at the door of Miles's red-lacquered carriage. "Next time you think we going to have *niggers* involved in Southern *business,* boy," said Forrest, "you better think *again.*"

Butch O'Gorman and Willy McKee were strolling down Beale Street in the cool evening of the first of May when they saw two boys scuffling in the dirt. One of the boys fighting was black, the other white—in fact it was May Clancy's son Clarence. The boys looked pretty well matched, so the men allowed the fight to proceed, in the interest of entertainment.

"Watching a fight always makes me thirsty," said O'Gorman.

McKee produced a steel flask.

"Aren't you a resourceful lad, though," said O'Gorman to his friend, and then to the boys, "Stand up and box, ye worthless buggers!"

The men pulled the boys apart, stood them on their feet, and stepped back.

The black boy kicked Clarence Clancy hard in the shin and threw a single punch that knocked him flat. Clarence rose groggily, wiped his nose, looked at the blood on his hand, burst into tears, and ran away.

"That won't do," said McKee, and clapped the black boy on the ear. "Why can't you fight fair?"

"Leave me alone," whined the boy.

Just then Clarence and his mother came steaming around the corner of Second. "Take that little robber in hand!" she called.

McKee snatched the boy by the hair. "Turn out them pockets, Sambo," he ordered. The boy, sniffling with fear, showed two pennies but refused to place them in O'Gorman's outstretched hand.

"Stealer!" cried Clarence.

"He *lie!*" protested the black boy. "We was lagging pennies. I wonned fair and square."

"Want to tell your lies to the *police?*" demanded May Clancy.

"Ay?" added McKee, shaking the boy's head vigorously by the hair. "Do ye?"

In terror the boy squirmed around and bit McKee hard on the arm.

McKee knocked the boy down, and stood over him, panting.

Suddenly they had company. Five of the black ex-soldiers from Fort Pickering—they had been mustered out only yesterday—stood watching from the middle of the street. "Let that there boy go," said one.

"He's a thief!" yelled McKee.

"I *said* let him *go.*"

McKee sauntered over and came up close in the soldier's face and said, "We are *calling* the *police.*" Indeed May and Clarence Clancy had already fled, and surely toward the station house.

Then he noticed the pistol, which had not been in the soldier's hand before.

"You don't scare me, you big baboon," said Willy McKee.

It was the last thing he ever said.

"Yonder they goes," whispered Aaron.

Sylvester followed the direction of Aaron's eyes to Miles Glory and Félice arm in arm as they disappeared into Fischbach's Colored Hotel. "Now I needs me a nigger," said Sylvester.

A pomaded swell in a lavender coat passed by. "That's him," said Sylvester. "Say, buck! Let me talk to you a minute."

When the man returned from his call on Miles in the hotel lobby, he said, "Say all he other girl ain't but a dime but this one fifty cent. That be some expensive pussy."

"Take this dollar," said Sylvester. "Fetch me the key and then keep the change."

The swell in the lavender coat grinned wide and headed back to the hotel.

"One dollar in the world, and this what you do with it," said Aaron. "You the stubbornest knucklehead I ever seen."

A narrow outside stairway rose into shadow. Each step sagged beneath Sylvester's weight.

He knocked.

"Entrez, entrez donc," came Félice's muffled voice.

She lay curled up on the bed, not looking. "Hey," said Sylvester softly.

She shook her head woozily, curled up tighter, and still did not look.

"It's me. Sylvester. I come to get you."

"I know it is you," she cried into the pillow, and Sylvester realized that she was weeping.

"I got me a farm, Félice. Mr. Joe going to let me farm sixty acre on share. I can cut wood right there for a cabin. Mr. Joe going to advance me a mule and some chickens."

"I cannot look at you," wept Félice.

Sylvester touched her shoulder, and she clenched as if stung. "I needs a wife," he said.

"I am not good," she cried.

"Aw, honey, they's a lot of bad days behind us," said Sylvester. "But they plenty good ones coming. Remember how you use to say? When we use to go swimming in the bayou?"

At last she looked at him, her eyes shimmering, her face twisted in shame. "You cannot trust me," she said, almost defiantly.

"You listen to me," said Sylvester firmly. "You listening? We going to get married. You going to come farm with me. We going to have us some babies. We going to love each other. I know he got you all tied up with laudanum. I is going to hold you tight till it let you go. You be all right."

And now, weeping anew, she was in his arms.

There were shouts from the street, and then gunshots. A man screamed. A police bell began to ring. There were more gunshots.

Sylvester looked out and saw three black men in blue Union army uniforms backing down the street holding out their arms to about a dozen policemen. The policemen stopped in front of the hotel, just below the window where Sylvester was standing, and fired a volley that dropped all three of the soldiers. One of the men raised his head, and was shot again.

Eventually a hearse arrived and carried the bodies away. The street was unpeopled and utterly still.

Miles Glory's red-lacquered carriage pulled up in the porte-cochère. Sylvester caught just a glimpse of Miles's tall stick-legged figure as he doffed his emerald-green topper to the woman preceding him into the coach, a plump and laughing pale-skinned girl in a spangled bright blue dress. As the carriage turned into the street, Sylvester saw Miles's face in the window, smiling mildly until he seemed to see Sylvester and his face went suddenly grave.

Another group of policemen appeared and stormed into a house across the street. Black men poured out of the windows and were shot down. No hearse came this time; the bodies lay there, stiffening, blood-crusted, crawling with flies, until night obscured them.

From near and far, all night, Sylvester and Félice could hear gunfire and screaming, and smell gunpowder and smoke. Through it all, Félice clung to him, trying to ignore the sensation of spiders on her skin as the laudanum waned.

The next morning, Sylvester saw Simon Bolivar Beaumont leading a posse of white men down the street; he was shooting into windows and yelling, "Come out and die, niggers!"

"The more I sees of white folk," said Sylvester to Félice, "the less I understands. Last week that man was saving my life. This week he killing niggers wholesale."

The Fischbach's lobby was jammed with people, many with news of the riot. The police were systematically burning every black church and black school in town, and beating the preachers and teachers, some to death. The Freedmen's Bank had been sacked and burned. A sixteen-year-old girl had tried to save an old man trapped in a burning house, and the white men who had torched it shot her and pitched her body through the front door into the fire. An old lady and her granddaughter had been sodomized, robbed of their life savings, and then drowned in the Wolf River lagoon. A black girl eating ice cream on the porch of an Italian grocery had been shot in the face at point-blank range. Two white judges had formed posses which were even now stampeding through the streets setting fire to the houses and gunning down black people as they fled the flames; Judge Creighton had been heard to bellow, "Boys, I want you to go ahead and kill the last damned one of the nigger race, and burn up the cradle, God damn them!" Other mounted mobs, under the leadership of aldermen, the county sheriff, the district attorney, even the mayor, were roaming the city setting fires and shooting Negroes. Hundreds of black people had been killed.

And through another night of death Sylvester and Félice clung to each other. In the morning, someone set fire to the hotel.

As Sylvester and Félice ran down the burning outside stairway, a post gave way beneath it and they tumbled to the ground. Sylvester hit his head and lost consciousness—only briefly, but long enough not to be able to prevent Miles Glory from getting hold of Félice and wrestling her into the red carriage across the street. Sylvester lunged forward, but someone tripped him, and he fell.

He turned to face the end of a shotgun barrel. "I'd advise you to leave well enough alone, my friend," said the policeman, jabbing Sylvester in the chest with the gun. "You'll be coming with me now."

Sylvester grabbed the gun and wrenched it away. He grasped the barrel and slammed the stock into the side of the policeman's head.

Sylvester ran blindly through the streets and kept running till he was out in the country, and then he realized that he was on the Hernando Road, the road . . . home. He sat on the roadside and bowed his head and wept.

A wagon creaked toward him slowly, loaded high with pinewood coffins. Aaron and another boy were on the driver's seat. There was a huge, moon-faced policeman behind them, sitting on a coffin, with a pistol pointed at Aaron's back.

"We gots to bury us some dead peoples," said Aaron, "and then we going to go on home Corelli plantation, so come on come with us."

In silence the three young men buried the coffins in a mass grave at the edge of the swamp. The policeman turned back toward Memphis.

As Sylvester stood over the big mound of sweet-smelling black earth, the third boy began to giggle. Then Aaron was laughing too.

Something gave way inside Sylvester; too little sense was being made. He ran into the swamp. Aaron splashed in behind him, and hauled him out flopping and squirming. Aaron grabbed Sylvester's head from behind by both ears and pointed it at the third young man, who took off his big straw hat and unwrapped his headrag and started wiping the lampblack off his face and said, "Yes, my love." It was Félice.

"You remembers how that Indian knife disappear out the evidence?" asked Aaron. "How that knife seem like it like to disappear and then turn up at the damnedest old time?"

"Aaron, you ain't kilt Miles Glory!" exclaimed Sylvester. Félice tried to snuggle closer, which was quite impossible.

"Naw, naw, knucklehead, I didn't kill him. We just had us a little discussion. About he special arrangement with the police department. About what the Ku-Klux Klan might do about that depending what they happen to knowed. Also we talk a little about how that knife in my hand seem how it got almost a mind of it own. All such as that."

Then Félice began to giggle again, and Sylvester was sobbing and then laughing. He danced to the top of the burial mound and laughed and laughed and laughed.

The morning sun splashed gold in the treetops and spilled in pools down the lawn.

While Aaron and Mattie strung strips of bright rag in the trees, and Caleb's cousin Cato rosined up his fiddle bow, Sylvester slipped into the forest and came to the Indian village. He sat on the moss and watched as a snake swam slowly across to the opposite bank. A red-headed woodpecker ratcheted up the diving-tree's trunk and rat-a-tat-tatted for breakfast. He rose and walked to the ruined Indian house where he had found his knife, that day, so long ago. A braid of blue-black ants was moving up and down the crumbling wall. So long ago.

Sylvester had lost his desire to know about the Indians; all his thought was of the future. He put his Indian knife inside one of the old clay pots, packed it with sand, and sealed it with clay—perhaps he would come back for it some day. The rubble in one corner of the house was deep; he buried the pot there.

Uncle Dunc had cut holes in an old straw hat of the master's, and Buster, Sylvester's new mule, was wearing it when Sylvester came up the path to the old slave quarters. Ribbons were woven in Buster's mane, and his tail was freshly trimmed in a triple-bell cut. Sylvester stopped to scratch the warm, damp place beneath Buster's hat, and the mule gave a placid sigh.

Luigi was under strict orders to keep himself scarce today, but Sylvester caught a glimpse of him mucking out stalls in the darkness of the stable—his new job.

People were everywhere. Bess and Senior were taking their ease on the master's white bench beneath the sweetgum tree, bantering with Aaron. Cato's brother Atticus was plunking idly at his washtub bass. The knob-headed blacksmith from east Shelby County arrived with his army drum, trailing what must have been two dozen children. A gang of Sylvester's prison friends from Governors Island were rolling dice in the courtyard. Caleb was sitting stiffly on a stool while Mattie gave him a haircut and Isabel looked on, giggling. Jonah Johnson had lost one of his feet in the war, but he had traded a baby raccoon for a ride on the Arkansas ferry and peg-legged it the rest of the way out from town. He still had another coon left, which Joe John was stroking.

A gleaming black carriage pulled in from the road but did not take the drive up to the house. It too came to the quarters, and from it descended Charity and Dr. Beau and the Preacher. Giovanni Corelli strolled slowly down the lawn to greet them.

Queen, Nathan Bedford Forrest's seamstress, had driven a wagon from Greengrove plantation yesterday loaded high with bushels of poke greens, sweet peas, butterbeans, turnips, potatoes, and onions, and now she and Hattie were setting out country ham, barbecued ribs, fried chicken, hogshead cheese, pickled trotters, egg-and-pea salad, potato salad, fried green tomatoes, mashed butterbeans, greens and turnips and dumplings swimming in pot liquor, lightbread, rising biscuits, crackling bread, persimmon preserves, peach compote, scuppernong jelly, swamp honey, corn relish, watermelon pickle, vinegar peppers, salted pecans, boiled peanuts, and a big silver bowl brimming with Creole punch. Finally they brought out a tall white cake.

Uncle Dunc and Aaron struggled to hang a big brass bell from a limb of the sweetgum tree.

Caleb brushed the Preacher's black coat, saying, "Preacher? You know that gal ain't nothing but a whore and a disgrace. Ain't no way this anything but a shame."

"You don't believe in redemption, old man?"

"No, sir, I does not."

The Preacher took out his Bible and gave Sylvester a nod. Uncle

Dunc began to ring the bell. People turned their heads and smiled and, murmuring, began to gather on the lawn.

Between the columns at the head of the manor house steps, Drury appeared, with Félice on his arm. She was dressed all in white. Giovanni Corelli began sniffling loudly. Aaron took his place beside Sylvester. Uncle Dunc, his banjo ready at his side, stuck out his big lower lip to its fullest extent.

And so Sylvester and Félice were married.

Part Three

1958

Across the last pasture, giving wide berth to his grandfather's bad-tempered bull, then through barbed wire again and past the tenant shacks, through chickens, guineas, ducks, turkeys, dogs, on into and through the dense young upland woods, down eroded red-clay breaks and into the shadowy bottomland forest Wordlaw Corelli made his way, wary, attentive, intent. Here and there were stumps of ancient trees, three, six, nine feet thick, mossed and crumbling. On the bank of the bayou sat an old colored man, fishing with a long cane pole. A brick-red hound sat next to him, watching the thick brown water.

"What you doing in here, boy?" the old man demanded.

"Exploring?"

"This ain't no place for a child alone."

"I'm going down there," said Wordlaw, pointing downstream.

"Shoot. Ain't even no trail down in yonder. You Mr. S. L.'s grandson, ain't you."

"Yeah," said Wordlaw, extending his hand. "How do you do?"

"How do. My name Wilbur Corey. This here is Second Samuel." Wordlaw scratched the dog's head; he seemed remarkably indifferent to the attention. "You know old Drury Woodson," continued Wilbur Corey. Drury was Wordlaw's grandparents' houseman. "Well, I am Drury's second cousin once remove. Whoa now!" He had a bite. "Naw, naw, Mr. Catfish, you keep off that snag. Don't give me no trouble. There you come, there you come." He hoisted the fish and deftly unhooked it. Second Samuel watched every move, wide-eyed but utterly impassive.

"Let me see him," said Wordlaw, reaching into the bucket of murky water where the fish was thrashing.

"Watch that spine on the back fin, boy!"

"Ow!" Fire coursed into his palm, up his arm, up his neck. "I thought it was the whiskers that stung."

"You better go on home and read you a book. Do your homework."

"It's *Friday!*" Wordlaw turned to go, catfish poison burning all down his arm.

"Boy?" called the old man. "Ain't I done told you that ain't nothing but swamp in yonder?"

Canebrakes, honeysuckle thickets, sudden plunging potholes made the going hard, and scary. He knew that if he stayed along the creek he could follow it back. But then there came a slough, flooded high this spring, its banks an impenetrable tangle of scrub willow. He would have to find a way around it. The only dry footing was out of sight of the water, and soon he had lost his bearings.

He looked to see where the sun had been, but it had clouded over. Above him hung a hornet's nest, silver-gray, turnip-shaped. His father had warned him that he was probably allergic to hornet stings. He was allergic to tons of stuff. Half the mornings of his life he woke up sneezing. His father had said that if a hornet or a wasp or a yellowjacket or a mud dauber or a bumblebee or even just a honeybee stung him, he might go into anaphylactic shock and die in less than a minute. Wordlaw was scared of anything that buzzed; dragonflies terrified him. He started to run, and then remembered that that was how you ran into snakes, not giving them enough time to get out of the way. Oak woods like this were where diamondback rattlers lived. Sometimes they were six feet long.

Raccoons and skunks carried rabies. There were rabid dogs, too, that the colored people had let run wild. If you got bitten you had to get shots in the stomach. There were water moccasins out here, and copperheads. Once Wordlaw had gotten poison ivy and run a fever of a hundred and three point six. There was quicksand in the swamp that would swallow you and leave no trace. If you went barefoot, hookworms would go up through the soles of your feet into your blood and breed in your brain and crawl out through your eyes.

Okay, okay, I'm chicken, Wordlaw admitted. Now what.

The walking here was easy. The trees were huge, and far apart. There was very little undergrowth, just dead leaves, uncurling ferns, and occasional tiny white stars of flowers on the forest floor. He had no idea where he was going, but the fear had left him. He wandered left and right, around in circles, kicking up oak leaves, looking at things.

There was a brightening ahead, a clearing. In it last year's high stiff grass still stood, a haze of new green glowing beneath. A hurrying swish of movement passed through the grass to the trees, and then there was silence. Wordlaw's fear returned in a rush.

But his curiosity overrode it. There was a gap in the grass where the sound had first come from. Above, now, vultures were circling, black silhouettes against the churning silver sky.

A deer lay curled in a muddy depression, its head twisted skyward, grinning—the cheeks eaten away. One back leg also had been eaten, and the hide peeled back from the rib cage. The guts lay in a heap off to the side, crawling with ants. There were big paw prints all around, and a long pair of parallel scrapes. The meat was fresh, the blood bright. It did not stink at all. Above, without a sound, the black birds wheeled.

Wordlaw found himself smiling, with no notion why. He did not move. He felt enclosed, sealed in this place and moment. The silence was as dense as stone. Was this stillness of the killer watching?

Suddenly he realized that the light was fading. At the edge of the clearing the forest, though just budding, was a mass of opaque shadow. He tried to retrace his route through the oak woodland, keeping to the high ground where the trees were sparser and the light better, but he could not find the willow-rimmed slough. He thought, The water has to be downhill. As he descended, the forest thickened, and the footing was rugged over fallen branches, creeping grapevines, gullies. Finally there was water ahead, its brown gone bluish gray, sky-bright. But it was not the slough, nor the creek. It was a cypress swamp, stretching far into darkness. He was lost.

The brightness of the water deepened the dark all around. He did not even have a match to make a fire. He would try to find a hollow tree and hole up in it. Would what killed the deer be hunting again?

There were night sounds now—scuttlings and scufflings, a whoof-whoof-whoof of big wings. A tree groaned in the rising wind. It started to rain.

But oddly enough, Wordlaw found that this real danger scared him less than the imagined ones of the afternoon—the allergenic hornets and anaphylactic shock, the poisonous snakes, the hookworms. There was something thrilling in this fear. He was on his own.

Well, it was mortifying, but he was going to have to do some hollering. "Help!" he yelled. "Please! I'm lost! Is anybody there?"

He kept it up till he was hoarse. It was full dark now, and cold, the rain had not let up, he hadn't even found his hollow tree. It occurred to him that he could die here tonight.

"Help!" he cried again.

A dog barked—probably one of the ones gone wild, rabid, coming to kill him. Then there was a crash in the leaves, and a thud. "*Dad* gummit!" growled a man's voice some way off. Through the misting rain Wordlaw could see the weak yellow of a dying flashlight.

"Over here!" he shouted, his voice cracking. "I'm over here!"

"Didn't I *told* you you was going to get lost?" came the voice. "Ignorant young monkey! I bust my head on a damn tree in the dark."

Wordlaw hurled himself against the overalls of Wilbur Corey and started to cry, clinging to the soft, soap-smelling denim. Second Samuel snuffled against Wordlaw's sting-swollen hand with his wet nose.

"We better get on out of here before I lose this battery outright," said Wilbur. "I don't half know where we at my own self."

Wordlaw told the old man about the dead deer, the sound in the grass, the footprints, but all he had to say in reply was, "Ain't that something?" The rain had stopped, and fog was gathering. They walked on in silence.

They stopped where Wilbur had been fishing, to pick up his pail of fish and his pole. Wordlaw took the flashlight now. It was fading fast, but Second Samuel, nose to the ground, led the way. At Wordlaw's back door, Wilbur Corey slipped into the darkness without a word.

"Bye, Wilbur!" Wordlaw called after him. "Thank you!"

"Better read you a book," growled the old man. "Do your homework."

Wordlaw's parents and his sister were in the dining room. "Come seven o'clock I was going to call the durn sheriff," said his father by way of greeting. His mother and Claudia stared into their plates and said nothing.

Sylvie brought in his supper—ham, turnip greens, sweet potatoes. "I done kept it hot for you, Wordie," she said, ruffling his hair "and there's hot bread coming." Sylvie Woodson was Drury's sister. She had raised Wordlaw, and still treated him like a baby. His hand was throbbing, so swollen it was hard to hold the fork.

In a rush of run-together words Wordlaw told what had happened. The look on his father's face was of disbelief, and disgust.

"That man, that Wilbur, he was in jail!" cried his mother. "I don't want that man on this property ever again, you hear me?"

"Yes'm," said Wordlaw, helpless in the face of such utter absence of sympathy.

Upstairs, the baby started wailing. "Shoot!" said Wordlaw's mother, getting up. "That child and her colic are driving me insane. Sylvie? Sylvie? Syl*ves*tra!" she yelled, ringing the bell, until Sylvie strolled placidly back into the dining room with a steaming basket of biscuits for Wordlaw.

"Yes'm, Miss Idie." Sylvie had special names for everybody.

"Shoot's crying again," said Claudia, who was five.

"Your sister's name is *Susannah,*" said her father.

"Is not," insisted Claudia. "Her name is Shoot."

Wordlaw laughed, sputtering crumbs, realizing that that was in fact what his mother said every time she heard or saw the baby doing anything. Sylvie must have started this. "Let's go see her," he said to Claudia. "Let's go see Shoot before she goes to bed."

His father was not amused. "Y'all's sister's name is Susannah, and I'll thank you to use it. Claudia, you may be excused. And you, Mr. Magellan, you're not going anywhere. First you finish your meal, and then you and I have got some business to transact. You know the rule."

The rule was that if he was late for supper he got a whipping.

"Go on," said his father. "Go get it." "It" was a particular belt that his father never wore.

Because he wouldn't cry, his father beat him harder, but with every lick Wordlaw was more determined not to cry.

Wordlaw always had Saturday lunch at the old plantation house and then spent the afternoon with his grandfather. "Well," said S. L. Corelli, "I do wish I could go out there with you, but I am not quite up to wilderness exploration any more. My old ticker is not right."

This was the first Wordlaw had heard of this. "Are you okay?" was all he could think of to say.

"I'm fine, I'm fine. Just have to take it easy. Listen. Let's ride down to the store, and then I'm going to show you something."

Wilbur Corey and a bunch of other old colored men were sitting on the porch of the general store, smoking cigarettes and drinking RC Cola. They fell silent as the white man and boy approached. "Hey, Wilbur!" called Wordlaw heartily.

"Hey, monkey," growled Wilbur, with a diffident touch of his hat brim to S. L. Corelli.

Wordlaw and his grandfather bought a bag of plaster of Paris, and when they got back to Corelli plantation his grandfather taught him how to make casts of animal tracks in tuna fish cans with both ends cut out. Drury's hunting dog—who didn't seem to have a name—watched curiously from her cage.

"You going to get lost again?" asked his granddad.

"I'm going to make Wilbur take me," said Wordlaw.

"What do you mean, make him?"

"He'll do it if I tell him to."

"That's probably so," said his granddad, "but it doesn't make it right. You can't just walk up to colored people who don't work for you and tell them what to do."

"Everybody else does," said Wordlaw.

"Well, you can't, and you won't. You hear me?"

"Yes, sir."

"Listen, son. All you're going to have to do is take a bearing off the bayou and then follow it back."

Wordlaw quailed at the thought of going alone.

"You look a little doubtful, boy."

"It's just—"

"You're not yellow, are you?"

"No, sir."

"Well, all right then. Look here." S. L. Corelli reached into his pocket and unfolded an old, leather-clad compass.

The Episcopalians had started having their eleven-o'clock service at ten-fifty so they could beat the Methodists and Presbyterians to the country club, but the staff had never yet adjusted to the onslaught of Sunday diners at the very stroke of noon. The waiters moved across the gleaming floor in slow motion, with dumbstruck gapes. It took Ree Billy a good minute to scrawl each order down. He could never keep straight who had what. "Ham sam bone jury," he whispered over Wordlaw's shoulder, "if them frog legs don't smell sweet!"

"I had the prime rib, well done," said the boy. Frogs were his friends, hidden in the swamp like himself, dropping from sight at will. Cows, on account of his grandfather's bull, he hated, and, so, gladly ate.

"Mrs. Corelli, was it you had the frog legs?"

"I swear, Ree Billy," said Wordlaw's mom, "nobody at this table ordered frog's legs. We are missing one fried chicken—for me."

"Yes'm, all right, but fried chicken take a while to cook, you know," said the waiter. "They fries it up from scratch. That's why it's so good."

"I know it's good. That's why I ordered it. And I *also* believe a family ought to have their Sunday dinner *together*. So please take all this mess back and keep it warm till my chicken's ready."

Ree Billy gazed lovingly on the unclaimed frog's legs. Somebody was going to have to eat them.

At this rate it was going to be three o'clock before Wordlaw could get into the swamp. "What's 'ham sam bone jury'?" he demanded when Ree Billy came round to top up their water glasses for the dozenth time.

"That's African talk," the waiter explained. "Mumbo-jumbo. What you say when your food be good. Keep the evil eye off of it."

"What in the hell are you talking about, Ree Billy?" demanded Robertson Corelli.

"Mr. Doc, tell you the honest truth, I ought to knowed I shouldn't said nothing about that," said Ree Billy. "White folks don't dig no mumbo-jumbo." He sauntered off, grinning.

"Robertson Corelli!" cried Wordlaw's mom. "How can you set there and let a nigra address you like that?"

"I like that old boy," said his dad, with a shrug. "I think we might be kin."

"What in the world has got into you today?"

"Well, he's another one of these Coreys, you know."

"Ree Billy's Ree Billy *Corey?*" exclaimed Wordlaw, momentarily forgetting his grievance against his father. His butt still stung. "Is he related to Wilbur Corey?"

"Hell, they're all kin to one another," said Robertson Corelli, "and probably kin to us. Ree Billy's granddaddy lived on the place. Corelli corrupted to Corey? Makes sense, doesn't it? Colored man would feel a damn fool with an Italian last name, don't you think?"

"But that old old crippled man, what was his name?" asked Wordlaw's mother. "The one that died when—why, Wordlaw, I plumb forgot! You were setting on that old colored man's lap when he just keeled over dead. Christmas morning, nineteen forty-eight. Aaron was his name. Aaron *Corelli.*"

"Yep," said Wordlaw's father, "Aaron always was different. Lord, he was ancient when I was a *child.* He was an actual slave."

"Dad, could we really be kin to Ree Billy?"

"Well, he might be kin to *us.*"

Wordlaw pondered this riddle in silence.

By the time he got home it was in fact too late to go to the swamp.

The morning sun splashed gold in the treetops and spilled in long pools down the lawn.

Beyond the slough was virgin forest—one of the last examples of old-growth upland forest in the whole lower Mississippi valley, his granddad had said. "I always thought I might see me an ivory-billed woodpecker in there. They're supposed to be extinct, but folks keep talking about how elusive they might be, and that place is classic ivory-bill habitat. Folks say there's a lot of money locked up in those trees. I don't care. I like it like it is, even if I don't go in there any more. I just like letting it *be* there. Absolutely devoid of utility."

" 'Devoid of utility'?" Wordlaw had repeated.

"Means useless," his grandfather had explained, smiling broadly into a laugh, and then seeming to look inward, as though remembering something, and still smiling. He had let Wordlaw spend Sunday night at his house, and skip school today.

Devoid of utility: that strange stilted phrase kept running through Wordlaw's mind as he walked among the giant trees, following his compass bearing.

The clearing was surprisingly easy to find. Most of the rest of the deer had been consumed. What remained was black with blowflies, and it stank to high heaven. The rain had smeared the tracks a little, but they were still clear enough. Then Wordlaw realized he had forgotten to stop for water at the bayou, and so could not make plaster. Rather than hike all the way back, he took a look around—and there, below a sharp drop-off on the far side of the clearing, right where the animal had fled on Friday, and then across a low plain of tangled undergrowth, lay Daylight Bayou itself.

Close though it may have been, the water was hell to get to. First there was the steep brambled slope to descend, and beyond that the vegetation was so dense that in places he had to wriggle under it on his belly—like a snake, and oh, Lord, *please* let there not be one. In other places the vines and fallen branches were layered so thick and so tightly interwoven that he could scramble across the top with the ground five feet beneath him. A box tortoise stared up at him, languidly blinking. Once, crawling, he looked up into the glittering eyes of a raccoon, which bared its teeth, hissed at him, and shuffled away. Birds whirred through the thickets invisible, and then burst forth, gold stars, in a green shaft of sunshine.

Again he climbed atop a mass of vine, as springy as a trampoline, with openings into dark mossed crevices deep below. His bucket caught on something behind him. He gave it an impatient jerk, and it flew from his grasp. It fell through a hole and landed with a loud clang.

There were no exposed rocks anywhere around here except gravel. The soil, granddad said, was hundreds of feet thick before you hit bedrock. Then what had that bucket banged on? Wordlaw pulled the hole wider, took a firm grasp on the best-anchored grapevine, and swung down through.

It was cool, dank. When his eyes adjusted to the dark, he saw—what was *this?*—two crumbling dirt-and-stick walls, no more than two feet high, joined at a right angle. Protruding from a heap of rubble in the corner was some sort of black vase, its mouth clogged with red clay. When Wordlaw picked it up, it came to pieces, and from within fell—a knife. The leather scabbard turned to powder when he touched it, but the knife itself, though heavily rusted, seemed sound. It had a handle of horn or bone, which, once dusted, gleamed.

He was able to use the knife at once, to hack his way out of the thicket. Soon he found the trace of an old path down to the bayou. Upstream, the channel narrowed and the foliage closed in overhead. Here the trees were draped with vines, the shoreline lined with willow, the sky only a winking and dappled absence in the forest canopy—the whole waterscape like a huge green room. A beaver slapped the water in alarm as he approached. He dipped his bucket.

He struggled back up the bluff and looked himself over. His shirt sleeves were ripped, his arms bleeding; one knee showed red through his jeans. He could not remember ever having felt so good.

He mixed his plaster, set his three tin cans carefully around the clearest prints, and took his casts. While they dried, he had lunch. A blue-black long-tailed wasp danced in the air above his thermos of sweet iced tea, and Wordlaw froze, his heart pounding. When his mother saw his clothes, she was going to murder him. The jeans were brand-new—well, had been. Good thing he'd left his jacket here. What creature *would* these tracks be of?

The clouds swept by overhead, their shadows racing into the trees.

The first thing Wordlaw heard when he stepped inside his grandfather's house was his father's voice. He skulked along the hall toward the library, and listened at the closed door.

"How long do I wait until I call the sheriff?" demanded Robertson Corelli.

"For heaven's sake," said Wordlaw's granddad. "I am sure the boy is perfectly fine."

"You know, I can't *believe* this," said his dad. "The more I think about it, the more incredible it gets. You actually putting him up to it, and then lying to both his mother and me. Why don't you get one of the tenants to go in there and look for him?"

"I insist that there is nothing to worry about."

"His allergies? You don't worry about him getting stung?"

"If you ask me, Robertson, all this alarmism is going to turn the child into a coward."

"That swamp is a menace. Mosquitoes, snakes, diseases, quicksand. It's just a sinkhole for money. Don't you realize we could be *rich?*"

"What is it you need that you don't have?"

"For Christ's sake, Pop."

"How many times have we had this discussion? The land is mine, and I will use it, or not use it, as I see fit. When I'm gone, and the way I've been feeling lately that may not be long, whoever I leave it to can use it as *he* sees fit."

The door swung open. Wordlaw looked up into his father's burning eyes. He was still wearing his white work coat, his stethoscope still looped in the pocket.

"I just got back," stammered Wordlaw.

Although his father had never hit him except under conditions of formal punishment, Wordlaw raised his arm, involuntarily, to ward off a blow. But his father strode past him and down the hall as though he was not there.

"Do you have any idea what time it is?" his grandfather demanded.

"No, sir," said Wordlaw.

"It is now twenty minutes past five. Your mother called the school, to see if they were keeping you late, and naturally they told her you hadn't been there all day. So she caught me in a bald-faced lie. I thought I could trust you."

Shame clamped Wordlaw's throat like a claw. He shut his eyes, and tears seethed through the lids.

"You got the casts?"

"Yes, sir," said Wordlaw weakly, fishing the best one out of his pocket.

His grandfather stared at it in astonishment. He pulled down a book and flipped quickly to a page. He shook his head as in disbelief, almost smiling now through his anger, and finally held out the open book in one hand and the plaster cast in the other, next to the picture—the footprint of a *cougar*.

"Also known as puma, panther, catamount, mountain lion," said Wordlaw's granddad in a hushed voice. "Considered extinct east of the Rocky Mountains."

"Wow," said Wordlaw.

"You're darn right wow."

"I love that swamp," said Wordlaw.

"You've got to go home."

"Yes, sir. I know."

"Come over tomorrow. After school. I want to talk to you."

"Yes, sir. I'm sorry, Granddad. I won't let you down again."

"See that you don't," said his grandfather, extending his hand.

Wordlaw took it gratefully.

1959

At last, at first frost, the pollens abated. A stark white-blue clarity gave every shape a black outline. Gray lichens yielded light as dazzlingly hued as a diamond's. The swamp maples burst into flame overnight. At last, Wordlaw could see.

He could breathe. He could *smell*—wood smoke, leaf mold, the vanilla of oak bark, fox pee at the base of a loblolly pine. For a solid month he had sneezed, and sneezed, fifty, a hundred times in helpless succession. His eyes swelled nearly shut. Noises throbbed in the fog in his head all night. And then at dawn came asthma, steel strap tightening around his chest.

A hard north wind brought chop to the water. Cypress needles clung in foamy windrows at the shore. There came a hammering above—Wordlaw swiveled fast, ever alert to the hope of an ivory-bill, but it was just another pileated. A late tiger swallowtail fluttered through the hickories.

The guys were gathering on Forrest McCracken's big side lawn, tossing the ball, hollering in their newly deep voices. "Well, if it ain't little Nelly Corelli," called Youngblood Venable, who though only a freshman was already playing on the varsity at Chickasaw High School, and the ball came hurtling at Wordlaw like a rocket. It caught him on his right middle finger and slammed tip-first into the tip of his nose. He started sneezing, over and over, as laughter spread across the lawn.

The Old Buzzard—that was what everybody called Forrest's grandfather, except to his face—appeared on the porch, followed by that tall blonde girl who was so beautiful, Cora something.

"Hey *hey,* Cora," he heard Forrest whooping. "When did *you* show up?" He heard the bold wet smack of the kiss she gave Forrest. Girls, too, to see me made a fool of.

In the choosing-up of sides, Wordlaw was as usual the last chosen. And as usual he fumbled punt returns, went into motion too early or late, flinched at the high-kneed onrush of runners, and was pummeled and trampled and elbowed and bullied to the brink of tears.

His last chance was a short pass he ought to have intercepted easily—he wondered indeed if Forrest had lobbed it straight at him on purpose—but he blew that too, as the Old Buzzard banged on a black iron skillet to end the fourth quarter.

"Don't worry about it," said Forrest, with a quick consoling shove to Wordlaw's shoulder.

"Y'all better watch out," called Wordlaw as he mounted his bike—"next time I'm *really* going to stomp some butt."

Blood Venable gave him the big-dick-in-hand hand sign and, as Wordlaw pedaled away down the drive, snarled after him, "Eat me raw, queerbait!"

On Thanksgiving night, Wordlaw got another baby sister, named Ivy Dee after her mother and promptly dubbed Junior by Claudia.

The day after was a still, soft day, the low sun warm through black branches and mist above the bayou. Wordlaw concentrated on stalking in perfect silence, heel peeling slowly to toe between stiff twigs and crisp leaves. In consonance with the Boy Scout creed—Be Prepared—he carried, in his new scout pack, canteen, compass, plaster casting kit, flashlight, one hundred feet of nylon parachute cord, first aid kit, waterproof match safe, emergency flares, rain poncho, and hatchet, as well as bird identification book, binoculars, sketchbook, soft pencils, India rubber erasers, turkey and dressing sandwiches, and his now shining and sharp horn-handle knife in the scabbard his granddad had had made for his birthday.

Crouched low in the weeds, he sketched the silhouettes of Wilbur Corey and Second Samuel at the fishing hole. At length Wilbur got a bite, and flipped his catch quickly into the tin pail.

"You keep hauling fish out like this," said Wordlaw, stowing his sketchbook, "there aren't going to be any more."

"Lot you knows," grunted Wilbur, not even turning around. The dog didn't turn either. "This ain't but the best catfish fishing in the whole of Shelby County."

"There's huge ones in the river, Granddad says."

"No doubt about that," said Wilbur. "I done grabbled for them."

"Grabbled? What's grabbling?"

"Go down in that muddy water bare-handed and grabble him up by the gill. That's all."

Second Samuel yawned in Wordlaw's face, foul dog breath.

"Wait a minute," said Wordlaw. "You are saying you have caught Mississippi River catfish with your *bare hands?*"

"I could have swore I just heard myself saying that," said Wilbur. "Sixty pound or more, that's all."

"Come on!"

"There ain't no limit to what you don't know, boy, is there? That's too much work, though—travel way over yonder clear past Horn Lake, get you a boat, worry about them big barge tows slapping you upside the revetment. I prefer to set here like a gentleman on my hind end and wait for these little ones. They much more sweeter eating anyhow. How come you don't catch your mama none?"

"I don't like fish," said Wordlaw. "Besides, she says catfish is—"

"Don't you say nigger food," said Wilbur.

"I wouldn't," said Wordlaw. "We don't talk like that."

"Just *think* it. I know what white folks are like. All this *we* talk. All this family."

"Haven't you got a family?"

"Naw. I like ladies. Too much sometimes. Get me in trouble."

"My mom said you went to prison," Wordlaw blurted.

Wilbur visibly started, and turned to give Wordlaw a hard cold look. "That's correct."

"What did you do?"

"Read books. Charles Dickens, William Faulkner, such as that."

"No, I mean to have to go."

"I know what you meant. Well, it was lady trouble. You know, old Dickens, he wrote long books, but they goes fast. Faulkner be shorter, but slow, slow. A jealous husband can be a mighty thing. That fool come at me with a axe. I had to defend myself."

"You *killed a man?*" gasped Wordlaw.

"Naw," said Wilbur, "just hurt him. Assault and batteried him."

"Wow."

"Man killed my dog! That was the other Samuel, which is how come this here one be Second." Wilbur scratched the red dog's head. "No-count worthless hound he turn out to be, too." Second Samuel's tail thumped the ground hard twice. "Don't know a coon from liverwurst."

Wordlaw thought he could see a slight resemblance to Ree Billy in Wilbur's high forehead, but Wilbur couldn't have been kin to the Corellis. His skin was basalt-black, with an ashy cast; his lips and nose were as African as a lion.

The porcupine quill began to jiggle, radiating ripples. "Your bobber's bobbing, Wilbur," said Wordlaw, mocking Wilbur's own dry tone.

Wilbur yanked so hard the line flew back over his head and hung up in the honeysuckle.

Wordlaw couldn't help laughing.

"Young monkey," growled Wilbur.

"S. L.," said Oscar Ballard, "I'm not telling you not to do it. I'm only advising you to reflect on the implications."

"I did my reflecting before I called you," said S. L. Corelli.

"I just hate to see you tie up your estate's most valuable asset. Practically its only asset at this point. What are you going to do about the tax? And what about your daughters?"

"Damn it, Oscar! I'm asking you to change my will, not run my life. I've heard your advice, for which I thank you but which I reject. One, the land to be held in trust until Wordlaw's twenty-first birthday. Two, a life estate for Cornelia. Three, figure out how much Robertson will need for the tax, and write that in. I've already provided decently for my girls, as you would have known if you'd bothered to refresh yourself on my current will."

"Who do you want for trustees?"

"You, you damn fool. And—I don't know. Get me some dimwit from the bank. Some nice *old* dimwit, who'll die before you and until then will do like you tell him to."

"And I thought it was lawyers who had the most cynical view of human nature."

"I'm not a cynic," said Corelli. "I'm a realist. How long will this take?"

"Just till I find you your dimwit," said Ballard.

"That shouldn't take long at the Planters Bank."

"You want to go duck hunting in Arkansas this weekend?"

"At that club of yours where they don't even heat the clubhouse? Drury's dog wouldn't go in that clubhouse."

"We got a stove," said Ballard. "Old pot-belly stove."

"The kind that's got a hundred years' worth of tobacco spit stuck to it," said Corelli. "The kind you tell the world's worst lies at."

"Exactly."

"I reckon so," said Corelli.

"Thank you very much," said Ballard, with a mocking salaam. "You do our humble stove honor."

"Drury'll drive us."

"Drury's half blind!"

"He's good company," said S. L. Corelli.

"Thank you very much indeed," said Oscar Ballard.

Cornelia stuck her head in the door. "Are y'all old no-counts about finished with business? Drury thinks it's time we had a drink."

"Drury knows whereof he speaks," said Ballard. "Cornelia, will you let your husband come duck hunting with me this weekend?"

"*Let* him?" she laughed. "You can *have* him."

Wordlaw had learned that not livestock but deer were the cougar's primary prey, and with the advent of hunting season many deer had sought refuge in the heart of the swamp. He patterned his movements on an imagining of the cougar's—one step and then pause, all awareness. Hoofprints converged on a jungle of cedar. He squeezed through the prickly limbs with his breath held, fluid, silent. He did get as far as once seeing the flash of a fleeing whitetail's white tail, but there was no cougar to be found, nor even one's track in the mud.

He tried to feel no disappointment. He was trying to teach himself that the reward of his explorations should be in looking, not finding. Similarly he had come to see these long days alone not as loneliness, not avoidance—in which, admittedly, they had begun—but as a savored solitude and self-reliance. He returned to the oak woods. Here on high ground the wind was sharp, the light cold pewter.

A triple crack of rifle fire rang from the bottomland and echoed in the oaks. He did not start, nor stir. He waited, watching, still.

At length Second Samuel appeared, and after a studious sniffing of Wordlaw's mud-clotted shoes sat to wait at his side. Wordlaw gave him a ginger snap. Soon Wilbur appeared, with a small deer over his shoulders and a rifle in the crook of his arm. Second Samuel gave a low, companionable *whuff*.

"I been getting right tired of fish," said Wilbur, grinning, as he slung the deer to the ground. "You know something, monk? I think that dog almost likes you."

"It's not very big," observed Wordlaw of the deer.

"That ain't no Piggly Wiggly supermarket in there, boy," said Wilbur irritably. "You takes what you can get."

"And the small ones make better eating," Wordlaw mocked.

"As a matter of fact that is so."

"Did you see any cougars?" asked Wordlaw.

"Naw, nor no elephants, tigers, nor grizzly bears neither."

The little buck's abdominal cavity was propped open with sticks, its tongue lolling out. Its eyes were wide open. Wordlaw tried to picture it, stepping from cover, turning its head to scan its surroundings with eyes, nose, swiveling ears, all awareness—but insufficient awareness, obviously—and then the utter surprise of sudden death. "How do you sneak up on them?" he demanded. "All I ever see is their damn tails running away."

"You watch your mouth, child," said Wilbur. "You come from downwind on their path till you get where they yarding. Then you go up in a tree and get comfortable and just bide quiet. Then after while Mr. Buck come, and you shoot him. See where I shot him? That's a lung shot."

"What about Sam?"

"He help me find the yard, and then when I tell him he just set on the ground back in the bushes. That's the stillest dog ever was born. I taught him that."

"Can you teach me? I get so restless."

"Naw, I can't teach you that. Boys is naturally restless. That's all right. You'll grow up, and then you'll wished you could move." Wilbur reflected a moment, twirling a finger in the deer's stiff leg hair. "Grass always greener on the other side to the fence. That's what I always tell myself when I smell T-bone steak cooking on some white folks' barbecue grill. Would I really wish to be one of y'all? Setting in that white church all solemn and nicey-nice-nice? I seen them in there. Look like dead peoples. No, sir, I'm going to eat neck bones and chitlins, and sweat and holler in church."

"Listen, if you're going to eat neck bones and chitlins can I have the deer then? I love venison." He fed Sam another ginger snap.

"You funny, ain't you?"

"I hate our church. Colored church sounds better. Can I go with you sometime?"

"Naw, you can't go with me."

"I bet you don't even go."

"I *got* to go, dad gummit. I'm on parole."

"Oh," said Wordlaw, sobered. "Wilbur? Is prison real bad?"

"I can't recommend it. Listen, I got to go." He hoisted the carcass to his shoulders. "Get up, dog. Samuel? I am talking to you. I know you rather set and eat cookies all day than go to work, but we got butchering and salting to do."

With a lingering look at Wordlaw Second Samuel sighed, farted softly, and rose.

"See you, Wilbur," said Wordlaw.

"Later," said Wilbur, turning toward home, wherever that was.

S. L. Corelli finally consented to Oscar Ballard's major-domo Horace doing the driving, but by then Drury had so set his heart on going to Arkansas that he came too. Ballard and Corelli, in the back seat of Ballard's big De Soto, read the papers while Horace and Drury, in the front, with Drury's reeking black-and-tan coon hound between them, listened to gospel music on the radio.

"I think I found you your trustee," said Ballard.

"When's my new will going to be ready?" demanded Corelli.

"I've got a draft to look at this weekend. If it's in order we'll have it ready to sign on Monday."

"Let me see it."

"Why don't you just enjoy the scenery?" said Ballard irritably.

"I want to see my God-damned will. I don't feel good." Corelli took the draft and, with a grunt of satisfaction, began to read.

Oscar Ballard frowned, snorted, and returned to his newspaper. Wide flat fields of farmland rolled by. From time to time the car would cross a long bridge above a relict bayou bed, the old serpentine watercourse, now dry, lined with brush and alive with bird song, the man-made ditch beside it full of water but otherwise bare and lifeless.

"Looks fine to me," said Corelli, folding the will.

Countless millions of birds funneled down the Mississippi flyway every fall, and in the intensively cultivated lower valley food and good cover were scarce. The hunting club's five hundred acres of rice and corn, therefore, were left unharvested, that ducks and geese might feast there. Amidst the fields were interspersed plentiful bayous, sloughs, ponds, groves of remnant floodplain forest, hummocks dense with shrubs, and islands of high grass—a paradise for waterfowl.

The clubhouse was a miserable big shack, unpainted and without telephone, electricity, or indoor plumbing. In a rough circle around the Franklin stove stood a dozen armchairs in a state of advanced demoralization. Whatever color the rug might once have been had long been obscured by grime, cigar ash, and spilled food. Dog-eared men's magazines and detective novels were stacked in the corners. The cabinets bulged with mateless socks, moth-eaten sweaters, disreputable long johns. Various wretched outbuildings were scattered around a muddy open lot; in these the hunters and their servants slept, in wheezing iron beds. The club did not have a name.

One shed housed a rackety old belt-driven machine whose rubber fingers ripped the feathers from the dead birds. Old oil drums stank of years of encrusted blood. Down drifted through the air and clung to everything. On the door, some drunken night long ago, some wag had painted, in blue, the legend "Pluck a duck."

Drury was standing outside that door, talking with Phineas, the club's dog trainer, cook, and duck plucker, as S. L. Corelli approached. Drury was indefatigable. He had been up all night hunting raccoons—the hounds could be heard yelling in the woods until nearly dawn—and had nonetheless insisted on coming duck hunting. Only members and their guests were allowed to shoot, but Drury had sat content in the boat with Corelli all morning, chatting and chuckling over Horace missing his coon last night. Even Drury, dim-sighted though he was, had gotten one. Not that there was that much to it. The dogs did the work, and then all you had to do was shine a light in the raccoon's eyes and blast him out of the tree. "That Horace, I tell you, Mr. S. L.," said Drury—softly, so as not to scare off ducks—"that old boy is a menace to society. But he ain't no kind of menace to coons!" Then, evidently having decided (unilaterally) that the ducks had stopped coming for the day, Drury raised his voice and called across the water, "Wake up, Horace!"—for in fact Horace, in the bow of Ballard's boat, was dozing—"Wake up, man! There come a coon swimming at you now! Get your gun!" and then he said, suddenly softly again, behind his hand, to Corelli, "Wonder should I borry him my spectacles."

After a long and vinous late lunch, Corelli had spent the afternoon napping off a painful bout of indigestion, but Drury was still going strong. "Hey, Mr. S. L.!" he boomed as Corelli approached the plucking shed. "Phineas say he can make me a raccoon hat."

"Like Davy Crockett," said Phineas.

"King of the Wild Frontier," sang Drury.

The sun was setting red behind the rice fields. Phineas in his black rubber apron and Drury holding the raccoon pelt comically above his head, both tinted dark yellow by the kerosene lamps, looked like figures in a painting. A deep, dull numbness began to travel down his arm.

"Drury, let me talk to you a minute," he said. He watched Drury walking toward him through the red and yellow light. The numbness was turning to pain, spreading into his neck and down his throat, and he could not breathe. The pain was heavy, dull, huge. It pushed him to his knees, and still he could not stay upright. He lay down, and the pain was on top of him like a heavy, heavy weight. Drury and Phineas were moving their mouths, but he could not hear what they were saying. The pain was very dark, and crowded out the sunset and the lamplight.

Wordlaw's grandmother clung fiercely to his hand throughout the funeral. Only when the casket was lowered into the earth did her hands fly to her face. One great sob burst from her throat with the violence of vomiting; she stanched it with a wadded glove. When she took his hand again, the steel had gone out of her grip. She bumped her head hard getting into the limousine.

"Stay with me," she whispered to Wordlaw at the door of his house, where there was to be a reception. "Stay with me every second, Wordlaw." She moved among the gathered family and friends of her husband of forty-nine years as though they were strangers, nodding blankly at their condolences, accepting cake and punch from Stella without even looking at her, turning airily away from Wordlaw's mother when she approached cradling the new baby in the crook of her arm.

"Where in heaven's name is Sylvie?" demanded his mother.

"She supposed to be bringing cookies from the bakery shop just like you said," said Stella, "but I ain't seen her." Stella Woodson was Wordlaw's grandmother's cook, and Drury's wife—thus Sylvie's sister-in-law.

"I have had it up to here with that woman," said his mother, for the millionth time.

"Wordlaw, will you please take me home?" said his grandmother.

Wordlaw's father intercepted them. "You're not really going to leave now," he said, "with all these people here just to see you."

"I hit my head, Rob," she returned, "and it hurts so badly I just feel like lying down."

"Well," said Robertson Corelli with a shrug, "suit yourself."

They took the back path, and his grandmother still seemed hardly to know where she was. She took a seat not in the library, where she habitually sat, but in the high mirrored parlor. It was getting dark outside; the room seemed very still, the air in it soft, almost foggy. She stared at the Christmas tree.

Drury appeared, out of his church suit and in uniform now. He plugged in the tree lights. "Let me get you some coffee, Miss Cornelia," he said gently, his thick lenses glinting Christmas colors. "Little toddy or something. Something to eat."

"What's that noise?" she said abruptly.

Wordlaw hadn't heard anything, but now he made it out—low moaning from the back of the house. Her hearing had always been acute.

"My sister's in the kitchen," replied Drury.

"Isn't it strange how grief strikes?" she wondered aloud. "Sylvie cries, and I can't. Are you all right, Drury?"

"No, ma'am, but I can't but get better."

"Wordlaw?" She turned to her grandson and for the first time all day really looked at him. "How are you, son?"

The fact was that he still had not felt very much, except guilty for not feeling anything clearer than this muddy puzzlement. He thought that if they had made him look his grandfather in the face, he would have flown to pieces for sure, but the coffin had been closed. "I don't know what it's going to be like not having him," he managed to say. "I can't imagine it."

"Drury," said Wordlaw's grandma, "Can I do anything for Sylvie, do you think?"

Tears shone on his dark matte cheeks. "It ain't account of Mr. S. L. she crying. That sheriff deputy, Riley, he hit her."

"My God."

"Deputy pull her over, right out on the highway. Say he looking for Wilbur Corey. Say he knew Wilbur and her been stepping out. Sylvie say she don't know where Wilbur at, and then he dump them cookies all over the shoulder of the road, them ones for y'all over yonder. She say she going to report on him for that, and that was when he hit her. With the stick. Say he will kill her if she report on him, and I believe him. That man been beating on colored folks nigh on twenty years and ain't nobody touch him yet."

"What's he want Wilbur for?" Wordlaw burst out.

"I don't have no idea, son," said Drury bleakly.

So Wilbur had been "stepping out" with Sylvie! Wordlaw was amazed—he'd never had the slightest notion of it. And now Wilbur was in dutch with the law again.

They heard wheels in the gravel out front, and Wordlaw could see his grandmother effortfully drawing herself up. "Drury," she said, "get that girl in the cellar and don't either of y'all so much as peep till I come get you. Go on, hurry up!"

The bell rang, and Cornelia Corelli made her way toward the front door with slow, stiff hauteur. She opened it on a policeman of precisely the type Southerners have nightmares of: knee-booted, barrel-gutted, red-faced, tobacco-chewing, face entirely expressionless. Wordlaw made himself scarce before the cop had seen him, but he stayed close enough to hear as Riley inquired, "You got a boy name of Wordlaw Corelli here?"

Wordlaw's grandmother considered this for a longish moment before replying in her grandest grande-dame style, "May I ask, officer, what your business is with my grandson?"

"Got something for him. Dog."

Curiosity overwhelming his fear, Wordlaw made for the side door, slipped out, and crept around to the front. Tied to the squad car's open back door, his brick-red coat gone nearly black in the dusk, sat Second Samuel. On the far side of the back seat Wordlaw discerned an unmistakable silhouette.

He looked back over his shoulder at his grandmother beneath the veranda's iron lamp. She flicked her eyelashes to indicate that she had seen him. "Well! Won't you come in?" she said with sudden, unaccountable graciousness. "Let's see if we can't find my grandson. Wordlaw?" she called, pretending she didn't know where he was. "Oh, Wooord-laaaw!" Riley followed her inside.

"Wilbur, what is all this?" whispered Wordlaw into the car. He reached, without looking or thinking, to scratch between Sam's ears, and touched wetness, crusted fur—a gash. The dog whimpered softly. Wordlaw looked at the blood on his fingers.

Wilbur's hands were cuffed in his lap. "Game warden get me with that little buck. I didn't have no license."

"Why *not?*" he whined, an exasperated Boy Scout.

"Where I going to get money for a hunting license, monkey? I don't even got enough to *eat* most the time. Then come to find out it's a parole violation. And my rifle, that's one too. That was Monday. So then today they sends this here officer Otto Riley to place me under arrest, but I wasn't home. I was fishing."

Wordlaw dropped his voice to a whisper. "He stopped Sylvie on the highway, and he hit her with his nightstick."

"I ain't surprise," said Wilbur wearily. "I'm sure he was looking forward to hitting me too, but first he come on Second Samuel. Samuel didn't do nothing! Just went out to look at him. You know he don't bark at nobody—except me when I don't do like he want me to, or if he want to tell me something. And old Otto he just whap Samuel upside the head with that stick. That's the first thing I heard—*whap!* I was on my porch, cleaning fish. I turn around and there go my dog going down like a tree, with his head bust open. And here come this police coming up on me. Looking serious ready for trouble, too—hand on his gun, man, the whole bit. He must have saw my fish knife. I put that knife down *real* quick, and says, 'Otto! Man, don't you know who this is?'

"We was little boys together, see. We done our fighting long ago. 'You under arrest, nigger,' he say, rearing back with that damn billy club. I say, 'Otto, put that stick up! This is Wilbur, man! Burr-head!' That's what them white boys use to call me when we was coming up. 'Naw!' he say, just a-laughing. 'Well,' he say, 'Burr-head, you dumb shit, you got to go to jail.' And I say, 'Otto, look what you done to my dog. You about ruint him.' So we work on Samuel till we get him back in the land of the living. And seem like Otto right sorry, so I ax him to ride me over here on the way to jail, to see if—will you take care of Samuel for me, monk?"

"Sure," said Wordlaw uncertainly. Oh, Lord. What were his parents going to say? "How long do you think you'll be gone?"

"There ain't no way to say that just yet," said Wilbur. "Might be some little while."

"I'll take good care of him, Wilbur." On some lame inspiration, he gave the Boy Scout sign. "I swear."

The front door opened again. "I just don't know what has become of that child," he heard his grandmother saying. "He's probably right out here in the yard playing."

"Grandma!" called Wordlaw. "Call the vet! Wilbur's dog's hurt!"

Riley turned slowly around, in ferocious false calm. "That there is a suspect under arrest!" he barked, clicking on his big flashlight and flaring wild circles through the bare oak limbs overhead. "Stand clear of the radio car! Stand clear, boy!"

"I didn't have no fishing license neither," whispered Wilbur, actually laughing a little, "but Otto too dumb to think of that."

"Stack," said Cornelia Corelli, reaching unsteadily, "would you please pass the, the—the dressing? I mean Rob. Heavens, I'm calling you by your daddy's name!"

"Dad," said Wordlaw, "do you think maybe they'll let Wilbur off? I mean, he just needed something to eat."

But Robertson Corelli was staring at his mother's face and frowning. She yawned. Her left eyelid was drooping. "Mama?" he said. "Let me look at your eyes." He stood over her, waving a candle back and forth, and lifted her eyelids with his thumb. "Now reach for that dressing again, Mama. I just want to see how you do that."

"I'm all right," she said thickly, yawning again.

Wordlaw's mother answered for her preoccupied husband: "A lot of these nigra men, Word, they think the world owes them a living. They'll take advantage of the colored women, they'll take advantage of whatever white people they can get their hooks into, they'll commit petty crimes like they think the rules just don't apply to them. Then it comes back and hits them in the face, like stepping on a rake that's been left laying upside down in the grass, and they act like they're so *surprised.* Well, I'm sorry, but the law's the law."

"But what about that deputy?" said Wordlaw. "Don't the rules apply to him? How come he can beat up Sylvie and get off scot-free?"

"Keep your voice down!" hissed his mother. "Do you want her to hear you? I know that wasn't right. But that's how things are between the races. A colored woman just can't expect to get away with sassing a policeman."

"Are you saying she deserved to be hit with a billy club?" demanded Wordlaw in outrage. "Grandma said she's going to talk to the sheriff. She said she's going to go see the editor-in-chief of the *Commercial Appeal* if she has to."

Wordlaw's mother pursed her lips and said nothing.

His grandmother was smiling vaguely. "I remember," she mused, "when that big tall black-colored man Wilbur Corey used to work in my vegetable garden, when S. L. and I were first married, and he'd bring that boy of his, Billy, to help him. That little boy was so *full* of questions. Wilbur would say, 'Yes, sir, Billy, yes, sir ree. Yes sir ree, Billy.' And pretty soon all the other little colored children were calling him Ree Billy. That's what I thought of just now."

"Ree Billy is Wilbur's *son?*" exclaimed Wordlaw.

"Oh, Wilbur's gone," said his grandma. "He went to jail."

"But he told me he's never been married," Wordlaw persisted.

"This is what I'm *saying* to you, Word," said his mother. "These nigra men have children all over the place—without getting married—and they don't take any more responsibility for them than a *dog*."

That last word reminded Wordlaw to slip Sam another bit of turkey under the table.

"One more time you feed that dog," she snapped, "and you will spend the rest of Christmas day in your room."

"It's Christmas!" cried his grandmother. "Let's open presents!"

"We already *did* that, Mama," said his father. "Don't you remember? The blue robe? Wordlaw's picture of the colored man fishing?"

"Oh," said Cornelia Corelli doubtfully. "I don't know what I was thinking of. I'm sorry. I have the most awful headache."

"That watercolor is of Wilbur Corey, Grandma," Wordlaw added. "And Second Samuel. Fishing in the bayou."

"Oh, Wilbur Corey's long gone," she repeated. "He went to jail. Years and years ago."

"You're mixing it up," said Wordlaw's father. "He's gone to jail all right—for poaching our deer. I saw to that right quick. But you're thinking of a long time ago."

"That's what I said, darling," said Cornelia Corelli. "I remember when Wilbur was just a little boy."

"Dad?" asked Wordlaw. "What do you mean, you 'saw to that'?"

"Well, I saw him big as life with it. We can't have just anybody going in our woods and shooting off our deer."

"Wilbur was my friend!"

"A very inappropriate friend," said his father. "But Wordlaw, believe me, I had no idea of sending Wilbur to jail. I thought he'd just get a fine. In any case, it's done, and I believe you'll be better off without him. He's a criminal, son."

Late that night Drury rang the doorbell and told Robertson Corelli that he'd better come quick. He had found Miss Cornelia wandering on the lawn in her new blue robe, without the slightest idea where she was.

"She's just not going to make it on her own," concluded Wordlaw's father. "We're going to have to make arrangements for her."

Robertson Corelli realized now that his mother may have had a subdural hematoma, incurred perhaps when she hit her head after the old man's burial. She might also have had a tumor, or any of a wide range of other problems, all of which could have been treated if only he had thought of them right away. But somehow his mind had just not been working in that whole range of thought.

Thus, by the time he got her admitted to the hospital, he had already had to begin concocting a medical history for her that would justify his not having taken prompt action. To her attending physician, his golfing buddy Dick Stahl, he had recounted a slow onset of forgetfulness, poor coordination, disorientation—all lies. As he had hoped, Stahl's diagnosis then was senile dementia. In which case there had been nothing to be done for her in the hospital. "Just see that she's as comfortable as possible," said Stahl unhappily. Did he suspect?

When she came home, Cornelia Corelli had lost the power of speech altogether, and could not even hold a pen to write a note. Only her eyes were articulate, and Wordlaw was too full of his own horror to try to construe the horror in them.

On the last morning of the year, in a light, soft snowfall, Wordlaw, Drury, and Stella stood on the steps feebly waving goodbye as Wordlaw's grandmother, strapped to a stretcher in the back of the Tatum Nursing Home ambulance, left Corelli plantation forever.

It was so cold the snow squeaked beneath his boots. Doves, puffed into balls, huddled in pairs on stiff branches and did not fly away at Wordlaw's approach. Daylight Bayou was frozen solid. Along the bank he saw the cougar's tracks. He did not try to follow them.

1960

"I usually have a little drink about this time of day," said Beau Echols before he was halfway in the door.

"Is there anything we need to talk about before he gets here?"

"Whoa—just one ice cube. I reckon we got to see what *he*'s talking about first. Main thing you got to know about Oscar Ballard is he fancies himself a gent. Real *gentleman.* You got your buddy to go see your mama again in the nursing home, didn't you?"

Luckily Dick Stahl had taken Robertson Corelli's history of his mother's symptoms as conclusive, but Corelli was still nervous. He had to keep telling himself that nobody would challenge the declaration of incompetence. After all, she *was* incompetent, now.

"Yeah," said Corelli. The bell rang. "Afternoon, Mr. Ballard. I imagine you know Beau Echols."

"Good to see you, Beau," said Ballard, eyebrows arched.

"Can I get you a drink, sir?" said Corelli.

"No, thank you," said Ballard, arranging his coat and hat on a chair. "Now. I didn't even bring the document with me, because I thought we might just visit about it first, as gentlemen."

Echols flashed Corelli a covert smirk.

"Dr. Corelli," said Ballard, "three days before your father died, he asked me to draw up a new will for him. It involved the establishment of a trust, so there was a couple of days' delay while I got trustees for him. I was to be one, and a man at the Planters Bank the other. Your father never signed anything, but he had read a draft—in my car on the way to my hunting club, that Friday afternoon—and he approved it to be drawn up without change. Drury and my man Horace and I all saw him do it. It was to be typed up for his signature that Monday, but of course he passed away first. Now, I want you to understand I'm not here on a matter of law"—Ballard nodded solemnly to Echols—"though I'm always glad to see my friend Beau Echols. This is really a family matter. I'm here not as S. L. Corelli's lawyer but as his friend—as it happens, the only one who knew his last wishes. Because his new will was never signed, naturally it has no legal standing. But I have hoped that you might honor his wishes nevertheless."

"What'd it say?" demanded Echols.

"I'm coming to that," said Ballard. "As you know, Dr. Corelli, your father's previous will provided that upon his death the plantation would be held in trust for you, with your mother as sole trustee, the trust to be dissolved at her death. By the way, let me say how sorry I am to hear about your mother's illness. She's a wonderful woman. How is she getting along?"

"Sorry to say, she's had to move into Tatum's," said Corelli. "What we call senile dementia. It had been coming on for a long time."

"I never noticed anything," said Ballard, startled.

"Well, these things are subtle," said Corelli.

"I'm sorry she's so unwell. A wonderful woman."

"Yes, sir," said Corelli. "Appreciate it. Now—"

"Well. The change your daddy made was to establish a trust for your son Wordlaw, to hold the plantation on his behalf until—"

"You've got to be kidding," said Corelli.

"Well, no," said Ballard.

"Until when?" demanded Echols.

"It was to mature on his twenty-first birthday."

"And what till then?" asked Corelli.

"The land to be maintained in its present condition by the trustees, and farmed by the present tenants. A life estate for your mother, and the farm income accruing to her."

"Shutting me out altogether!" cried Robertson Corelli.

"No, it would have gone to you in the event of your son's death should that event have preceded dissolution of the trust. And there was a cash bequest for you as well."

"Oh. I see. Great," said Corelli. "Really great. You know something, Mr. Ballard? I can't believe you have the nerve to walk in my house and give me this crap. I can't believe any of this."

"There's no reason to get all worked up here, Rob," said Echols. "He doesn't have a leg to stand on."

"Do you think we might discuss a compromise that would at least partly honor your father's wishes?" asked Oscar Ballard. "His greatest concern was preservation of the forest and swampland. We could certainly discuss the agricultural portion."

"Oscar, I got to say you do have a pair of nuts on you," said Beau Echols.

"You can go," said Corelli to Ballard.

"Well, thank you for your time," said Ballard grimly, pushing himself to his feet. He put his old chesterfield coat on, slowly adjusted his fedora, and walked to the door.

Neither Corelli nor Echols rose to see him out. Corelli just sat on the sofa shaking his head until Ballard was gone, and then said yet again, "I really can't believe this. You know, Beau, my daddy used to threaten me with all kind of things, but I never thought the old son of a bitch would do something like this. It's kind of hard to take." There were tears in his eyes.

"Son of a bitch is the word," said Echols. "Have a drink, boy."

S. L. Corelli had left the contents of the house to be squabbled over by his son and three daughters. In the end, Wordlaw's Aunt Anna took the Italian paintings that had come from their maternal grandfather Augustus Robertson, but she disdained the works of her own forebear Angelo Corelli. Nobody else wanted them, either, so the canvases were left to molder in the attic. Aunt Aurelia got the dining room and parlor furniture, Aunt Augusta the library. Besides the silverware and china Wordlaw's parents found little to their taste. The siblings agreed that the quite substantial number of valuable things that none of them wanted should be auctioned off.

By noon the drive was packed with cars all the way down to the road. Wordlaw's aunts, in a cloud of perfume, poured sherry—to loosen the bidders' purse strings, they giggled. His mother sat up front throughout the sale and noted down each winning bid.

Wordlaw took Sam to try again to visit Drury's nameless dog at her run. The two hounds detested each other with a hearty relish, and this bothered Wordlaw. "Such a *nice* dog," said Wordlaw to Sam, scratching Drury's dog's ear through the wire. In response Sam merely raised his hackles and glared out of his own enclosure, of stillness.

Drury's dog started barking, but not at Sam—she was looking past him. Drury was coming around the side of the barn.

"Don't shoot! I'll come peaceful!" cried Wordlaw, raising his hands, for Drury was carrying his beat-up old rifle.

"You better go on home," said Drury. "I ain't got time to mess with you."

"What are you doing?"

"I'm fixing to shoot my dog."

Wordlaw blinked and shook his head. "What are you *talking* about, Drury?"

"Go on home, Wordlaw. I got to get this over with. I got a bus to catch."

"*Bus!*" cried Wordlaw, reeling, groping for words. "Drury, tell me what—"

"Ain't nobody had the gumption to even tell you, I reckon. Me and Stella is going up to stay in Chicago for a while. My brother Skeeter got a record store up there, and I going to work in the store, and this old dog just can't come. They won't even take her on the bus. Nor the train neither. Besides, Skeeter say there ain't no place to live up yonder but a apartment, without no yard or nothing, not to mention no coon to chase nor tree to chase him up."

"Drury, will you please tell me what you're talking about?"

"We don't have no job here no more, son. We don't have no place to live."

"Wait a minute. Let me talk to my dad. I'll take your dog. Just wait a few minutes. I could get her a pen, just like this one."

"She ain't a house dog," said Drury. "She's a hunting dog. And you know these two wouldn't do nothing but fight if you give them the chance. Listen, son. I done already axed your daddy, and he say no. It was him that fired us, don't you see? I don't have no hard feeling. What would we do, if your folks ain't going to move over here?" The dog had taken shelter in her doghouse; you could see her eyes in the shadows. "Dog never was much count anyhow."

"Drury, no! I'll get Dad to find you a job so you can stay."

"I got a bus to catch."

"Please!"

"*No!*" Drury roared—Wordlaw had never heard him sound like this. "Get *out* of here, boy!"

"Will you write to me, Drury? Please?"

Drury sighed, and collected himself. "Write to you? Letters? Well, I ain't much of a penman, but I suppose I could do that. Now go on, son. Go on home."

Wordlaw buried his head under his pillow, but he still could hear in dire clarity the first crack of the rifle and the second and the final third.

Robertson Corelli and his father-in-law were leaning over a blueprint on the dining room table. "You'll get your flow from the Interstate down this here way, along Forrest," Wordlaw Wickham was saying. "That sucker's going to have to go to four lanes right quick."

"It takes forever to get road work done in this county."

"Not when Beau Echols is dealing with the commission. Who you think got that exit put in? It wasn't cheap, but him and them guys, Bumpers and Farr, they're going to flat clean up on that strip they bought along Forrest. Gas stations, seven-elevens, they even got a Pentecostal Holiness church moving out from town, with five hundred members. We going to have to kick in with Beau and them, but we'll make it right back and then some on the traffic down that four-lane."

"We're going to have to have a light," said Corelli.

"Red light? We're going to have three of them! With a forty-second-delay left-hand-turn arrow, right straight in. Now," continued Wickham, "when we want to expand, you just dogleg back and follow down along here. We can near about double our footage that way, and you can still reach everything in the plaza in less than a quarter-mile walk."

"That creek floods."

"We going to ditch it out! Ain't nothing we ain't thought of."

"What about the tenants?"

"I'm going straight to Silverstein right off the bat. I built that old bastard's house. He knows every Jew in Memphis. We get him, we're sitting pretty. You put your Silverstein's here, see, what you call the anchor position. Then a bunch of little stuff: Singer sewing machine shop, bakery, pharmacy, cosmetics, maybe a little jeweler's. Here at the corner, what I'm dreaming of is a big bowling alley, twenty-four lanes minimum, with automatic pin setters, snack bar, pro shop, everything, and next to that a nice family cafeteria. Then a big grocery store, and around the corner for your low-rent row—services—your barber shop, beauty parlor, laundrymat, hardware store, shoemaker. Might even get us a book shop, for tone, if we can find us some old lady with more money than sense."

"You've done a fantastic job, Dub"—this was Corelli's nickname for his father-in-law, short for the initial W. "I've got to admit it. What are we going to call it?"

"Just simple and elegant: Chickasaw Plaza Shopping Center."

"Chickasaw Plaza," said Corelli, savoring it. "That sounds mighty fine to me."

"And look a-here, across the highway. It ain't a mile from that little niggertown in the bottom, so your niggers can walk to work."

"We don't want too many of them. I don't want nigger stores."

"Listen, Rob, there's not that many niggers left even now. Time we get done with the subdivisions, there's not going to be no place for them to live except down yonder in the bottoms, and them ones'll keep on using the same old stores they're used to. They don't like change."

"You said it," said Corelli. "You should have seen old Drury and Stella when they got on that bus to Chicago—bawling like babies."

"There's going to be a bunch more getting on buses before we're finished," said Wickham. "Now I got one more little thing to show you," he went on, pulling out a smaller blueprint. "She sets way back up from the highway, all white brick, French Provincial style—that's what you call a mansard roof, see? With a big long old yard, serpentine blacktop driveway, plenty of parking around the back. And look at this here—that's a *fountain*. Read what it says in the box."

" 'Medical arts building'? Dub, you old booger!"

"I just thought I'd run it by you. You could walk to work just like the niggers," laughed Wickham.

"What does Beau say about the financing?" asked Corelli.

"Shoot. We got banks elbowing each other out of the way!"

"We're going to make us some money, aren't we, Dub."

"You bet your sweet ass we are, boy."

Soon, for Wordlaw to reach the swamp he would no longer traverse pastures and long, flat fields of cotton. He would have to navigate a sea of parked cars.

Eudora Wickham had taught herself not to omit the *r,* and the result was four syllables: li-buh-ray-ree. And now the crowning delight of her devotion had come, in the form of the chairmanship of the board of directors of the Chickasaw Public Library. She unrolled the blueprint on her daughter's kitchen table.

"One hundred thousand dollars," she said.

"Lord have mercy!" Ivy Dee Corelli gasped. "Mama, you have finally lost your mind."

Sylvie came in with Junior in the crook of her arm and Shoot toddling along behind. "Book!" declared Shoot when she saw her grandmother.

"Well, let me just see," she replied, rummaging through her carry-all, the closest thing the little town had yet had to a children's library. "Do you like duckies, darling?"

"Book!" repeated the child.

Eudora permitted herself a small smile of triumph as she handed the little book over. "You'll enjoy this one, Shoot," she said.

"I wish you would call my daughters by their names."

"Seriously, Ivy Dee, I am expecting you to be generous," said Eudora in her you'll-recall-I-*am*-your-mother voice.

Sylvie got Junior settled in her bassinet and was now spooning pudding into Shoot in the highchair. "That that new liberry you been raving about, Miss Eudie?" she inquired, wagging the gloppy spoon.

"Sylvie, the word has *two r*s in it," said Eudora Wickham primly. "Li-buh-ray-ree."

"That's what I said," said Sylvie. "Liberry. Is that it?"

"Yes, it is."

"Where's the colored entrance at?"

"Well, Sylvie," stammered Eudora, "there's not one."

"Y'all going to build a integrated liberry!" she cried. "God bless y'all. I mean that."

"Sylvie, would you kindly fetch Wordlaw for me?" asked Ivy Dee quickly. "I'll finish feeding Susannah."

"Yes'm," said Sylvie glumly, understanding now.

The instant Sylvie was gone, Eudora began to rub her forehead hard. "What am I going to say?" she implored her daughter.

"That woman has reached her limit," said Ivy Dee. "I really don't give a hoot what you say. Just put that darn blueprint up and let's be talking about something else when she comes back."

The door flew open and in flew Wordlaw. "Hey, Grannie!" he sang out. "Sylvie says y'all are going to have an interracial library! That's *great!* I thought there was nothing but bigots in this town."

" 'Bigots'?" mouthed Eudora silently, as though to say, Where did this boy learn such a word?

Sylvie cast a cold high-headed glare on the assembled white folks, turned, and strode out.

Wordlaw's mother put her arm softly around his shoulders. "It's a white library, Wordlaw," she whispered. "I understand how you feel, darling, but you know the colored people don't read books."

At the honeysuckle-encircled sycamore grove on Daylight Bayou where Wilbur Corey used to go fishing, there was now a low concrete bridge, and across it on a new gravel road passed scores of truckloads of gravel each day bound for the cypress swamp.

A swamp was not, of course, the easiest place to build an Interstate highway, but Beaumont Echols had persuaded the county commission, and they in turn the federal authorities, that if Memphis and Shelby County and indeed the tri-state area expected to make the most of the rapidly changing distribution of the population, they had better pay heed to the booming unincorporated town of Chickasaw. The economic development of the region, as well as the inevitable expansion of the Memphis city limits, would depend upon suburban population growth, which was bound to follow the Interstate highway system, and if Chickasaw were to be passed by—which would hinder its growth significantly—then both the county and the state would be missing out on a source of tax revenue that stood to be substantial. Echols talked about artesian water, low electrical and sewerage costs, the proximity of railway access, and the high income and law-abiding nature (which was to say, white skin) of the new residents of the town—all in contrast to the countryside to the east, through which the highway had been planned to pass—but what most impressed his audience was his multicolored chart showing a projection of Chickasaw's population growth, which he had cooked up out of thin air. He did not have to mention that white people were pouring out of Memphis, and that Negroes were registering to vote in unprecedented numbers, and that it would not be long before the voting population of the city was more than half Negro; he did not have to mention that the rapid growth and in due course the annexation of Chickasaw would insure years of continued white control of Memphis.

(In the late nineteenth century, the state line had been moved some four miles south, to follow the true Thirty-fifth Parallel, and thereafter Corelli plantation and the whole area that was to be known as Chickasaw lay no longer in Mississippi but in Tennessee.)

In the hallway outside, Echols had mentioned to Butch Pollard, the commissioner of highways and roads, that the businessmen of the community favored additional study of the economic effects of the growth in suburban transportation, and that they had authorized the expenditure of twenty-five thousand dollars for such a study, payable in cash and in advance; he did not have to mention his knowledge that Pollard operated a small consultancy that specialized in such studies.

Thus had it come about that the Interstate was to be routed through what had been impassable lowland wilderness.

Wordlaw rather liked the grunt and pungency of the earth-moving machines, but the high banks and wide path of the vast highway now under construction did make it harder to get where he wanted to go. Obliged now to range farther, he discovered that the swamp went much deeper than he had ever imagined, and in those far reaches seemed wilder yet. He was determined that one day this year he was going to make it all the way to Nonconnah Creek.

As it curled into the trackless depths of the bottomland swamps, Daylight Bayou divided, looped back on itself, spread out in shallow willow-choked ponds, dropped into bottomless kettles, sank through gravel and percolated under quicksand and oozed forth in green-scummed sloughs without discernible current. Streamside briars raked Wordlaw's face and fumbling hands. Leeches clung to his ankles. He tripped on a cypress knee and smashed his nose on an overhanging limb. He wondered if there might still be alligators here, although his grandfather had been sure there were not.

When dry land came at last, it came so suddenly that Wordlaw fell yet again. He stood up to see that he was at the base of a little crooked hill vaguely the shape of a truncated pyramid.

This was strange, and seemed stranger when he climbed up and realized that he was at the center of a nearly perfect circle of stones, on several of which he could discern flecks of bright paint. He felt a chilly breath of air. He looked down the back side and saw a low opening in the hillside—a cave! It too was certainly man-made: leading up to it were crumbling bits of rough clay-and-straw bricks, which seemed to follow a faintly steplike pattern.

The sky was darkening fast. The cypresses and tupelo gums of the floodlands leaned against each other, creaking softly in the wind. A great blue heron stalked through the shallows below, and with a sudden dart speared a frog. And then out of a canebrake came a boy.

"What the fuck do you think you're doing here?" the boy yelled. He looked half animal—barefoot, bare-chested, covered with mud. There was mud even in his black hair. And he looked, well, *insane.*

"My family owns this land," said Wordlaw, not quite sure if that was really so this far from home.

"Nobody owns the swamp! It owns *us.*"

Pretty weird, pretty weird. "What is this place?" asked Wordlaw, hoping to touch earth with some less chimerical subject.

"That's for me to know and you to find out," said the guy.

"Did you see all those big feathers down by the water?" Wordlaw tried again.

"Turkey feathers. I saw them."

"I think it might have been a bobcat got him."

"Shit," said the strange boy. "It was a owl. I saw it happen. Owl tore that damn turkey all to pieces."

"An owl in the middle of the day?" wondered Wordlaw.

"Shit, no," said the guy. "Night. Full moon last night."

"You were here at *night?*"

"What's your name?" demanded the boy.

"Wordlaw Corelli. What's yours?"

"Colbert Fox. You better go home to your big fancy house on the highway or you'll be here all night yourself, and you'd be *scared.*"

"How do you know where I live?"

"I know a lot that you don't know."

"It is getting sort of late," said Wordlaw, looking for the sun, which was invisible in the overcast. "Are you going back?"

"Well, yeah, I got to get home." Colbert Fox scrambled into the cave and emerged with a burlap sack. "Let's go."

They spoke hardly at all—which was just as well, since Wordlaw was out of breath the whole way, so fast did Colbert slip through the swamp. He *was* like an animal: silent, running low beneath the dense vegetation, zigzagging but always to the way of least resistance. At last they emerged, at dusk, on the raw swath of the expressway bed.

"I go south from here," said Colbert.

"Where do you live?" asked Wordlaw.

"We're just renting a trailer on State Line Road while my pa looks for work."

"My dad says the new construction's bringing in a lot of jobs."

"I hate this fucking highway," said Colbert bitterly.

"Well, until it's paved," said Wordlaw, "this mud will be a good place to look for tracks. I found cougar tracks in the swamp once."

"There's no cougars left here," said Colbert.

June the 25th.

My Dear Wordlaw:

Well here we are in Chicago. It is ever so differt up here. My Brother Sketers record shop the land lord rase the rent on him & he had to close so he & I are both out of a job. My wife Stella has work as a day made for a lady but only 2 days a week & she dont like her. Also she has to ride the bus a long ways & last week there was a robery. But you know she has fath in the Lord so we will get by. Sketer is playing on friday & satday nites in a band.

Sketers boy was by here last nite & you know Wordlaw he remind me of you. He has so much curiousity just like you. He plays the saxophone so good some times he set in with Sketers band, he is not but thirteen just like you.

We have red your letter, thank you for the picture of my old rocking char. It is the 'spitting image'! In reply to your question I remember yes there was wolfs in the swamp when I was a child, they got in my Mamas chickens one time but there was not so many & I have not knowen of none for a long time. Your Great-Grand-Daddy use to trap them. His wife had a wolf colla coat. Well we surely do miss your Grand-Daddy & Grand-Mama & all the Home-Folks. God bless you Wordlaw, I remain

Cordially Yours,
Drury Woodson.

"Robertson, please, for the ten millionth time, please do not slam that screen door!" cried Ivy Dee Corelli.

"I had a real bad day today," said her husband through gritted teeth. "I seem to be having a run of bad luck with appendectomies. This one was a little girl. I think I may get out of the surgery business and just do medicine."

"Rob, is she all right? She's not—"

"She's going to *be* all right, but they took her away from me, and now I have to go before this damned *board*."

"What happened?"

"Technical mistake. I need another drink."

"Another?"

"I stopped by the club."

"Rob, you know I know you drink when you get up at night."

He went to the bar and poured himself a nearly full glass of bourbon. Wordlaw came strolling through, whistling. "Your mother and I are having a conversation," said his father.

"That's fine with me," Wordlaw shrugged, flopping onto the floor and turning on the television.

The news showed another lunch counter sit-in in Nashville, to which Wordlaw's father diverted his surging wrath. "*God* damn these people!" he burst out, and made for the bar. When he returned, calmer, he said to his wife, "You've heard about Nut Bush, I suppose?"

"No." Nut Bush, Tennessee, was her mother's old home town.

"Haywood County's filling up with agitators. They've got the colored all worked up, and now the God-damned assistant attorney general of the United States himself is up there, kissing their butts. I can just see them coming here next, *ruining* the shopping center. Sitting in, marching, driving off business."

"Dad," said Wordlaw, "all they want to do is register to vote, and then their landlords evict them."

"Sit in today, marry your sister tomorrow," said his father. "Take over the country day after that."

"I mean, they vote here, don't they?" Wordlaw persisted. "Why shouldn't they vote in Haywood County?"

"That's enough out of you, boy."

Claudia tiptoed in, tears of wonder in her eyes. "Daddy?" she sniffled. "Is it bad to marry a nigger? Are niggers bad?"

"Jesus," said Robertson Corelli, rubbing his brow. "*A,* Claudia, we don't use that word in this house, *ever*. *B,* we don't eavesdrop in this house. If you want to come into a room with the door closed, you knock. *C,* you had darn well better *not* marry a colored man. *D,* there are good ones and bad ones just like anybody else."

"But I want to marry Ree Billy," she pouted.

Her father threw back his head and guffawed long and loud. In mystification, wiping one slippered foot across the other, Claudia watched him till her eyes spilled over, and with a sob she ran out.

Her mother rose to go after her, turning as she left to hiss at her husband, "Have *another* drink, Rob."

Wordlaw rose and crept out.

Robertson Corelli sank back into his chair. "I need some air," he said to the empty room. "I'm going out for some god-damned air."

He put the Cadillac's top down. The air was thick, dense, oven-hot. Behind the old manor house the sun was setting above the bulldozers and the raw clay of what had been the pasture. Smoke lay in streaks above heaps of felled trees. A mist began to fall, fogging his glasses but cooling his brow.

He headed south. The faster he drove, the cooler and better he felt. On an impulse he turned, tires shrieking, onto the gravel of State Line Road. There was no traffic. The road was a straight shot. He gunned it to sixty, seventy, eighty. The mist was actually chilling him now. Ninety. He groped for the heater knob.

The noise of the impact was not loud—just a soft *whump*—and as the shape flew dimly into the brush on the left he was pretty sure it was just a dog. Some colored person's dog run off, or maybe a wild one. He did not want to stop, but the bent fender was scraping against the front tire, and after a half mile more he had a flat.

It was very quiet on the road. The soft rain was still falling, but without the onrush of speed the air was hot again. Corelli got out of the car and stood there for a long while, not knowing what to do.

A single headlight appeared back down the road, coming fast. Corelli stood staring into the oncoming light. A battered pickup with an Oklahoma license plate slid to a stop in front of him. A fat man with long black hair climbed down from the truck and waddled slowly up to him. The man stank of sweat, dirty clothes, beer. He was dark-skinned, but not a Negro. An Indian—an American Indian. "You killed my daughter," the man said. "You didn't even slow up." Corelli noticed only now that the man had a small black pistol in his hand.

"I'm a doctor!" was all he could think of to say.

"Get in the truck," said the Indian. "I've done called the sheriff already."

"I can help her."

"She's dead, man."

The gouged earth was dark yellow, the clay banks ochre with veins of dark orange, the far horizon the brown red of dried blood. In India ink he sketched in the ancient trees split, smashed, pushed into heaps and set afire: spastic hand movement, jagged lines smeared and smutted. The trees still wore their green leaves and would do no more than smolder. Charcoal smudge for the layers of smoke then, thick-spattered tempera leaves, more deep red in the flameless fire. He took dirt from the bulldozer's blade and black grease from its joints, and rubbed them into the paper with his thumb, obscuring the whole image beneath a brownish gray pall. For the dark red horizon, the color of dried blood, the only color he applied on top of the dirt and grease, he used his own blood.

With a hot coal from the barbecue grill he burned a ragged black edge. He sawed a section of a porch plank from one of the demolished tenant shacks, salvaged several dozen old square headless nails, and drove them through the board into the mud. On the mud-clotted side he then impaled the picture, riddled thus with fiercely protruding spikes. On the other side, in crude block letters, with his wood-burning tool, he engraved this legend:

CHICKASAW ESTATES * AD 1960 * CORELLI FECIT

It was his final work for his summer art course at the temporary library, an old house behind the Methodist church. "That is completely unacceptable," Mrs. Pardue said. "I couldn't even bring myself to touch it. A person could get lockjaw just touching such a thing."

Chickasaw Estates was the name of the new residential subdivision into which Robertson Corelli and Wordlaw Wickham poured their energies as soon as the shopping center project seemed to be firmly on course. None of the tenant farmers had had leases, so the evictions were easily accomplished. Five hundred acres of weed-choked old fields and pastures were scraped bare, the utility lines ditched in, a grid of roads graded. The segment of Daylight Bayou that flowed behind the development and on past Chickasaw Plaza was straightened and deepened, its shoreline fenced, its flood plain cleared and filled. As was customary with suburban housing tracts of this sort, and in order that the lot prices be kept as low as possible, all the landscaping was to be left to the individual residents; not one tree was left standing. Corelli had thought that the hardwood might bring a good price, but although there were tons of it there was still not enough to interest the mills, and so it had had to be burned.

Corelli was in a hurry to get the first houses up, because he needed money. For one thing, he had been suspended from the practice of medicine, at least until his appeal was heard, and who knew how long that might take. Second, he had promised one of those first houses—free—to Delbert Fox, whose daughter he had killed. And now Beau Echols was telling him that the various criminal charges he was facing—negligent homicide, driving while intoxicated, leaving the scene of an accident—were probably going to cost him a hundred thousand dollars in cash. It was dangerous, too: that money had to go straight to the governor of Tennessee. (The Foxes' trailer was on the Mississippi side of State Line Road, but the girl's body had been thrown to the north side and so into Tennessee jurisdiction.)

But by August everything seemed to be pretty much under control. The governor had seen to it that the charges were dropped. Corelli was still under suspension, but he had learned that one of his old fraternity brothers was chairman of the appeals board. And now, in a little bungalow on the landfill along what the developers were calling no longer the bayou but the *creek*—"bayou" being deemed too swampy and old-fashioned a word—the Delbert Foxes became the first family to move into Chickasaw Estates. A neat fit they were, too, chuckled Echols, having learned that Mr. Fox was a *Chickasaw* Indian!

Wordlaw and Second Samuel walked along the edge of the channelized ditch that was all that was left of the bayou behind the Foxes' house. He had gone seldom to the swamp this summer. Sticking resolutely close to home, he had painted a suite of watercolors of his grandparents' house—boarded up, already peeling—and then the series on construction and destruction that culminated in the piece his teacher had refused to touch. He knew he had been denying to himself a great many deep feelings, not least the fear of meeting the brother of the girl his father had killed, but he told himself that avoidance itself fueled his work, that the things denied would find expression in his pictures, and give them their power, as indeed he felt they did very successfully in *Chickasaw Estates*. Yet he felt, too, a longing for birdsong, silence, beds of moss, cypresses and tupelo gums, the green slant of light through the canopy, the rich dense smells of the swamp. And so at last, unavoidably—it was in the oak forest, where no footstep left a visible trace—his path crossed that of Colbert Fox.

Colbert was asleep, curled up in the ferns like a real fox, oblivious to the horseflies buzzing around his head and clinging, blue jewels, in his hair. Wordlaw sat down very quietly, settled Sam beside him, and waited for Colbert to wake.

"Shit!" gasped Colbert. "You scared the piss out of me. I can't believe I didn't hear you."

"Listen," Wordlaw made himself say, "I'm sorry about your sister."

"Wasn't your fault," said Colbert. But his eyes said something else.

"What grade are you in?" asked Wordlaw.

"Starting eighth."

"Me too. You going to go to Chickasaw?"

"Where else would I go?"

"Well, I didn't know if you were Catholic or something."

"Naw, I'm voodoo. We have sacrifices. You drink the blood. You cut out the hearts for curses of revenge."

"You are *so weird,*" said Wordlaw.

"You want to track a fox to his hole?"

"Sure! Where'd you learn that?"

"We was on this army base in Texas, and me and my pa would kill baby coyotes. You pour gasoline in their hole and burn them up."

"I don't want to kill any fox," said Wordlaw. "I love animals."

"We're not going to kill the fox. It's just pretend."

"You blur the line between real and pretend, Colbert."

"There is no line."

When Wordlaw went to Colbert's house to see if he wanted to go exploring, Colbert's father answered the door, a huge, dark, glowering man in a dirty undershirt. "I know who you are," he growled. "You tell your paw this house is no damn good. It's sinking. It's crooked. The foundation's cracked. Colbert! You got a visitor."

Once they'd gotten well away, Wordlaw said, "My granddad used to say there might be ivory-billed woodpeckers in here. And I keep thinking maybe some day I'll see an alligator."

"Nah," said Colbert. "They're all gone. But there's spirits of them."

"That sounds real Indian."

"My pa says the old spirits, the spirits of the animals and the plants and the weather and all the dead ancestors, they're all going to rise up and destroy the white man. I hope I don't count. My ma's white."

"Did he ever find a job?" asked Wordlaw.

"You don't know? *Your* father got him one. About as low as a job can get, my pa says. Loading shit off of trucks at the shopping center. The man holds a grudge, you know. He's still mad about stuff that happened hundreds of years ago."

"Does he know a lot of Chickasaw history and all?" wondered Wordlaw.

"Nah. He don't know much of nothing. Typical Indian. You ever been to Oklahoma, where they got all them reservations? It's pathetic. Chickasaws ain't even got a reservation any more. Used to be a big deal, the Chickasaws, Pa says, but now there's just a few of them, broke, broke-down, and ignorant. I don't think there's nothing more ignorant than a Chickasaw Indian. Still, you know, for some reason, all of us are proud. I don't know of what."

Colbert froze in midstep. Ahead on the path a water moccasin opened its white mouth. "Don't move," he whispered. "Give me your knife, quick." He ripped down a willow switch and waved it, and when the snake struck he seized it by the neck and with one stroke beheaded it. But he did not stop with killing it. Teeth bared, eyes wild, oblivious, he hacked the snake to bits and flung them off in all directions.

Second Samuel cowered low. Sam had never warmed to Colbert, and Colbert never touched him.

"Man," said Wordlaw, "I guess you killed that snake."

"I guess I did," said Colbert foggily, teeth still bared.

Wordlaw did not realize until the next day that Colbert had not given him his knife back. Well, school was to start Monday. But Colbert Fox did not show up for school, and was not at home either.

As Wordlaw crept along on hands and knees, watching a wood

duck preen on the bank of the bayou, he heard behind him a heavy thunk and a quivering whir, and whirled to see his knife sunk into the bark of a tree. Colbert sprang out of a thicket. "Don't ever assume you can sneak up on me," he said. "I am an Indian. I will cut your heart out. I will do to you what I done to that snake."

"Okay, okay," said Wordlaw. "Jesus. What's eating you?"

"Nothing *much,*" sneered Colbert. "Just they won't let me even *register.* They say I'm a *nigger.* Chickasaw Indian can't go to a school named Chickasaw. Funny, ain't it? And my pa got fired. And you know who's responsible for both those things?"

"Who?"

"Your father, asshole."

"Oh." Wordlaw did not doubt this for an instant.

"Remember my pa telling you our house was sinking? Remember him telling you to tell your father? Did you do it?"

"No, I didn't," Wordlaw confessed miserably. "I don't talk much to my dad."

"Well, he knew. My dad called him on the phone about twenty times before he got through. He knew, and he didn't do shit. Now there's plaster falling down, and night before last in the middle of the night there was that tremor—you felt it?"

"No."

"Well, it was like a little earthquake, and a bunch of our windows busted. The whole house is falling apart. It's fucking *sinking.* Finally my pa found this lawyer, and tells him about my sister and all, and your pa getting off. So then this Mr. Ballard—"

"I know Mr. Ballard!" said Wordlaw. "He's a great old guy."

"You may not think he's so great if you'll let me finish what I'm saying. So he starts talking about compensatory damages and re-opening the police investigation and a bunch of stuff. And he calls up your father. Next thing we know—this is yesterday—my pa gets fired, and it's like registration day for new students, right? And they tell me the school is *white only.* I just hollered, 'My ma's white!' And they says, 'Lots of niggers have white blood, but they're still niggers.' "

"I'm really sorry, Colbert. Listen: Dad's lawyer, Mr. Echols, is on the school board. Maybe he can do something."

"*Echols* was the name on the letter they showed me telling me I couldn't register. He's the son of a bitch that's behind it."

"I guess I should have known."

"Mr. Ballard says we can destroy your father," said Colbert coldly. "Says we can take every cent he's got and then send him to prison for the rest of his life. Then you're going to be the one stomping around barefoot."

"I always thought you went barefoot on purpose in here," said Wordlaw. "I thought it was like this Indian deal."

"I got one pair of shoes, Wordlaw. I can't get them muddy."

"I thought your dad just got out of the army. Soldiers get paid okay, don't they?"

"He's been out of the army for three years. They threw him out."

"Oh," said Wordlaw.

"He's a dangerous man," said Colbert Fox darkly.

But so was Beaumont Echols. Echols soon discovered that the military police had an outstanding warrant for Delbert Fox's arrest. Colbert's father had not, as his son thought, been thrown out of the army—he had just been AWOL for three years, after nearly killing a fellow soldier in a bar fight. Oscar Ballard declined to represent Mr. Fox further. He did offer to bring suit against the school board on Colbert's behalf, but then, the day after Delbert Fox was extradited to Texas, Shelby County declared the Fox residence unsafe for habitation and sealed the door. Without a Shelby County address, then, Colbert had no standing to sue.

Colbert and his mother sneaked back in for the next three nights, while his mother spent the days trying to persuade the owner of their old trailer on State Line Road to let them come back on credit. Finally she found a week's employment picking cotton—somewhat to her surprise, since machines were now doing much of the work and Negro children were still being dismissed from school to work in the fields at harvest time. But many of the farmers of the hard clay hills of north Mississippi were too poor to buy mechanical cotton pickers, and many Negro parents were now objecting to child labor, and Leeann Fox was willing to work cheap and ride the yellow bus far. The Negroes had never seen a white woman picking cotton before, and thought it hilarious, but she toiled grimly on, ignoring them. The owner of the trailer agreed to accept the farmer's scrap of promissory paper as a deposit, and the week after that she was able to get welfare. Colbert enrolled without difficulty at a white school in Mississippi.

A condemned house was bad publicity for a new subdivision, so the little bungalow on the landfill was promptly demolished. In its place CorWick Properties put in a seesaw, a sandbox, and a swing set, laid down some sod, and announced the establishment of a playground, free to all residents of Chickasaw Estates. Despite Robertson Corelli's objections—he claimed to be uneasy about raising questions of race unless it was absolutely unavoidable—Dub Wickham insisted on posting a sign there that read, "White Only (Or Maid In Uniform)."

Sylvestra Woodson, without explanation (and none was requested), resigned her job in the Corelli household and went to join her brothers Drury and Skeeter in Chicago.

Oct. the 30th.

My Dear Wordlaw:

Well Sylvie is with us now but it is hard times. Stella lossed her job so we have to get well fare. We all have been looking for work but there is not much. Alot of the white peoples here in Chicago have white servants too. Sketers boy Sylvester got beat up by a gang then the police come & they beat him up too. They knock out sevel of his teth & cut his lip. He is so sad acount he can not blow his horn. One good thing is election day coming up, they give you mony here to vote for Mr. Kendy. Sylvie says a big hug for my boy. Stella says one from me too & a kiss too.

God bless you Wordlaw, I remain

Cordially Yours,
Drury Woodson.

"Damn wild dogs are killing off the deer," said Colbert Fox, fingering a faint footprint in the mud.

"I've never even seen one," said Wordlaw.

"There's a lot you don't see," said Colbert. "It's a crime, what man's made of the wolf. Wolf's the most beautiful and intelligent animal in the world, and it's wiped out now, and all that's left is *dogs.* Sit, shake, roll over, *beg?* Slobber all over you. It makes me sick. I mean, the more you kick a dog, the more he loves you, right? If that ain't sick. You know how white people's dogs'll only bark at the niggers? Like when the egg man comes—he's a nigger, right?—these neighbor dogs of mine, they go crazy, but you let the milk man come, a white man, and them dogs just set there. It ain't the dogs' fault. They been bred to it—just empty spaces for their masters' thinking to fill up. Nothing but human ideas in animal shape."

"That's a pretty weird theory," said Wordlaw uneasily, glad he had not brought Sam to the swamp today.

"Yeah, well," said Colbert.

"How's everything going?" Wordlaw ventured. He had not seen Colbert since Colbert's father was arrested and their house condemned.

"It's right bad in the physical world, but Pa called me on the phone and he says the spirits are rising up. He's been reading in prison. He found all his ancestors all the way back to a Chickasaw warrior named Lakowea. Lakowea lived here. Lakowea's son fought in the Civil War, for the South; his name was Red Fox; he was my great-great-grandfather. They came to my pa in a dream and said the animal spirits are rising up. The wolf is rising up."

"You are getting strange beyond belief, Colbert."

"Don't fuck with me, man." Colbert's eyes were black pits. "You think I'm crazy. What I am is *clear.* I can see the inside of things. What makes things like they are. I'm intelligent. I'm mystical. I'm having visions." He pointed a tremulous forefinger. "Do you know what that is?"

"Anybody knows what cow shit is."

"Growing on it."

"Those little mushrooms?"

"We eat them and see the truth. Light shines out from the inside of the world. Here, try one."

"Yuck! And what do you mean, 'we'?"

"Indians, dumb shit! I ate some an hour ago, and I'm okay."

"There isn't going to be any more cow shit," said Wordlaw. "They're going to build more houses here."

"No, they ain't."

"Well, look, Colbert, I hate to mention him to you, but it's my dad that's building them, so don't you think I ought to know?"

"The spirits are rising up," said Colbert.

"Oh, right, I forgot. Well, look, Colbert, I've got to go."

"You tell anybody about this and I will kill you," said Colbert. "I'll slit your belly open and eat your fucking heart."

"Nobody'd believe me anyway," said Wordlaw.

The first dead dog, a German shepherd, was found in the country club driveway, its belly slit open and its heart removed.

"Wordlaw, darling," said his mother through his bedroom door, "I know it's awful, but evil things do happen from time to time, and we can't let them rule our lives. For every horrible incident like this there are a thousand Christian kindnesses. So come on down and have your supper, won't you?"

He still could not say anything, or move.

"The boy looks sort of green, Ivy Dee," said his father.

The next week a collie was killed and mutilated, and the next week a poodle. The community was hysterical.

The sheriff's department tried stake-outs and infrared photography and bloodhounds and everything else anybody could think of, to no avail. The killings continued—a cocker spaniel, a dachshund, a Labrador retriever, a Schipperke, the Echolses' Doberman, Forrest McCracken's fuzzy-muzzled mutt Albert.

There was a sudden cessation of demand for houses in Chickasaw Estates.

And then one morning Sam was not sitting at the side of the bed staring at Wordlaw. The new maid, Estherine, in tears, confessed that she had let Sam out late the night before and gone to bed without remembering to get him back in.

Wordlaw could no longer not tell. "It's Colbert Fox!" he cried. "Get the cops to Fox's trailer on State Line Road!"

"Oh, Wordlaw," sighed his mother, "he's just a child."

It all came pouring out in a rush—the mushrooms, the Indian spirits rising up, Delbert Fox's imprisonment, Colbert's visions of revenge, his threat against Wordlaw.

Shelby County sheriff's deputy Otto Riley and his counterpart from De Soto County, Mississippi, served a search warrant on Mrs. Leeann Fox and found, on her son's closet shelf, a large glass jar in which were preserved in blood-clouded formaldehyde ten dogs' hearts. She was arrested on a charge of failure to exercise proper supervision of a dependent minor.

Wordlaw ran north along the path of the Interstate and into the heart of the swamp. He found fresh barefoot prints along Daylight Bayou, and fresh dog prints the right size to be Sam's. At the slough the tracks veered away from the water, and in the oak woods they disappeared.

There was a sound in the leaves behind him, and then the low *whuff* of Second Samuel. He sniffed his way toward Wordlaw's feet and with austere dignity presented his brick-red head to be patted.

"I knew you'd tell if I took Sam," said Colbert, who had materialized out of nothing.

Wordlaw could not speak.

"But you didn't tell before that, did you? That's why I didn't kill him. They're after me now, huh?"

"Yeah."

"Well," said Colbert, "They're going to have to find me."

Wordlaw held Sam tight against his chest and kept his eyes closed until Colbert had gone and the swamp was silent again.

1970

Far out in the channel an uprooted tree rose from the current like a river monster's claw. It raked the air, swirled on an eddy, and was gone. Low clouds rode a mat of warm air out across the flood plain to a blood-red line of sunset. A hydrocarbon sheen floated above the moving water.

Throughout the Mississippi valley, the great river's tributaries and their tributaries and theirs, all the way up to the merest of part-time trickles, had been ditched and straightened and shorn of trees; all but a few of the vast lowland swamps had been drained, timbered, plowed, and planted; where once water had pooled, spread, meandered, soaked slowly through marshes, lazed around oxbows, loitered in sloughs, transpired into the heady air of wet-footed forest, now it shot down a deep straight ditch to another deep straight ditch to another and another and into the Father of Waters in a hurry; and so when it rained, as it had now for a week and a half, the monstrously swollen Mississippi gorged itself on silt and gobbled at its banks and ripped trees up and spat them out and roared. Contractors and their patrons in the Army Corps of Engineers stood ready to repair the chewed revetments, scour out the silt-clotted channels for the thousandth time, shoulder and shove the errant sandbars back where they belonged, build a new wing dam, dredge a new diversion, and in every way seen fit (by themselves, with no need of anyone's advice or consent) chide and chasten the monster—and charge you for it.

Wordlaw turned away from the river. Most of Main Street still wore a plywood face these two years and more after the King assassination riots. The upper stories, toothless and blind, gaped down on trash-spattered emptiness. An occasional pimp tooled by, pink-hatted, big-Afro'd, and drew flocking whores to his Rolls Royce window.

It was dangerous here, which was fine with Wordlaw. Indeed he almost wished someone would confront him, some spade in a dashiki, with a chrome forty-five and a bad-ass goatee. Wordlaw would give him a timid Black Power fist and the spade would sneer, Fuck that shit, give me your money, honkey.

There was a disturbance up ahead—a man and woman yelling in the parking lot of the Lorraine Motel, famous as the site of the martyrdom of Martin Luther King, now a fleabag brothel. Suddenly someone was running straight at him—a white man, fat and unsteady but running flat out, with his pants bunched in his hands, with a woman, black, in red high-heeled sandals, red bra, red panties, and nothing else, in hot pursuit. She paused to get her breath, shrieked, "Cheap-shit pervert, I'll cut your dick off and feed it to the rats!" and only then caught sight of Wordlaw. "Hey, honey," she said.

"Hey yourself," he replied.

"You want to party?"

"Thanks," he said, "but I've got to get home to my parents."

She gave a sharp hoot. "Well, merry Christmas," she added.

"Yeah, you too," said Wordlaw.

But wait just a God-damned minute! He *knew* that man. It was—naw!—well, it *was*—that had been *Mr. Frobisher!*—the principal of Chickasaw High! First time he'd seen the old booger in five years.

Well, well, well.

Daylight Bayou was ditched out too, a zigzag gouge behind a chain-link fence, a drainage ditch. The oak woods had been cut down, the cypress bottomlands drained and filled. The sloughs, the gullies, the kettles, quicksand, cedar swamps, thickets, tangles, darknesses, depths, all were gone. The fields, the pastures, the leaning shacks, the old black people, all were gone. In all directions to the horizon stretched young white suburbia—little brick houses, young trees some still guyed to stakes, bird feeders, tricycles, Chevrolets.

Christmas Eve, a Sunday, Wordlaw, Shoot, Junior, and their parents went for lunch to the country club. " 'Hill in the shape of a truncated pyramid,' you say? Yes," said Robertson Corelli, "there was a thing like that out there, way in the middle of the worst part of the swamp. It was a damn Indian mound. Dragline operator goes to the contractor and the contractor comes to me, because the last time he hit something like that, God dog if they didn't have the state historical commission and a bunch of professors and archaeologists and I don't know what-all tying the project up in knots. Tied it up for three years while they went through that damn Indian mound with toothbrushes and flour sifters.

"Now, this thing of ours, the first big mouthful the dragline takes out of it comes up full of human bones—skulls and everything—and that's *it* for the operator. Says he won't go near it. Colored man, you know. Superstitious. I thought, well, let's get us another operator in here quick and just mow the sucker down. White man, this time."

Wordlaw caught sight of a slim girl in dark sunglasses and a tiny black miniskirt in the vestibule, with blond hair frizzed out to her shoulders and, very visibly, no bra beneath her thin white angora sweater. Despite all he'd just been hearing, he had to laugh out loud.

His mother held a water glass in midair as Claudia Corelli sashayed in, home from her first semester at Radcliffe.

"Hey, you guys," she said, distributing kisses.

" 'You guys'?" echoed her father, otherwise struck dumb.

Shoot and Junior whooped and gushed, clinging to their glamorous sister's long black-stockinged legs.

"You look *great,*" said Wordlaw.

"I'm starving," she said. "We drove all night."

"What y'all going to have?" asked Ree Billy, running an appreciative eye up and down the gorgeous girlscape.

"Reeble!" cried Wordlaw, pushing out of his chair to exchange a power grip with his old pal. This was Wordlaw's first visit to Memphis for a year.

" 'S happening, bro," said Ree Billy, black-militant cool in his voice but warmth in the handshake.

"Feel like some chess?" inquired Wordlaw.

"All right."

"Pool house? Three o'clock?"

"You want the frog legs?"

"Put me down," said Wordlaw. "Ham sam bone jury."

It was freezing in the locker room, but it was the only place they wouldn't be hassled. "How you feel, Reeble?" asked Wordlaw.

"Stoned."

"Me too," said Wordlaw, starting to set up the board. "My sister brought some powerful shit home from Boston."

"What you think I'm talking about?"

"She's a nice girl."

"You better keep her away from me," said Ree Billy solemnly.

"*Look* out!" laughed Wordlaw.

"That's all right," said Ree Billy, and suddenly, in that phrase, Wordlaw heard Ree Billy's father.

"Let me ask you a question. Whatever became of Wilbur Corey?"

"Shit," said Ree Billy, making four syllables of it. "That Wilbur, he mess up good."

"What happened?"

"Arm robbery. In the state of Mississippi."

"They got him?"

"They got him. They killed him. Sentence him twenty years in Parchman Farm," said Ree Billy. "And then—I don't know. They *say* he was trying to excape. I don't believe that. I seen him not a month before they killed him. He say he was going to finish reading some big bunch of books. History of the world, that's what it was. Said it was going to take him a year. That don't sound like no plan for a breakout to me."

"But he did commit the robbery?"

"Oh, yes," said Ree Billy. "He did do that."

"Who the hell's move is it?"

"Stoned to the bone, ain't you, Wordlaw?"

"That is a fact, Reeble."

Wordlaw found the perfect spot from which to see down the long bright corridor of neon and traffic at dusk to the dark shape of his grandparents' house. It would be difficult to bring off the extreme contrast, but the idea of a picture with so dark and empty a center appealed to him. He wanted to evoke a sense of standing on the edge of a bottomless hole. He would blur the blazing lights of the fast food joints, gas stations, and shopping malls as though the viewer were plunging past them down a well of lurid color and into a light-sucking vortex. The asphalt of the highway would be streaked with silver headlights and red taillights, and the sky would mirror them in red-streaked silver.

But he could not even start the painting.

Why did his father not tear the house down? He'd long since given up practicing medicine, so he had nothing to do but continue his bulldozing rampage across the landscape. The paneling, the brass, the mantelpieces, the carved moldings, even the plumbing had all been ripped out in wave after wave of vandalism, every last window shattered. The wallpaper hung off in strips. Beer cans, broken bottles. Half-burned mattresses, limp condoms.

I love this, thought Wordlaw. I love what's dead, what's ruined, what's doomed.

"Come look at this," called Claudia, holding a dirty manila envelope. "You remember what Grandma used to call her treasure cave?"

He did—a little cabinet set into the wall inside her closet.

Wordlaw opened the envelope to find the watercolor he had given her the last Christmas of her life, of Wilbur Corey fishing on the bank of Daylight Bayou and Second Samuel sitting stolidly beside him.

"It's not very good, is it?" he managed to say through the tightening of his throat.

"I think it's lovely," said his sister. She studied his eyes. "How are you, brother?"

"I'm having trouble working."

"You ought to live in New York, you know. You do realize that."

"I hate *scenes*. I don't like other artists. I want my work to succeed on its merits, not because I go to the right cocktail parties. RISD"—the Rhode Island School of Design, pronounced "rizdy," from which he had graduated last year—"was one continuous cocktail party."

"But aren't you worried about being pegged as, like, 'regional'?"

"Look, Claudia, if my work is good it'll be seen for what it is."

"Wouldn't it help to be around other artists who are getting good work done, with sort of the smell of success on them? Instead of a bunch of dopers and drunks, if you'll pardon my saying so."

"There is more to my life in New Orleans than dopers and drunks. What the hell do you know about it? One trip when you're fucking seventeen years old. It happened that I was going through a bad time last summer. But I'm trimming back on the bad associations."

Shoot and Junior came storming in, tired of spying.

"Let me see," said Shoot, reaching for the picture.

"Poor Sam," said Junior. He had died just this year, at last, white-muzzled and arthritic. "He looks like such a puppy."

"Why doesn't Dad do something about this place?" Wordlaw asked.

"We like it," said Junior. "It's the only thing in Chickasaw that's not, like, orange plastic."

"It's our Link to the Romantic Old South," added Shoot.

"Where did you get such a mouth?" demanded Wordlaw.

"I have multiple personality syndrome," she answered primly.

"Y'all certainly are an unusual couple of girls," said Claudia. "Y'all should come visit me in Cambridge and let me show you off. I have that old Cotton Carnival picture of me in a hoop skirt, you know? And they really think that's what we live like. My roommates have started calling me Maggie—short for The Magnolia? So you two would make a nice surprise."

"Is sincerity foreign to this whole family?" wondered Wordlaw.

"You hogged it all," answered Claudia with a faint smile.

"Can we smoke marijuana with y'all?" asked Junior.

"No, you may not," replied Wordlaw.

"Can we if we come to visit you?" Junior persisted.

"I think y'all are more the heroin type," said Claudia.

"I want to lose my virginity to a Yankee," said Shoot. "A black Yankee Harvard student."

"If you do," said Wordlaw, "be sure you come home pregnant."

Claudia was blushing. Hm.

On Saturday night, Forrest McCracken invited Claudia and Wordlaw to his coffee house, the Black Hole of Memphis. He had grown long hair, which he kept in a luxuriant pony tail. "Hey hey!" he boomed in greeting. "Wait'll you hear this girl."

Her name was Mimi Fontaine. She was a very pale and fragile-looking person—pale brown hair, pale cream skin, pale violet eyes—and she moved to the piano as hesitantly as if she feared it might explode at a touch. She began to sing so quietly that Forrest had to move the mike closer and boost the gain. For minutes on end she did not open her eyes, and when she did it was only to look at the keyboard. But her voice was at once hoarse and sweet, ingenuous and world-weary, untutored and perfectly pitched. Her songs were shockingly candid:

"My father refuses to feel disappointment.
He turns it to hate.
He hates me.
I've always loved anyone I've ever loved too late.

"My love, you refuse me your deep disenchantment.
You tell me it's fate.
You leave me.
I've always loved you, but I've told you so too late.

"Anyone I've ever loved I've always loved too late."

The applause at the end of the set was long. Mimi Fontaine's eyes flicked briefly at Forrest, skipped past Wordlaw, and settled on Claudia, to whom she sent a shy smile. "Can we meet her?" asked Claudia, with a quick glance at Wordlaw.

"Sure," said Forrest.

"Excuse me," said Wordlaw, and headed for the bathroom.

"How well do you know my brother?" asked Claudia.

"Medium," said Forrest. "Why?"

"I think he's smitten."

"Him and every other guy that's ever seen her." Forrest waved her over. "Have a seat, cutie pie. Mimi Fontaine, Claudia Corelli. Oh, and here comes Wordlaw Corelli. And no, he's not married to this child. He's her brother. Are you planning to sit down, cement-head, or are you going to stand there all night?"

"You are *incredible!*" blurted Wordlaw at Mimi, without even hello first. This was most unlike him. "I love your lyrics."

"Good," said Mimi, with a little giggle. "I didn't write them."

"And your voice," was the sorry best Wordlaw could manage.

"She lip-syncs a tape," said Forrest.

"Forrest tells me you're an artist," said Mimi.

"Intermittently," said Wordlaw glumly.

"What do you do the rest of the time?"

"Brood."

"I know what you mean," said Mimi with evident sincerity.

Wordlaw turned to Forrest. "Is it possible to get something to drink in this place?"

"Long as you don't mind hiding it in your coffee," said Forrest. "I've got a bottle in the back. Claudia, come help me."

Forrest fumbled through boxes in the storeroom.

"You're stalling, aren't you?" said Claudia. "You seem to know him well enough."

"Well enough to know he needs a girlfriend," said Forrest.

"He's so gloomy," said Claudia.

"She'll like that," said Forrest. "So's she. *And* she lives in New Orleans."

"Machiavelli!" cried Claudia.

"Y'all are the only Italians I even know."

"Have you ever given a straight answer?"

"What was the question?" He cranked up the volume on the sound system, which was playing some bizarre atonal sort of square dance tune in five-four.

"What in heaven's name is *that?*" she demanded.

"Hampton Grease Band, from Atlanta. Friends of mine," he said, opening the door a crack. "Come, take a peek."

Wordlaw and Mimi were deep in conversation, their foreheads almost touching—an artifact perhaps of Forrest's adjustment of the volume, and then again maybe not. "He's telling her about all the pictures he hasn't been painting lately," hypothesized Claudia.

"Who was that Italian fellow you mentioned?" asked Forrest.

"Give me a swig of that, will you?"

"My dear," Forrest scolded, "you are a *minor.*"

With the approach of closing time on Saturday nights, the Reality Rangers Central Commando Unit, as Forrest's circle of friends called themselves, would begin to gather at the Black Hole, and later there would usually be a jam session later by a subunit of the R.R.C.C.U. known as the Highly Irregular Jug Band and Marching Choir. To the tune of "Walking the Dog," they sang "Dodging the Draft"—"just-a, just-a, just-a d-d-dodging that draft" (which every last one of the males present was doing). They sang "She'll Put Anything in Her Mouth," "My Girl's Ugly but She's Poor," "Why Do You Think They Call It Dope," "Jerry Lee Lewis's Mother's Lament," and a particularly tasteless number called "What, My Lai?" with a chorus that ran, "How could I know there was gooks in that hooch?" Somewhere in the midst of all this, Wordlaw and Mimi disappeared.

"My parents are going to kill me," said Claudia, looking at her watch, which read two-thirty.

"Let's us just elope and get it over with," suggested Forrest.

"You're twenty-five years *old!*"

A huge black guy with a shaved head pulled up a chair backwards.

"Hey hey!" yelled Forrest.

"Bubba Bohannon," said the guy, extending a foot-long hand.

"Claudia Corelli."

"Wordlaw's sister? Hi."

"You haven't seen the son of a bitch, have you?" asked Forrest.

"He's out in the parking lot with your singer, talking like he's been in solitary confinement for a year."

"Aptly put," observed Forrest.

"I'm going to go get him," said Claudia. "Inconsiderate lout."

"Cute," said Bohannon when she had gone.

"Go ahead, she's all yours," said Forrest McCracken. "That's what I do. Find girls for other guys. Soften them up a little bit, little sweet talk, get them in the mood, and then I hand them over."

"Whoa, whoa!" protested Bohannon. "She ain't even *legal.*"

"Speaking of illegal, give me a toke of that." Forrest wiggled his fingers at Bohannon's fat Jamaican spliff.

"Narcotics squad!" yelled Wordlaw through the front door. "You're all under arrest."

"And obliterate the intellectual riches of this metropolis in one fell swoop?" said Forrest. "A whole generation bereft of leadership?"

Mimi and Wordlaw started kissing and showed no sign of stopping soon. Finally Claudia grabbed a handful of his ratty old tweed jacket and pulled him backwards toward the car.

"I'll call you," he said, probably for the hundredth time tonight.

"I'll be back on the fifth," replied Mimi, ditto.

"I said you needed a girlfriend," said Claudia, "but this is ridiculous."

"I know," said Wordlaw, grinning.

1975

It was rare for Mimi Fontaine Corelli to write a song she did not have to labor for note by note, but this was such a moment. She was in that sort of trance which even a particle of self-consciousness could shatter. She had been in it for hours, concentrating so hard that she stayed utterly rigid in all but her hands and ankles. And now as the trance fell away, spent, she sighed in sweet joy for its having sustained itself so long that the song was finished in this one sitting. It was as if the song had already been composed somewhere inside her and she had been merely retrieving it from memory.

It had all come so easily, she realized only now, because every phrase was exactly the same kind of variation on the previous phrase, in such a way that twelve phrases brought you right back around to the first. The only problem was in the lyrics she had been working from: the third line of every four-line stanza would now need to be shortened by one iambic foot to make it fit, and the lyricist she worked with, Alice Pelletier, tended to be coolly disinclined to alter a single word once it had been enshrined on the creamy hundred-percent-rag paper she employed to fortify her work's finality. At the thought of their confrontation, which would have to come tonight at their weekly dinner out, an acrid chill bloomed in Mimi's gorge.

There was still work to be done. She raced through the arpeggios over and over, scratching fiercely at the score paper. A dull ache grew cold in the knuckles of her right hand, and she faltered. The hand looked all right, but it hurt like hell.

When she went to the bathroom for some aspirin, the smell of burning leaves came in the window, and at once she was engulfed in a memory she thought she had successfully dammed back, of the last time she had seen Willy Newman.

It had been a tingling fresh Indian summer night just after a storm, with shreds of mist still clinging in the hemlocks along the river. She and Willy were standing on an old wooden bridge over the rapids, and Willy was saying that that big round silver thing up there was the West Virginia moon, not the same one you saw in other places.

This was four years ago—November of 1971. Mimi had been married to Wordlaw Corelli for only eight months, and Willy was living at the commune in West Virginia with Barbara Potts. Willy and Barbara and Mimi had been students together at the University of North Carolina, and from sophomore year onward Willy and Barbara had been steady sweethearts, but all through the fall of their senior year Willy had also engaged in an agonized flirtation with Mimi. Mimi had refused to go to bed with him unless he gave up Barbara, to whom he seemed more enslaved than actually attracted. Then, suddenly, at the end of the semester, Willy and Barbara had dropped out, and Mimi had seen neither again until Willy tonight.

Mimi's first album had just been released, and she was on tour to support it. When she played Charleston, there was Willy at a front table, alone. Wordlaw was home in New Orleans, not painting.

She had sung wonderfully, and she was dizzy with fatigue and exhilaration. Moreover she was at precisely that point in a young artist's career when there have been just enough challenge and just enough triumph—and little enough failure—that the world lies ahead with all the fragile grace of an autobiography still to be written. By the next spring, she would find that her album was not selling, and the record company had dropped her cold, but tonight she was armored in glory, and she felt sure she could afford a bit more of the tantalizing suspense that had made the fall of '68 such fun.

Willy Newman was also a songwriter, but he was not a singer, and because these were the salad days of singer-songwriters Willy had not been able to find suitable performers for his work. There was a new sadness about him, an air that he was already resigning himself to disappointment—which made Mimi, ever fearful of infection, wary. Giddy with success, then, and at the same time as cautious as if success were a crystal bowl in her unsteady hands, Mimi Corelli walked with Willy Newman up the mountainside toward the still unfinished geodesic dome in which he and his fiancée and their comrades all lived.

Mimi was to sleep in a funny little circular room at the top of the dome, where the only semblance of a window was at top center, in the form of a turret that was actually an intricately modeled miniature of the entire house. This could be lifted on a hinge, and, as Willy proudly demonstrated and Mimi then saw for herself, if you stood on a chair you could poke your head out into the dark and silent mountainscape, over which shone the famous West Virginia moon. She stepped down from the chair and into his arms.

And oh, she felt herself slipping, he was so tender, he was so sweet—but for God's sake! she was still a newlywed, practically. And yes, in love with her husband, and no, Willy, no, she just couldn't. He understood, he smiled, he went downstairs.

In the middle of the night he returned. He sat on the edge of the narrow mattress and massaged her shoulders, her back, the backs of her legs. When he reached between her legs she had to move just ever so little to receive his hand. She lay utterly still, while Willy caressed her inside and out, until, shuddering, gasping, biting her lip, trying not to cry out, she came. Words floated into her mind, "Do with me what you will," and, laughing a little, she spoke them.

Through the propped-up miniature dome at the top of the room, then, the scent of burning leaves had descended.

She had not seen Willy again.

And now this afternoon four years later, in New Orleans, in November of 1975, the scent of burning leaves rose from the lawn, where Wordlaw was burning his rakings and staring into the meager flames. Mimi flexed her right hand. The first and second knuckles of the index and middle fingers were cold and stiff and sore.

Seven mornings a week, Wordlaw Corelli would shut himself up in his studio and call plaintively on his muse, but it had been two years since he had finished a painting—a beautiful portrait of Mimi that he had done in the spring of '72, after her contract had been dropped and she had entered on a deep depression.

He had then set out on a more ambitious project, a self-portrait as American citizen. In smeary, hurried charcoal he had sketched out a gleefully overwrought allegory, in which he was seen, a colossus, from far below, holding a bleeding bald eagle in his hands, while all sorts of symbols—crosses, fish, rockets, his old Indian knife—whirled like the stars around a cartoon character's conked noggin. In the background he put two landscapes. On one side there was a big hydroelectric dam and reservoir, into which he sketched himself again, as a grinning water skier. Little boats bobbed here and there, and high-tension wires rode off over the horizon. On the other side he concocted a street in Vietnam: a version of the famous photograph of the Saigon police chief blowing the brains out of the Vietcong suspect, but with Wordlaw's own face on the executioner. It was going to be huge, and he was really excited about it, but somehow he had not been able to get beyond the drawing.

As Wordlaw's will to work sank, Mimi's depression lifted. It was her theory that not only Wordlaw's art but his whole sense of well-being fed on her suffering. Invariably, when she was doing well he would be pitched into gloom. And these days she was doing very well indeed. With the mournful little songs that were the fruit of her search for a new style in the past two years (a period corresponding exactly to Wordlaw's artistic impotence), Mimi had developed something of a cult following. She did not like to travel, and gradually she had made a small club in the French Quarter virtually her own, and to it her sad-hearted acolytes, mainly lonely girls, trooped from all over the South. She had played there five nights a week for six months now, and the house had rarely been much less than full. Her self-assurance had grown apace, followed like a mocking shadow by Wordlaw's despair. Now she was going to take six weeks off to record a new album, this time only for a small local label but with a generous budget, Alice as producer, and an eagerly waiting market among Dixie's young, female, and woebegone.

Alice Pelletier was too beautiful, too rich, and too smart to fit the servile role that Mimi would have preferred for her lyricist, but Mimi had to admit that the role that Alice actually played—serene grande-dame-to-be, and amateur dabbler quietly better than vulgar mere professionals—she played very well. Ever since their freshman year at Chapel Hill, when, as they liked to joke, they had been the two unmatchables left over when the computer had finished assigning roommates, Alice had breezed through life, never setting goals yet always excelling, while Mimi lumbered along behind, earnestly berating herself for her inadequacies and frequently living down to her expectations. Nevertheless it was Alice who admired Mimi, for her triumphs, and Mimi who derided Alice, for the hollowness of hers. One of the latter was Edmond Delafosse, a thirty-five-year-old "private investor" of old Creole stock with whom Alice was living while he good-naturedly waited out a hideous divorce. Whenever Edmond and Alice came to see Mimi at the club, she stumbled through her patter, missed high notes, and got Alice's lyrics painfully wrong as Edmond in his Savile Row suit and relentless smile and Alice in her crisp linen dress and erect debutante poise shone as though themselves spotlit amidst that glum gray audience.

At the restaurant Alice had chosen, Alice recommended the oysters Poulette, Alice explained the redfish Gelpi, Alice ordered the Chassagne-Montrachet—the '71, not the '73—and somewhere hidden beneath the sweetness that Alice spun round her replies even to Mimi's most peevish demands there was cold steel resolve.

Thus when Alice, without even having heard the new song, smiled and said she'd be glad to change the lyric so it would fit, Mimi wondered aloud what Alice might be up to.

"Why, Mimi, *darling,*" breathed Alice. "Really."

"Answer the question, Alice."

"Well, I'm worried about you. You look tired, darling."

"What's that supposed to mean?" demanded Mimi.

"No more than it says. You live out on an edge, Mimi, that most of us can't even go near. It's what makes you such a fine performer."

"And now suddenly you think an argument with you might put me over this edge?"

Alice sighed. "Would you rather we argued?"

"No, no, of course not, Alice. I'm sorry."

"I just want you to be strong and happy when we go into the studio."

"I know," admitted Mimi.

"How's Word?"

"Next question."

"Where are y'all going to spend Christmas?"

"Wordlaw's sister is flying home from New York, and he wants us to go to Memphis to see her. Where is that damned waiter?"

Alice caught the waiter's eye and motioned for him to refill Mimi's glass. "Isn't this wine delicious?"

Wordlaw roamed New Orleans in vague dejection, studying the interplay of holiday lights and wet asphalt beneath the dull pewter overcast while Mimi toiled happily, night and day, in the windowless recording studio, oblivious to the time and the season; she said she'd just as soon skip Christmas this year, and Wordlaw fled to Memphis.

Claudia arrived from New York with not only her two roommates in tow but also a middle-aged Japanese-American ex-surgeon (with no explanation of the "ex") who had recently moved in with them and around whom there seemed to swirl dark currents.

Lisa Gruenthal was a dark-eyed, long-legged, stupendously sexy girl whose brash laugh and bold leer immediately intimidated Wordlaw.

Marian Jennings was an art dealer—a species Wordlaw tended rather to deprecate—and fairly exuded Old New York Money, but she was much more the watching-from-the shadows type than Lisa, and it took little time for Wordlaw to feel quite comfortable with her. Marian was elegant, slim, beautifully dressed, green-eyed, with a frequent wry twinkle of amusement and at moments a cool hard stare of assessment. When she was amused, she would tuck her chin down toward one shoulder, and her long, fine, light brown hair would fall forward over one eye, and then she would toss it back with coltish grace. He watched her, and she saw him watching him.

Claudia fluttered and fussed, all hostess, making sure the divinity and candied pecans got passed. As she proffered the silver tray, she smiled her brother a smile of unfrank and incurious sweetness. She was hiding something; this was a previously unknown phenomenon. Meanwhile Dr. Susumu Watanabe, peeking furtively out from his curtain of long black hair, sniffled with every other breath, cracked his knuckles, and hummed to himself like a lunatic.

The old manor house had at last been demolished, and above the Corellis' den mantelpiece there now was displayed a watercolor of it that Wordlaw had painted when he was thirteen. The house at that time had just begun to deteriorate, and, especially as Wordlaw had portrayed it, it made for a very gloomy picture. His father's hanging it here now must certainly have been a pointed gesture, although toward what Wordlaw could not have said.

Robertson Corelli and Wordlaw Wickham had bulldozed flat the low hilltop where the old house had stood, and in its place had erected six stark rows of cheap "cabana" apartments. There was a glut of such housing on the market just now, and the developers, much to Wordlaw's amazement and their own chagrin, had had to accept black tenants. Meanwhile, some dozen or more of the little tract houses that had been built on landfilled swamp had begun to settle, tilt, and break apart, just as the Foxes' had done fifteen years before, and a number of lawsuits were in progress. This Wordlaw found nearly as gratifying as his parents' having next-door neighbors of African descent.

Casting frequent sidelong glances at his father, who was engrossed in a bowl-game preview on television, Wordlaw loudly recounted to Watanabe the rise and fall, or sinking, of Chickasaw Estates.

He responded with hectic nodding but no comment.

"So, Dr. Watanabe, you're a friend of Claudia's from Vietnam?" Claudia had taken a year off from Harvard to work in various field hospitals in the howling midst of the war.

"Right," was the reply in full. After some deliberation, Watanabe added, "Call me Sam, man, okay?"

Wordlaw felt his asthma coming on—not without remembering how grateful to it he was, for having kept him out of Vietnam.

"Boy, you still smoking?" demanded his father.

"No, sir." (Hack, hack.) "I quit smoking two years ago."

"Well, what the hell are you coughing about?"

"Bronchitis or something, I don't know."

"Bullshit," concluded his father, and then hollered across the room at Marian Jennings, "You want a drink, miss?"

"Thanks, I think I'll wait for lunch," she replied, with a fleeting twinkle at Wordlaw.

"You might as well learn to drink in this house, girl," yelled Robertson Corelli. "Only way to survive. Boy, you ready for a drink?"

"Yes, sir," said Wordlaw. The asthma loosened its grip.

"How about that Chinese fellow? Want a drink, Mister uh—?"

Claudia spoke up: "Daddy, don't you remember? It's *Doctor* Watanabe, but he wants you to call him *Sam.*"

"That's right, that's right. Fellow physician. Hey, Sam, you want a drink, son?"

Sam hotfooted it right over. "You kidding me?"

"Got us a drinking man, Wordlaw," said Robertson Corelli.

"Why, you mean old mud rat!" cried Ivy Dee Corelli in high-pitched baby talk. "Have you forgotten your little sugar?"

"Mama!" cried Claudia in horror.

"Honey, I tried for fifteen long years to convince your daddy he was a alcoholic, and he never would admit it, and I just got tired of being the high and mighty teetotaler." It occurred to Wordlaw that his mother may already have been drunk.

"Old Japanese proverb," chuckled Sam Watanabe, his mood improving rapidly: "No can rick dem, join dem."

"Pour your mama a drink, boy," said Wordlaw's father. "Put some Co'-Cola in it."

"I still can't *stand* the taste," his mother giggled, rolling her eyes, and then threw down half a highball glass of faintly cola-darkened bourbon. She gasped and did a little shivering dance and shrieked, "Get 'em, dogs!"

"Old college cheer," explained Wordlaw.

Marian and Lisa looked on in bafflement. Claudia fled the room.

Shoot, now seventeen, and Junior, sixteen, tried to slip in the back way, but their mother collared them, trailing two boys of the flop-hair dull-stare ilk. Wordlaw had thought that Shoot and Junior would be entranced by beautiful Lisa and elegant Marian in their cashmere, silk, and pearls, as once they had delighted in Claudia's racy bohemian blacks, but in one indifferent glance they declined even to taste this rich slice of New York; teenage Chickasaw had its own fashions, and unlike their elder siblings Shoot and Junior had no ambitions of taking flight. The boys pulled at their crotches; the girls snapped their gum and mooned out the window.

"I'm so *proud* of my girls?" gushed their mother. "They've gotten *so* involved in their church work? St. Stephen's has this Outreach for Youth remedial reading program? It's the envy of the whole city. Boys like Wayne and Lee Dan are getting a whole new chance, thanks to my girls. It just goes to show, doesn't it? what the presence of Jesus can mean in a young person's life?" She took a long pull on her bourbon and Coke. "Isn't that right, Lee Dan?"

"Yes'm," said Lee Dan wanly.

"Expect a visit from my little sisters later," Wordlaw warned Lisa and Marian behind his hand. "In quest of drugs."

Some bowl game had begun. The elder Corellis drew close to the tube, turned the sound up, and lost themselves in drinking, cheering, and groaning. They had five dollars bet on the game.

Marian stood in a ballerina's third position, one hand on her hip, head cocked, chestnut forelock fallen across one eye, poised as calmly as an owl in a tree. "Maggie told us you were funny," she said.

" 'Maggie'?" wondered Wordlaw. "Oh, right, the Magnolia, y'all call her."

"But she didn't say how funny."

A memory flashed through him, of Wilbur Corey's diatribe on white people's easy family solidarity—"All this *we* talk," Wilbur had said. "All this family." But had Marian meant a plural or a singular you? "Y'all" was a useful locution.

"What are you thinking?" she asked.

"Sorry," said Wordlaw. "I guess I drift away sometimes. Whole bunch of stuff. This family, this place on the map."

"Ah, families," she said, trailing off.

"Marian? Once we get through Christmas, do you think y'all might like to have some *fun?* I need to have some fun."

"I'm having fun now," she said simply.

"But you've probably never heard the Highly Irregular Jug Band and Marching Choir."

"I put myself in your hands," said Marian.

"Oh, Lord, don't say that," said Wordlaw, flushing.

She gave him a reserved but inquisitive smile in reply.

Progressing toward the new year and a final mix, Mimi began to receive visitors from the record company, their eyes closed in what seemed to be approval as the VU meters twitched. Neil O'Neill, the president, was a fidgety, fiftyish man who always dressed in black and wore his thinning red hair pulled back in a tight, short pony tail. Tonight, as always, he was accompanied by a young German in black leather and sunglasses, named Helmut, who rarely uttered a word.

After having one song played back five times—the same one whose lyrics Alice had changed—Neil put his arm awkwardly around Mimi's shoulders and growled, "Mimi, listen. I want to tell you. This album is going to be a monster. Mimi? I want to go all out. I want to hire a special promotion man for you. I want you on the road as soon as the product is in the stores. I want you visiting the stations, Mimi. I want you in the press. Have you been working with publicity?"

"Not yet," she replied. The guy's fidgets were rattling into her.

"Mimi? The day you finish mixing—Helmut, you on this bus?"

"Yeah, why not? I talk to Liz, yeah?"

"The very *day* you finish, Mimi, I want Liz Chisholm here. I want you to talk to her without holding back. I want a bio that jumps off of the page. Mimi, I want press on you personally, your whole life-style. This is what moves product. Your husband is like a painter or something, right, Mimi?"

Uh oh. "Yes."

"I want both y'all to just sit down and rap with Liz, okay? That's a girl. Mimi, you take care now." He squeezed a few last heebie-jeebies into her and was gone.

Alice simply closed her eyes and shook her head.

Night after night, after Christmas, Wordlaw entertained the honored visitors—or, that is, he turned them over to Forrest to be entertained.

"Hey hey *hey,*" cried Forrest, a connoisseur of girls, on first setting eyes on these. The Black Hole was no more—"Imploded," Forrest explained—but McCracken Global Systems now operated Bar-B-Q Billiards (offering both, plus beer), Quicker Liquors (wines and spirits, with a drive-up window), and the Parnassus Hi-Tone Theatre (movie classics). At BBQB they ate ribs and played eight-ball, at Quicker they plundered the cellar of Château Lafite, and at the Parnassus they were treated to a private screening of Russ Meyer's "Mud Honey." They played frisbee beneath the cold eyes of the equestrian statue of Nathan Bedford Forrest in Forrest Park. They picnicked one warm midnight on the Mississippi bluff as cold gusted in, nimbuses boiling above the horizon and lightning veining the dark starlight between them. They went to the drag races. They played miniature golf in a snowstorm.

Sam Watanabe was far gone into cocaine addiction. "You got yourself a world here, don't you, Wordlaw," he would say, "all these interconnecting lines of force and affection and, like, back into history. I saw so much Southern culture in 'Nam, you know, black and white, all tangling up. It's far out how much you people all have in common. Those Southern dudes over there *knew* each other even when they didn't know each other, know what I mean? All this, like, seamless, like, web, of, like, irony and, like, authenticity," and then poof! his eyelids would droop, his mouth would hang open, and Claudia would take him in her arms like some crippled child.

"He was wounded, real badly," she said, as if that explained everything.

"Claudia," said Wordlaw later, in private, "how are you, really?"

"I always have wanted someone to take care of, and now I have one. Sam is such an interesting *challenge.*"

"What ever became of Quigley Seymour?" Quigley had been her boyfriend for years, from way back at Harvard.

"Oh, Quigley," said Claudia with an impenetrable smile. "We're still just as close as we can *be.*"

Lisa took rather a fierce shine to Forrest, although he could sometimes be seen looking past her toward Claudia, after whom he had intermittently pined for years.

This left Wordlaw with Marian. They had a better time together than either of them quite wished to. For all his difficulties with Mimi, Wordlaw continued to believe that his marriage could be made to work, and Marian certainly did not want to get in the middle of it.

"You know I'm keeping my distance from you," she said.

"Saying that only makes me like you more, which is precisely what neither of us needs," replied Wordlaw.

"I take it back then," she laughed, looking out across the river. The wind lifted her hair.

"Even when you're not looking at me, you know," said Wordlaw, "I feel sort of scrutinized."

"You should talk."

"Painter's job. What's your excuse?"

"I suppose I was eventually going to have to tell you I'm kind of a writer, in a way," said Marian. "A would-be way."

"Really? And what would you be thinking of writing about?"

"Your sister?"

"This thing with Sam is so weird," said Wordlaw.

"Have you ever thought of painting her portrait?" asked Marian.

"Oh, what haven't I *thought* of painting?"

"Are we going to have fun Wednesday night?" That was New Year's.

"Big fun," he assured her. "Big fun."

New Year's Eve started small and mild, gathering mass and lunacy as it accelerated through a carefully planned succession of bars. The Reality Rangers Central Commando Unit, in addition to Wordlaw, Forrest, Sam, Claudia, Lisa, and Marian, was comprised tonight of Peter and Paul the Indistinguishable Farrs (twins, also Chickasaw High alumni, who claimed to be unable to tell each other apart); Flip and Annie Mayhew (junk sculptor and sex poet, respectively, twice divorced from each other but still cohabitant); and Bubba Bohannon (recently retired from the Green Bay Packers and now a municipal bond salesman). In the course of the evening the R.R.C.C.U. conscripted in addition three nameless lounge lizards, at the Lizard Lounge; the entire Highly Irregular Jug Band and Marching Choir, fresh from being hooted off the stage at Mamie's Mop-up; and, at the Vapors, four gum-chewing, bubble-haired "foxes"—Forrest's word—of sensational fatuity.

The Vapors Club's dance floor was a vast, teeming sea of rednecks and their molls, and somewhere in it Sam Watanabe went under. He surfaced in the parking lot, where Wordlaw and Marian, out for a breath of air, spotted him engrossed in conversation with several members of the Living Dead Motorcycle Club, an organization infamous throughout the Mid-South for its savagery. You couldn't hear a word they were saying for the thunder of their engines, but Sam had hold of one Living Dead leg and was twisting it hard.

"He's nuts," said Marian quietly, starting forward.

"Oh, no, you don't," said Wordlaw. He had her firmly by the shoulders. "Those guys are for real."

But it was too late to stop Claudia, who had come up unseen from behind and was swallowed into the Living Dead's midst.

With one voice the Reality Rangers breathed, "Oh, shit." Then, as the Rangers conferred worriedly behind the Farr twins' van, there went Forrest after her.

"Great," said Wordlaw. "Now we can all get killed."

Sam had stopped twisting the guy's leg and had come to no harm, but Claudia was still nowhere to be seen. Forrest was gesticulating; the cold stares he got in response looked most uncongenial.

"Well," sighed Bohannon, "I reckon we're going to have to see if they want every brother in Memphis coming down on them." And off he marched, alone.

"Really great," said Wordlaw. "Race war. Happy New Year."

As Bohannon, huge, bald, and grim, approached, the motorcycles fell silent, and the Living Dead drew themselves into a knot. The first thing he did was grab Forrest by the scruff of his blazer and send him stumbling back toward safety. Then he spoke a few quiet words, and there was a long, tense pause, and finally Claudia was produced from the shadows. Sam grinned at her sheepishly, and she fell into Bohannon's arms. He propelled her softly back toward the Rangers. Sam caught up with her and tried to take her hand, but she shook him loose.

As they came within earshot, Sam was raving, "For Christ's sake, sweetie, they weren't going to hassle you! I fixed that dude's leg for him at Pleiku, that's all, no big deal, *Jesus*, and now we got this gorilla back there laying God knows what kind of trip on the dudes!"

"Just shut up, Sam, please!" cried Claudia.

Forrest gathered her up and took her home to change clothes, while the Mayhews stuck a joint in Sam's mouth to keep him quiet.

Now Bohannon turned on his heel and simply walked away from the Living Dead. Watching him, Lisa Gruenthal was aglow. "That,

I believe," she purred, "is what is known as a baaad mother *fucker.*"

So much for her shine for Forrest.

The motorcycles roared to life, and the Living Dead roared past in single file. When the last one was gone, Bohannon sank to the asphalt and buried his face in his hands. "McCracken," he said, not knowing that Forrest had already left, "don't *ever* do that again."

Lisa knelt beside him and asked, "Is there anything I can do?"

He gave her a look, and grinned.

"Well, maid Marian," said Wordlaw, slipping his arm around her waist, "how do you like Memphis so far?"

"How close would you say that was, really?"

"Real close. Real close. That Sam is a bundle of laughs."

Now it was Marian who drifted off.

"Hello?" said Wordlaw softly.

"Sorry," she replied. "I was thinking how to describe all this."

"How serious would you say this writing deal is, really?"

"I've been putting it off. Getting serious, I mean."

"Don't put it off," he said. "Take it from one who's gone wrong that way."

"Well, aren't we the dead end kid! What about all those prizes? Maggie talks about you all the time."

"School prizes. I've been out of school for six and a half years."

"I've seen your work. I will remind you what I do for a living."

"What the hell do *dealers* know?" he snarled.

"You're good, Wordlaw. That picture you sent Maggie—"

"*Three years* I tried to turn that piece of shit into a painting. I sent it to her because I'd given up."

"You think it's supposed to be easy?" she shot back.

He could not speak.

"Wordlaw, why did you leave Memphis?" she asked.

"To go to school."

"No, I mean to say, why didn't you come back? This *world* you have here, all these amazing friends."

"I don't know."

"Are you very attached to New Orleans?"

Hm. "I've been trying to make up my mind about that."

"A painter should probably be in New York," said Marian.

Wordlaw had been about to open the car door for her. With his hand still on the handle, he moved his face in front of hers, and, yes, she was ready for him to kiss her, so he did it.

Firecrackers popped, car horns blared, and a great Rebel yell rose from the throat of the city. It was midnight, it was New Year's. He kissed her again.

1976

The Reality Rangers reconvened at Flip and Annie Mayhew's already insanely overcrowded bungalow (they had an indeterminate number of housemates, whose own New Year's party had been in progress for some thirty-six hours). The Highly Irregulars whanged out their Greatest Hits of All Eternity and Possibly Beyond, including "Whole Lotta Wha'?" "How Can a Whiskey Six Years Old Lick a Man of Twenty-eight?" "Why Do You Think They Call It Dope?" and their deathless masterpiece, "She'll Put Anything in Her Mouth":

"Rancid sausage, rabbit pellets, mongoose musk,
navel lint, infected walrus tusk,
mystery garbage from the ASPCA,
second-hand feminine hygiene deodorant spray;

"whatever's hosed out of the showers at the Y,
buzzard gizzards sizzling in a pie,
gobs of greenish phlegm from nursing home spittoons,
discharge from a VD'd VC's wounds;

"guinea hen and quiche lorraine,
foie gras and roasted crown of pork,
shrimp soufflé and goose paté,
purée of afterbirth of stork;

"DDT and mercury,
phosphates, enzymes, herbicides,
plastic grass, leaded gas,
seagulls drowned in oily tides;

"rats and mice and ticks and lice and trails of snails,
scrapings from a sewer worker's nails,
bleeding stumps of freshly amputated limbs,
thems and those and its and hers and hims."

Lisa and Bohannon promptly disappeared into the depths. Claudia danced with Forrest while Sam, waving his skinny arms, harangued Marian:

"Who is this dude? This McCracken. I mean, was it my fault she made such a hassle over at that night club? She humiliates me. I don't know what the deal is here."

Meanwhile, Wordlaw went out on the front porch, swept the beer cans from the swing, and breathed in the warm wind, which bore north the sweet sump-smell of New Orleans.

The wind soon also bore to him the ripping roar of unmuffled internal combustion, as the headlights of the Living Dead M.C. came sweeping around the corner and down the Mayhews' cul-de-sac.

"Happy New Year," said Wordlaw, to no one, moving quickly inside to spread the bad news.

A knot of nervous Rangers met their callers at the curb.

"Hey hey," said Forrest, essaying a stern smile. "What's happening, friends?"

"Where's the nigger at?" opened the negotiations.

Bohannon had prudently made himself scarce, and the Rangers thus had no information to impart or conceal. "Um," said Forrest.

"We want the nigger," repeated the ambassador.

"I don't know who you mean," mumbled Forrest.

Impatient with such tedious parley, the Living Dead shouldered past the cowering Rangers and roamed the house. One of the intruders, two expressionless black eyes in a nest of black hair, shot a hole in the living room ceiling, then lowered his big black pistol in a slow arc till it came to rest pointing at Marian's face. "Now, don't piss me off," he said. "We need to know where that nigger is at."

"I really don't know," said Marian hoarsely. "Really."

"Ho now!" exclaimed the gunman, with a gold-toothed grin. "Got us a Yankee girl. Little Yankee girl. Where you from, bitch?"

"New York."

"Nooo *Yawk!* You want to step out with me tonight, Noo Yawk? Go for a ride on my sex machine?"

"No, thank you," said Marian.

"Ho now. No thank you! Say them Noo Yawk girls tough, ain't that right? Ain't that right?"

"Not me."

"I'll treat you sweet, bitch. You ain't got nothing to worry about. You worrying about anything?"

"The gun," she answered. "Please."

"This here? This old thing won't hurt you. It don't kill nothing but niggers and queers." He looked at it fondly. "Reminds me. Where's that little *slope*-eyed faggot at?"

He had been distinctly absent, but suddenly and most assertively Sam was there now: flying through the air with a foot-long knife in his hand. He did a perfect flip in midair and crying "*Banzai!*" landed on his feet six inches in front of the guy with the gun. He brought the knife down so fast toward the guy's wrist that the hand seemed certain to be severed, but somehow the gunman snatched his hand back, dropped the pistol, and was out the front door all in a blink. Sam switched the knife back and forth in a silver blur under the noses of the remaining L.D.s, who simply stared, struck dumb, until a wailing of sirens gave notice of the advent of the law. The Living Dead fled.

Bubba Bohannon emerged from the back of the house, where the toilet was flushing over and over as God knew what substances went glugging down. "Can you feature this?" he was saying. "*Beëlzebubba* calling the *Memphis cops?*"

Flip Mayhew met the police outside and thanked them very much for their prompt response and assured them that the trouble, if there had been any, was over.

The head cop lopped off a brown drool of chaw with a wipe of his finger, craned his neck to peer into the dark and quiet interior, looked back at Mayhew, smiled very unpleasantly, and said, "Shit."

"Do you think, like, a letter of thanks to the chief would be something we could do?" asked Mayhew. "You know, commending y'all?"

"We been watching this house," the officer said. "Waiting for a opportunity to bust y'all's ass. I know this a drug den, sex orgies, I can't even say what all. Don't fuck with me, boy." He turned away.

"Well," sighed Mayhew as the patrol cars pulled out, "I think this New Year's is about complete."

The Mayhews withdrew, leaving Bohannon, Wordlaw, Forrest, Lisa, Marian, Claudia, and Sam on the scruffy patch of front lawn.

"By the way, Sam, old buddy," said Wordlaw, "I'd like to thank you for a truly outstanding martial arts demonstration."

"Oh, Wordlaw, shut up!" cried Claudia. She turned to face Sam now, her lips a thin line. "Don't you realize you're taking your self-indulgence a little too far when you endanger other people's *lives?*"

Sam might well have replied that far from endangering them he had *saved* people's lives. All he said, however, in his joke-Japanese accent, was, "Rife cheap." Then he took Claudia's arm and pushed her roughly ahead of him around behind the house, muttering under his breath, "You and me got to rap."

"He's hurting her!" said Forrest, heading after them.

Lisa and Marian intercepted him. "I know you're concerned," said Lisa, "but we've seen this kind of thing before with them. The best thing you can do is leave them alone."

Ten long minutes passed. Claudia emerged from the shadows in tears, holding her upper arm. Sam had grabbed it so hard that he'd left a five-fingered bruise. This time Forrest would not be stopped.

But Sam was nowhere to be found, and with exhausted goodbyes the Rangers dispersed, Forrest guiding Claudia gently to his car, Bohannon and Lisa already obliviously entwined in the back seat.

Wordlaw and Marian walked toward the railroad yard at the end of the street. The wind had turned cold. Black shapes of boxcars and steel towers loomed against a faintly less black sky, with stars like wounds through a membrane from a bright world beyond.

"I'm going back to New Orleans today," said Wordlaw.

"I know," said Marian.

"And you're going back to New York."

"Yes."

"I want to kiss you again," said Wordlaw, "but I don't know if you want me to."

"I want you to," she replied.

It was a long, serious one.

"Oh my word," said Marian, breathless, breaking away.

"What," said Wordlaw.

"This is really getting to me," she said.

"Me too."

"I feel this terrible sort of *yearning*, and—and sadness. As if I know somehow this is the end of it."

"And you wish it weren't," he said, not quite asking, not quite stating.

"Is it?" she asked, eyes black in the blackness.

"Ah," breathed Wordlaw, looking away. He did not have enough to give this girl; he was not worthy of her; he was bound to disappoint her, sooner or later.

"Oh, God," prayed Marian.

Wordlaw could not think of anything to say, until, lamely, he tried, "I've got to get my work up and going. I want you to see it."

"Do you?" she said, moving her head so he would have to look at her. Her hair fell across one eye. "I do so want to."

He smiled sadly at this Yankee patrician locution, token of their distance, and pushed the hair back from her white forehead, her black eyes. He traced the dark line of her eyebrows, held her cheeks in his palms, kissed the tip of her nose. "Let's write each other letters," he said, with earnest false cheer.

"I get sent out to see artists sometimes," said Marian, holding his face too, not letting him look away.

He kissed her again, and unhappiness filled his veins like lead.

A small, long-haired figure approached. "There's like this tunnel down into your mind, you know?" said Sam without prelude, "and all these crystals like inside a geode, that are perception mechanisms, right?—perceptions before they've got any content, just *forms,* right?—ready to refract any input to the various receptors, right?—but then you get this light that breaks up into all these colors and doesn't make a picture, just a big dazzle, too bright to look at, and you try to straighten out the colors, and these crystals are *sharp,* they'll snag you, man, they'll cut your ass to pieces. I'm down in there, man, and I'm in a fucking panic. And every way I turn there's like a fragment of despair, a shrapnel-piece of rage, everything is shattered into a zillion pieces and every piece will cut you. It will *rip* you, man. I don't know what to do. I don't know what to do."

What does one say to this kind of thing? "Sam," essayed Wordlaw, "I think this whole evening has been kind of a—purging for you? and now you might want to go through a little period of re-orientation? maybe smoke a joint and, um, maybe ease up on the coke? We're all going out to eat a barbecue, so why don't you come on with us and we'll just have a few beers and just let things flow, okay?"

Sam was trembling. His eyes were wild, wet, all black pupil. "I don't want to see your sister, man. No offense. I'm just going to get a room somewhere, and split in the morning."

"That's fine, Sam, that's fine," said Wordlaw, trying not to betray his relief.

"Marian," said Sam, all business suddenly, "would you mind seeing that my stuff gets back to New York?"

"Glad to."

"Dig you later, then," said Sam.

"I hope not," said Marian under her breath.

"Claudia?" boomed Wordlaw's father through a mouthful of eggs. "How come little old Doc Wakinaki hasn't come down to breakfast?"

She burst into tears.

"Ivy Dee? What the hell's the matter with your daughter?"

"Robertson Corelli, you are so *insensitive* I just can't stand it! Can't you see you're embarrassing Claudia in front of her friends?"

Claudia cried harder. Shoot and Junior gaped; Lisa and Marian looked into their laps; Wordlaw wanted to touch Marian but could only squint at her through parched eyelids. He had slept hardly at all, lying wedged into the narrow bed of his boyhood beside her, unable to stop wishing that he had plucked the moment when it was ripe, unable to stem his regret.

Liz Chisholm carried Neil O'Neill's style of sinister tenebrosity to a demonic extreme. Her witch's cape and hood were black, her waist-long hair was black, her fingernails were painted black. Her skin was the color of a corpse washed up on an English detective story beach.

While Mimi and Alice finished mixing down a song inside, Wordlaw and Liz played pool in the outer room. She asked him nothing about himself or Mimi; she talked nonstop about herself. She *was* a witch, in fact—met weekly with her coven, in a tenement in the Quarter.

She snapped open a black lacquered cigarette case, withdrew two pills, gulped them down without benefit of liquid, and proffered the case. Within were neat rows of tablets and capsules, each nestled in a black velvet cavity.

Wordlaw could only stammer, "Uh, no, no, thanks." He slowly chalked his cue. Looking up, he saw her kohl-lidded eyes fixed on his hand, reading a meaning he had by no means intended. As her eyes slid to his, Alice and Mimi emerged from the studio. Mimi looked haggard, bloated, terrible.

Liz produced a cassette recorder and proceeded to read from a typed list of asinine questions—favorite color, what for breakfast, sun sign, moon sign, influences on musical style. Much to both Mimi's and Wordlaw's astonishment, Alice dominated the interview, bragging shamelessly about their new songs and even about Wordlaw's painting. Liz, black eyelids drooping, edged ever nearer to coma, but she braved it through to the end of her list and staggered foggily out.

"What's the latest medication of choice?" asked Alice.

"Percodan," answered Wordlaw, grinning.

Mimi, rubbing her hands, mumbled, "Maybe I can still catch her."

"She shouldn't be too hard to catch," laughed Alice nervously. "She's probably passed out in the parking lot."

"What in the hell is this?" demanded Wordlaw.

"It's my damn *hands,* Word!" Mimi half-sobbed over her shoulder as she ran outside.

Wordlaw looked at Alice, and Alice looked back at him, and neither spoke a word.

In accordance with his marriage's one inexorable principle, Wordlaw began to be able to work again. He filled up half a dozen big canvases with life-size bodies—many of them images of Liz—in every manner of union, whorls of Rubens pink and Watteau blush and Reynolds pale and Bacon crimson-purple writhing on a ground of purest black.

Every morning now, Mimi awoke with the knuckles on the first two fingers of her hands swollen and hurting. She would rub and flex them, and as the day went on the pain would subside. By late afternoon, however, she would be exhausted, and before long she could not even lift a frying pan.

Mimi's album was due out in March, and much of her tour was already booked, so she should have been rehearsing every day, but it hurt too much to play the piano. She knew she could have hired a piano player and practiced her singing; she was going to have to hire one anyway for the tour. She knew that the next step forward in the life she desired depended on singing the whole depth of these new songs over and over in town after town as if each audience were new, but she was too sad and too sick to sing.

Neil O'Neill summoned her to his office. The walls were covered in black patent leather, with chrome studs. Helmut offered Mimi a

Russian cigarette, and lit one each for Neil and himself. "Well, darling," said Neil. "Liz tells me you're not feeling well. I'm so sorry. Have you been to the doctor?"

She shook her head.

Helmut frowned.

"That won't do, darling," said Neil O'Neill. "I've got a good doctor for you. I want you to see him. Today. I'm counting on you for my second quarter. *I want you to make that tour.* Darling."

She nodded meekly.

"And darling? I want you to work on your appearance. I want you to have all the wardrobe you can shake a stick at. I want you to get your hair cut some way wild. Get me that checkbook, will you, Helmut? I want you to have a little advance, darling, let's say two thousand, and just spend it all on your appearance. And, Mimi, ah, you lose a little weight—you hear?"

She heard.

"Get Liz Chisholm in here," said Neil O'Neill the instant Mimi was gone.

Helmut brought her. "I want you to *watch* that bitch," said Neil. "She is getting fucked *up*. I want her *happy*. You understand?" He handed Liz Chisholm five one-gram vials of cocaine.

M. v. B.J.

26 Feb 76

Dearest dearest Wordlaw,

Not a day has passed when I have not thought of you, and yet I find, to my chagrin, that it has taken something of a crisis for me finally to write.

I'll just plunge right in. Your sister has told me that she hasn't told you any of this, and she's given me her permission to do so.

Sam was back amidst us three days after we returned to New York—nagging, whining, threatening, sulking, complaining, and blasted on drugs worse than ever. Weeks of hell ensued.

Then one night last week, when Claudia was out of town on

business, I came home to the most horrible scene. What I *thought* it was was that Sam was raping Lisa. I opened the door, and there he was, slamming into her, pinning her wrists to the floor, and Lisa screaming bloody murder. What else could I have assumed? Anyhow, I grabbed him by the hair to pull him off, and—I broke his neck. I didn't kill him, but he's still in the hospital, and it's not clear whether he's going to be all right or not.

And it turned out that it wasn't rape at all. Sam and Lisa had taken LSD, and it was just plain old drug-crazed sex.

Your sister forgave them (of course), and all of them seem to have forgiven me, but naturally it hardly seems appropriate for us to go on living together. Lisa has already found an apartment, and Maggie's looking, and I'm alone.

And I'm going bananas. I need very badly to see you.

Wordlaw, let me come and see you. Call me.

Your
Marian

He did not call; he did not write back.

He was still determined to try to save his marriage. But Mimi called his kindnesses pity, his suggestions criticism, his sympathy contempt. After a while, he simply tried to steer clear. He wrote a note to Marian, apologizing for being so withdrawn but begging her indulgence. He was painting all day long every day, and, since Mimi could no longer do it, cooking every night—like a maniac, typically.

One night he made a dish of the Brothers Troisgros—*oeufs pochés et frits à la purée Stéphanoise,* it was called.

First he had to poach eggs, which he had never done before. To come out with four, he used up fourteen. Then he had to trim their edges with scissors—and trashed two more. He went back to the store for a new half dozen, successfully poached three, trashed one of them, and finally had his four. He had made a fond blanc de volaille the previous evening—six hours' work on behalf of the cup and a quarter of stock the egg dish called for. With the stock he made a velouté sauce, which was to be enriched with cream and egg yolks (another trip to the grocery). But he added the hot sauce too fast and curdled the yolks, and the whole business had to be thrown out. He made another batch of sauce, thanking God he had extra fond blanc. Now he had to dip the poached eggs and coat them with the sauce. He broke another one, and decided to make do with three. The eggs now had to be refrigerated to firm up, so he turned to the purée Stéphanoise.

In three pots of boiling water, he cooked string beans, asparagus tips, and peas. He soaked and sloshed the spinach till the sand was out, which alone took fifteen minutes, and then peeled the stems and veins from the leaves. It was now eight o'clock—at which hour he had planned to serve this god-damned dinner—and he still had not even begun work on the main course, a lobster fricassée. He sautéed the spinach in Normandy butter; reserved a quarter of the beans, asparagus, and peas; added the rest to the spinach in his new fifty-dollar red-enameled casserole and cooked it all together for half an hour; and pushed the lot through his new Mouli food mill. The result was a vague-tasting green glop.

On the fifth try at beurre noir, he managed not to burn it, and poured himself a stiff bourbon.

Now came the hard part. He whipped a raw egg and some peanut oil in a soup plate and rolled the sauce-coated chilled poached eggs in that. Then he rolled the now unbelievably sticky little bastards in bread crumbs—which he had also made last night, from day-old bread from Lascombe's, the best bakery in New Orleans, which he'd had to drive clear across town to. For the life of him he could not figure out how to pick up the eggs without leaving naked finger-spots in the bread crumb coating. Trying to, he broke another egg.

He heated oil in his new electric deep fryer to a precise three hundred and fifty degrees, and lowered the two surviving eggs into it with his new Chinese skimmer. He was supposed to keep the eggs swirling in the fat the whole time they fried, and doing so he burned holy hell out of his arm but of course could not stop to attend to it.

He lowered the fried eggs gently onto a paper towel, put them in a low oven to keep warm, and heated up the green glop in his new Pyrex double boiler. He reheated the reserved peas, beans, and asparagus in his new bamboo steamer. He warmed the plates for the eggs and sprinkled the eggs with sea salt. He spooned the hot purée onto the plates, arranged the vegetable garnish artfully round about, hollered for Mimi to open the bottle of Meursault-Perrières (gift from Edmond and Alice), drizzled the beurre noir over, and raced to the table. It was almost ten o'clock.

Mimi was still in front of the TV. "Didn't you open the wine?" demanded Wordlaw.

"Huh?"

"The wine!" he yelled.

"Where is it?" she asked.

"In the refrigerator!"

"This white?" She was moving in what looked exactly like movie slow motion.

"It's the only bottle in there, Mimi! *Please* hurry. The eggs are getting cold."

"Where's the corkscrew?" she asked.

"On the hook where it always is!" he yelled back.

"I can't get the what-do-you-call-it, the lead thing, off."

"The capsule! Bring it to the table! Please!" He pulled out her chair, and she half fell into it and did not scoot forward when he tried to help her.

"What happened to your arm?" she asked blurrily.

Wordlaw's egg was brick-solid straight through, and managed to be at once burned on the outside and cold on the in. Mimi's, however, was perfect, the brilliant yolk oozing garishly over the green purée.

"This is incredible," she said. (Incredibly gross, said the look on her face.)

"It sucks, doesn't it?"

"No, no. It's real good."

"It sucks. And I never even got to the lobster. Let's go down to Felix's and get something to *eat.* Oyster poorboy or something."

"I'm really not hungry," she said. "This was fine. You go."

———

The bus lines were offering a ticket that allowed you to go anywhere in the United States for a hundred and fifty dollars.

"Why don't you take the car?" asked Wordlaw.

"I don't know," she replied.

"Where are you going to go?"

"I don't really know."

"What's going on, Mimi? Tell me. Let me love you."

"I don't know, Word. I wish I could. I can't think."

"How are your hands?" he asked.

"They hurt. And my wrists, and my feet, and my knees, and my hips." She was near tears, but the Valium held the line.

"Have you thought of giving up cocaine?"

"I haven't done any coke for two weeks, Wordlaw. Liz got fired, for failing to save me."

"That's too bad."

"Fuck her," said Mimi.

"Have you talked to your parents?"

"*Please,*" was all she said. Mimi's father was a congressman, her mother a Washington social climber, both habitually much too busy to give a damn what was happening to their daughter, whose way of life they considered a personal disgrace and, worse, an embarrassment.

"Well," said Wordlaw hopelessly, "how about dinner at Galatoire's?"

"Okay. Sure. Why not."

Mimi only picked at her food. Wordlaw ordered a half bottle of champagne to go with dessert, but just as the waiter uncorked it Mimi started crying and they had to go.

Standing dazed and bus-worn amidst the squalor of Eighth Avenue, Mimi found herself dialing the number of Claudia Corelli's new apartment. Mimi was not as passive an actor in this brief scenario as she tried to think. Wordlaw had told her about his sister's strange involvement with Sam Watanabe, and it was not really to Claudia but rather to the combination of medical expertise and drug abuse personified in Sam that Mimi in her pain was drawn.

Claudia chose, characteristically, to believe that the honor was all hers, and she gushed and fretted exuberantly over Mimi. Claudia insisted on fixing her hair, topped off with a flourish of lavender grosgrain—"because look how it picks up your *lovely* violet eyes!" When Sam laid out coke after dinner, however, the real bond in this visit was instantly evident. "*I*'ve got to go to work tomorrow," cooed Claudia, "but don't mind me. I just want you to have the *best* time in New York. Give me a hug, Mimi. I'm so happy to *see* you."

"So," said Sam mildly when they were alone. "The Cajun queen. I dug the shit out of your album."

"Thank you. I've got a new one coming out."

"What's the matter with your hands?" he demanded suddenly.

"You a mind reader or what?"

"Just a doctor. Used to be."

"My doctor thinks it might be rheumatoid arthritis."

"Bummer. This'll fix you right up," said Sam, razoring out eight sparkling lines.

Sam and Mimi snorted cocaine for five straight days and nights, bludgeoning themselves into occasional brief and restless sleeps with sledgehammer doses of downs. Sam had little to say, but Mimi had never talked so much in her life. Claudia drifted through from time to time, in from work, out to dinner, dressed to the nines, here and then gone hardly noticed, leaving behind her the ashtrays cleaned and the throw pillows plumped.

"You ever try freebasing?" asked Sam.

She had never heard of it. Sam prepared the pipe.

Instantaneous transport to paradise. She decided she was in love with Willy Newman. Why had it taken her so long to realize it?

She slept for twenty hours straight. Sam and Claudia saw her off at Port Authority.

———

There was no furniture at Liz Chisholm's, only cushions of velvet and beaded suede. A false ceiling, also of velvet, deep purple, made of the long low room a kind of tent.

She rinsed out a dirty glass and downed a big white pill and two little blue ones. "Can I get you something? Valium? Quaalude? No coke, I'm afraid—as you may have heard, I got fired. Beer?"

"A beer would be great," said Wordlaw.

"You ought to try a Quaalude," said Liz.

"One of these days, maybe. What's it like?"

"Ludes? Just smooth, man. Smooth. Makes you feel like—liquid." Indeed she soon became notably fluid, undulating into a nest of cushions. "You look mobile enough to maybe put on a record?"

"Sure," said Wordlaw. "What do you want to hear?"

"Not your wife."

"Don't worry."

"Just something—smoooooth," crooned Liz.

Wordlaw found a Brazilian samba record.

"Oh, yeah," she sighed. "Oh, *yeah.*" Albeit through darkness both physical and mental, she was looking at him hard. "Listen," she said, "Wordlaw. You want to make love?"

Before he could speak she was talking again:

"I kept thinking when I was seeing Mimi all the time that I might get a chance to get to you. I even did a little spell. Ate a shitload of luck-in-love powder. But man, you lays low—always dissolving right out of the room. Hard to get, right?"

"No," he said, trying to sound equally nonchalant. "Easy."

She moved toward him through the dark purple light. "Let me do that," she purred, removing his hands from his shirt button.

Yes, liquid was the word. She was slippery as a dolphin. Everywhere, she was so soft she seemed swollen. She sweated, she slobbered, she oozed. She seethed.

"Turn me over," she commanded.

"Yeah, right, okay," Wordlaw panted as, near exhaustion, he kissed again Liz Chisholm's mucous, sucking mouth.

Finally he invited Marian to New Orleans.

She frowned at the big black Liz pictures. "I don't like these much, I'm afraid," she said. "They seem so out of sorts."

"Yeah, well," said Wordlaw.

"These, however, I adore"—his most recent work: thick gloppy constructions on board, landscapes on the model of his childhood piece *Chickasaw Estates,* incorporating material from the actual places represented—mud, sticks, stone. "I *feel* you in these," she said, standing close to him, his bourbon on her breath. "Kiss me?"

Well, shoot, of course he would; and very happily did. It came back to him then what he'd reared away from so fearfully in Memphis the Christmas before: he was not ready for love as vertiginous as this. But this time he was swept over the edge and was falling, falling. "I don't know if this is—"

"Shhh." She kissed him again.

"I mean—"

"Shut up, turkey," murmured Marian. "Just hold me."

He was weightless, spinning through space. Yet there was, it seemed, gravity enough to draw them to his studio cot; and, at the same time, little enough that, laughing, entangled, as it were wind-borne, they could fairly float to the floor.

Afterward, she rose, walked to his easel, and studied the canvas in progress, hand on her hip, bare ass cocked. "Oh, Lord," he muttered, mostly to himself.

She heard him, though, and turned, smiling, the very picture of ease. She tucked her chin down toward him, and her hair fell forward over one eye. "What's on your mind, sailor?" she said, throatily.

"Turn around," he said, and, again, as she complied, "Oh, Lord."

She looked back, over her shoulder, through her hair again. "What is it?"

"I'm getting this urge to, um, paint you," he said.

"Like this, you mean? Flushed? Rosy? Happy?"

—•—

The bus was hot, close, foul. Mimi was running a fever, and she had never felt so depressed. The joints of her fingers were on fire. At the station in Washington, where winos wheezed on the benches and larcenists cruised coolly past surveying her luggage, she tried again to phone Wordlaw, and for the third day straight there was no answer.

She called her father's office. "Miriam! Mimi baby!" he boomed. "Listen, babe, I've got a quorum call staring me in the face. Where can I get back to you?"

The maid said that Mimi's mother was at a Democratic luncheon at the Watergate.

In the bathroom mirror Mimi saw that an angry rash had spread across her cheeks and the bridge of her nose, in a kind of butterfly pattern. She wanted to cry, but could not. She wanted cocaine.

The slashed unhealing mountainsides of Appalachia crept by. Faces peered longingly at the gleaming bus, as though perhaps there might be a movie star within. Pickup trucks with broken mufflers clattered down the hills backfiring. Broken-hearted miners scowled from porches. Women snatched at their children's clothes.

At the woebegone gas station that was her stop, it took her half an hour and twenty dollars to persuade a drunk old man to drive her to Willy Newman's mountaintop dome.

"If I'd knowed you was coming, I'd'a baked a cake," said Willy, unsmiling.

"I should have called," said Mimi.

"That's true."

"I'm sorry," she pleaded. "I just wanted to see you."

"Well, I'm delighted you're here." He did not look it.

"How's everything?" she asked, trying for sprightly but bull's-eye on brittle.

"Lousy. Commune's hit rock bottom—it's just Barbara and me and T.C. and Sara now. Three years ago we had eighteen people."

"I guess the sixties really are over," she said.

"I haven't had a new song recorded since '72. My manager dumped me. I'm broke. All in all, I'm doing quite poorly. How's the brilliant career of Mimi Fontaine?"

"I've got a new album in the can," she said, "ready to be released. But I've got to tour to support it, and right now I can't play because I've got something the matter with my hands."

Here at last she seemed to have reached him. He took her hands. They were swollen, stiff, ugly. "Jesus. What is it?"

The sun was setting. Big dark pines rose above the hardwood trees just leafing out along the ridgeline. She had not even considered that spring was here. She bit her lip to keep it from trembling. "It's probably rheumatoid arthritis. It's an immune system thing. Where your body's defenses turn against your own tissue as if it were foreign. Nice resonance in that concept, wouldn't you say?"

She felt a chill return of Willy's unsympathy in this long pause. He had never had much patience with other people's troubles. "Couldn't you just sing?"

"I don't know," she said. "I feel so awful."

"How's your husband?" Willy's face was blank.

"I don't know," said Mimi. "I've been in New York for a week, and he's not answering the phone. He's painting, I guess. He always paints when I'm fucked up. He feeds on the suffering of others."

"He must be well fed," Willy shot back.

"Do I look that bad?" she asked, helplessly.

"No, no," he said, "you misunderstand me. I just mean there's a lot of suffering out there. You look fine."

"Willy, Willy, Willy," she said, softly, trying to call up the softness that used to come into her voice when they were alone. She touched her cheek to his shoulder.

"What, Mimi." No go.

"It's just—you seem sort of distant."

He snorted, and stepped back. "And telling me so is really going to help. Look, Mimi, I haven't seen you or even talked to you in five years."

"I'm sorry," she said. "I'm just upset—I mean, I'm tired. How about a walk, down by the creek?" Like before.

"Sure, okay, why not," said Willy. "What the fuck."

As they walked, the West Virginia moon rose. When they came to the bridge, they turned to each other in silent appeal, but fear stood between them, adult fear now, of the consequences of anything bold, the black-gloved fear that at first caresses and comforts but ultimately clutches and strangles those who have had courage before but can no longer summon it up. Mimi knew she looked awful, and her hands hurt terribly, and this Willy Newman was not the one she had half-dreamed in her freebase frenzy in New York.

"Willy, do you by any chance have any coke?"

"Yeah, I think we've got some up at the dome."

Mimi strode fast up the hill. She waited for Willy at the door, tapping her foot. Barbara and Sara and T.C. were watching television, and barely looked up when Mimi and Willy came in. She joined them, Barbara rather grumpily making room for her on the sofa.

"Long time no see," said Mimi.

"Yeah," said Barbara. "Let's catch up on the gay old times after the show's over."

It was just some bullshit sitcom. Mimi tried to watch, picking at her cuticles. The canned laughter made her want to scream. Somebody had farted. Fever washed over her in sickening waves.

Willy called from the kitchen: "Pepsi okay?"

August, a Sunday, hot, raining, quiet. Marian's fifth visit since spring.

Mimi had called early this morning from her parents' place in LaFourche Parish, where at last, out of money, out of drugs, she had gone to fall apart. As she seemed now always to do, she had broken into tears within her first minute on the phone. For Marian's sake, perhaps for his own, Wordlaw had kept a stone face, murmured noncommittal reassurance, and rung off as quickly as possible.

Then they had made love, gone out for coffee and beignets, read the paper, and, beneath a dripping umbrella, stood outside a black church listening.

Three hours now remained before she had to leave for the airport. He watched as she finished packing.

"I find," said Wordlaw, "that I have begun to enjoy most of all the last moments before you leave. Not that I want you to go—far from it. I actually sort of savor the *sadness*. Isn't that strange?"

She gave him a small, speaking smile, but said nothing.

"*Oh,*" he said finally, the light dawning. "I get it!"

She smiled more broadly, sweetly.

"I'm *learning!*" laughed Wordlaw, picturing a cartoon light bulb over his head. "Right?"

"It's nothing you didn't already know," said Marian softly. "How could I ever have loved you if you didn't, deep down?"

He kissed her. "Do you think you could ever live here?"

"Are you inviting me to?" She gave a nervous, deflective laugh.

"I don't really know if I'll be wanting to come back myself."

"*What?*" She went pale.

"Well, I've been thinking about going on the road. Friend of mine's got an old van for sale."

She put a hand over her mouth and studied him with wide eyes. Then she kissed her own fingers and touched them to his lips. "One second you're talking about me coming here, and the next you're buying a van and leaving. Or are you just looking for a house sitter?"

He laughed glumly. "I'm sorry, Marian. My mind wanders. It's just I've been thinking about the future, my so-called career. I mean, suppose I do go on the road for a while. I'd be missing you, I'd be miserable. Maybe also enjoying missing you and being miserable—as the gospel according to Marian teaches. I have this idea that I'll do a bunch of bleak, lonely landscapes. And then I'm going to be ready for a new phase. One with less solitude in it."

"Oh, Wordlaw," she whispered, hiding her face on his shoulder. The baby-soap smell of her hair filled him with tenderness.

"But it's going to mean a long time when we don't see each other at all. Things happen to people when they're apart for a long time. I'm not a gambling man, and this seems risky."

She looked at him now. "I'll still be there," she said.

"We can talk on the phone a lot."

"I want to see my picture again."

He had finally finished it, and only this weekend shown it to her. In it she stood, as she had stood that day last spring, at his easel, nude, looking over her shoulder, hand on cocked hip, chin tucked in amusement, hair fallen softly across one eye. For the canvas that had actually been on the easel—yet another Liz-derived sextravaganza—he had substituted one of the landscapes that Marian had liked so much. It was vertical, on board, a dark, gold-streaked view into the cypress swamps of Lafourche Parish—where Mimi had been born and raised. Marian studied the picture, and smiled. "Want to borrow it?" he asked.

"No, no," she laughed, blushing. "Amos would go insane." Amos was Marian's brother but also in a sense her father, being twenty-three years older and having acted the official parent role after their parents' early death.

"It's good, isn't it?" he could not help saying.

"The only thing better is hearing you say that," said Marian.

"I owe you so much," said Wordlaw.

"I will accept a down payment," she said then. "Something to keep me warm on the plane."

"It's going to be a long time till I see you again," Wordlaw said between kisses.

"I can wait," said Marian, after another.

1977

Gunmetal Texas savanna; blue treeless Nevada mountains; wind-gutted prospectors' cabins tiny at a Utah salt flat's edge; junked cars heaped into a sweep of canyon bank in Idaho; coastal hills soft as young love's breast, hogback ridges hard as old villainy's bones: the landscapes of the American West were huge, but Wordlaw rendered them small. He saw this as a gesture simultaneously of conquest and of the gesture's own futility—I make this place little enough to carry under my arm, this place is too big to paint big.

Working on a small scale was in any case a physical necessity, since he was maintaining both residence and studio in the back of his van.

"At last!" cried Marian. "I thought you were *dead!* Oh, my dearest, how are you? Where are you?"

"I'm cold. I'm at a truck stop near Billings, Montana. It's twenty-two below, and they say it may get cool tonight."

"Well, Happy New Year," she sighed.

"I'm sorry I haven't called."

"Yes, well."

He *had,* at first. But the calls had not gone well. She seemed to assume he needed helping, comfort; from this he shrank. Eventually it was easier just not to try. From time to time he would crate a piece and send it, with a note: "I do love you"—as if denying that he didn't. He didn't know what to say now.

Marian broke the silence: "Work going all right?"

"It's all crap." His Western landscapes were not succeeding as externalizations of his inner solitude, which was what he'd had in mind. They were lonely, and beautiful enough in their loneliness, but they did not make contact with the source he had meant to tap: his long young days in the swamp, immersed in stillness. What he had wanted—so badly!—was to express the swelling of the heart that he used to feel there, alone, but these pictures had failed to do that.

"The things you've sent me are definitively not crap, Wordlaw. But listen. There's another reason I've been wanting to talk to you, besides missing you. You may recall we had Vicente Ortega Montes scheduled for April. Well, he's had some sort of freakout, and we can't even get him on the phone in Mexico to find out what's going on, but it looks as though there'll be nothing to hang. So I carpéd the diem to show your stuff to Yves, and—guess what."

"Jesus," muttered Wordlaw. Dread sat on him like an elephant.

"A one-man show, Wordlaw! At Yves Olivier! I'm so happy for you—for us both. Aren't you? *Say something,* for heaven's sake!"

"You've been so kind to me, Marian." Bitter wind was whirling into the booth and up his pants legs.

"You must be lonely."

"Put it another way: I am trying to learn to enjoy solitude, with varying degrees of success."

"I've got so much to tell you," she said.

"Uh oh."

"Why do you say that?"

"Prefaces usually mean bad news. Good stuff you say right out. What is it you want to tell me?"

"*A,* I love you. God knows why. I really love you. I've been working on this, and it's never been so clear."

"I love you too, Marian."

"*B,* I want to see you."

"Well, I guess I'll be coming to New York in April, won't I?"

"I need to see you before that. I need to know if this thing is going to go somewhere."

"Tick tick tick tick."

"Yes, damn you!" she cried. "The clock is running."

"Give me a couple of days?"

She sighed.

"Do you see?" he said. "Somehow, Marian, somehow we don't quite get along."

"Okay. *C,* about that blowup in New York last February? There's something I didn't tell you. There's this guy—"

The breath went out of him as though he'd been punched in the belly. "Say on."

"I don't even know if I like him that much. I know I don't love him. But I guess there's something there, or I wouldn't have kept it from you. I sent you the catalogue for our Karl Watters show—those big photo-realist pictures of insects? Well, this guy, this entomologist, came to the opening. And that night when I came in on Sam and Lisa?—he was just bringing me home from our first date. And he sort of saw me through all that, when you didn't write me back or anything, and I was very grateful to him."

"All this time, almost a year, you've been seeing him?"

"Only intermittently," she said. "What I've really been doing is waiting for *you* to settle down a little and see where your real interest lies, and then—then come to me."

"What's his name?"

"His name is Walter Pinckney," said Marian.

"Do you fuck him?"

"Oh, Wordlaw."

"Right. Okay. Marian, let me ask you one question. How do you think I could ever trust you?"

"It's not that *serious,*" she pleaded.

"An entomologist."

"I think you'd find his work interesting, actually, with your cotton-planter roots. He's looking at a parasite of the boll weevil. It could have tremendous application in IPM—integrated pest management?

It's the wave of the future. It could replace a lot of dreadful insecticides."

"I'm so glad," said Wordlaw.

"Asshole!" she cried, trying to laugh. "You're jealous! Oh, you are! I want so much to see you. Don't you think we could just try to talk through everything, and really focus on what's *good* between us? I'm sorry I didn't tell you about Walter. I guess I didn't want to seem to be manipulating you, trying to make you jealous. Do you want me not to see him any more? Tell me, and I won't. Tell me."

"I can't tell you what to do," said Wordlaw.

"Tell me," she pleaded. "Tell me not to."

"I can't take that kind of responsibility for you."

"That's what's wrong. You're so wrapped up in your damned self-sufficiency! People need to depend on each other!"

"You always want to change me," said Wordlaw. "It's a thread that's run through all our conversations, from way back when. If only this, if only that. But I don't have the energy to go on a big self-reformation campaign. It's all I can do to make these shitty pictures. I *wish* I could be like you want me to be. I wish I could *try* to be."

"You're wrong about a 'massive self-reformation campaign,' Wordlaw. I'm not making demands on you. I'm offering you a gift. It fell out of the sky on me after that Christmas and New Year's in Memphis. We've talked about this before, but I've wondered if we ever quite reached closure on it. The gift was seeing that it wasn't necessary to be negative about everything, the way you and I both have a natural tendency to do. I've come to understand that in me it was just a bullshit self-defense, a withdrawal. I know how hard it is for you. I remember your saying you carried all that inherited negativity around inside you. And I think I was attracted to you because at some level I felt the same way about myself. But you know who brought this home to me? Not by anything he said but just in what he was? Forrest McCracken. He just bathes everything around him in warmth. And then I started really watching Claudia. Your sister certainly hasn't inherited any burden of evil. When that beam of light of hers comes to rest on someone, that golden glow of her empathy, they just absolutely *bloom*—like one of those time-lapse photographs of a flower opening."

"Like Sam Watanabe," said Wordlaw acidly.

"Exception to the rule. You shithead. Listen to me. I could have avoided breaking Sam's neck if I'd understood him and Lisa a little—and I *could* have understood them a little if I'd brought some empathy to bear. But I have the gift now. It's finding delight in the world. Not laughing at it; not amusement. Knowing even tragedy, betrayal, horror, as somehow beautiful."

"You're so full of shit I'm amazed you haven't exploded."

"You're hurting me on purpose, Wordlaw."

"Well, you're talking *nonsense,* Marian. By your reasoning I'm supposed to take pleasure in you fucking Walter Pinckney behind my back. I'm supposed to celebrate the ruin of the Indians, slavery, the Holocaust."

"All right," she said bleakly. "I'm tired. It's after midnight."

"I'm tired too."

"I want to talk to you some more before you write me off."

"Sure, okay," said Wordlaw.

"You'll call me? You promise?"

"Sure."

But he didn't.

The sight and smell of the Atchafalaya cypress lowlands filled Wordlaw with longing, for his own lost swamp, and with dread, of the doom awaiting this one: from the north, the Mississippi, swollen with the runoff of its thousands of scalped, gutted, and hemorrhaging tributaries, threatened every spring to burst its banks and rampage through this wilderness of still waters; meanwhile, from the south, spilled oil, draglines, and river silt were moving inland, clogging the marshes, salting this sweet water, killing all that lived therein.

He paid no mind to the strange car at the curb, but he entered his house to a dense stink of marijuana. Trembling, checking his footing, he flipped on the lights. The living room was strewn with newspapers, beer bottles, ashtrays, chicken bones. Then he noticed a light on in his studio out back, and the door open.

Mimi was standing in front of the portrait of Marian, smoking a joint. She turned, saying, "Liz?"

He was invisible in the darkness of the courtyard. "No, it's me."

"Word?"

She looked like a concentration camp survivor, all eyes and bone. "What are you doing here?" he demanded.

"It's nice to see you too," she said.

"Sorry. I just thought you were in Washington."

"I guess you haven't been reading the papers," she said. "Come with me."

He followed behind her to the house and into the littered living room. She walked strangely, stiffly, now. She picked up a *Times-Picayune* and shoved it at him.

REP. FONTAINE RESIGNS
IN BRIBERY SCANDAL

Washington, Feb. 26.—Rep. Roy V. (Ti-Bubba) Fontaine, Jr., Democrat of Louisiana, resigned today from the United States House of Representatives. Mr. Fontaine has been implicated in a widening federal investigation of the awarding of construction and oil exploration contracts in his home state. He pledged to cooperate fully with the Federal Bureau of Investigation.

U.S. Attorney Elwood Fish declined to comment on reports that Mr. Fontaine will be indicted on federal racketeering charges later this week.

Sources close to Congressman Fontaine have suggested that he may link several other prominent Louisiana political figures to the alleged bribery and kickback scheme. It has been speculated that Mr. Fontaine might be granted some leniency in return for his cooperation. . . .

"Holy shit," said Wordlaw.

"And I guess all this reminded Neil O'Neill of my existence," said Mimi. "He's finally decided to release my album. So I'm going to try to play the club. Just a week. Alice found me a piano player."

"You must be feeling better," said Wordlaw.

"You think so?" She thrust out her hands. They were curled into horrible claws.

"I'm sorry, Mimi."

"I need money," she said.

"I haven't got any," said Wordlaw.

"What do you *live* on?"

"Well, I've got that little trust fund from my granddad, but you know that half of that wouldn't be enough for anybody to live on."

"How much do you think your father's worth?" she demanded.

"You know perfectly well I'll never see it till the bastard's six feet under, and my mom too. I'm not sure I want it anyhow, considering where it came from."

"Oh, Mr. Morality! You make me sick."

"Listen, Mimi, I'm going to go sack out in the studio. Let's talk when you're straight."

"I'm never going to be straight!" she shrieked. "I'm going to stay wrecked till I die."

"You and Liz are friends again?" he asked, coolly.

"And she's ready to testify for me too."

"You're divorcing me, finally? And cutting her in on the proceeds?" He supposed he oughtn't to be surprised at Liz.

"You'll take that money when the time comes," said Mimi.

"Well, at least I have a reason now to wish my father good health," said Wordlaw.

Sadness kept him up all night. The morning light mocked the darkness in his heart; these unpainted canvases were the very image of all he had failed to do with his life. Only the portrait of Marian could not be disfigured by his mood. In it she was always smiling, always about to speak: "Like this, you mean? Flushed? Rosy? Happy?"

There was no phone in the studio. Well, let Mimi hear if she must. He tiptoed into the kitchen, and dialed.

"Did I wake you?"

"No, no," lied Marian drowsily, then bolted awake. "*Wordlaw?*"

"Listen. I need to see you."

"You are incredible."

"I've been up all night, looking at your portrait."

"You dropped off the face of the *earth.*"

"I know. I said I'd call you."

"Eight weeks ago. Eight weeks can be a long time, Wordlaw."

"Yes, I know," he said. Soft piano chords came from the living room: Mimi was up.

"Well," said Marian, and took a deep breath, "Wordlaw, I'm going to marry Walter Pinckney."

"Oh."

"You broke my heart, you son of a bitch."

"I'm sorry, Marian."

"So am I."

"Is it too late?"

"Yes."

"I guess I'll see you anyhow in a couple of weeks."

"Yes, I suppose so," she said.

Mimi had never seen him look so bad.

"Peter Elias—Wordlaw Corelli," she said.

The black-furred paw Peter extended was a pretty odd substitute for Mimi's own pale, thin, once delicate fingers. She saw Wordlaw thinking the same thing, stealing a glance at them as he mumbled hello.

Alice came sweeping in the front door, in apple-green linen dress, spectator pumps, ribboned straw hat—belle of the garden party. "Wordlaw! Darling!" she cried, enveloping him. "Back from the desert! Suitably shriven? Soul white as snow?"

"Soul black as hell's asshole," said Wordlaw.

"Won't you stay and hear our new song?" asked Alice. "Isn't it wonderful, Word, having Mimi back in action?"

Mimi waited for Wordlaw to find a reason to clear out, but he just kept sitting there. He had always hated her rehearsals.

Peter had done his homework—it was extraordinary how perfectly his playing emulated her own rippling arpeggios. She closed her eyes. The new anti-inflammatory was pretty good. She hadn't even felt obliged to get stoned. She began to sing:

"I respect the pleasure police.
I condone their excesses.
My overripe burdens languish in jail,
sharing their secret caresses.

"I respect the solitude thieves.
I admire their rages.
My insolent alibis fly from my mouth
into their golden cages.

"The worst will be blindness:
touch his soft skin, and believe.
He will bathe you with kindness
and button your sleeve.
He will tell how the mornings glisten,
and you'll sit and touch him and listen.

"The years descend
and rise marinely.
We did love the sea.
I see the end.
It comes serenely.
Come inside, and see:

"Light the candles.
See us lying there.
Your arms are folded.
There's a ribbon in my hair.

"See the mourners.
Some are deep in prayer.
My hair is gold,
and there's a ribbon in my hair.

"In the distance
see my golden hair.
My hair is gold,
and there's a ribbon in my golden hair.

"Remember how
it seemed unending,
timeless, weightless, free.
I need you now.
No use pretending.
Be afraid with me.

"The best was the morning.
I lived alone, by a lake.
He'd arrive without warning
and kiss me awake.
He would tell how the morning glistened,
and I sat and touched him and listened.

"I respect a passionate age.
I delight in dramatics.
My heedless remorses watch their TVs,
with mongoloids locked in their attics.

"I respect an empty life.
I know the terror it covers.
The arid planets turn in space,
timeless as waltzing lovers."

Wordlaw looked at Mimi, and she saw for an instant the face of the man who had loved her so much, so long ago. "It's a beautiful song, Mimi," he said. "It's very sad." She heard him close the back door, and then his studio door.

He set up three fresh canvases, each one foot square.

"So," said Sam Watanabe, "how's all God's chillun in the town that care forgot? Give me five, bro."

He slapped Sam's outstretched palm. Sam's apparently complete lack of self-awareness was rather comforting, to a person who doubted his own. "Eating crawfish and drinking Sazeracs all day and night."

"Let me get you a drink, man," said Sam. "Claudia's just gone out for some lobsters. Nothing but the best for number one brother." He gestured toward the elaborately decked-out dining table in the corner of the loft. It was set for four.

"Who else is coming?"

"Who you think, bro? Important Manhattan art dealer!"

"Oh," said Wordlaw, with a gulp. "And the, ah, fiancé?"

"Out of town. Bug fanciers' jamboree somewhere. Scotch?"

"Thanks. Rocks," said Wordlaw. "Will this be, ah, the first time you've seen Marian since, ah—?"

"Yeah," said Sam. He was still wearing a neck brace fourteen months later. "Going to be a good night for interesting vibes."

The jawlike elevator door slammed open, and out came Claudia and Marian together, arms around each other's waists. "Look what I found downstairs!" cried his sister, hurrying to hug him, even in the midst of which he could not take his eyes off Marian as she crossed the shining expanse of floor. She was wearing tight jeans faded nearly white, a soft, lustrous, rather clingy teal-blue silk shirt, blue cowboy boots, a silver-tipped belt way too long so that the end dangled and swung in front. Lord, she was good-looking. Her eyes found his.

She presented her cheek to be kissed. "I came early," she said.

"You, ah, look, ah, incredible," Wordlaw stammered.

"Why, thank you." She smiled, one hundred watts.

This cool self-possession was maddening. She followed his words with deep-drinking eyes, but her body language, before and all during dinner, shut him resolutely out.

Claudia announced that she was going over to Mulberry Street to pick up some Italian pastries. "You'll walk me, won't you, Sam?" she asked with a flutter of hands toward the street, as if teeming Soho at ten o'clock was too dangerous for a girl alone.

"Babe, listen," Sam protested. "I haven't seen Marian for three coon's ages."

"*Come,* Sam," hissed Claudia.

The instant they were gone, Marian's body language turned soft, opened out, drew him in.

He took her hands—the left one wearing a fat oval sapphire engagement ring—and pulled her out of her chair. He kissed her. She kissed him back.

But no. She broke away abruptly, and walked fast across the wide floor, boot heels clicking, derrière splendid in those jeans. She held her hands in a little rooftop in front of her mouth, back still to him. She turned, and smiled across the distance. "I really don't have the nerve to hang the portrait," she said—characteristically leaping miles away while somehow at the same time staying on the inner subject. "Of course it's your picture, but I'm asking you."

"It's okay," he said, trying to sound unbothered. "I brought a replacement." I can ride out a detour, he told himself. Still he did wonder how much time they would have before Sam and Claudia got back. Well, even if not tonight, he would find time. If anything in his life had ever been, this woman was worth pursuing.

He unzipped a portfolio and folded out the new triptych, three foot-square canvases encased in rough black wood: Marian's face on the left panel, faint pink in a washy pink mist; Wordlaw's own on the right, crude black gouges in black impasto; and in the center, a ghoulish countenance which on examination revealed itself to be a composite of Marian's and Wordlaw's faces—not the formal and expressionless ones from the side panels but something from a nightmare of agony—leering double-exposure mouth, vacant dead eyes, hair on fire. The effect of the light pink on the left, the gunky black on the right, and the lurid smears between was of imbalance, discord, violence, madness.

"My word," gasped Marian.

"Hideous, isn't it," said Wordlaw. "See this?" He pointed to an ivory-white lump floating in the darkness of the composite face's gaping mouth. "That's my wisdom tooth."

"And that's the lock of my hair you asked me for last summer, isn't it?" she said, not quite touching it.

"My talisman," he said, coming close to inhale the baby-soap smell from the crown of her head.

"Quit it," she said, shifting away.

"You don't like the picture," he said.

"Wordlaw, *liking* is hardly an appropriate response to something like this, don't you think? It's very powerful."

"It is quite recognizably *you,*" said Wordlaw. "Is that going to be a problem for you? I mean, with Walter. I mean, what have you told him?"

"Do you feel like walking a little?"

They walked all the way from Prince Street to East Sixty-third, often not talking, holding hands the whole way. Marian avoided the subject of Walter Pinckney, and Wordlaw did not press her, simply letting the heat and propinquity of his reburgeoning love act on her as they might. It was raining, the same dense fine-grained rain that had fallen that Sunday last August. In New Orleans it had blurred the outlines of the lacy ironwork, red brick, whitewashed wood, dimming all to gray pastel; in this New York springtime it exploded the streetscapes into starbursts of color on slick obsidian black. In the narrow canyon of Mercer Street she said, "You should paint this." In Washington Square, he kissed her again. At Gramercy Park, she kissed him. In front of the dark white Morgan Library, the magnolias were swollen just short of bloom; Marian seemed uneasy now, saying only, "I know I seem to drift in and out, but bear with me, be patient, my dearest, won't you?" Her pace quickened. This marble, this much-painted black iron, this shining brass, this glowering dignity—this, this was her New York. They passed through the echoing emptiness of Grand Central and into the foursquare valley of Park Avenue.

"I could learn to like this town," he said, aching for her.

As they neared her building, an extra inch opened between them: there loomed obviously the question of whether she would invite him in. Beneath the canopy, she took a breath, squeezed his hand tight, and, with a curt smile to the doorman and not a word to Wordlaw, hauled him across the lobby and into the elevator. "We had an elevator man until recently," she said as the doors closed, and put her arms around him and closed her eyes and let her mouth fall just open.

The first thing she said in the morning was, "That was a mistake."

"No," he said, stunned, pulling the sheet under his chin as she strode up and down beside the bed, already dressed. "Marian, listen to me. It was not a mistake."

"Yes, it *was!*" she yelled. She pulled back the curtains, and sunlight gushed in. Softly, she added, "I don't know."

Here was a straw to grab at. "What don't you know?"

She spun around. "You'll drag me down," she said, still angry but also, it seemed, feeling vulnerable. "You'll turn me back into the depressive I've escaped from being. I need someone I can *count on.* That's much more important than just love. Why am I even saying love? Lust. We're still in the stupid *lust* phase, Wordlaw. Everybody knows that dies. Then what? Then you have to live."

"You'll drag me down," she had said: the future tense, not the conditional. He waited.

"I suppose I do still love you, you bastard. But this morning I don't think I can afford it. All that time when I didn't hear from you—it hurt *so much.* I felt so, so, so *abandoned.* I changed."

"I'm going to be here for three weeks," said Wordlaw. In the heart that was hammering in his chest, three weeks was an inconceivable eternity. "Let's just feel our way through it."

"Walter's coming back on Sunday." She moved toward him, peering down into his eyes—he still had not even sat up.

"So you'll have to sneak out," said Wordlaw, with an overhearty laugh, throwing off the covers, reaching for her.

"Stop that," she replied, tossing her hair but then looking back. "Seriously. It's not fair."

"Come here," he urged, running his finger up the inside of her leg.

"*No,*" she said firmly, stepping away.

"You'll think about it, though, won't you?"

"What the hell else do you think I'm going to be able to think about?"

The people at Wordlaw's opening tended, at first, to sort themselves into two distinct groups, both figuratively and literally north and south, at opposite poles of the narrow exhibition space. At one end—as far as possible, Wordlaw noted, from the triptych—stood Marian Jennings, serenely sipping champagne, surrounded by her tribe: her brother Amos, his wife Jenny, their drop-dead-beautiful sixteen-year-old daughter Kitty, and their two other younger daughters; Marian's sister Elisabeth and her husband Whitney Simon; an Episcopal priest named Curtis Emerson who had been Amos's roommate at Harvard; Claudia's old college boyfriend Quigley Seymour, now the Jennings family lawyer; Lisa Gruenthal and her current flame, a famous (and married) movie director; and assorted Old New York grandees of a type that Wordlaw really had never quite believed to exist, the men in English suits, hair slicked straight back, mouths not moving when they talked, the women emaciated, dressed to kill, eyes Antarctic-cold. Meanwhile, at the other, southern (Southern) end, in a melancholy ill-at-ease hush, milled Wordlaw's contingent: his falling-down-drunk father and pertly smiling mother; his goggling giggling sisters; the drastically stoned Flip and Annie Mayhew; Paul and Peter the Indistinguishable Farrs, with two gum-chewing adolescents they'd picked up in some singles bar last night; Bubba Bohannon, huge and gawking; and Forrest McCracken watching in dismay as Claudia Corelli and Sam

Watanabe, on either arm of the glamorous Yves Olivier, gaily herded Wordlaw back and forth between camps.

Shoot and Junior found Yves to be the most amusing creature they'd ever seen. Camping it up as Dixie air-heads, they asked breathlessly if it was *true?* that he lived in a real live *penthouse?* And wasn't their brother the most *adorable thaing?* Well, certainly, Yves looked forward to knowing him better; his work was most promising. Had Yves ever been to Memphis? In fact, once, when he was working at Paris, he had delivered a most *dreadful* Renoir to Mr. Elvis Presley—such a vulgar person, and oh! that house! Shoot and Junior said they'd been there too, once, when they were little, they'd snuck in with the phone man and seen Elvis screwing a blond starlet on the floor in the mirrored living room, he had the hairiest ugliest *ass?* Yves touched five fingers to his chest, bugged out his eyes, and pursed his lips.

Amos Jennings sought out Wordlaw and subjected him to the Old New York eyeball. "My sister tells me you are immensely talented," he said, looking every bit as powerful, expensive, and microscopically observant as Claudia described him.

"Well, shoot," stammered Wordlaw, letting pass that his talent was on view and therefore eligible for the man's own evaluation. "*My* sister tells *me* you're pretty hot stuff yourself."

"Your sister has been a marvelous friend to Marian," said Amos. Was there an inference to be drawn here?—"as you have not," something like that?

Wordlaw sneezed; the room was getting smoky. "Vice versa too," he mumbled through his handkerchief. "Marian tells me you're quite a connoisseur. I'd be interested to hear your opinion of my pictures."

"I've not had a chance to look at them well," said Amos. "I hope to come back this week. My office is just down the block. But they do seem very sad, and yet, mm, peaceful."

"I'm trying to learn to love sadness," said Wordlaw. "You know, like when you feel real lonely, but there's something enjoyable in the melancholy? Loving what's dying, or doomed? They're also attempts to capture the spirit of a place—to recapture the feelings I once had for the place I grew up, which is now completely trashed."

"Mm. Yes. I see that. I understand that you come from Chickasaw, Tennessee?"

"Well, I'm afraid Chickasaw doesn't exist any more, as such," said Wordlaw. "It was annexed into Memphis a while ago."

"Mm," said Amos. "Well, you know, I've got an old friend from there. I wonder if you know her. Cora White?"

"Sure, I know Cora," said Wordlaw. "I mean, I used to know her, a million years ago. We went to the same high school. She's a couple of years older than me. Where is she now?"

Amos darkened suddenly. "I don't actually, mm, know, just at the moment. I was just, mm, wondering, if you knew. Excuse me," he said, and disappeared into the crowd.

What the hell was this?

He searched the room for Marian. She was talking to a guy who looked as if he'd wandered in from a Come-as-a-Creep Fifties party—ill-fitting brown plaid suit, plaid shirt with a different-plaid tie, scuffed black shoes, smudgy black-framed glasses sliding down his nose. When Marian caught sight of Wordlaw scrutinizing him, she grabbed the guy's hand, dragged him through the crowd at full steam, and pushed him into Wordlaw's face. It was, of course, the dread Walter Pinckney.

"I've heard quite a lot about you," said Walter, his little blue eyes fixed stonily on Wordlaw's. "Oh, and, very interesting work," he added, gesturing toward the walls but still not moving his eyes.

"Yeah, it's a big night for me, said Wordlaw inconsequently, staring back. "I owe it all to Marian."

As he might have expected, she cut in. "Wordlaw, see the guy over there in the ascot? That's Rupert Henry, from the *Times*. That's Anastasia Kovacevic next to him, from *Art News*. I want you to meet both of them. And somewhere in here we've got people from *Art in America*, and the *Voice*, and the *New Yorker*, and—oh, and there's Kimberly Sturges, from the Whitney. Hi, Kimba!" she mouthed, wiggling her fingers over the sea of heads. "You've absolutely got to meet her—my brother-in-law's on her board." Then, "Freddie!" she cried suddenly. Wordlaw looked back with a start—he'd been searching the crowd for the Whitney curator—and Marian was kissing the air on either side of an old man's chalk-white pate. Wordlaw stood waiting to be introduced, but she just continued yakking away at old Freddie, hand on his arm, eyes bright, teeth flashing.

Wordlaw took a glass of champagne and wandered into the back room. There was an Ortega Montes on the wall—pretty, but shallow, just a bunch of pretty colors. He sat down, daydreaming idly of scooping up Marian and running away. A good while passed.

"Aren't you supposed to be mixing and mingling?" came Claudia's voice from behind him.

"I'm having a hard time," said Wordlaw.

"From the moment you called me from Marian's, that first night you were in town, and said you were spending the night, I knew you were going to have a hard time," said Claudia.

Wordlaw smiled sadly. "She says she needs to think."

"I hate to say this to you, brother, but I think she's just trying to get you through the show. She's determined to marry him."

"Jesus *Christ!*" cried Marian, streaming through the door. "What do you think you're doing? *Two hours,* that's all I asked: that from six to eight p.m. you try to act in your own interest for once. I am *furious!* Rupert and Anastasia have already left. Freddie Blum, who's only one of the most important collectors in the *world*—I turn around and you're just simply *gone,* without a by-your-*leave.*"

"I'm sorry, Marian," was all he could say.

She exhaled long and loudly through her nose. Then she took a deep breath and said, "Sorry, Maggie."

"No, I should have realized," said Claudia, and slipped out.

He bent to kiss Marian. Her lips did not yield. For a long minute, Wordlaw and Marian gazed at each other, unblinking, in ambiguous silence.

"Well, come on, turkey," she sighed finally, taking his hand. "Let's see what we can salvage."

He stayed her. "Is there a chance for us?" he asked.

"Let's just get through tonight, okay?"

Aha. Was Claudia right? "I'm thinking of going home tomorrow."

"No!" expostulated Marian, bowing her head beneath his chin.

He breathed her hair-scent in and lost his resolve. "Please don't go," she said. "Not yet."

At the dinner afterwards he got only a brief private moment with Marian, in which she agreed to meet him in the park at noon.

"I've absolutely got to be back in an hour," she said.

"Let's go to your apartment," said Wordlaw.

"I need time," said Marian.

"I need *you.*"

"Listen, Wordlaw. I haven't slept with Walter, either, since that night with you last week. I just need some time. Oh, Wordlaw, *look* at those flowers!"

" 'Oft, when on my couch I lie in vacant or in pensive mood, they flash upon that inward eye which is the bliss of solitude,' " he recited; "and then my heart with pleasure fills, and dances with the daffodils.' "

"I do love you," she muttered, hiding her face on his shoulder.

"I can't stand this," said Wordlaw, holding her tight. "I'm going to New Orleans. Call me when you've made up your mind. I'll be on the next plane, I swear."

He looked back once more, to see her still standing in the host of golden daffodils.

Apr. the 4th.

My Dear Wordlaw:

Well I wonder how long has it been since last I wrote you a letter, it must be ten years or more. I am a old man now & I do not get out much so I was thinking, Why not write my pen pal Wordlaw again?? The ocassion for me thinking this was a visit from a friend of you & me, Mr. Wilbur Corey Jr. the one evrybody call Ree Billy, the mater d. at your Mama and Daddys country club. I always think of Memphis on this day April 4th because it was the day they kill Dr. Martin L. King Jr. Ree Billy come to Chicago on vacation & say you are an artist now & I am not surprise, you allways could draw so good. He said your Mama & Daddy was going all the way up to New York city to see your paintings in a fancy art galary. I am so proud of you boy!! He said you live in New Orleans, that was allways a place I wish to visit. I said I wish to write you a letter so Ree Billy get me your adress from your Daddy. May be you will write me back & tell me all about New Orleans & New York. Do you remember I use to tell you about Skeeters boy Sylvester, he allways played the saxophone? He live in New Orleans too!!—& still playing that horn. But now he has what they call a stage name, it is Saxophone Chicago. I think thats right different as a name but thats what they call him, he says he is going to be famous but that boy was allways a big talker. His daddy Skeeter dont feel so good, he had a heart attack, he is 81 year old. Sylvie my sister is doing just fine, she works in a school kitchen, she sends you her dearest love. My wife Mrs. Stella Woodson past away in 1971. Well I am tired now & so will close.

God bless you Wordlaw, I remain

Cordially Yours,
Drury Woodson.

"It's me."

"Marian!" he boomed. "At last! How *are* you? And how am *I?* Selling like hotcakes, right?"

"Well, no, not yet," she said, guardedly, "but Yves is going to make some calls."

"But when the reviews start coming in, that's when it'll pick up, isn't that what you said?"

"I hate to just say it out like this, Wordlaw, but it looks as though there aren't going to be any reviews."

He could not speak for a moment. "How can that be?"

"Well, it can be hard, you know," she said, "for a young artist to break in."

"Young my ass! I'll be thirty next month."

"Listen, Wordlaw," she retorted sharply, "I can't help that. I got you the show. I got people here to see it."

What was this tone? "But the great Yves Olivier!" he yelled, losing equilibrium. "And what about all the great connections of Marian Jennings? Isn't that the deal? Your great connections?"

"Of course it helps to know people, Wordlaw, but they do have to like your work."

"Then how about at least some *bad* reviews?"

"I'm afraid it doesn't usually work like that," said Marian. "Generally they'll review only what they consider significant."

"So my work is not—significant. And I just fall into a vacuum. All this, and nobody reviews it and nobody buys it and you just stick it in the back room and it doesn't exist?"

"Collectors are what matters, not reviews. Yves has been out of town, and he's promised to make some calls."

"What are *you* going to do, Marian? Huh?"

"Wordlaw, get hold of yourself."

He said nothing, paralyzed with rage.

"I am trying to be patient with you," said Marian icily. "This is hard for me, too. We've all done our best. The climate for art is unpredictable. You know your work is good, and so do I. The next time, you may be the darling of the whole art world. Meanwhile you just have to keep working. I can understand your wanting to blame someone—me, or yourself, or the critics, or the public, or whoever. Maybe I shouldn't have encouraged you to do the landscapes. Maybe you'd have done better with those big nudes. But what's to be gained in post-facto recrimination?" Tick tick tick. "Say something, Wordlaw."

But he couldn't.

"You have a wonderful inner strength, you know that," she continued, softly now. "It shows in your work, and I know it in your heart. I do want so badly for you to succeed, you know. It's been very difficult for me, too—seeing Yves's enthusiasm just evaporate, just because a couple of his jet-set darlings didn't like the show. But *I* care. I'm trying so *hard,* Wordlaw. I'm terribly tied up in you. You know that. Wordlaw?"

Silence.

"Are you there?"

"I'm here."

"Are you hearing what I'm saying?"

"Yeah. You're saying you're going to marry that pie-faced moron," he sneered.

"Wordlaw, I'm going to go now, and I'm going to call you back when you're in less of a state. I'm starting to get angry, and that's not going to do either of us any good."

He did not reply.

"I'm going to ring off now. Goodbye."

He could not even bring himself to say goodbye.

"Good*bye,* Wordlaw."

Still he could not speak.

"If you don't say anything, I'm just going to have to hang up, and that's going to leave a very ugly mark on both of us. Goodbye. I'll call you tomorrow. Goodbye? Oh, Wordlaw, Wordlaw—*please.*"

He said nothing.

She hung up.

A thin, eerie saxophone melody, unaccompanied, came from down the rain-slick street, the tune of "Rain, rain, go away, come again some other day—wish I may, wish I might, have the wish I wish tonight." And again (Wordlaw supplied the words): "Ladybug, ladybug, fly away home—your house is on fire, your children will burn."

The music was coming from a row of cellar windows in a crumbling brick warehouse. There was a crude hand-lettered sign on the wall:

BLACK HOLE OF NEW ORLEANS

Performance Art

Hot Dogs

Oysters

Beer

A Division of McCracken Global Systems

TONIGHT:
SAXOPHONE CHICAGO QUINTET

Drury's nephew! And playing in—a Forrest McCracken joint? Forrest, who had sworn never to leave Memphis even for vacation? Wordlaw opened the peeling steel door and descended a dimly red-lit flight of creaking stairs. He came to a second steel door, on which was plastered a poster:

Genio del nuovo jazz
SAXOPHONE CHICAGO
ed il suo combo

Club Buco Nero di Roma
10–14 settembre 1977

Weirder and weirder. He had been in Rome himself then, on the lam from his twin New York disappointments (his Liebe and his Arbeit both shot to hell). And wait a second. Didn't Buco Nero mean Black Hole? Wordlaw opened the second door on a low, lurid, irony-drenched vista.

The hand of McCracken was everywhere evident—in the dangling clusters of lame-brained kitsch, the baby dolls leering through holes in the plaster, the Hell-style lighting, the absolutely perfect sound system, and, most unmistakably, the crowd, which much resembled Forrest's old Memphis clientele (miscellaneous misfits and cause-related kooks, lethal-looking Negro males, booze-embalmed beat-niks, oversexed professors on patrol for beautiful girls, beautiful girls) but with a good deal of uniquely New Orleanian character mixed in (a gang of uproarious conventioneers, an old black lady in a go-to-meeting hat, a couple of dark-suited and heavily cologned young men present presumably on behalf of the local organized crime chapter, a quartet of transvestites in prom gowns). Forrest himself, however, was nowhere to be seen. The red-haired gum-snapping hostess—gorgeous (another McCracken trademark)—seated Wordlaw at a tiny table with the two young hoodlums, who nodded gravely and looked away. A Wild Tchoupitoulas album was blasting, "Meet the boys on the battle front, 'cause the Wild Tchoupitoulas going to stomp some rump."

"Sally!" boomed an inimitable voice. "Dom! Hey hey! And *Wordlaw?* Hey hey! Back from the land of the dead?" Forrest was wearing a purple sharkskin tuxedo, and had replaced his ponytail with a platinum crewcut.

"I think *this* may be the land of the dead," said Wordlaw, surveying the room. "What the hell are you doing out of Memphis?"

"Y'all need a beer or anything?" inquired Forrest of the Mafiosi. "Couple dogs?"

"Nah," they said, and resumed brooding.

Forrest returned his attention to Wordlaw. "I'm so homesick I could puke. I've been out of town for four days. Going back tomorrow morning, thank God. It's scary out here in the world. I'm starting a chain, see? A Black Hole in every port. You saw the Rome poster?"

"Shit, McCracken, I've been *living* in Rome for the last six months. Were you there?"

"Nawww," drawled Forrest at the absurdity of the notion of foreign travel. "It's a franchise deal. This Italian guy that was working at Memphis State? He was in Memphis to do research on the Chickasaw Indians? I heard you were in Europe. I should've written you about the Buco Nero. Well, disirregardless, what brings you back?"

"Divorce," said Wordlaw. "Mimi's really sticking it to me, too. I'm going to have to get a job."

"No shit," said Forrest in solemn sympathy. "That's terrible. The job, I mean."

"It doesn't matter that much," said Wordlaw, declining to be amused. "I've hardly painted a thing all year."

"How is Mimi?"

"She is completely fucked, Forrest. She's got major-league arthritis, she's depressed beyond belief, she's destroying herself with drugs, and now she's gone paranoid. Thinks the whole world is conspiring to get her money, and money she doesn't have yet, like my inheritance. I feel real sorry for her, but she's gotten so unpleasant that I just can't handle it. You know her father's going to jail?"

"Yeah, I heard."

"I made a big mistake, feeling sorry for her. I let her divorce me. I could have sued *her,* for Christ's sake, for abandonment. And I didn't sell a single picture in New York last spring. They even sent me a *bill* for the fucking *shipping.* And as you may know, I finally fell head over heels in love with Marian Jennings, just slightly too late. She married some dickhead."

"Yeah, I heard," said Forrest again. "I talk to your sister every once in a while."

"I'm feeling sort of snakebit, you know?"

"Well, wait'll you hear this guy," said Forrest. "He will fix you right up."

"Do you remember the last time you said something like that to me?" demanded Wordlaw. "The last time you said wait till you hear this musician, and then you introduced us?"

"I feel it's most unlikely that you'll marry Saxophone Chicago, somehow."

"Never mind marrying him, I'm already related to him, practically."

Forrest gave Wordlaw a quizzical look, but at that moment four members of the band, all dressed in black, filed onto the little stage, and Forrest went to help them set up. They had dozens of instruments—a row of reeds (four saxophones, a clarinet, an oboe, a bassoon), a row of various fretted instruments, an electric violin, assorted exotic percussion (gongs, rattles, African drums, some sort of marimba, other stuff altogether unidentifiable), several species of accordion, a Dagwood sandwich of electronic keyboards. A furry face peeked out from behind the keyboards and waved—Peter Elias, the big bear who'd been playing piano for Mimi before she got too sick to go on. While Wordlaw went forward for a quick handshake, Forrest got the high sign from the sound booth, stepped into the purple spotlight, and announced, "Ladies and gentlemen, the Saxophone Chicago quintet."

The three saxophones and then the bassoon joined in a shimmering long chord. The lights went down. The lights came back up, and there stood the fifth musician, Saxophone Chicago himself, a tiny little guy, also dressed all in black, his eyes squeezed shut. His alto sax came in hesitantly, adding a weak, sweet, high note to the still sustained chord. From time to time, one player or another would pause for breath and then take up another long note; there was no melody, no beat, only this slowly shifting chord. Minutes passed; the chord went on and on.

The audience, restless at first, grew still. There was something awesomely peaceful in this sound. Wordlaw felt enclosed, sealed in this place and moment. At last, one by one, the first four instruments fell silent, and for a minute after that, the only sound in the room was the thin, weak note of the alto, until it too faded into silence.

The name-tagged conventioneers were the first to shatter the hush, with a burst of whistles and cheers, but they suddenly stopped as they realized how wrong that sounded and how alone they were; the goombahs at Wordlaw's table gave each other a bad-clam look and clapped hard three times each; the cross-dressers had lost their saucy smirks, and deeply moved human beings could now be discerned behind their makeup; Wordlaw himself was so moved that he could not move. The initial response, in short, was as various as the responders; but slowly, as the music continued sinking in, the applause swelled into unanimity.

Only as the room grew quiet again did Saxophone Chicago open his eyes and allow himself a smile. "I am a liar," he said. "Nothing I say is true. I'm a Möbius strip." He pronounced it with a proper German umlaut-O. "The sky is blue, blue—that's what I see when I close my eyes and play my horn. It's my sky; it's inside. I make it blue, I make it mine. Anything I say is true is false," he said, and began to play again.

This was a less unorthodox piece, a simple Italianate melody in the alto around which four obbligati merrily swirled—a concertina, the marimba, a double-bass, and Peter Elias's synthesizer emulating a celesta. It had the bright, pretty surface of an old-fashioned divertimento, but there was something indefinably, threateningly dark and huge hidden inside this light, small tune. Wordlaw had thought he was going to hear jazz, but this was not jazz. For one thing, it was clearly quite strictly composed, and it was ensemble music, not a showcase for soloists. No sooner had this thought surfaced, however, than the band broke into a rollicking, bluesy parody of the tune, and from there into five wildly intertangling simultaneous bebop improvisations. From moment to moment Wordlaw would feel invaded, infected, possessed, and be seized with a desire to resist, close his ears, leave—the music seemed too powerful to be given free entry. But soon he gave himself up to it, closed his eyes, floated. The piece ended with an abrupt crash of cymbals and bells and then sudden silence, like a bus hitting a wall.

"My great-granddaddy, of record, was a slave," said Saxophone Chicago. "After the Civil War, he married his former owner's mistress, who was seven-eighths white but had been a slave too, and they had one son, just the one, my granddaddy. My daddy used to tease my granddaddy that he looked more like a certain no-good half-black half-Indian freeman who'd been after my great-grandmama all through the war. That's what my uncle Drury used to tell me. Uncle Drury used to run his finger down my nose and say, 'That sure do look like a Injun nose,' and I'd laugh and whoop and jump up and down, and I'd ask him, 'What was that half-breed's name?' And he'd say, in a low, secret-telling voice, like he didn't want my daddy to hear him, he'd say, 'That old zambo's name was Miles Glory.' " Saxophone Chicago turned to show his profile to the room, and ran his finger down it; it was, in fact, long, narrow-bridged, hooked. "Great-granddaddy?" he called into the invisible sky. "Is that you?"

He took up the clarinet and started to play. This was almost unbearably beautiful, a soaring, swooping, spiraling, plunging solo melody swallowed up in tumultuous fugue of organ, accordion, twelve-string guitar, and furiously strummed banjo, and then struggling through the surface again in a triumphant minor-key jig. One by one the players changed instruments, clarinet to tenor sax (played through a synthesizer), organ to electric piano, accordion to drums, acoustic guitar to electric, banjo to electric bass, and the piece metamorphosed into rock and roll, a lurching farrago of—what? anguish? joy? Again the end was sudden, mid-measure.

What *was* this stuff? For the first time in his life, Wordlaw knew himself to be in the presence of indisputable genius.

"Happiness? Happiness? Happiness? Happiness?" chanted Saxophone Chicago, over and over and over, giving each repetition precisely the same bemused and faithless intonation. Then he paused, looking out across the audience from face to rapt face. "Say it enough," he said at last, "*think* it enough, and it stops making any sense at—all." The band had manned the bank of percussion, and at that last word "all," they slammed into a short, savage, all-rhythm piece. At unpredictable intervals they would shout, in unison, a wordless, primeval "*Yah!*"

They played for an hour in all, the pieces always separated by Saxophone Chicago's bewildering little anecdotes, riddles, enigmas. The performance concluded with another long chordal piece—or perhaps it was the first one again, transformed by the intervening invasion and draining of the listener's mind. Saxophone Chicago thanked his band each by name, and then all five filed offstage.

Wordlaw kept his seat as the audience milled slowly out. He wandered toward the quilt-screened corner that served as the dressing room. Four of the musicians were laughing together, digging out beer from a cooler. Saxophone Chicago sat alone, apart, looking exhausted. A waitress brought him a tall green slush-drink with an orange straw and a little lavender parasol, and he looked up and smiled, and noticed Wordlaw hanging back.

Wordlaw came forward, saying, "That was the best music I have ever heard in my life."

Saxophone Chicago smiled more strongly. "That's nice to hear. Thank you."

"What the hell is that you're drinking?" asked Wordlaw.

He laughed, and held it out, offering a taste. "Chartreuse and some damn thing."

Wordlaw made a cross with his fingers to ward it off. "Forrest McCracken creation, I'll bet."

"I forget what he called it. You know Forrest?"

"We grew up together," said Wordlaw. "Where shall I start? That was my great-great-great-grandfather your great-grandfather took your great-grandmother from."

Saxophone Chicago sat bolt straight, eyes wide. "You have got to be kidding me."

"Wordlaw Corelli," said Wordlaw, extending his hand.

Saxophone Chicago stood up and seized it and shook it, and shook it some more. "Come on! No shit? My uncle Drury been beating me over the head about Wordlaw Corelli ever since I was twelve years old."

"He used to write me about you, too. Skeeter's boy Sylvester, plays that horn so good."

"Sylvester's my slave name. Call me Sax. Y'all two were big letter writers."

"We still are," said Wordlaw. "I got a letter from Drury just last spring. It's sitting on my desk. I keep meaning to write him back. He's going to be so glad we finally met."

"He's dead," said Sax.

"No!"

"Him and my daddy both died last summer. My father had a heart attack, and then Drury had one trying to get him down the stairs. Took the cops thirty minutes to get there, and the ambulance twenty minutes more. They won't even send an ambulance in the ghetto till the cops have checked you out."

"Jesus," said Wordlaw.

"Yeah, well," said Sax, and sucked up some slush.

"Hey hey!" boomed Forrest, strolling in with his own green drink. "How you like that Grand Wizard, Sax?"

"Grand Wizard, that's what he calls it," said Sax to Wordlaw.

"General Nathan Bedford Forrest was the first *Grand Wizard* of the Ku-Klux Klan," explained Forrest. "He was a relative of mine."

Saxophone Chicago was staring in renewed astonishment at Forrest. "Listen, I know all about Nathan Bedford Forrest. He was Wordlaw's great-great-great-granddaddy's best friend."

"He was?" said Wordlaw.

"Shoot," said Sax, "he *sold* my great-granddaddy to Giovanni Corelli. He sold my great-grand*mama* to him."

"Wait a minute," said Forrest. "Are you saying that that rap you did tonight, about your great-whatsits who were slaves—they were Wordlaw's family's slaves?"

"I told you we were practically related," said Wordlaw.

"I can't believe this," said Forrest.

"I can," said Wordlaw.

"So can I," said Saxophone Chicago.

Forrest had to go pack to leave for home; Wordlaw and Sax went out for a drink. Wordlaw heard all about the great wooing and winning of Félice Renard by Sylvester Woodson against the rivalries of their master the opera-singing Giovanni Corelli, the dreaded slave dealer and soldier Nathan Bedford Forrest, and the notorious trickster Miles Glory; the corn-shucking parties and jug bands of the slaves; the murder of Forrest's valet Jerome, and Sylvester's trial for it, and his exoneration by the judge who had once been the Preacher; the ludicrous Battle of Memphis; Sylvester's escape from Corelli plantation through the swamp; the heroism of Sylvester's friend Aaron at the Fort Pillow Massacre, where he killed a white man; the epic walk home of the blinded Joe John from Mobile to Memphis; the race riots and night riders and lynchings of Reconstruction—"You do *know* this shit, don't you?" said Wordlaw, agog.

"That is a fact," returned Sax, in Drury's voice, so real it gave Wordlaw a shiver: "Dat is a fack."

"But *how?*"

"I come from long line of listeners, and rememberers, and history telling."

"This is amazing. But look. If Giovanni's family stayed in Italy, how come I'm here?"

"Well," said Sax, "it wasn't simple. First of all, it looks to me like his boy Alexander was queer. Mr. Joe wanted him to come anyhow, because he was his only male offspring. His wife was still carrying on with that cardinal, and Alexander was kind of a gossip, so they were more than willing to get rid of him. So the cardinal dug up this wall-eyed bastard girl and married Alexander to her. She wasn't but seventeen. She had the baby the day they arrived in Memphis."

"This would have been Hamilton—"

"Hamilton Forrest Garibaldi Corelli."

"Wait a minute, Sax. How in the hell did the *blacks* know about all this shit going on in *Rome?*"

"Well, I think my great-grandmama must have kept up some sort of relation with old Giovanni. She was how Uncle Drury knew all that stuff about the war years. She always managed to know things."

"Did she keep on with Forrest too?"

"I don't think so. Old Forrest just went from bad to worse. He never could get used to paying blacks, so he sold his plantations, and kept on trying to build that railroad till he went broke. His wounds never healed right, and he had malaria and dysentery to boot. Died in '77. Fifty-six years old, but they said he looked ninety.

"But at least he missed the yellow fever. The white folks thought it was Giulietta—your great-great-grandmama—that brought it back from town. They had two daughters by then, Annamaria and Désirée, and they were the first ones to go. Throwing up black bile. But our folks figured it was Alexander brought it, because he was always sneaking off to these dives on the waterfront in Memphis. Anyway both your great-great-grandparents were dead inside of a week. We were supposed to be immune, but old Uncle Dunc died of it, too.

"Memphis was in a panic. Anybody that had the money to get out did. Doctors, nurses, preachers, all of them left. The little towns out in the country raised militias—gave them orders to shoot to kill any stranger that tried to enter. Sick people were roaming up and down the countryside begging for shelter, stealing food, dying."

Sax drained his glass in one long chug. Wordlaw beckoned for refills.

"The people left in town were the ones too poor to get out, most of them black, the rest Irish. There was corpses piled up in the streets, too many to bury. The dogs and cats and rats all got fat, then they died too. Old women started menstruating. Some of the sick people would get a wild sex drive, and have these death orgies. Some folks couldn't stop laughing. Volunteers came from all over the world, and most of them died, too. September and October were almost as hot as August, and the epidemic just kept going. Finally there was a frost, and it was over.

"Funny thing was, old Mr. Joe died that same year, of cancer.

"Memphis was just wiped out. It literally ceased to exist, even as a legal entity.

"Now, the Wordlaw line comes in in '86. That's when Ham married Miss Opal Etta Wordlaw. She was sixteen. Daughter of a moonshiner from Tallahatchie County named A. J. Wordlaw, Jr."

"No, that's not right," protested Wordlaw. "It was my mother's father that was the Wordlaw—Wordlaw Wickham."

"Well, he wasn't the first. Opal Etta was the granddaughter of that man that Aaron killed at Pillow."

"Jesus."

"Anyway it wasn't long before they had a baby, name of Stacker Lee. Weighed twelve pounds at birth, Uncle Drury said."

"My granddaddy."

"See how quick it comes down? Hey, bartender, my man! Another J&B, double. Wordlaw?"

"I'm okay."

Sax's eyes were bright, and focused far away. "That Ham Corelli was a mess. See, he was raised up by the colored folks, and they just couldn't do nothing with him. He run that place like it was slavery time all over again. By '88 he had my great-granddaddy seven hundred dollars in debt.

" 'Where you planning to find that kind of money, Sylvester?' says Ham. 'This ain't a charity operation, you know.'

" 'No, sir, Ham, I knows that,' says Sylvester. 'I seen the price of furnish up yonder at the crossroads store, and from what I seen up there this here commissary business must be doing all right.'

" 'How come you don't speak your mind, boy?' " Sax did a perfect Old South white accent.

" 'Well, sir—'

" 'I *meant* it seemed like you *already* spoke it,' says Ham."

"You're making this shit up," said Wordlaw.

"It's true enough!" Sax insisted. " 'Yes, sir,' says Sylvester.

" 'My granddaddy let y'all folks push him around, you ask me,' says your great-granddaddy. 'Seem like it's the people that don't pay taxes that's doing all the voting these days, and that don't set right with us younger folks. Seem like the colored are getting above themselves. I wouldn't say that to you unless I knew you trusted me and I knew you knew that it's not you personally that I'm talking about, Sylvester. It's just a general observation.'

" 'Yes, sir,' says Sylvester again.

" 'You know, Sylvester,' says the white man, 'I'm going to be twenty-one next week. You going to have to call me *Mister* Ham.'

" 'You going to have you a birthday party, Mr. Ham?'

" 'You always did love a piece of cake, didn't you, uncle?'

" 'Yes, sir,' says Sylvester, 'that is a fact.' "

Sax seemed no longer to be telling the stories to Wordlaw, but just to be telling the stories.

"Well, Ham and a bunch of his buddies stayed up late after the party, drinking whiskey and carrying on, and one of them threw a cigar butt in a dry spittoon where somebody else had thrown a candy wrapper, and somebody else shoved it back behind some lace curtains, and late that night was when the old manor house burnt down.

"And Ham was so cheap he hadn't renewed the insurance."

"I never knew any of this," said Wordlaw.

"By and by, the Army engineers got the river stabilized for shipping, and people cut down all the hardwood forests in the flood plain, and that was the best cotton dirt in the world. The bankers and brokers and factors got rich, wearing patent leather shoes and building big gingerbread mansions, and Memphis got made a city again.

"And the white folks were getting real down on the blacks. There was a new state constitution in Mississippi that said that anybody that wanted to vote had to either be able to read and write any clause of that constitution that the registrar might choose or else be able to interpret it when the registrar read it to them. Well, you can imagine how many of our people could do that.

"Another part of that constitution was a new state line, and all of a sudden Corelli plantation wasn't in Mississippi anymore.

"Tennessee didn't have the bad voting laws yet, so Aaron and Sylvester went down to the schoolhouse to register. But Ham meets them outside, and he says, 'Now, y'all listen to me. There's a bunch of old boys looking for trouble, because so many of y'all come into the county with this thing of moving the state line.'

" 'Well,' says my great-granddaddy, 'I's much oblige to you for giving us that warning.'

"But Aaron didn't like this one bit. 'What you talking about, Sylvester, you damn knucklehead?' he says. 'Bunch of rednecks going to stop me from *voting?* Huh! That's my right as a American citizen.'

"About this time these white boys come out of the schoolhouse, and one of them tosses a rope over the tree limb where the swing set is, and gives Aaron and Sylvester a grin.

" 'Hell *fire,*' says Aaron.

"I've about talked myself dry," said Sax.

"You can't stop now!" cried Wordlaw. Listening to Sax talk was like listening to his music.

"Get me a drink, will you?"

Sax would pause for a stiff slug from time to time, but he kept talking. "Let's see. Nineteen hundred was when Aaron went out duck hunting with Ham, and Ham got drunk and shot him in the back of both knees. Aaron never walked again. My great-grandmama and great-granddaddy were just scraping by, but they couldn't hardly not take their best friend in."

"My grandfather was so different from his father," said Wordlaw.

"That's so. Your grandmama saw to that. Anyway, let's see. Fourteen was the year that Ham decided to drive his new Cadillac into the lobby of the Gayoso Hotel, and him and Opal Etta were both killed. The house he'd built to replace the old one was already falling down, and Mr. S. L. and Miss Cornelia decided to replace it. They found a bunch of old Angelo Corelli's paintings rolled up in the attic, including one of the big house that had burned down in '88, and that's how they come to build that replica of it. Is it still standing?"

"No. My father tore it down."

"I ain't surprised. Well, I know it was quite a place; we had a picture of it. Took six years to build, and everybody they'd ever known came to that housewarming. Sylvester and Félice were there, of course, along with my granddaddy Lafayette Woodson and my grandmama and six of their seven children and twenty-nine of *their* children. Aaron was there, in his wheelchair. That old blind man Joe John was there. And Miles Glory was there—richest Negro in the South.

"And Sylvester comes up behind Miles, all quiet, says, 'You ain't got no prettier in you old age, is you.'

"Old Miles turns around and says, 'Is that you, little nigger? How come you ain't dead yet?'

"About then my great-grandmama comes up. 'Phyllis,' says Miles—he never did pronounce her name right—'Phyllis, you looks like a rose in bloom. Now tell me why I ain't seen y'all for what—forty year? Y'all oughts to come see my park. I done built a amusement park, ever since they close the city parks to colored. We got rides, and games, and velocipedes for rent, and a lake with white swans a-gliding on it. I just bet you would fancy seeing them swans, Phyllis, and you ought to drag this old sprout with you. Shoot, I might even let y'all in free.'

" 'I sees enough poultry right here,' says Great-granddaddy.

" '*Damn,*' says Miles.

" 'It been longer than forty year,' says Sylvester. 'Last time I sot foot in Memphis was the year 1873. How long that, Lafayette?'

" 'Forty-seven years, Paw,' says my granddaddy. 'I was five years old. I remembers that trip.'

" '*Boy,* huh,' says Miles, grinning. 'Gray-headeder than he daddy. I knows Lafayette. He come to town from time to time.'

"Well, my great-granddaddy didn't like hearing that. I can just see him with his head filling up with pictures of gambling parlors, whiskey bars, low women. But Lafayette wasn't nothing but a old potbellied farmer in overalls, not a hell raiser.

" 'He is a very fine son,' says Félice.

" 'And good-looking,' says my granddaddy—Drury loved to tell this about his pop— 'and intelligent. And re*fined.*'

" 'He play the guitar,' says Félice." Sax's French accent was pretty good too.

" 'You ought to come play on Beale Street,' says Miles. 'I knows all the musicians. I'll introduce you.'

" 'I is glad to see you still working you good influence on the young peoples,' says Sylvester.

" 'Ain't he a paw?' says my granddaddy. 'But you know, last time a Woodson goed to Beale Street it was my boy Skeeter, and we ain't seen him since.'

" 'Skeeter Woodson is you boy?' says Miles. 'Hell, I knows Skeeter. He in St. Louis, playing in a band.' That was my daddy.

" 'You see him, you tell him we got cotton need picking,' says Sylvester.

" 'You pay a dollar a day like that tavern in St. Louis do?' says Miles.

" 'I just glad to know he doing all right,' says Lafayette.

" 'You don't know nothing,' says Sylvester.

" 'That's my paw,' says my granddaddy.

" 'You must be right proud, Phyllis,' says Miles, real quiet and serious. 'Fine son and grandchildrens and great-grandchildrens like all this here.'

" 'I am happy enough,' she says.

"Miles Glory died that winter. He was eighty-eight years old, and still living with two women in different parts of Memphis. At the funeral, one of them tried to shoot the other."

"You are making this shit *up!*" cried Wordlaw.

"Nuh-*unh,*" said Sax, waving the bartender over. His speech was slurring by now, but it didn't slow him down a bit. "So about here is where the second Wordlaw comes in, your granddaddy. What kin he was to that first one didn't nobody ever figure out. He come into the area in '33, deep Depression. S. L. Corelli was going broke. Fourteen tenant families were still living on the place. Your daddy's daddy had to sell some land, and it was Wordlaw Wickham that bought it.

"Then of course your daddy married your mama, and old Wickham built them that house that you grew up in. Wickham used to drive

Mr. S. L. crazy with all his plans. He was the one that started calling that little settlement Chickasaw; it didn't even have a name before that. Said S. L. was plumb stupid not to start in putting up houses for all the G.I.s coming home. 'You going to wish you had sense!' he hollers. 'Someday you going to wish you knew how to listen and didn't just live in a dream world.'

" 'It's true that I choose to live in a world some would call antiquated,' says your other granddaddy. 'Maybe some people do see it as a kind of dream. But I happen to like it, sir.' "

How could Sax possibly have Wordlaw's grandfather's voice down so right?

" 'God damn it, man!' says Wickham. 'If I'm going to make a go of this thing, we going to have to get the damn niggers out of here. You know we can't have a nice suburb right smack upside a bunch of niggers in a bunch of falling-down shacks.'

" 'I'm going to ask you to leave now,' was all your granddaddy said.

"Old S. L. didn't even come to your christening, you know. Account of your name, I reckon."

"I had no idea."

"Only way you ever got to see Mr. S. L. and Miss Cornelia when you were a baby was because my aunt Sylvie would bring you over there.

"I remember Uncle Drury telling me two things about that next year—'48, now, I'm talking about. One was about the sheriff shooting a mangy, scrawny old bear back in your granddaddy's swamp. Mr. S. L. was fit to be tied. That was the last bear left, folks said.

"And the other was my great-grandmama and great-granddaddy's little old shack burning down to the ground. Aaron got out, some way. Uncle Drury put a blanket on him and got him back in his wheelchair.

" 'We live so long,' says Aaron, 'and still it ain't long enough.'

"And he just keeps talking, to nobody in particular. 'I quit trying to get in and out the bed last year,' he says. 'I just sleeps in my chair. Such as I sleeps at all. I said, "When you going to fix that stove, knucklehead?" I always did call him a knucklehead. And what he say? Say he like to live dangerous. And then he give me that smile, like he half crazy, same as he done ever since we was back in slavery time. That's how I get out. I seen them flames go up on they bed, and them a-thrashing at the burning cover. But they was too old. They couldn't but just thrash around, and that fire just go *whumph* all in the house. I couldn't do nothing but wheel on out and tumble down the step. I could smell them burning up. I was in a battle in the war one time and I smelled that. Mens burning up. I never could eat no barbecue after that. Smell just like old-time pork barbecue. I couldn't help them, son. I would have died my own self if I could.'

"Uncle Drury just says, 'Yes, sir. I know you would.'

"Finally old Aaron started crying. Everybody just stood around watching that old man with his face in his hands.

"Then Aaron opens his eyes, and says, 'I is too old for no grieving and moaning. Shoot—they live long enough.'

"Your grandmama was there by then, and she asks him, 'How old were they, Uncle Aaron?'

" 'Best I can recollect,' he says, 'me and Sylvester both born 1842, young miss. One hundred and five year old. Félice she were two year older. What I going to do, miss?'

" 'You come on home with us,' was what she said.

"Aaron Corelli died on Christmas Day that same year. He was playing with you on his lap, and he just fell over dead."

"Listen, man," said Sax, "I need to ask you a favor. My girlfriend said she was going to kill me next time I come home drunk again, and I am drunk. I will admit I am drunk. Wordlaw, old bud, can you put me up for the night?"

"Shit," said Wordlaw. "I don't live but just around the corner."

"That's what I like about the South," said Sax into his empty glass.

"Fuck the South," said Wordlaw, into his.

"That's what I mean," said Sax.

1980

There was no answer to Wordlaw's knock at the studio door, so he went on in. "What do you want?" mumbled Sax, still in bed.

"I was actually thinking of trying to do some drawing," said Wordlaw. "You still here?"

"Leave me alone," said Sax, pulling the covers over his head. "I got a hangover."

"Well, so do I, but I'm starting a new life today."

"Where have I heard this before?"

Wordlaw pushed his way through Sax's heaps of instrument cases, stacks of scorepaper, scattered music stands, wire-snarled recording equipment, dirty clothes. Still on the easel, under plastic wrap, was a moldy half-finished canvas Wordlaw had not touched in what? a year? He pulled it down, chucked it into the junk pile in back, and tacked up a sheet of paper. He made several charcoal swipes at it, sighed, and stopped. "I've got to go to work in half an hour anyhow," he muttered. He could not get himself even to make sketches any more. It wasn't that the results were unsatisfactory; there weren't any results; he never got that far.

Meanwhile, Sax's career had bloomed: three albums for a major label in two years; mounting acclaim in the rock press, the jazz press, the popular press, and even in university-based new-music circles; mounting sales, thanks particularly to a tune that he'd done as an affectionate parody of the techno-pop disco style and which now was a hit in discos all over the world; sold-out performance tours, no longer in clubs but in auditoriums; and for the first time in his life, serious money.

Nevertheless Sax remained reluctant to entertain any notion that his success would be permanent. He seemed untouched by praise, fame, affluence. He *liked* living half his life in crummy motels, he said; he liked eating in crummy cafés. After he had taken part in a conference at the Yale School of Music on the Future of Composition (and had gently skewered the sterile academic dominance thereof), and been put up at the dean's splendiferous house on the Connecticut shore, and been augustly fêted by what he termed "a bunch of old white guys who didn't know a Fender from a Farfisa," he had come home in a state of nervous exhaustion and stayed drunk for a week. His girlfriend had kicked him out for good then, and he had moved the rest of his stuff over to Wordlaw's studio, where in any case he had already been practicing with the band, doing most of his composing, and spending at least half his nights in town.

It was not a very good move for either of them. Both Wordlaw and Sax had already been drinking too much, and there seemed to be a certain alcoholic synergy between them. It did not, however, keep Sax from working. Drunk as the devil, he could still play like an angel. Wordlaw, on the other hand, when not manning the counter at Cannizaro's Wines and Spirits, was either too depressed to work or too drunk. He had welcomed Sax in the hope of inspiration, but so far all he had gotten was friendship.

Jesus, he thought, what am I doing complaining about Sax? As if it were his fault that I'm a fuckup. Best friend I ever had. Believes in me too. Who else ever did? I just wish—

He had this thought often, "I just wish—" The sentence was always unfinished. An image of Marian would flicker through his mind, and he would say to himself, No, fool! that's not what you wish, you *know* it's nothing more than a convenient fantasy-shape to pour your damned longing into. And what was his damned longing *for?* He did not know. He had forgotten—strenuously—the lesson of Marian's portrait, the paradoxical and profound sense of delight she embodied. He had not even spoken to her in—it would be three years next month. She had never really had faith in him, he told himself, never really loved him. Did he really believe this? He did not ask. He would banish all thought of her with the ritual excantation, Okay, okay. *Okay, okay,* it was my fault, but I couldn't help it. He waited, with gritted teeth, for time to make the formula's continued repetition unnecessary. Okay, okay. She wasn't so great. After all, when it looked as if he wasn't going to be a big famous artist right away, when she'd seen how inept he was socially, when all in all he was just sort of not working out, she'd dumped him, and married that entomologist. So, okay, okay. Fuck her. I just wish—

"Wordlaw, my friend," said Edmond Delafosse, "what's drinking well these days? With rack of lamb."

"With garlic and stuff?" asked Wordlaw.

"Yes, and rosemary."

"Well, you know, the conventional wisdom says Bordeaux, but why don't you try a Rhône? We've got an incredible Côte-Rôtie. Or a Barbaresco. Are you willing to plump for a Gaja? It's got this minty nose that really says lamb."

"Plump how much?" smiled Edmond, good-naturedly.

"It's expensive." Wordlaw pulled the bottle and turned it to show the price.

Edmond perched a pair of half glasses on the tip of his long nose. "That's fine," he said. "Let me have six."

"Like to try a little sample first?"

"Well, you've never let me down, Wordlaw—but I certainly won't object."

"Come on in the back," said Wordlaw, trying not to seem too eager. "How's Alice?"

"She's fine."

"We just got some more of that Puligny that she likes so much—the Leflaive Combettes?"

"What an excellent idea. Six of those too, then? Oh, and pick us out a case of champagne, won't you?"

As soon as Edmond was out the door, Wordlaw slugged down

another glass of Barbaresco, and then another quick half a glass. Well, it did have sort of a mint taste, though you could just as easily have said socks.

Later that afternoon, old man Cannizaro confronted him with the half-empty bottle. "*Mis*ter Corelli," he intoned sepulchrally. "Is this *yours?*"

"On the strength of that taste, Mr. Cannizaro, I sold two cases of very expensive wine."

"This *taste,* you call it?"

"You want me to pay for it?" snapped Wordlaw.

"I do. Yes. I do indeed."

Sax said he was going to be doing some heavy-duty rehearsing with some guys out in the country. Be back in a couple days.

Would he be back in time to go see *Parsifal* in Houston?

"I don't know, I don't know. I'm not sure. I can't say." There was something decidedly strange in his manner, sort of slowed-down.

"I need to know," said Wordlaw. "Those were expensive tickets."

"I'll be back when I get back, okay?"

"Okay, okay." Jesus. There was a point past which Sax was utterly impenetrable.

He stayed gone for a week. Unable to find anybody else willing to entertain the thought of forty bucks to see *Parsifal,* Wordlaw ended up selling the ticket outside the auditorium for half price.

Then one day when he came home from work, there was Sax on the living room sofa, tootling woozily on his bass clarinet.

"What's the matter with you?" demanded Wordlaw. "You look weird."

"Absolutely nothing," said Sax.

"Why don't you open your eyes?"

"I'm sleepy."

"Sax—are you drunk?"

"Nooo. Absolutely not." He played a little lilting phrase several times over. "Oh, yeah. You're supposed to call your sister."

He did, but Claudia had already left for Memphis, so it was Sam who gave him the news. Wordlaw's father had driven his Cadillac the wrong way down an exit ramp onto the expressway in the rain this afternoon and hit a tractor-trailer head on. His mother was in the car too. They had both been killed instantly.

Sax had treated himself to one extravagant indulgence, a red Corvette convertible. Choogling up the Interstate through Mississippi with the top down and Sax in the passenger seat honking on his tenor seemed to Wordlaw an infallible recipe for getting slam-dunked into the torture chambers of some county jail and never seeing light again, so when the inevitable blue strobe came whoop-whooping up behind he gave serious consideration to high-tailing it for the bridge ahead over Hickahala Creek and plunging in, but in the event he just sat waiting as the textbook-perfect Mississippi highway patrolman (gut, swagger, mirrored sunglasses) approached in the mirror, hand on holster.

"Driver's license, please, sir?" said the patrolman.

"Anything wrong, officer?" said Wordlaw helplessly.

"Registration, please, sir?"

"It's his car," bleated Wordlaw.

Sax, with his most dazzling stage smile, reached into the glove compartment and produced the document.

"Thank you, sir," said the patrolman. "I'm going to have to make a little radio call? If y'all'll please just set tight a minute I'll be right back."

"How fast were you going?" asked Sax.

"Fast enough."

"Goddamn Democrat speed limits."

"I don't need to hear any more of you threatening to vote for Reagan, okay? And will you please quit playing that damn horn? He's *coming,* Sax." Sax played more quietly but didn't quit.

The cop gave Sax a long look. "Sir?" he said. "Haven't I seen you somewhere before? Are you a musician?"

"I sho am," said Sax, grinning again.

Sho indeed.

"It says here you're Sylvester Woodson the second, but you look mighty like a fellow—I forget the name—"

"Saxophone Chicago?"

"Why—"

"That's me. That's like my stage name. Mr. Corelli here is my attorney."

"Pleased to meet you," said the cop to Wordlaw. "Everything's in order with y'all's papers," he continued, handing them back, "but you *was* speeding a mite." He looked at Sax again. "You know that song of yours, that 'Narcosis'—how'd you get that sound?"

"You mean that *zzzwwwmmm* kind of thang?"

Thang?

"That's it, man!" exclaimed the policeman. "That sounds just like it!"

"That was an electronic music synthesizer," said Sax.

"Electronic music synthesizer! Isn't that something! Me and my wife love that song," said the cop. "Listen, uh, Mr. Woodson—or do you say Mr. Chicago? Could you give me a autograph, do you think? My wife is not going to believe this."

"Call me Sax, man. What's her name?"

"Name Louise."

"And what's yours?"

"Tommy."

Across the half-finished speeding ticket Sax inscribed, "With best wishes for Louise and Tommy," and signed, with a flourish, "Saxophone Chicago." "There you go," he said.

"I can't hardly give you a citation that's got this wrote on it, can I?" laughed the policeman. "Y'all drive safely now, and have a nice day."

Chickasaw.

"Now," said Wordlaw, pulling over to the curb, "this is where the slave quarters were, arranged around a courtyard right down there at the bottom of the hill. There was only an old barn left when

I was a kid. This was pasture down along here, till you got to a fence line, and then there were some shacks—some little houses—"

"Shacks is fine," said Sax, "Mr. Liberal."

"Fuck you," said Wordlaw as he drove on. "Then somewhere around here the woods started, and you see how it still slopes down a little? See those boarded-up houses, all crooked? They sank into the landfill my father laid over the flood plain. And back behind the houses, you see that chain-link fence? There's a drainage ditch back in there. That was Daylight Bayou. It flowed north, through a cypress swamp, up toward Nonconnah Creek, which is where the Union lines were. It's bound to have been the same swamp that your great-granddaddy made his escape through. I spent the happiest days of my life in that swamp. My great friend back in the swamp was an old man who was some kind of cousin of Drury's, named Wilbur Corey. Wilbur was Ree Billy Corey's father. Didn't you know Ree Billy?"

"Just the name," said Sax. He was unnaturally quiet, distracted—trying, perhaps, to see the world that was gone?

"As far as I know, Ree Billy's still the headwaiter at the country club, so you'll meet him this evening."

"Listen, Wordlaw, if it's okay with you, I think I'm going to pass on this funeral. I was thinking of going to see Forrest. I mean, do you think there has ever been a single black guest in that club? Or even the church?"

"Yeah, okay." Sax had already gone his extra mile. "Well. So. These were all our cotton fields, all through the mall and all the way up to the apartments where my grandparents' house used to be. Mostly blacks in those apartments now, by the way. Lot of blacks moving in all over Chickasaw. My old school is almost a hundred percent black, and of course it was all white when I was there. All the whites are in the seg academies now. That big ugly Spanish-style mansion we passed down near the state line? That used to be my maternal grandparents' house, till they moved to Arizona, and it's just been bought by a black *politician*. Some kind of crook, I think." They turned into a street of trim, close-set houses. "Would you *look* at these for-sale signs?" exclaimed Wordlaw. "This is all white flight."

"You can't even tell which houses have the blacks in them," Sax observed, with a rueful half-smile. "I mean, they don't have those cars with the leather static strips hanging down in back, or anything."

"This is upward mobility, man! The new bourgeoisie!"

"I guess this isn't bad, in a way," mused Sax, "but I don't know. It feels so—like they're losing something. I know, don't tell me, Hubert Humphrey, they're gaining too. Wordlaw, old bud?"

"Yeah, what?"

"I think I've had enough for today."

They had lunch with Forrest at Bar-B-Q Billiards. They hadn't seen much of Forrest since the Black Holes Division had gone broke. His Parnassus Hi-Tone Theatre was currently showing the one film ever made starring his old Chickasaw High School girlfriend Cora White. He was still living at his grandfather's, in the underground bomb shelter. With his jaunty "Hey hey!" and nonstop comic monologues, Forrest seemed chipper enough, but there was a sad tinge to him. But then there seemed a sad tinge to Memphis. Wordlaw left Sax at BBQB and went home.

"Nice car," said Shoot, who had just arrived from Boulder, where she and Junior were allegedly in college. She ran a long red-lacquered nail down the Corvette's same-red fender. "Real funereal."

Claudia and Junior came down the front steps and joined in a big four-way sibling hug. Their aunts Anna, Aurelia, and Augusta and their Wickham grandparents lurked within, in a grim, hushed, covetous knot, wolfing down cake. Luckily there were phone calls to be returned, and Wordlaw could leave the familial grieving for a while in the care of his sisters, who were much better at such things anyhow.

Beaumont Echols informed him with lugubrious gravity that his bequest was "substantial," and that they should sit down together to discuss the disposition of noncash assets.

The rector of St. Stephen's Episcopal Church, Father Brown, whom Wordlaw had never met but who insisted on being called Mike, said he had composed a "really neat" homily.

The third was from a Mr. David Graves—what a name for a funeral director!—seeking to effect the purchase of two coffins, which Claudia had described in her note as "ghoulish beyond belief." Mr. Graves offered also to take charge of floral arrangements, musical accompaniment for "the viewing," transportation, the burial wardrobe, and other details, at an astronomical package price. He did not ask to be called Dave. Wordlaw gave him carte blanche.

He meditated for some minutes on the fourth scrap of paper before he returned the call.

She answered on the first ring.

"It's me," said Wordlaw.

"Oh, Wordlaw!" cried Marian. "Are you all right?"

"Wake up, Hawk," said Wordlaw, shoving Sax's shoulder. His hand came back gritty. Twelve lanes of roaring turnpike had covered them both with grime; they liked keeping the top down no matter what. By now they were heroes of their own road-buddy movie, Buz and Hawk.

It was one of those diamond-clear April nights, with big white clouds scudding past a klieg moon and the skyline of Manhattan glittering like—"Oz," said Saxophone Chicago. "The Emerald City."

"Yeah, as long as you look at it from five miles away, across a river, in the dark."

Sax raised his tenor and tore out a caterwauling "Over the Rainbow" in the surging convergence of cars at the Lincoln Tunnel tolls.

"What's happening, beautiful sister?" hollered Sax, between saxophone phrases, to the fat, brown, dull-eyed woman in the booth, who gave him a bovinely affectless stare in return.

"The town so nice they named it twice," said Wordlaw.

"One thing you got to say about this place, Buz, old bud," said Sax as they emerged from the tunnel and swerved to avoid a wino stumbling through the traffic, "it's a *place.* You come back, and you look at it, and you say, yeah, that's right, that's New York. Could not be *no* place else. You know what I'm saying?"

"Yeah, I've been thinking about the same kind of thing. When I was trying to show you all those places the other day—you know, this is where the swamp was, this is where the fields were? There really is nothing left. There is no *place* there. It could be anywhere."

"So what do we do," said Sax, "with our famous Southern sense of place?"

"You're not Southern," scoffed Wordlaw.

"All black people are Southern," asserted Sax, with a grin. "I mean, all native American black people. These Caribbeans who've been coming in, I don't know what they are but it ain't Southern."

"What about Africans?"

"Some Africans are right Southern," said Sax.

"Do you reckon they're going to cover Africa with shopping malls and expressways?"

"I think it'll be more like East Germany," said Sax. "You know, concrete-block housing projects? You ought to see East Germany, man."

"We don't have those in Chicago, do we, Hawk?" snorted Wordlaw. "Or New York, or New Orleans. Shit, they've got them in *Rome.*"

"So do we just go ahead and shoot ourselves, or what?"

"We're almost there," said Wordlaw. "Start looking for a parking place."

"We are putting this baby in a *garage,*" said Sax. "You seem to forget: you is rich now."

It seemed a strange moment for the death of his parents to hit him at last, but Wordlaw's eyes misted over so quickly that he had to pull into a bus stop. "I'm sorry," he said.

"Put on your flasher," said Sax.

"Right," said Wordlaw, letting himself cry now.

"Feels good, doesn't it?" said Sax after a while.

Wordlaw found himself smiling through his tears. "Asshole," he said hoarsely, starting to laugh.

Sax wetted his reed and held the horn to his lips but did not play.

Wordlaw and Marian dawdled, admiring the cherry trees, pink petals scattered on the bright green grass, the blue-uniformed kids from the Lycée Français playing frisbee and shouting in French, the babies in strollers and their gossiping nannies, the radio-controlled miniature schooners on the sailboat pond, all the exultant bustle of a Monet-perfect April day in Central Park, as the figures of Saxophone Chicago and Cora White moved on into the middle distance. They made a funny pair, Sax so short and brown, Cora so tall and blonde. "What is it with you and people from my home town?" asked Wordlaw. "At my opening, when I found out your brother knew her, I asked him if he knew what had become of her, and he just sort of turned green and disappeared. Now here she turns up with you. What's the deal?"

"It's a long story."

"It sounds like an interesting one."

"Well, the short of it is that Amos was very ill that fall, and Cora came to see him in the hospital, and I was there, and we just hit it off. And then when I was in the teeth of my divorce, she really saved me. Divorce is hard, isn't it?" She turned toward him in silent appeal. She bowed her head; her hair fell forward over one eye. He touched her cheek briefly, and they walked on.

"Sounds strangely parallel to Sax," mused Wordlaw. "I haven't been doing so well, but I don't think I'd be functioning at all if it weren't for him."

A long-legged girl, short-shorted, tank-topped, was sunning herself on a sparkling schist boulder, paradigm of blooming youth, unscarredness, spring. "Ugh," grunted Marian.

"What?" said Wordlaw, though he thought he understood.

"I feel so old."

"Twenty-seven!"

"Not yet," said Marian. "July."

He doddered along on an invisible cane, an ancient thirty-three.

They came to the same bed of daffodils where they had parted, a world ago. It was blooming again.

She smiled sadly. "We made a big mistake here, Wordlaw, didn't we?"

"Do you think we can undo it?"

She did not reply, and turned so that her face was hidden.

I shouldn't have said that, he was thinking. Better to have let it work itself out in action, free of words, if it was going to.

"I said *we* made a mistake, but really the mistake was mine," she said finally.

Which was not an answer to his question, but he let it go.

Some of Sax's musician friends were playing at a club downtown, and Cora leaped at the chance to go with him. Marian shot her what seemed to be a warning look.

"She's just coming out of an awful time," said Marian as soon as they were gone. "Much worse than anything you or I have been through."

"It's hard to imagine," said Wordlaw. "She looks so fresh, so perfect."

"She is good-looking, isn't she?" said Marian. "But Cora was very, very sick. She had a bad drug problem, and then a dreadful illness, and she was involved with some extremely unsavory people, and there were money troubles, and she had no one she could trust, and everything just fell apart on her at once. I'm not violating a confidence—she tells everybody. It's one of her ways of keeping from backsliding."

"Wow. So, what's on the agenda?"

"I made a reservation for dinner at Le Cirque. I think you'll find it a very amusing place, with your taste for urban anthropology. Have you got a jacket and tie?"

"My whole funeral outfit."

It had not profited from three days in a shopping bag in the Corvette's trunk, and Wordlaw felt rather rumpled amidst the ferociously tony metropolites eyeballing him as he squeezed past.

"Busy night?" said Marian to the restaurateur as he kissed her on both cheeks.

He answered with a hundred-tooth smile and widespread hands in benediction over the glittering, jam-packed room: my circus.

"The more I see of this city," said Wordlaw, "the more I realize how huge your apartment is. Nobody has any *room* here."

She looked hard at him. "Wordlaw, how is your work?"

"Ah," he sighed, looking away. "Let's say I am about to embark on a period of unprecedented productivity. I no longer have to work in a liquor store. I have inherited."

"Was it money that kept you from working?"

He returned her unflagging gaze. This was one matter-of-fact woman. He loved her, but he could not live with her. Not yet, anyway. First he would have to prove himself, to himself; and that might then be the qualification—for one *would* have to qualify, for all her air of gentle generosity and her doctrine of compassion. "You know the answer to that, of course," he said.

"I'm sorry," she said, knowing she must have hurt him.

"It's all right," he said. "I'm helped, you know, by seeing you also in the position of having made a drastic mistake."

"Asshole."

He waved this off. "And I'm helped just by being with you—bathing in your golden glow. You know? I'm going to be okay."

"Am *I?*" she demanded, as though he could know.

"I do hope so," he said, wishing he could.

"The gravlax is out of this world," said Marian, opening her menu.

"This is some wine list," said Wordlaw.

They made love that night, for a long time and slowly.

The morning sun splashed gold in a vase of white roses and spilled in pools down the blue Qum rug. "My God, Marian, wake up!" yelled Wordlaw. "Sax didn't come home! What'll we do?"

"Well," she said, with a knowing smile, "the first thing we do is call Cora."

But Cora had left Sax with his friends at two-thirty. They were doing drugs, she told Marian, and she had felt it was time to make herself scarce.

"Sax doesn't do drugs!" hollered Wordlaw. "He won't even tolerate anybody doing them." Yet surely there was no reason to doubt Cora's word.

The police said to wait a while and see if he came back.

Sax finally drifted in about four that afternoon.

"Where the fuck have you been?" demanded Wordlaw, furious.

"Big night," said Sax thickly.

"I've been worried out of my mind!" cried Wordlaw.

"Sorry, *Mom.*"

Wordlaw waited to get himself under control. "This really isn't like you, Sax," he said.

"You don't know what I'm like," said Sax. "You don't have no fucking idea."

"I don't get this."

Sax handed Wordlaw the car keys. "I met some interesting new people," he said. "Musicians. We may work something up. I'm going to stay here for a while. I'll fly home. Where's Marian?"

"She's at work."

"Tell her thanks for her hospitality, will you? I'm just going to pack up my stuff."

"*This makes no sense!*" Wordlaw pursued Sax into the guest room and spun him roughly around. He held him by the shoulders and tried to see into his eyes. They were blank, the pupils cold pinpoints.

"Some things don't," was all he replied.

"Please don't do this to yourself," pleaded Wordlaw.

"Fuck you," said Sax.

Wordlaw chose a wide horizontal format to paint the Saxophone Chicago Quintet as they had appeared that first night he had seen them—the single downstage line of black-clad figures in purple light, playing four saxophones and a bassoon, the racks of other instruments piled dense behind them. On a second canvas the same size, fitted flush below the first, he rendered the foreground sea of heads, including the red-haired hostess, the transvestites, the conventioneers, the beatniks, the Mafiosi, Forrest in his punk haircut, and himself, listening, face upturned, eyes closed. He appended a third canvas beneath the first two, depicting the rain-refracted scene outside—the slick dark sidewalk, the old brick wall, the bright cellar windows, the hand-lettered sign. His first go was shadowy, smudgy, crude, his inveterate black palette, but in the overpainting a bright crispness began to appear, whites and silvers; the faces moved from caricature to gently comic verisimilitude; the colors and contrasts grew clearer, the detail more precise. He was breathing light into the scene. It grew less cruel, less sad.

It took less than a month to finish. Somehow, he knew what he was doing now. It had been like this ever since he had gotten back from New York.

He talked to Marian from time to time, but essentially he was alone. "That inward eye which is the bliss of solitude" found subjects everywhere: recollections in tranquility like the one he had just finished, as well as present observations—himself at the wheel of Sax's Corvette, with an imbecile grin on his face; Mr. Cannizaro glaring out from behind the counter with a long cigar in his teeth; the dark gleaming heap of Sax's disused instruments in a corner of the studio; Mimi on her mother's screen porch, peering through the haze of her pain, her gnarled hands gripping the arms of a white wicker chair. Perhaps some of his treatments were sentimental, perhaps even trite, but those were judgments for others to make—he was working from his heart. Whatever his paintings turned out to be in the eye of the beholder, he knew that the process of their creation was authentic, and the best he could do.

He did not know what had happened; he was just glad that it had. Absent from her, he found that his craving for Marian lessened. They were both content to have their love on hold. Wordlaw suspected that it might remain that way indefinitely. Which, while sad, was fine—there was even a certain pleasure in this sense of suspension, perhaps because it was voluntary and mutual. A positive move by either of them would have been met by a positive response, and yet neither moved. Why, he did not know. It was enough that the status quo was satisfactory.

He would see her in Memphis at Christmas: she was coming with Cora White to meet Cora's mother, and Wordlaw and his sisters were then at last going to clean out their parents' house so that it could be sold. Cora's mother was awful. Wordlaw preferred to think that the real reason Marian was coming was to see him.

Sax had still neither come back nor even called. Sam Watanabe had gotten his hooks into him somehow, and though that was probably a bad thing for Sax it did mean that Claudia could report to Wordlaw that Sax was working away with his new twelve-piece band in New York. Then Sax called Peter Elias to ask him to come up and join the new group, and also asked him to get the Corvette from Wordlaw and store it in his garage. Peter said Sax said to say hi.

Wordlaw decided that he was better off with Sax out of his life: Sax was so overwhelmingly talented that his presence had acted on Wordlaw as a depressive. In the end, he had felt invaded, oppressed, his autonomy compromised, by all Sax's knowledge, his genius, all that X-ray intimacy. And then there was the whole business of drinking, which Wordlaw was doing only very moderately now. Sax had certainly seemed to be headed in the opposite direction. With this sadness and absence, too, then, Wordlaw was, all in all, content.

He began work on a still life: white roses just going brown, a spilled glass of wine, a glistening catfish, one of his old cougar footprint casts, his grandfather's leather-clad compass, a faded photograph of Second Samuel, an ear of corn, a cotton boll, a polished cypress knee, a stuffed baby alligator in a terry cloth bathrobe and straw hat, a bowl of wild persimmons.

A flyer came to him in New Orleans:

McCracken Global Systems
presents
the world début
of the
SAXOPHONE CHICAGO DODECATET

in a
Christmas Concert

Thursday, December 25
8 p.m.
Orpheum Theatre
Memphis

The next day, he got a phone call: "Hey, Buz."

"Hawk!" cried Wordlaw in delight. "Sax! I got the flyer. What's the deal?"

"I just thought Christmas was the time and Memphis was the place to introduce my new work. Twelve days of Christmas; twelve pieces, one for each of the disciples, and, you know, a bunch of other shit that comes in twelves; Memphis because the piece is kind of a history thing, and because I owe it to Forrest, for all the good stuff he did for me when I was getting started. You coming?"

"Wouldn't miss it. I was going to Memphis for Christmas anyhow. Been working hard?"

"Man," said Sax.

"Me too, at last."

"That's good, that's good. Listen, Wordlaw. I been thinking, and I don't think I can handle another tour on a bus with a bunch of damn musicians. Especially now there's twelve of us. So, um, how would you feel about driving the 'Vette up to Memphis for me?"

"Sure. No problem. You think it'll start?"

"Peter's brother went and jumped it, and he says it's ready to roll. He's going to call you and drop off the key."

"Okay," said Wordlaw.

"Listen, thanks a lot," said Sax.

"Glad to do it. Sax—"

"I hate to cut you off, man, but I got to go. We'll get together in Memphis, all right?"

"Sure," said Wordlaw.

"Later," said Sax, and rung off.

So all he'd really wanted was his fucking car.

Wordlaw staggered down from the attic with a steamer trunk and added it to his pile. Shoot was rocking in the rocking chair he had claimed earlier. She had always had little use for material things, and had no pile of her own. Claudia's and Junior's were mountainous. "Did you even look in that thing?" Shoot demanded.

Marian smiled up from the book in her lap.

"Isn't this where the old paintings are?" puffed Wordlaw.

"You ought to have looked," said Shoot.

He opened the trunk. Most of the stiffly rolled canvases were ruined.

"Ooh," said Marian.

"Can't they be fixed?" he asked.

"I'm afraid not," she said, and touched his arm, knowing how this hurt.

"Y'all need anything at the mall?" asked Shoot. "All this dead people's stuff gives me the creeps."

Wordlaw culled several of the pictures that had not been too badly damaged. Marian helped him stack books on the corners to hold them open. He threw back the curtains; low winter light sliced in.

"They're really not very good, are they?" he said.

Marian smiled sadly. "Well—"

Wordlaw looked out the window at the Christmas Eve traffic, backed up all the way from Chickasaw Plaza.

Marian stood close behind him and wrapped her arms around his chest. He turned and held her tight. She nestled her head below his chin. He breathed the baby-soap smell of her hair.

"Word*law!*" came Junior's voice from somewhere upstairs. "Telephone!"

"Coming!"

On the way up he passed Claudia. "I found something of yours," she said, and reached into her pile. She turned back, grinning, brandishing the horn-handled Indian knife he had found in the swamp, so long ago. He wondered what might have become of Colbert Fox. Probably in some prison somewhere. Blonde, smiling, so generous, his sister was lovely today. Wordlaw swore to himself never to forget this picture and moment: Claudia at the foot of the stairs, the knife raised over her head, the Christmas tree behind her in the otherwise empty living room, its lights reflected in the polished floor, the inexplicable joy that welled in his chest at the sight of that knife.

"*Word*law!" yelled Junior. "It's Forrest, and he says it's, like, *urgent!*"

"Okay, okay," he called, and ran the rest of the way. "Forrest?"

"Have you seen Sax?" demanded Forrest, without even hey hey.

"I keep waiting for him to show up. I've got his damn car."

"He was supposed to be here at two o'clock for the sound check and it is now *four*."

Marian stayed with Wordlaw, holding his hand as he fretted, until midnight. "Merry Christmas, my dearest," she said then, and kissed him. Neither of them made a move to go further.

"Merry Christmas to you, too," said Wordlaw as he helped her into Cora's mother's rusting Plymouth.

At one-thirty-two in the morning—he would never forget—there was a sudden series of sharp popping noises from the cabana apartments next door. Wordlaw woke sitting straight up in bed. There was a second burst. He heard men yelling, and crackling voices on a two-way radio, and, a few moments later, sirens.

He dressed and ran downstairs and outside. Spotlights were being set up next to the cracked and empty swimming pool in the apartment courtyard. Policemen in bulletproof vests were squatting behind cars, with rifles. His sisters appeared in the front hall, and within minutes scores of neighbors, many in robes and slippers, were milling on the lawn. Nobody knew what had happened. Half an hour passed.

Then, in a burst of static, an electric bullhorn: "All clear. Perpetrators in custody. Hold your fire. Hold your fire." A cluster of policemen moved through the silver-blue light and shoved one, two, three, four, five handcuffed black men into the back of a paddy van. A stretcher followed, the form on it covered completely.

Wordlaw shouldered his way closer, and found a group of black people from the apartments. What had happened? Somebody had shot at a cop, they'd heard, and then the cops had shot him. Probably the dude that had borrowed that whore's apartment. Word was he was selling drugs. There was a whole bunch of them in there, in and out at all hours. Cops didn't get half of them.

Wordlaw went back to bed, but he had not yet fallen asleep when the phone rang down the hall, clangorous in his parents' empty room.

It was Sax: "Say, listen, bud, I got to have my car."

"Do you realize what time it is?"

"Yeah, I'm sorry about that, but I'll just be dropping by in a minute, all right?"

The doorbell rang three minutes later. "How'd you get here?" Wordlaw peered over Sax's shoulder.

"Walked," said Sax. "I like to walk." He grabbed Wordlaw in a quick, hard hug, and then stepped back. "I'm sorry about all this rush and all. Tell you all about it later. It's just I got to go." Sax held his head funny somehow, sort of thrust forward; it made him look even shorter.

"Well, merry Christmas. Hey, Sax? Did Forrest get in touch with you?"

"Oh. Yes. Yes, he did. Well, look, thanks, brother Buz. I got to run. Merry Christmas. I'll call you in the morning."

Which he did not.

Who did, however, was Forrest McCracken. "I'm going out of my mind," he said. "I can't find the son of a bitch anywhere."

"He said he'd talked to you," said Wordlaw.

"*Said?*" yelled Forrest. "You've seen him?"

"He came to get his car, in the middle of the night. There's been a lot of weird shit going on around here."

"He has *not* talked to me," said Forrest.

"You heard about the shoot-'em-up?"

"Yeah, my granddad told me this morning. You can't hear a damn thing down in the bomb shelter. Listen, Wordlaw, you've got to help find Sax. I've got twenty-two hundred tickets sold. Not to mention that I'm worried about him."

"Have you called the cops?"

"I guess I'm going to have to," sighed Forrest. "It's just that there's something fishy here, you know?"

"Call them. I'll be right over."

He called Marian—not that she could do anything, but just for the comfort of hearing her say, as he knew she would, "Oh, Wordlaw, my dearest, I know you must feel *awful.*" Better still was what she said next, "I'll meet you at Forrest's. I want to be with you."

The police called Forrest back within five minutes, and told him that a red 1980 Corvette with Louisiana license plates had been found at 2135 Tupelo Drive in Chickasaw Estates, but there had been no sign of the driver.

Marian called Cora to ask her to help with the search, while Wordlaw phoned home for Claudia, Sam, Shoot, and Junior. Forrest recruited Bohannon, the Farr twins, and Peter Elias. They all met at the Tupelo Drive address. The house sat next to the expressway, one of the ones boarded up and abandoned, with the drainage ditch running behind. The Corvette had scored deep ruts across the weedy unmown lawn, smashed down a spindly redbud tree, and sunk up to its axles in mud. A yellow plastic police tape was strung around it. The neighbors had neither seen nor heard anything, and they were rather irritated to have to be repeating what they'd already told the cops to a bunch of civilians smack in the middle of Christmas and the Sun Bowl game—Mississippi State was playing Nebraska, for Christ's sake. Bad enough having drug murders in the neighborhood.

They fanned out. Where kids had breached the chain-link fence, there was a gap. Wordlaw helped Marian down into the drainage ditch that had once been Daylight Bayou. There was hardly any water in it anymore; you could walk on its concrete bottom as easily as on a sidewalk. He followed it under the Interstate, downstream, toward what had been the cypress swamp and was now a vast air-freight complex, while Marian went the other way. The roar of traffic prevented him from hearing her yelling until she was right behind him.

"I found him," she said. She covered her mouth with her hand and closed her eyes, and took one deep breath after another.

Marian struggled to keep him from going to look, but he tore his way out of her arms.

Sax lay sprawled face down in the trickle of filthy water. It was a warm day for Christmas, and there were flies.

The autopsy found that Sylvester Woodson II had died of an overdose of heroin.

The horizon is near the bottom of the canvas, occupied by a front elevation of the Chickasaw Plaza Shopping Center, behind which the sun has just set or is about to rise. The brightness of the neon signs and the stores' unpeopled interiors is just beginning to equal that of the natural light, or just ceasing to.

In the foreground, seen from a low and close point of view, stands a nude figure of an adolescent boy with his arms crossed over his chest. In one hand he holds a long horn-handled knife, its blade pointing skyward. The figure looks as if it is straining against invisible bonds: sweat is running down the torso in glistening threads; every cord of muscle in the legs stands out rigid as steel cable; the toes are gripping the black asphalt so hard they seem to be clawing into it; veins bulge purple in the neck, which is twisted as though in convulsion. The boy's arms, however, are relaxed, and might be seen as moving into a tender embrace of himself.

His head is thrown back in transport, his mouth drawn into a toothy rictus. His eyes gaze over our heads into the distances behind us, beyond the world and into the encircling darkness.

It is the face of Colbert Fox.

Above the shopping center and the boy in the parking lot floats the blue, blue sky of Saxophone Chicago, and in it, just over the bowling alley, there hangs a single icy star.